MAYHEM IN THE MOUNTAINS

MAYHEM IN THE MOUNTAINS

JANE LOEB RUBIN

First published by Level Best Books/Historia 2026

Copyright © 2026 by Jane Loeb Rubin

This novel is entirely a work of fiction. The names, characters, and incidents portrayed in it are the work of the author's imagination. Any resemblance to actual persons, living or dead, events, or localities is entirely coincidental.

Jane Loeb Rubin asserts the moral right to be identified as the author of this work.

First edition

ISBN: 979-8-89820-263-7

Cover art by Level Best Designs

This book was professionally typeset on Reedsy.
Find out more at reedsy.com

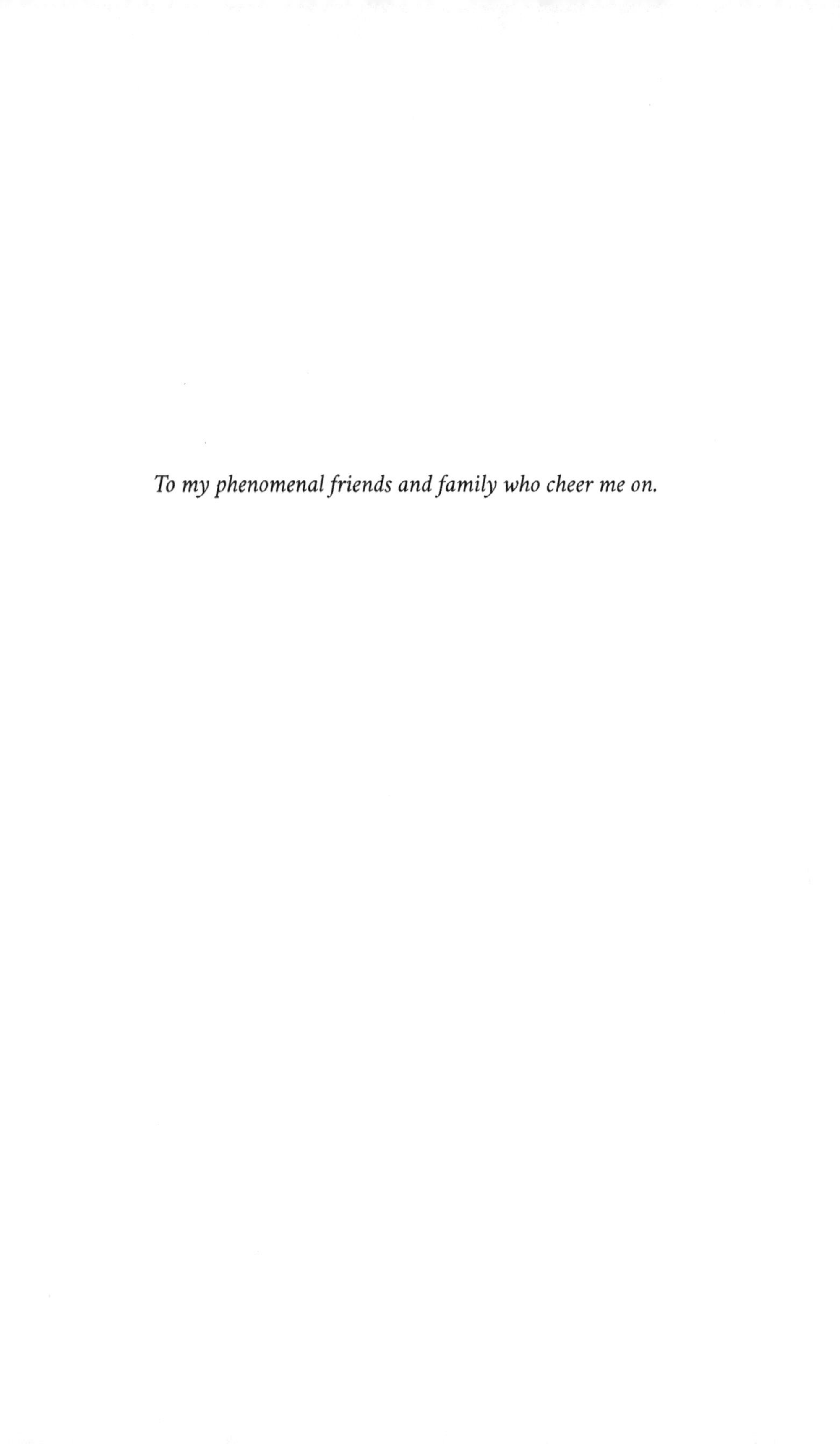

To my phenomenal friends and family who cheer me on.

Praise for the Gilded City Series

Praise for **MAYHEM IN THE MOUNTAINS**

"Settle in before you start *Mayhem in the Mountains*—this coming-of-age adventure will keep you reading straight through to the end. The novel vividly evokes 1920s America through the eyes of 18-year-old Ella Levine, a determined young woman who finds unexpected belonging among her extended Jewish family in the Catskills after years of neglect. But danger lurks as Ella crosses paths with notorious gangster Dutch Schultz and, with her family, faces the antisemitism of the rising Ku Klux Klan. Rich and unforgettable, *Mayhem in the Mountains* is a story of resilience, identity, and family that kept me turning pages late into the night."—**Mally Becker,** 2025 IPPY "best mystery" gold medal winner & Agatha Award-nominated author of The Revolutionary War mysteries

"Rubin masterfully immerses readers in the unpredictable, dangerous world of 1920s New York's Hudson Valley. Though the landscape exudes tranquility, the narrative pulses with tension—bootleggers defy prohibition, ruthless gangsters run whiskey, and the sinister presence of the KKK brings a chilling undercurrent of antisemitism. In this fourth installment of Rubin's Gilded City series, the story stands on its own, yet devoted fans will delight in watching familiar, skillfully crafted characters evolve over time—characters who linger in your mind long after the final page is turned."—**Linda Rosen,** *bestselling author of The Emerald Necklace*

"Readers are in for a treat with Rubin's fresh historical fiction. Exploring a little-known sliver of 1920s history, Mayhem in the Mountains has it all: strong female characters (especially the firebrand heroine), complex family dynamics, really bad, bad guys (the KKK) and a hopeful, satisfying finish. This tale of an industrious Jewish family in the Catskills is sure to delight."—**Samantha Greene Woodruff**, *bestselling author of The Trade Off* and *The Lobotomist's Wife*

"Jane Loeb Rubin transports us to the Catskill Mountains in 1924 in her riveting and action-packed new novel, *Mayhem In the Mountains.* As the story opens, Prohibition fuels crime and the Ku Klux Klan has drifted north, threatening those they consider outsiders. Against this turbulent backdrop, Rubin follows three characters struggling with family bonds and sweeping change. Whether you're a fan of Rubin's earlier novels or new to her stories, you'll race through *Mayhem In the Mountains*, cheering for her characters to overcome all obstacles."—**Marlie Parker Wasserman**, author of *Inferno on Fifth* and *First Daughter*

Praise for **OVER THERE**

"I am in awe of Jane's courage, on and off the page. What a privilege to spend time in the world she has created in *Over There*."—**Bess Kalb**, Emmy-nominated comedy writer and the bestselling author of *Nobody Will Tell You This But Me*, a *New York Times* Editor's Choice

"Bravery and daring, compassion and patriotism are the forces that push and pull Jane Loeb Rubin's latest historical page-turner *Over There* and tug at the heartstrings. It is a captivating tale of three medical professionals who join the American Hospital Corps and American Red Cross during WWI. Gut-wrenching and heroic, Rubin's rich characters draw you into a world where duty calls, love waits, and surgeons, medics, and nurses are the true heroes forced to redefine their lives while saving others. The price tag of war is devastating and heartbreaking—but in the end, Rubin's evocative tale proves that love ultimately wins."—**Lisa Barr**, *New York Times* bestselling author of *The Goddess of Warsaw*

"Jane Rubin has truly captured the horror of war and the dedication and selflessness of the medical personnel who also sacrificed so much to care for the troops wounded in battle. With superb writing, she weaves a complex story of World War 1, through the eyes of four members of a family of extraordinary people."—***Harriette Sackler,*** Agatha-Nominated short story writer

"This fast-paced historical fiction is the third book of the Gilded City trilogy, yet it easily stands alone. Set during World War I, 'the war to end all wars,' *Over There* between New York City, pastoral upstate New York, Paris, and the trenches at the French front. The novel takes its title from the 1917 patriotic war song 'Over There' by George M. Cohan.

The story is told in the voices of four characters from the previous novel in the series, *Threadbare*. Some chapters are about Hannah, a mother and the head of the obstetrics department at Mount Sinai Hospital. Her husband, Ben, the chief medical officer and highly experienced surgeon at Mount Sinai, enlists and serves at the rapidly growing American hospital in Paris. He devises a process to save as many viable limbs in the field as possible rather than automatically amputating. He eventually specializes in multiple lengthy operations needed for traumatic head and face wounds.

Miriam, Hannah's niece, is a passionate and consistently active nurse at Beth Israel, despite needing to wear a leg brace after contracting polio. Miriam recently married Dr. Eli Drucker, a rising star surgeon at the same hospital who volunteers his talents to the war effort and is sent to mobile hospitals near the trenches. Medical staff drastically leave in droves to serve overseas. Hannah stays in New York, caring for her children and patients for long hours. She feels responsible for her niece Miriam, who begins scheming to go to France to serve her country more meaningfully, and to be closer to Eli. Meanwhile, a new influenza is attacking at the front and reaching back home.

Over There discusses politics and financial challenges between the military and its physicians, between the needs of doctors serving the war effort while funding is needed for the hospitals in New York City to progress. The author pays great attention to the particular challenges of surgery in the field. The medical staff and soldiers persist while faced with understaffing, exhaustion, and disease. Rubin examines both their trauma and that of their families awaiting their uncertain return. In particular, she focuses on the Jewish American population who helped defeat Germany in the Great War.

This is a highly recommended read, whether as a stand-alone or as the conclusion of Rubin's series. The author well conveys the misery of war as well as the sparks of humanity, care, and hope that can exist during the most difficult of times."—***Miriam Bradman Abrahams***, reviewer, Jewish Book Council

"A meticulously researched novel immersing the reader into the indelible impact of war on the soldiers and medical personnel in the war zone, as well as the families at home. In this emotional, engaging story, set during WWI, we follow the characters Rubin brought us in the first two books of her Gilded City Series. Read this evocative novel as a stand-alone but be prepared – you'll be anxious to read the whole series."—***Linda Rosen***, bestselling author of *The Emerald Necklace*

Praise for **THREADBARE**

"Rubin's novel, *Threadbare*, is a classic, delicious immigrant story with a twist. Set in 19th century New York City—not the 20th—it's loaded with history, and its protagonist, Tillie, is a headstrong, visionary teenage girl. Although Tillie becomes a woman far too fast, her indomitable spirit prevails. Her compelling story is one of resilience in the face of discrimination, economic hard times, and epidemics—and it resonates for the 21st century."—**Susan Jane Gilman,** bestselling author of *The Ice Cream Queen of Orchard Street*

"In *Threadbare*, Rubin weaves a vivid tapestry of hope, heartbreak, and resilience amid breath-stopping challenges, opening a window to a transformative time in women's history."—**Audrey Blake,** USA bestselling author, *The Girl in his Shadow, The Surgeon's Daughter*

"Full of research and fast-paced storytelling, Threadbare explores many critical, ever-relevant issues, including poverty, childbirth, reproductive freedom, women's place at home and in the business world, rampant disease, immigration, and the value of community. Rubin's contrasting depictions of rural Harlem and New York City during this period are as vivid as her description of Tillie's frustrations, failures, accomplishments, and successes as a daughter, caretaker, wife, mother, partner, and business-woman."—**Miriam Bradman Abrahams,** reviewer, Jewish Book Council

Praise for ***IN THE HANDS OF WOMEN***

"The author deftly captures the social challenges for women of the era, when sexism restricted their access to the best protections that science could offer. One can't help but be impressed by the rigor of the author's research ..." and "The depiction of the era in which Hannah lives is so vividly instructive that it makes this a worthwhile read, especially at a time when its principal lessons seem on the verge of being forgotten"—***Kirkus Review***

"Rubin has written a fascinating novel, well-paced and brimming with historical detail. It's 1905 in New York City, a time and place of dramatic social changes. Hannah Isaacson has graduated from a major university with an MD in obstetrics but faces widespread discrimination as a professional woman. She encounters chronic antisemitism, realistically depicted. One can't help cheering her on as she fights for decent health care for women, for equality within the medical profession, and for respect in her own personal relationships. Ultimately, In the Hands of Women is a compelling and heartwarming historical novel."—**Libby H. O'Connell,** Chief Historian Emeritus, History Channel, and author, *The American Plate*

Acknowledgments

In May 2025, after Mayhem's completion, I decided to retire from writing, nervous I might be running out of time. After all, I was in the under 1% of ovarian cancer survivors living into my sixteenth year. I've always tried to be honest with myself, at least intellectually honest, if not psychologically (that's far more difficult). I knew I couldn't live forever, and nothing would disturb me more than having a half-finished novel sitting on my desk.

But the compulsion to write, to begin telling a much more personal, fictionalized story of my formative years in late high school and college, pulled at me. I waited two weeks for the feeling to pass, but it was irresistible. I began writing a new novel. In 2027, I will be publishing a fifth book in the Isaacson series. Right now, it has the working title "Moxie" while *The Eve of Destruction* plays in the back of my head.

Many people have helped me along the way. They are all incredible, spurring me to continue the saga and arrange venues to share my novels. But the stories would not have been written without the genius of my unsurpassed medical team. They have embraced ground-breaking treatments, always respectful of my need to enjoy life to the fullest. They have encouraged me to pursue the activities I love: family time, writing, travel—fulfilling my dreams. My family, every child and grandchild, has bolstered me with their unique spirits. Together, we have all learned to stop, really stop, and savor the special moments of life, saturated with our love and energy.

My husband, who lives with me day in and out, shares a judgment-free life, both immersed in our own pursuits, yet treasuring our time together. His unwavering support for my treatment decisions and my life as a writer are not small—and never taken for granted.

ISAACSON
FAMILY TREE

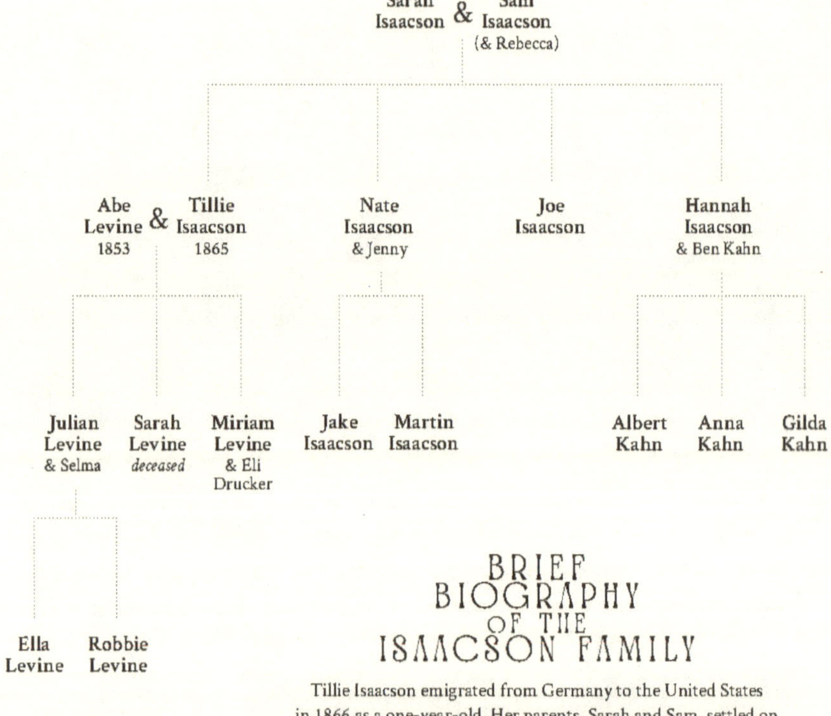

BRIEF BIOGRAPHY OF THE ISAACSON FAMILY

Tillie Isaacson emigrated from Germany to the United States in 1866 as a one-year-old. Her parents, Sarah and Sam, settled on a chicken farm in Harlem, NY, and had three more children: Nate, Joseph, and Hannah. Nate moved north with Sam and his step-mother, Rebecca to Sullivan Country when the farms in Harlem were leveled, making room for the city's expansion. He eventually took over management of the farm. Hannah, who was raised by Tillie on the Lower East Side, became a physician, a testament to the family's commitment to education, and later married Ben Kahn, a surgeon. Tillie's daughter, Miriam, studied nursing, later marrying Eli Druker, a surgeon. Their lives and values embodied the upward mobility of the Jewish immigrants through devoted family support, education, community, and business.

Foreword

At the turn of the twentieth century, upstate New York's Sullivan County, situated in the Catskill Mountain range one hundred miles north of New York City, was a peaceful and bucolic region. By the 1920s, danger lurked around every corner. Not only had it become a thoroughfare between Canada and New York City for gangsters moving whiskey, but it was the eventual home to Dutch Schultz's distillery. Worse yet, it was a northern spawning ground for the Ku Klux Klan. If history had played out differently, we never would have experienced the magnificent hotels that eventually comprised the Borscht Belt.

"If you reveal your secrets to the wind, you should not blame the wind for revealing them to the trees."

—Khalil Gibran

Chapter One: Ella

June 1924

"I'm never going back!" I shouted at the menacing river, turning to grab Robbie's trembling hand. I squinted with determination, rooted to the shoreline. "Come hell or high water, we're going to Uncle Nate's farm."

When we left Brooklyn that morning, there was not a cloud to be seen. But now, the June sky was blanketed with dark grey shadows, sending a bracing chill through the air. We were in for a rough Hudson River crossing.

Robbie pulled on my hand, forcing me to turn my eyes away from the distant ferry, still a brown smudge on the water, chugging its way slowly east, where we waited at the Dyckman Street Pier in New York City. I scrutinized his unwashed face.

Robbie's soulful brown eyes filled with tears. "I'm hungry, Ella."

I patted my satchel. "I made cream cheese and jelly sandwiches for the boat and tossed in a hunk of cheese on the side. And I filled the Stanley thermos with cold milk." I laughed brightly, attempting to lift his spirits. "It was a miracle Papa had food in the icebox."

The sky was about to break open and rain. A rumble of thunder came from the west. Robbie's body trembled. Time to adjust my plan. I threw my arm around his narrow shoulders.

I pointed to a bench near the entrance. "Thought we'd eat on the ferry, but maybe we should sit and have lunch now. Not sure the rain is going to hold off much longer."

Moments later, the ferry's horn blasted as it approached. We gobbled down our sandwiches, then tugged on the sweaters I'd dug out of our single valise. "Let's get on the ticket line so we can board early and find a dry spot on board. The rain's gonna come down hard any minute." I slung the satchel over my shoulder, picked up the valise, and reached for Robbie's hand, hoping Uncle Nate and Aunt Jenny wouldn't mind a couple of surprise visitors. I'd assumed a lot.

Robbie pulled back; his brows drawn together in concern. "We've never crossed the river. Does this make us runaways?"

I gave his small hand a reassuring squeeze. "It'll be fine. We're going to visit family." The fact that we were not expected hung in the air.

Moments later, we boarded the ferry. I spotted a low wood bench in the boat's center near the beverage bar, fully protected from the rain. I crossed my fingers, hoping the squall would pass before we reached the opposite shore of the Hudson.

Robbie's face relaxed, his eyes glimmering with an excitement I hadn't seen on his innocent face in months. "Can you hold my seat so I can watch the cars drive on board?"

"Of course. Just stay on the ferry. Somewhere I can see you. And try not to get wet." I called after him as he scurried to the bow of the boat where automobiles, one by one, were driven aboard.

I studied the people while Robbie drifted to his vantage spot in the front of the boat. Most passengers were young families with small children, watching the sky, probably hoping the squall would clear and not spoil their outing. Holding blankets and picnic baskets, they were dressed for a day outdoors by the river. Women wore colorful calf-length, smartly belted gingham dresses and straw wide-brimmed boater hats. Men dressed casually in open-collared shirts and loose pants. Some sported boaters, others felt work caps. I hoped the bad weather would pass over quickly for these lovely folks.

Digging back into my memory, I couldn't recall one happy outing with my family. From my earliest years, my parents loathed each other; arguments flared at minor missteps. They clung tightly to failed expectations, never shared out loud. That is, until they divorced. Then they stopped speaking altogether for a while.

I had Uncle Nate's address in my pocket on a folded paper. It was time to consider how we'd get from the Englewood ferry dock on the New Jersey side to his Liberty, New York farm. I knew there were trains and buses to Monticello, but from there, it was a long ride to Liberty by car. We'd need to call Uncle Nate or hitch a ride if there wasn't another bus. Fortunately, we were flush with one- and five-dollar bills in the pouch beneath my blouse. I had taken them hours earlier from Papa's stash.

I startled when the ferry captain blasted the horn, jerking the boat away from the dock. My eyes searched for Robbie. Where did he disappear off to? I hated it when he didn't listen. I heard Robbie call my name just as I began gathering our belongings to search for him.

"Ella, come look. An Austin Twenty!" All heads turned his way as he stretched his arms far apart. "A real one, all the way from England. And it's gigantic, just like in the pictures."

With a firm jerk of my hand, I signaled him over to my seat. "Come here and stop shouting. I told you to stay where I could see you. Almost had to give up our seats."

Robbie stood before me, his eyes popping with the moment's thrill. "But, Ella, the man let me sit in the driver's seat and pretend I was driving. He said it can go seventy miles an hour!"

I smiled, relieved he wasn't still upset about running away. I let him ramble on. Robbie had been fascinated by any object with wheels since he could hold a toy wagon in his hands. Now that he was seven, I watched his interests narrow to machines with motors. He collected every issue of Motor and American Motorist magazine he could lay his hands on. At twenty cents each, far too rich for our blood, he got his copies by reaching his arm into a barber shop when the operators were busy. Then he'd nick one. Mama would punish him if she found out, but Papa was another story. He would chuckle, amused by Robbie's mischief.

"Robbie, sit by me. You can show me the car when we dock on the other side." I leaned forward to peer through the ferry windows and noticed the clouds separating, hints of pale blue peeking through. "Take a look at that. Clear skies are coming our way."

The pitch of the ferry passengers' conversations lifted as they took notice, too. Voices shifted from concerned to jovial and relieved, laughter overtaking the serious din. Moments later, we were docked on the New Jersey side of the Hudson River.

Robbie jumped up and grabbed my hand. "Come with me, I want to show you the Austin before he leaves."

I grabbed our things and followed Robbie through a short, tight corridor to the front of the ferry, my valise bumping against the walls as we wormed our way forward. Several cars were lined up on a platform. Right away, I spotted the Austin, standing out among the unassuming Model Ts. It was a grand car, robust, ready to hit the road with a flourish. A grown man of average size and well-cut brown hair was opening the driver's door, about to step in. He lifted his fedora, tossing it onto the passenger seat.

"Hey, mister!" Robbie shouted. "This is my sister. Can she see your car, too?"

I pulled Robbie back, speaking in a hushed voice. "What have I told you about speaking to strangers?"

The man turned his head our way, a cigarette dangling from the center of his mouth. A broad smile crossed his face as he bit down on his smoke, causing it to tip upward. "Hey, kid." His eyes scanned my body, taking it all in, smiling. "Now, ain't you a tall drink of water?"

Heat rushed to my face. I was accustomed to catcalling and whistling on the street, but the man's comment felt far more personal, smoldering, in fact. I cleared my throat, "I'm sorry my brother was bothering you. He loves cars."

Robbie pulled me closer to the car until we stood beside the passenger door. "Can Ella look inside? It's swell!"

The man chuckled. "Sure, kid. Where're you headed?"

Robbie scrambled inside the car before I could stop him, not answering the man's question.

"Robbie, come out of there right now," I ordered, then turned my eyes to the man. "North to my uncle's farm. I'm sorry for his boldness. This is the first time he's traveled out of the city." I caught Robbie's eye and tilted my head, lips squeezed together in annoyance, letting him know I meant it. He smiled back at me.

The man, standing at my height, looked me straight in the eyes. "Let the kid have his fun. I'm heading north, too. I have a turkey farm up there in the Catskills. What town are you headed to?"

My body relaxed, knowing he owned a neighboring farm. But his suit and fancy car didn't fit my image of a farmer. I studied him a little closer, feeling emboldened. "You're a farmer? Pretty swanky car for a farmer."

He leaned back and guffawed at my comment, his mouth hanging open. "You're a feisty thing, ain't ya?" Collecting himself, he said. "My farm's a big business and takes me to the city distributors every week, like clockwork. There's a year-round demand for turkey cold cuts. It's all the rage. Big money if you run the business right."

His explanation made little sense to me. Uncle Nate raised chickens his whole life and was a wise man. I was almost sure he didn't drive an Austin or own anything so flashy. However, this man's lightheartedness was a welcome change from my previous worrying.

He cocked his head to the side, "How're you planning on getting there? I'm happy to give you a lift. I can drop you off wherever you're going on my way to my place. It'd be nice to have the company."

Robbie interrupted, begging, "Oh, could we, Ella? Could we? Please? I want to see how fast the Austin goes."

I looked from Robbie to the man and sighed loudly, "I don't think we've been properly introduced. My name is Ella Levine."

He reached out his hand, winked, and shook mine. "I see. So, you're one of the Jewish tribes, too. Dutch Schultz here, but my friends call me Dutch."

Chapter Two: Ella

In its wake, the rain squall left the air cool and fresh smelling. Or was the pleasant scent simply the country air in New Jersey, free from the dirt and grime of New York City? Dutch insisted on driving with the convertible top tucked behind the rear seat, where I sat with our valise. Robbie rode in the front, his hair blowing in the wind, singing his favorite tunes into the sky, every song he'd ever learned since his early days in a crib. His all-time favorite was, *My Bonnie Lies Over the Ocean.*

I stewed, my apprehension burning, knowing I'd heard the name "Dutch" before. I just couldn't place it. Was it at school? Mama didn't have extra coins to buy newspapers, so I had no idea if Dutch had been in the press. I kept my eyes and ears open, waiting for a clue, knowing in my gut it had to be bad.

Dutch reached the farm in record time, driving the entire way like a reckless maniac. Robbie's constant encouragement egged the man on. So, he pressed on at top speed, passing farm animals strolling on the highway and speeding through red lights. I wiped my clammy hands on my skirt. Beads of sweat rolled down my back as I gripped the back seat, bracing for the inevitable crash. But it never came. The Dutchman had unworldly luck—his hands were always steady on the wheel as if he was driving a getaway car like in the cinema.

Robbie blurted through the noise. "I want to be a race car driver when I'm bigger and have a fast car! Just like this one."

Dutch threw his head back and laughed, his mouth gaping open. "This is the life, kid." He glanced at me in his rear-view mirror, taking in my grimace. "Don't worry your pretty face, Ella. I'll get you there alive. This is me, driving careful."

Careful my keister, I thought, as we careened around a group of milk cows wandering onto the highway. I screamed and reached forward to grab Robbie by the shoulders so he wouldn't fly over the windshield onto the hood.

Dutch veered around the small herd, steering the car onto the grassy shoulder, then corrected his course back onto the highway. "See what I mean, doll? Got it under control."

I was never so happy as when we arrived at the top of the hilly driveway leading up to Uncle Nate's house. Dutch stepped on the brake with a flourish, sending a spray of gravel and dirt from the driveway into the front flower garden while his brakes emitted an ear-splitting screech. He lay on his horn with a prolonged blast to cap off our arrival.

Oh my god, what will they think of us? Not only were we unexpected, but Dutch also destroyed the flower beds to boot. What a showboat!

Aunt Jenny opened the front door, peering out as Robbie and I scrambled from the car. She was much older than I remembered; her lined face framed with an untethered spray of loose gray curls partially secured at the nape of her neck with a bun. She wore a frown that spoke volumes, midway between disdain and fury. Would she turn us away?

I moved back to Dutch, who was opening his car door. Anger broiled in my belly. With a sneer, I walked close to him. "Please, just go."

Turning back to Aunt Jenny, I waved my hand timidly, walking from the car to her, whisking the dust from my clothing. I attempted to flatten my unruly chestnut hair. Hair that had turned into a wildly tangled bird's nest from the drive. "Aunt Jenny, I'm Ella, Julian's daughter." I reached for my brother. "And this is Robbie. Could I talk to you and Uncle Nate?"

Aunt Jenny glanced at Robbie, her eyes softening, then shifted her gaze to the chicken coops down the hill where a bent, older man was walking up to the house, surveying the commotion up the mountain. That must be Uncle Nate. We stood and waited for him to join us. In the meantime, I grabbed my suitcase from the back seat and set it beside the steps, glaring back at

Dutch.

Relieved to have our feet on firm ground and having tolerated my fill from Dutch, I tried again to get rid of him before Uncle Nate reached us, stepping his way a second time, leaning into his face. "Thanks for the ride. I can take it from here." But Dutch didn't budge an inch. Instead, he smirked at me.

Having collected herself from the surprise, Aunt Jenny opened her arms to us. "Come here, both of you. It appears we have catching up to do." She glanced upward at Dutch with her brows raised, waiting for him to leave. But he still wasn't going anywhere. Not yet.

While we waited in a huddle for Uncle Nate to climb the hill, Dutch stood apart, rambling on about meeting us on the ferry and offering to drive us safely to the farm. "You have nice kids. Pretty smart, too." He pointed to Robbie. "And this one knows a hell of a lot about cars."

I wanted Dutch to stop his yammering. His efforts to break the ice with my aunt sounded phony, like the Fuller Brush man who visited Mama's apartment every month, selling her things she didn't need. I was afraid Aunt Jenny would distrust my judgment, taking a ride from such a man. But my worries were in vain. Once Uncle Nate reached the driveway, his wide eyes immediately told me he knew exactly the type of character he was dealing with and would handle things his way.

Dutch shot out a hand. "Nice to meet you. Dutch Schultz here. As I was saying to the missus, you've got a great couple of kids. Just drove them up from the ferry."

Uncle Nate shook his hand quickly, withdrawing it with a wary eye fixed on Dutch's face. "Thanks for getting them here safely. Don't want to hold you up. You can get on your way now."

But Dutch wasn't leaving so fast. He said flatly, "Can I trouble you for a glass of water? We've been riding with the top down. I'm parched."

Aunt Jenny ran into the house for the water. I figured she knew Uncle Nate wanted the man gone as quickly as possible. Standing on the top of the driveway, we waited for her to return. I broke the silence, "Uncle Nate, I met you years ago at Bubbe Tillie's. I'm Ella, Julian's oldest, and this is my brother, Robbie. I can explain everything."

Uncle Nate could not contain his surprise. "What do you know? You were just a little girl when I last saw you." He then focused his eyes on Dutch, speaking to me all the while. "We'll talk in a few minutes."

Meanwhile, Dutch still didn't take the hint. Instead, he launched into a speech about his turkey farm in Ulster and the volume of poultry he produced. "Turkey is big business these days. More expensive than chicken, but tastier and not just for Thanksgiving anymore. I got processors hungry for as much meat as I can produce—for their delis in the city. Cold cuts are a year-round rage. They use every part, from the neck to the legs." He kept glancing at Robbie, who was mesmerized, hanging onto every word as if this man were a god.

All this traveling and tension was taking its toll on me. I watched my uncle's face, his jaw twitching with impatience. Would he be angry and send us back to Brooklyn after Dutch finally left?

"You betcha, raising turkeys has turned out to be quite a success," Dutch's words cut through the air, filling the space with his rambling monologue. "How long have you been at it? You know, with the chickens?"

Uncle Nate cleared his throat, taking his time. His voice was terse and direct. "Farm's been in the family for more than forty years."

Dutch eyed him thoughtfully, "Ever consider renting rooms to the city folk? I hear many farms like this are doing just that. Making a few extra bucks on the side." He looked around, pointing to the massive pond in the distance. "With a watering hole like you got there, you could make a tidy sum when the heat gets bad."

Aunt Jenny returned with a glass of water. Dutch took it from her hand and drank the entire glass in one long gulp. "Thanks for the hospitality," Dutch squeezed the moisture from his lips with his thumb and forefinger, handing back the glass. He then turned to Uncle Nate with a tight-lipped smile. "Let me know if you decide to rent rooms. I've got plenty of provisions I can offer you." He leaned his head close to Uncle Nate's, whispering loudly, "If you know what I mean."

Uncle Nate's eyebrow twitched, his mouth in a tight frown. "I'll keep you in mind if we need anything."

Dutch walked back to the Austin, reached beneath the rear seat, and pulled out a newspaper rolled around a bottle. With a wink, he handed it to Uncle Nate. "Here's a sample for you—on the house."

Uncle Nate nodded, his face hard as granite.

Dutch reached out his hand to Robbie. "Nice to meet you, kid. One of these days, you can come to my farm, and I'll give you another ride in the Austin." He winked at me.

Robbie was star-struck, his eyes wide. "That would be the bee's knees!"

With Robbie's excitement hanging in the air, Dutch hopped into his car and turned on the engine. As he pulled away, he saluted with two fingers on his forehead.

Chapter Three: Ella

"What in tarnation were you thinking, Ella? You know, taking rides with strangers is dangerous!" Uncle Nate admonished me. "You both could have been killed."

Robbie interrupted, still bubbling with excitement. "But Uncle Nate, Dutch was so much fun and let me sit in his car on the ferry, pretending to drive."

Uncle Nate turned to Aunt Jenny, lowering a voice laced with gravity, "Take Robbie inside and get him a drink. I want to speak to Ella alone."

My belly sank. My next nightmare was about to happen. We'd be sent home with a tongue-lashing to go with it.

Uncle Nate led me around the house into the backyard. He pointed to a wooden picnic table with benches set in the shade of a large oak tree. "Let's sit, Ella."

I sat on the splintered bench, not making a peep, trying not to move. My stomach clenched. Here it comes.

Uncle Nate sat opposite me, interlacing his gnarled fingers, hands accustomed to a lifetime of hard work. For the longest time, he sat as if waiting for his thoughts to organize and his anger to cool. "There's so much I don't know, Ella. Why don't you start from the beginning? What made you decide to bring Robbie here? Did something happen at home?"

Dumbstruck by his straightforward delivery, I wondered how to explain what it felt like to be unloved my whole life—an afterthought, an inconvenience, the offspring of an unhappy marriage? I had no idea where to start.

My thoughts drifted back to earlier that morning, when I was packing sandwiches. Papa hadn't returned home from his Friday night outing, and my decision to run away hit me hard. It was the perfect time to leave. I couldn't spend one minute more in his stifling hot Brooklyn apartment watching out for Robbie instead of planning my future. A few weeks back, Papa had screamed at Mama, telling her it was his right to have us live with him when school let out. That, legally, it was his parental time since we lived with her during the school year. Now that I was eighteen, I wasn't so sure about that. Mama, afraid of his temper, typically gave in. She'd say, "Sometimes his anger was so fierce, it could melt the wallpaper off the wall."

We last saw Papa Friday morning, before he left for work at Metropolitan Life, a job over the Williamsburg Bridge in the city he detested. Before the war, he'd been a loan analyst at the Jarmulowsky Bank on the Lower East Side. But by the time he returned from his duty in France, the bank had closed, filing for bankruptcy. Over the course of the Great War, too many Jewish immigrants had withdrawn their life savings to help relatives escape war-torn Europe, and the Bank could not recover. For some reason, he took it as a personal affront that the Bank wasn't waiting for him upon his return from the war. I didn't understand why he cared either way, since both his loan analyst job at Jarmulowsky Bank and his current job involved managing other people's money, certainly not ours.

Friday morning, before he left for work, Robbie and I had been sitting at the table eating oatmeal. All the while, he shouted at us to find summer jobs and help pay for our keep, telling us that the ice haulers down the block needed workers. Papa sneered at me the whole time. "Especially you, Ella. The free ride is over now that school's out. You have your diploma."

He hadn't said a word about coming home for dinner. On Fridays, he got paid, and who knew where he'd go. I'd bet my last penny Papa was passed out at a friend's place after hitting the speakeasies.

It was only one week into summer break and I was already brimming with anger and boredom. Was he serious? Ice hauling? It was one of the most dangerous jobs for a girl my age. All those dirty men with hands, hungry to paw. And Robbie was only seven and skinny as a rake, not strong enough to carry a twenty-five-pound block of ice up anyone's apartment stairs. Papa didn't give a damn about us. I knew in my heart he'd only taken Robbie and me for the summer to cheat Mama out of support money.

Saturday morning, I made a quick breakfast of toast and butter. I packed a few clothes and two blankets. Mama had bought a cheap brown valise for Robbie and me to share when we moved to Papa's for the summer. It was plenty big for the rest of our things: some underwear, a second skirt, knickers, a couple of shirts, and sweaters. I didn't know where we might be sleeping on our way to Uncle Nate's. But we still needed money. I knew Papa didn't put much in the bank. He might have hidden some in the apartment. But where?

A half-hour later, after rummaging through drawers, his jacket pockets, under the mattresses, and in a couple of shoe boxes stored high up on a shelf in the bedroom closet, I was losing hope, running out of places to look. He may have had a bank account after all.

Robbie was spread out on our shared bed, rereading his favorite book, The Story of Dr. Dolittle. He called out, "Ella, do you think Uncle Nate takes care of sick animals, too?"

"Don't know, Robbie. Why don't you ask him tonight when we get to the farm?" His excitement calmed me. The farm would be a great relief from the summer heat and grime of the city. I just hoped Uncle Nate would be as excited to see us. He'd never met Robbie, but Papa had brought me to a Passover meal in Bubbe's Lower East Side apartment when I was small, and Uncle Nate was there with his family. My grandmother, Tillie, still alive back then, was hosting, trying so hard to keep the family connected. Uncle Nate and Aunt Jenny had told me we were always welcome to visit them in the country. I hoped he remembered.

I sat on the parlor chair, thinking about money, how to get to the farm if I couldn't find any. I'd saved fifty cents and knew it wouldn't stretch far. Ferry fare was a nickel apiece, and I had no idea what the train would cost. My eyes scanned the walls and stopped at a picture of the Brooklyn Bridge, hung between two sturdy bookcases holding Papa's precious book and stamp collection. He might not have liked his kids, but he loved his small library. We'd get our knuckles rapped if he caught us even looking at his stuff. "Get yourself to the public library if you want to read," he'd say. "Stay away from my books, or there will be hell to pay."

I lifted the frame from the wall, hoping to find an envelope of money taped to the back. Nothing but cardboard. As I rehung the picture, my eyes caught a ripped piece of paper sticking out of the top of a book Papa had placed in the bookcase. I reached for it, sliding the book carefully off the shelf so I'd know where to replace it. *Bread Facts*, by Ward Baking Company. The book was probably left behind when Mama moved out. As I opened it to the bookmark, Robbie called out again, startling me, sending the book flying from my hands into the air, falling onto its spine with a thud.

The pages sprang open, and a shower of one- and five-dollar bills shot into the air. Go figure, just like the greedy bastard to hide his money in a book about bread. A smile crossed my face as I gathered the cash, stuffing it into a pouch I planned to wear under my shirt. I knew I could outsmart the old geezer.

I gathered the suitcase and placed the wax-paper-wrapped sandwiches in my cloth satchel. "Time to hit the road, Robbie. We have everything we need."

"Aren't we going to say goodbye to Mama first?" Robbie asked with a hitch in his voice.

I sighed, knowing a stop at Mama's apartment would derail my plan. What if Robbie told her we were going to the farm? She hated Papa's family. Said they were uppity German Jews with their Americanized accents and high school diplomas. Thought they were too good for the Russian Jews living in Brooklyn.

I sat beside Robbie on the bed. "We don't have time now, but we'll write to her tonight when we're safe and sound at the farm. That way, she won't worry. Right now, she probably thinks Papa is watching us." What a joke. Moments later, we were riding the train across the East River to board a streetcar north to Inwood and the ferry dock to New Jersey.

Uncle Nate broke his patient silence, drawing my thoughts back to the picnic table behind his farmhouse. "Ella, did you hear my question? Can you answer me?"

I studied his compassionate, tawny eyes. He wore a brown tweed work cap barely shading his face from the sun. Uncle Nate's weathered skin suggested he'd seen more of life than I could possibly imagine. My eyes misted as I struggled to hold in tears. Braced for a tongue-lashing, I was ill-prepared for his gentle compassion. "It's such a long story. I…I don't even know where to start. My parents hate each other…." My voice hitched as I hiccupped a near-sob. "Well…they hate us too. At least Papa does."

Uncle Nate reached for my hands, pulling them across the table, slowly massaging my knuckles with his thumbs. "We had no idea. I'm so sorry."

My body trembled. I couldn't fathom Uncle Nate's kindness. Perhaps it wasn't every parent who drove their children to run away. Why couldn't Papa be kind, like his uncle?

Admitting my predicament aloud added an unexpected gravity to the situation. I'd said enough for now. Uncle Nate understood why we'd run away and was silently offering me permission to share the full story of our childhood misery at my own pace, or not at all. Maybe it would remain bottled up inside me forever. With a meek voice, I said, "I never forgot Passover at Bubbe Tillie's when I was much younger. You told us we could visit you and Aunt Jenny in the country any time. This morning felt like the right time to take you up on your offer."

Uncle Nate spoke softly. "I meant it, too. I was just surprised. Didn't expect you kids showing up out of the blue."

I blurted out, "Is there any way we can live here this summer? Robbie and I can help you on the farm." I shifted my gaze to the rolling hills and orchards. The sun was setting in the western sky, casting hints of pink and red overhead, layered against the massive blue, as the air cooled. I had never witnessed a sky as expansive and vibrant. "It's more beautiful than in my dreams. I had no idea."

Lifting himself off the bench with a moan of discomfort, Uncle Nate said with a slight smile. "Yes, heaven on Earth here in the Catskill Mountain range." His voice took on a more official tone. "Does Selma, er, your mother have a phone?"

I nodded. "Got one about a year ago."

"Good. Then the first order of business is calling her and letting her know you both are here with us. I don't want her worrying. And be sure you get her permission to stay a while. We'll talk about the summer after you two speak."

As we walked toward the back door of the farmhouse, he turned, hands on hips. "And, Ella, I want to know if you see that man, Dutch, around here again. He's as crooked as a corkscrew."

* * *

I'd seen screen doors on small storefronts in the summer, attached for the blistering summer months. The screens allowed cool breezes in and kept flies out. But I'd never seen one on the back door of a home. Entering the kitchen, I was careful not to let it slam and disturb Aunt Jenny, who was preparing dinner, arms flying from the icebox to the counter, then to the stove at a fantastic speed. She'd tidied her bun and now wore a crisp white apron, her hands purposefully moving, chopping carrots, picking stray feathers off the chicken skin. Robbie sat at a small oak kitchen table covered with a red gingham tablecloth. On top of the table were piles of snap peas and a saucepan. I could hear Wendell Hall's voice singing in the background, and I wondered if they had a gramophone. "I love that phonograph record."

Aunt Jenny laughed, "That's not a recording, dear. He's singing at the radio station in Albany. *Ve* can pick up the station on our radio."

"You have a radio?" I marveled. "Papa said they're too expensive." My world was growing in leaps and bounds. I planned to listen to the radio a lot while we visited.

Robbie hummed along with the tune, *It Ain't Gonna Rain No Mo*, as he pinched off the end of a pea, carefully pulling the string along the spine, dropping it on a pile of food debris. He then placed the peas in the pot of water. "Hey, Ella, see what Aunt Jenny taught me to do?" Eating one raw, he said, "They even taste good before cooking, and she uses the strings to fertilize the garden."

I smiled. Watching Robbie engaged in a harmless activity, bouncing his head to the music instead of rereading his books in the hot, dark apartment, lifted me. In just one hour, our world had been transformed. I imagined teaching him to swim in the sparkling pond down the hill and scattering feed for the chickens. I hoped Mama would let us stay, at least for the summer. Aunt Jenny glanced at Robbie with a satisfied smile. It was impossible not to love that kid.

"Uncle Nate wants me to call our mother. I hope that's alright. Then, I can help you with dinner." I looked at the three chickens Aunt Jenny was coating in melted butter, salt, and pepper. "Isn't that a lot of food? Robbie and I don't eat much."

Aunt Jenny's eyes shifted away from her cutting board, sweeping them up my body, until meeting mine. "I can see that. You're both skinny as rakes and need to eat much more. You're growing children. Besides, I invited your Aunt Miriam and Uncle Eli to join us for dinner."

My heart swelled at the thought of meeting more family. Why had Papa and Mama kept them hidden from us? Could Mama hate German Jews that much? From this little corner in the farmlands of New York, all I saw was a happier, more welcoming world for Robbie and me.

Thankful Mama had installed a phone, I dialed not expecting her highly emotional response, shattering my newfound fragile contentment. "Mama, stop crying. We are both perfectly fine. Everyone is kind here." I pursed my lips with frustration, shaking my head. "Why don't you talk to Robbie for a minute, and then we'll speak again?"

I handed the phone to Robbie, whispering, "Try to calm her down. Don't say anything about Dutch."

He eagerly took the phone. "Mama, we're having so much fun. Aunt Jenny is swell. She's making a big chicken dinner right now and taught me how to string peas from her garden. I want to stay here all summer."

Robbie listened, then his face pinched in pain. He was on the verge of crying.

I grabbed the receiver from his hands and walked as far from the kitchen as I could, stretching the cord to its full length. Speaking a smidge above a whisper, I said, "Mama, you're upsetting Robbie. Did you know Papa hasn't been coming home at night?"

Now Mama, barely calm, sounded regretful, her voice taut and slow. I knew she was about to cry again. "I'm sorry. He won't allow you to stay home with me this summer. All he cares about is cheating me from child support."

My stomach roiled thinking about stealing Papa's hidden money earlier today. How long before he realized it was missing? Would he come to the farm, demanding it back? I'd better come up with a hiding place quickly.

Trying to settle Mama further, I said, "We are safe here, and I haven't had a chance to talk to Uncle Nate about the summer. But you should know that we're both happy, and it's much better than staying in Papa's suffocating apartment for the next few months."

I could hear her breathing through the receiver, slow and deep. Knowing Mama, she was thinking it over. I knew what she worried about. Mama was a proud, old country woman sickened by the thought of accepting charity. I knew her decision could swing in either direction. I needed to come up with a way Mama didn't feel beholden to Uncle Nate—and fast.

"Mama, how about I call you back on Monday? I know Uncle Nate could use extra help around the farm, and Robbie and I can earn our keep that way. In the meantime, please don't worry. We are perfectly fine, and Robbie has been miserable since we got to Papa's." I needed to hammer in a bigger nail to seal the deal. "Did Robbie mention Papa was going to make him work for an ice hauler?"

That did the trick. Mama gasped, her voice growing louder, angrier. "No!" Here it comes. Mama's mercurial rage. Or as Papa called it, her Hungarian temper.

"Yup, and me too. Trust me, when I tell you, we are much safer here." I let out a slow breath, hoping this final pitch would work. I waited for her tirade.

She shouted into my ear, "That man is *meshuggah*. He's a *chazer*! What did I ever see in him?" She caught her breath. "Yes, stay there and call me next week. I will speak to you and Robbie then."

"I'll do that. We miss you, Mama."

Mama paused. "And Ella, I want you to watch out for Robbie. You must take responsibility for him."

"Yes, Mama." I exhaled a breath of relief. Inwardly, I laughed, knowing I'd have been responsible for Robbie even if we'd stayed in the broiling city.

After setting the receiver back in the cradle, I heard Uncle Nate and Aunt Jenny speaking in hushed voices in the kitchen. I inched closer to listen.

Uncle Nate's whisper was scarcely audible. "That man, Dutch, is a gangster. A bootlegger. His name's been all over the news. How the hell did they get tangled up with a character like him?"

Aunt Jenny gasped. "Oh my, it was all innocent. Robbie told me he saw his fancy car on the ferry. The Dutchman let him make-believe drive."

Uncle Nate emitted a loud tsk. "As much as I hope we've seen the last of him, I'm not counting on it. There's something about this place that caught his fancy. And honey, it's just Dutch, not the Dutchman."

My blood boiled listening to them. Just as I suspected, Dutch was up to no good. And to add to the problem, he'd seduced Robbie with his phony charisma, wealth, the Austin, and even promises of more rides. I wasn't sure how I could manage my brother's pull if Dutch appeared again.

Thinking of Robbie, I wondered where he'd gotten off to. Walking out the front door, I spotted him down by the pond, climbing into an old rowboat secured on the shoreline. I cupped my hands around my mouth and shouted, "Robbie, get out of that boat and stay away from the water. You can't swim!"

Robbie turned to me and ran up the hill, his eyes full of wonder. "I saw fish in there. Do you think Uncle Nate will show me how to catch them?"

His excitement tore through my frayed nerves. It hadn't occurred to me that a farm would have dangers of its own.

I walked midway down the hill to meet him, talking to Robbie as I drew close. "Tomorrow, we start swim lessons. No fishing or hanging around the pond until you can pull yourself out on your own. I haven't a clue how deep the water is. And absolutely, no swimming alone. I promised Mama I would keep you safe."

"Yes, Ella."

As we approached the house, we heard a car's engine rumbling on the main road. The car turned into Uncle Nate's gravel driveway. My heart raced in anticipation. I grabbed Robbie's hand, both running the rest of the way to greet them. It must be Aunt Miriam and Uncle Eli.

Robbie and I waved wildly, running alongside the red Model T as it pulled up to a stop beside us in front of the house. Uncle Eli jumped out, then opened the back driver's door. To my delight, two young children scrambled out. I watched Aunt Miriam move slowly from the front seat, her leg brace swinging out of the car first. I vaguely recalled hearing about her brace over the years but could not recall exactly when or from whom. She lifted her body out, embracing a small baby swaddled in a pink cotton blanket.

Uncle Eli extended his hand to me with an open smile. "Welcome, fugitives from Brooklyn. Too hot for you in the city already? Aunt Jenny filled me in on your escapade."

Robbie's brows knit with confusion. I figured he didn't know what the word "fugitive" or "escapade" meant.

"He's teasing us about running away," I said.

Robbie placed his hand on the hood of the car, stroking it with admiration. "Wow, I've never seen a red Model T. She's a beaut!"

That was precisely how Dutch referred to his Austin. Now Robbie was mimicking him. It was a good thing Dutch was long gone. Robbie would have better men to admire in our own family.

I leaned forward to give my aunt and uncle a quick hug, excitement racing through my veins, as I tried to act as mature as I could muster. "I've heard so many great things about both of you, especially your bravery during the war."

Aunt Miriam patted her children's heads. "Jake and Tamara are twins, named after their cousin Jake, who died in the war, and Tamara, after her grandmother, Tillie. They're both five and start school this fall. The baby is Sarah. She's named after both my older sister and great-grandmother, who both passed before I was born."

I caught my breath, my delight fading. "I didn't know there was an Aunt

Sarah." I thought briefly. "Did Papa have a sister?"

Holding the sleeping baby closer, Miriam's eyes drew wide with amazement. "You mean your father never told you he was a twin? His sister, Sarah, died from pneumonia in infancy, before she turned one."

My head spun. I had no idea. Another damn secret. Why on Earth would Papa keep something that important from us? As if his sister's life held no significance. An anger burned inside me. How much else hadn't he told me about his side of the family? After all, it was my family, too.

Aunt Miriam called out to Uncle Eli, "Honey, don't forget to bring the dessert inside."

Robbie's eyes sparkled. "Dessert? Yummy. What is it?" He leaned into the car through the open window to inspect the plate.

Aunt Miriam laughed. "Oh Robbie, I bet you'll like it. Pineapple upside-down cake. It's all the rage."

Robbie stood back, studying Uncle Eli's eye patch while he reached into the car to pull out the cake. "Are you a real pirate?"

"Robbie!" I scolded, "That's not polite."

Uncle Eli tussled Robbie's hair playfully with his free hand. "You bet I am. And there's an honest-to-goodness war story to go with the patch. If you behave yourself, maybe I'll tell you about it one day."

* * *

An hour later, I sat at the picnic table with the grown-ups, watching Robbie play tag with Jake and Tamara. Running barefoot, they crisscrossed the wide grassy slope like untamed puppies, enjoying the first warm days of summer. Meanwhile, baby Sarah slept peacefully on a blanket tucked into a wicker basket beside the picnic table, without a care in the world. I couldn't recall a more idyllic setting. One I'd only experienced in novels and dreams.

Miriam's voice cut through the spell. "Ella, I'm a bit concerned. I would like to hear more about your father. I don't remember him acting so indifferently toward family when we were growing up. I can't get over the fact he didn't tell you about his twin sister. What in the world is going on with him?"

I caught her probing eyes, wondering how many awful stories I should share and why I knew so little about my very own family. I stalled for time. "When's the last time you two spoke?"

Like an unexpected squall, her eyes clouded with concern. "Far too long ago. Your Papa seemed to slip away from the family after he left for college. He was so smart back then. Did you know he had a full college scholarship? He was gifted with numbers. Could do arithmetic in his head quicker than anyone I'd ever met."

"Did you see him before you left for the war?" I asked, looking at her anxious face.

Aunt Miriam shook her head. "No, we had little contact before the war. I know he told Bubbe Tillie about you and Robbie when you were born. She and your Grandpa Abe visited you in Brooklyn for a time. Then Bubbe Tillie fell ill, and the next time I saw my brother was at her shiva. He left quickly after the service, before we could talk. And he didn't come to your grandfather's shiva. At that time, Julian, I mean your Papa, was at a military training camp in Ohio." She sat still; her eyes fixed on the distant mountains. "I saw him one time after we returned from France. I always meant to reach out again, but I had my hands full helping Eli heal."

Eli softly took her hand and cupped it to his slightly hollowed cheek, a gesture so small, yet powerful. My parents had never exchanged such a tender and heartfelt moment.

I sighed, "Papa was lucky he was never hurt, but I know he lost a lot of friends who were shot in the trenches."

Aunt Miriam said, "There are other ways men were injured besides bullets. I worried that he kept to himself because he suffered from shell shock. But then I heard Julian had a good job with a bank when he returned to Brooklyn. None of it made sense, and I decided not to interfere. Afterwards, life got busy for everyone." She leaned down to kiss the baby, inhaling her sweet fragrance.

As hard as I tried, I couldn't recall Papa enjoying Robbie and me. For that matter, he never expressed appreciation for all Mama did either: cooking, washing, and keeping the apartment. "He's plain mean. Hates all of us. Calls Mama a greedy cow. That she spends all his hard-earned money." A moment of shame passed through me. It was awful to speak about my father that way, airing out our private family business. Still, I'd do just about anything to avoid returning to Brooklyn. "He told Mama that going into the trenches was a vacation compared to being married to her."

Aunt Jenny gasped. "*Chazer*! Doesn't he know we lost our beautiful boy, Jake, in that war? It's nothing to joke about!"

My stomach twisted as a wave of guilt traveled through me. The last thing I wanted, was to stir up painful memories for my poor Great Aunt. "I'm sorry to bring that up, Aunt Jenny. It's like I said, he's mean. He doesn't want me to go to college, either. And I graduated at the top of my class. Said girls are only good for housework and motherhood – though not exactly in that order." I caught myself hiccupping an unexpected cry, quickly swallowing it down. I couldn't go on.

Aunt Miriam searched Uncle Nate's face, shaking her head. "Mama must be rolling in her grave. My education, Julian's education, was her top priority. She and Papa tried so hard to help both of us in any way we needed. I can't imagine what could have gone wrong with him. He never went without anything, especially love." Darkness passed over her face. "Nate, I wonder if he's still...."

Uncle Nate sliced off her words, studying my glum face. "I think that's enough for now. Ella, what did your mother say about staying up here this summer?"

I sat for a moment before answering. "I'd be lying if I said Mama wasn't upset, both with me for running off with Robbie and at Papa. After she blew off some steam, she settled down and agreed to let us stay as long as we called her next week with a plan for summer. She especially wants us to be helpful. Mama won't take charity, even from family."

A smile crossed Uncle Nate's face. "There's plenty of work around here. That'll be the easy part. After all, it's a farm. But there is a little fly in the ointment. We're expecting boarders this summer, so we'll need you and Robbie to share a room. We thought we'd put you in our boys' room with the two beds, where they slept when they were young." His lips broke into a smile. "How wonderful to have family here again."

"Last summer, we added more bedrooms upstairs, a hot water tank, and an extra bathroom, expecting boarders this year. Jenny and I moved our bedroom to the first floor."

An unexpected laugh erupted from my mouth before I could squelch it, causing everyone to turn their eyes to me. "Sharing a room is no problem. Right now, Papa has us sharing a bed."

Aunt Miriam's face turned bright red as she choked out the words. "What the hell is the matter with that man? He's blown a gasket!"

"Don't worry. We never wake each other up." I had a sense that I had better shut my trap before I made matters worse. The more detail I spilled; the more Miriam's concern grew.

"It's not right. Julian has plenty of money to buy proper beds," she said, her face reddening. "I've got a mind to ride down to Brooklyn and have words with him."

That was the last thing I needed right now. I didn't want my newfound family up here finding out about the money I stole. And I was sure it'd be the first thing Papa would tell her because money made him tick. I needed to change the subject fast. Bending my head to the side, I searched her face. "Who watches the children while you're working at the clinic? Do you need help with them?"

Uncle Eli looked at Aunt Miriam, nodding, "You were just saying you need a new sitter for the summer." He glanced at her leg and brace. "Between the patients and the children, you're on that leg of yours too much. Looks like we may have the answer."

I was grateful Uncle Eli helped me change the subject. Then he turned to me. "Are you up for watching the three children? The clinic is beside the house, so we'll be close by if you need us. And of course, we'll pay you properly. What do sitters make these days? A couple of bucks a week?"

Excited, relieved, and curious all at once, I said, "That sounds perfect. I've been watching little ones in Mama's apartment building after school for extra money. Plus, I've always wondered what nurses like Aunt Miriam do." I turned to her. "Can you show me sometime?" Then I realized I'd be leaving Robbie for long hours every day. "But there may be a small problem. Mama wants me to watch Robbie. Can I bring him along, Aunt Miriam?"

Without giving her a second to answer me, Aunt Jenny interrupted with a gentle smile. "Oh, *ve* have plenty for him to do here at the farm. And I'll keep a careful eye out." A wistful look crossed her face. "I do miss the old days with our boys, Martin and Jake, and later, Albert. Nothing's better than raising young boys on a farm. Those boys were always up to shenanigans, teasing the chickens, climbing the apple trees, and running all over the place. Time passes by so fast." Collecting herself, she added, "Martin and his wife live down the road a way, and he works with your Uncle Nate caring for the farm. Eventually, he'll take it over, and I hope there'll be lots of children running about again. They're expecting their first baby at the end of the summer." A somber look crossed her face.

Uncle Eli changed the subject again. He had a quick sense for when a different conversation was needed and when it was not. "Nate, Miriam tells me you're taking in boarders. Many of my patients are doing the same thing. The men leave the family in the mountains for the summer and go back and forth to the city for work, returning on the weekends."

"That's right." Uncle Nate answered. "The family is arriving next Sunday from Brooklyn. We've been writing to each other all winter. They seem like good, honorable folks."

As I listened to the men's conversation, one thing became crystal clear. There was a reason Uncle Nate had not told Dutch he was taking in boarders.

Chapter Four: Ella

The next morning, I woke before the rest of the household and set a pot of coffee to perk on the stove. Once the coffee was done, I took my cup to the backyard and sat on the same bench I'd occupied a few hours earlier, absorbing the dawn. A heavy mist hovered over the valley, engulfing the pond and orchard, obscuring the outline of the trees. It was a glorious sight.

A moment later, I was joined by Uncle Nate and Aunt Jenny, both still wearing their nightclothes. I slid to the end of the bench making room for them, avoiding the splintered wood.

Uncle Nate slurped his coffee, licking his lips. "How'd you learn to make coffee? This is delicious, a treat to wake up to."

We sat in silence, watching the sky open its arms to the dawn. A virtual light show of intermingling streaks of pale blue and pink. "This is magnificent. I've never seen a sky so beautiful." I shifted my thought to the pond. "I was wondering how deep the pond is."

"Very deep, probably between twenty-five to thirty feet in the middle," said Uncle Nate. "It's fed by springs under the ground. Be careful, especially in the middle."

Within minutes, the sun was visible in the eastern sky. It was time for the day to begin. Aunt Jenny announced, "Time to get dressed and put on breakfast. What do you and Robbie like to eat?"

"Whatever you're making," I said, knowing that everything about the day would be new and beyond Robbie's and my day-to-day imaginations.

CHAPTER FOUR: ELLA

* * *

By Monday morning, it felt like I'd been sucked into a country life where time was suspended. Here, the minutes passed in a gentle, unhurried manner. Meals were eaten slowly, vegetables exploded with the freshest flavors from the garden, and every bite was savored.

The massive sky, framed by mountains, trees, and silos, welcomed me after dawn when I woke and gazed out my bedroom window. I pinched myself, barely believing it was all real. Even the sun appeared to linger in the sky, shining longer each day so we could swim in the evening before bed. There was a strange thing about summer. While each day was stretched out like a rubber band, the days also had their way of passing quickly, meal to meal, day to night. Right now, I wouldn't trade it for the world.

Robbie's excitement hadn't waned a minute. It was as if he'd landed in the heart of Steeplechase Park at Coney Island, riding the mechanical horses encircling the grounds and the massive carousel—never told to get off. Each ride had cost ten cents. The farm was free!

I'd spent a good part of that first weekend teaching Robbie to float and swim. After hours of lessons, I was satisfied he could drag himself out of the pond if he fell in. His sloppy, splashy stroke needed more refinement, but I would tend to that in the evenings and weekends. In the meantime, I asked Aunt Jenny and Uncle Nate to read him the riot act about not going into the water or the boat alone. The rules were crystal clear. If Robbie disobeyed, he'd be sent straight back to Brooklyn. There was one thing about Robbie—he knew when I meant business.

On Monday morning, Aunt Miriam arrived at 8:00 am to pick me up for a day of tending the children. I'd just finished the most delicious breakfast of my life: oatmeal with cream and raisins, scrambled eggs, and toasted challah with jarred strawberry jelly Aunt Jenny had made from last year's berries. It was ecstasy. Instead of my skimpy portion at Papa's, she filled my plate and bowl, urging me to eat seconds. Robbie and I could get used to this life in a big hurry.

Before leaving, I scurried to help clean up the dishes and place them away in the cupboards. Aunt Jenny kept repeating, "It's so nice to have a pretty helper. What a blessing you are."

***

Aunt Miriam's home was at the edge of Liberty's Main Street, a short ride west from the farm. She pulled up to a charming house with a long porch stretched across the front of its two entrances. One door held a sign for Uncle Eli's medical practice. The second was unmarked. Aunt Miriam explained, "There's a door inside connecting the clinic to the house. Let's go in, and I'll show you around."

She led me through what she called their tiny cottage. Triple the size of Mama's apartment, it didn't feel little to me. With a kitchen that included a breakfast table with four high-back chairs, a separate dining room, and a large parlor on the first floor, there was plenty of space for everyone. Numerous children's toys were organized on the lower shelves of bookcases. Endless activities would fill their summer days. I bent beside a white wooden rocking horse, stroking its mane, admiring the leather saddle and bridle. "What a pretty toy. I dreamt about having one just like it when I was small."

Aunt Miriam cast a sad glance my way. I figured she felt mighty sorry for Robbie and me by this point. I'd have to watch what I said, or she'd be sure to call Papa and give him a scolding. "A local craftsman makes the rocking horses and other wooden toys for stores in the city. He's a patient of your uncle's, so we got a good price."

Although the home's interior was much smaller than Aunt Jenny's farmhouse, the space was uncluttered and decorated with modern touches. In the parlor were two fluffy dark-gold couches set on a wool carpet with black-and-white geometric designs. Aunt Miriam had none of the dated Victorian frill filling most apartments I'd seen. A mantel ran across the top of a large stone fireplace. Beside it were floor-to-ceiling bookcases. The shelves held books, knick-knacks, and numerous framed pictures of family and friends, some in military uniform.

She guided me to the mantle. "First order of business, you must call Eli and me by our first names. Now that you're eighteen, I think you're old enough to drop the formal conventions. After all, there's not much of an age difference between us. I could be your young aunt." She pointed to the first picture and said, "Let me introduce you to some of the family you may not know."

It was the first time anyone had permitted me to dispense with the formalities of my childhood station. I was thrilled to be treated as an adult and intended to surpass her expectations.

She pointed to a large hand-painted photograph, painted in human-like colors. "This is your grandmother, Tillie, and your grandfather, Abe. Your Papa is standing beside them, and I'm on your Bubbe's lap. Your father must have been around nine or ten years old. I was two. The other girl is your Aunt Hannah. She's five years older than your father. Did you know she's a doctor?"

I nodded my head, transfixed. "She grew up with you?"

"Yes, ever since she was five. There's a long story behind it. When your Bubbe was seventeen and took Hannah into her tenement home months after birthing her own twin infants. She and your grandpa, Abe, raised Hannah. They were very generous people."

I was shocked. The idea of raising Robbie on my own was unthinkable. "I had no idea."

Miriam continued, "Did you know Uncle Nate's chicken farm was originally in Harlem before that part of the city was leveled to build apartments? His father, your great-grandfather, Sam, brought the chickens up to the Catskills at that time. His entire community moved together: shul, school, and homes. But your Bubbe Tillie had just finished eighth grade and was dead set against leaving the city. In fact, she desperately wanted to attend high school. Despite her frustration and heartbreak, Bubbie's father and stepmother would not allow it, nor could they afford it with the big move. So, she decided to marry Abe, hoping he'd allow her to finish school."

I listened, astonished at this new family history. Married after eighth grade? How could her father permit that?

"The rabbi introduced her to your grandfather, Abe, and the two of them moved downtown to the Lower East Side where your father and his twin sister, Sarah, were born a year later. Bubbe was only seventeen when the twins were born." Her eyes, glazing over, drifted back to the photo. "Lots of stories to share, but we'll save them for another day."

Although Papa had told us part of the story in bits and pieces, usually after a whiskey, Aunt Miriam's explanation finally glued the scraps together, forming a tapestry of Bubbe's young life. "And that's where Sarah, Papa's twin, died?"

She nodded.

"Were you born there, too?" I asked.

The corners of Miriam's mouth turned up in a nostalgic smile. "As a matter of fact, after baby Sarah passed, your Bubbe insisted they move to a modern apartment with a toilet, running water, and a furnace, not too far from the filthy Lower East Side tenements. They both worked in the Garment District and wanted to live close to their friends and customers. Years later, I was born."

Just then, Jake and Tamara trotted down the stairs in their nightclothes, giggling loudly.

Aunt Miriam scolded them in a hushed voice. "Shh, the baby's sleeping. Tiptoe into the kitchen, and Ella and I will fix a nice breakfast."

My curiosity piqued as I took the children's hands. I whispered to Miriam, "I can't wait to hear more. I have so many questions." Married at sixteen? A mother of twins at seventeen? What a fright that must have been, especially with her dream to continue school. I wondered if she ever had the chance.

Ten minutes later, baby Sarah woke. I took over the skillet, scrambling eggs for the twins. After bringing the baby downstairs, Miriam settled into an armchair, positioned a pillow under her forearm, and nursed the baby. Swallowed up in their domestic bliss, I couldn't think of anywhere I'd rather be. I set the eggs and buttered challah toast before Jake and Tamara and asked, "Aunt, er, Miriam, what can I make for you?"

She drew her eyes from Sarah with an appreciative warmth. "A cup of milk and scrambled eggs would be lovely. Before the war years, Eli did all the cooking, but I took it on after his injury." It was clear to me that his injury had complicated their lives, marriage, and careers. Without knowing all the gritty details, I understood their happiness was hard-earned. So much more complicated than what appeared on their content surface. And Miriam was another matter. Her brace from polio was no small matter. I could see the limp fatigued her. I had to hand it to them both – they never complained.

Perhaps there was hope for me, too. I had spent so much of my childhood feeling sorry for myself, wishing my parents could be happy and grow closer together. Instead, as time wore on, their arguments became fiercer, until Papa drifted away, disappearing little by little, until he was no longer there. Later he was gone altogether in France, leaving Mama in a constant state of despair, alone with me—pregnant with Robbie.

By day's end, Miriam had scooted back and forth from the adjoining clinic three times to nurse Sarah. When she did, I took Jake and Tamara outdoors and kicked a ball around in the backyard. While the baby slept, we played Parcheesi and Uncle Wiggly on the parlor floor, a few rounds of War with the playing cards in the bookcase and read a half-dozen books for what seemed like hours. I was beginning to worry that summer was going to seem endless and boring. I reassured myself that if I saved every penny, I could afford to go to college, and the slow hours would be worth it.

Around 4:30, Eli and Miriam walked through the adjoining door into the kitchen, buzzing with a discussion about their last patient. The twins and I had just finished a second game of War and were cleaning up the toys.

Eli winked, "Looks like you've all had a busy day. Did the kids beat you at everything?"

"Of course." I laughed.

"I'll take you to the farm on my way to make house calls," he said.

I looked at Miriam, concerned. "Don't you need help preparing dinner?"

She waved me off with a flick of her hand. "I'll take care of dinner tonight, but tomorrow is a long clinic day, and then I'd appreciate your help."

As Eli and I approached the front door, a young man with a mop of dark brown curls walked straight into the house without knocking, setting us both off balance. "Whoops, sorry. I wanted to make it home in time to meet my cousin, Ella." He stared at me, his mouth gaping. "I thought you were a little kid."

I laughed, "Robbie is the little kid. He's seven. I'm eighteen. I just finished high school. Who are you? Another cousin?"

His light brown eyes sparkled, extending his hand to shake mine. "I seem to have lost my manners. I'm Albert, your Uncle Ben and Aunt Hannah's son. We're cousins, but not in the traditional sense. I'm Ben's son from his first marriage. My natural mother was killed in a carriage accident when my younger sister, Anna, and I were very small. Then Papa married Hannah a few years later and adopted Anna and me."

Another family member, popping up out of nowhere with a story of his own. "I had no idea. Nice to meet you."

Judging from Eli's smirk, he was finding our awkward conversation amusing. He tossed the car keys to Albert. "How about you take Ella back to the farm? You two can catch up along the way. I'll stay here and give Miriam a hand with the children while she makes dinner. I'll head out later to make house calls."

"Mind if I put the top down?" Albert asked.

Uncle Eli nodded, still looking amused. "Just secure the top back on when you get home. I don't want to open the door to a wet seat if it rains."

Moments later, we were driving east on Mill Street, the wind blowing through my hair. Rather than exhaustion from a day of entertaining the twins, I had caught a second wind. Who was this darling cousin? Another missing piece in the family puzzle Mama and Papa never discussed? "Albert, you're my mystery cousin. Tell me about yourself. Do you live with Miriam and Eli?"

He gave me a side-long glance. "Me, a mystery? What about you and Robbie, our long-lost family? I'm dying to hear about your trip up to the farm. I heard you met a gangster."

I cringed. Dutch had become gum on my shoe. "Seems I'm never going to live that down. Can we talk about it another time?"

Albert's curls blew in the wind. "We can leave it for now, but I'll get it out of you one of these days." He drew a breath. "You were a surprise, too. No one talks much about your side of the family."

The more family members I met, the more resentful I grew toward my parents. What was wrong with my father? What did he do to alienate all of us? It must have been something horrible to justify depriving Robbie and me of a lifetime with these warm, happy people. What was Papa hiding?

Albert's smile vanished, sensing my discomfort. "Didn't mean to insult you. It's just your father pulled away from everyone, and as a kid, we never met."

"It's alright. I hope you don't mind all my questions, either. I'm just curious. Don't your parents live in the city? What brought you all the way out here?" I asked.

He turned his head to face me and smiled. "It's a long story, but one summer during the war, I moved to Uncle Nate's and worked at his neighbor's farm, training horses for France. After the war, I wanted to stay and did. I like to imagine that my living at the farm after the war helped Aunt Jenny and Uncle Nate weather their grief."

"Of course it would have helped them." I began to realize that life up here in this beautiful country had its share of misfortunes.

Albert continued, "Last month, I graduated from Pharmacy School in Albany and am opening a drugstore in the middle of town. We're almost finished with the building. I'll live in an upstairs apartment. The second floor should be done by September."

I was astonished. "You never returned to New York, even after your father returned from France?"

He shook his head. "Just for visits. I love it here. Felt like I was trapped in a bird cage in the city. My sister went back and still lives with our parents on the Upper East Side while she attends Barnard. Pop understood what I needed. We're very close."

His parents must have dropped from heaven. Boys had so much more freedom than girls. "So now you're living with Miriam and Eli?"

"Just for the next few months. The pharmacy's down Main Street near Chestnut. A terrible fire occurred in 1913. The whole area was scorched to the ground. Once the lots were cleared and empty, the land went up for sale at bargain prices. My father and I invested, and now I'm opening my pharmacy. The Fourth of July is the official opening date."

Albert's story kept getting better. I couldn't get over how lucky he was. The freedom to stretch and grow was pulling at me, too. But I couldn't figure out how to navigate my future on my own with no money. And then, what about Robbie? How could I leave him behind in Brooklyn?

I was eager to hear Albert's opinion about a million questions circling in my head. Still, I hardly knew where to begin: college, choosing a profession, or starting a business. I could only imagine the opportunities ahead for me if I played my cards right. In the end, all I said was the truth. "I'm jealous. This month, I graduated at the top of my class, and my father wants me to work hauling ice blocks. Can you imagine? You've no idea how lucky you are."

Albert pulled up in front of the house. "I do know. But it was tough for me in a different way, during the war." He seemed to think for a moment and changed the subject. "How about I pick you up in the morning, and we can talk some more."

As I stepped out of the car, he said, "And Ella, welcome to Liberty."

Chapter Five: Albert

I spent the week immersed in a delightful new rhythm, gathering Ella in the morning from Nate's farm and returning her home by dinner, growing more dazzled each day with her irresistible charm. How on earth had the family kept her hidden from me all these years? Although her tall, athletic bearing, hazel eyes, and shiny chestnut waves were undeniably attractive, it was Ella's keen intelligence and endless curiosity that captured every second of my attention. I had met many girls in college, but they were often the product of overly protective Jewish parents, pushing their daughters to find husbands, bringing little stimulation to our dates. Conversations consisted of an endless list of interrogations and rules. Marriage suitability was their primary purpose.

Ella was different. Her curiosity about my life rang pure beneath the cautious recitation of her upbringing. Ella's willingness to slowly share her past, admitting her difficult childhood, stirred me, making it natural to share back, something I rarely did.

I was driving Ella back to the farm at the end of the first week when I confessed. "You remember I told you I moved out here the summer before high school and never lived in the city again."

She turned to me, her curious eyes sparkling as the late afternoon light hit the gold specks in them. "Why was that?"

"It's strange. I can't remember everything. All I recall is how scared I felt for my father's safety. My fear wouldn't quit, day and night, not being able to do a damn thing to help him. The other boys at school were worked up, too. Someone always said something to start a fight. I had a black eye practically every week."

"That's horrible."

"Hannah decided to bring Anna and me to the farm one summer to help Uncle Nate and Aunt Jenny. Straight away, Uncle Nate saw my need to blow off steam and got me a job working at the horse farm next door. Since Uncle Nate and Aunt Jenny had two sons, Jake and Martin, he understood boys and realized it was the perfect way to settle me down," I said.

"You know how to ride a horse?" Ella asked. "Could you teach me this summer?"

I laughed. "I didn't know how to ride when I got here, but within a week, I was helping train the war horses. It was the best summer of my life. I finally felt as if the storm inside me had quieted."

I found myself thinking about Ella all day while I wiped the dust from the freshly installed display shelves in my pharmacy. The following Monday, I decided to invite her for a walk down Main Street before taking her back to the farm. I wanted to show off my progress.

As I unlocked the front door, Ella gasped, "This is amazing! Do you have any clue how lucky you are? Having your very own business? I'd kill for a chance like this."

I laughed, "Kill. Kind of a strong word."

She peered through her inquisitive hazel eyes, "You know what I mean. Everyone around you cheers for your success. And this pharmacy will be an important store for the town as it rebuilds the rest of Main Street. Like Eli and Miriam, everyone will need you when they get sick. You're guaranteed to succeed."

I hadn't thought about it that way, riding the crest of my family's continual support and love. I couldn't help but wonder what it was like for Ella, clawing her way through life. But I had to hand it to her. She was one sharp cookie, with a heap more street smarts than me. She viewed everything around her with a fresh perspective.

That evening, after dropping Ella back at the farm, eating dinner with Miriam and Eli, and helping with the children's bedtime routine, Miriam, Eli, and I sat in the parlor, sharing news of our day. The pharmacy was approaching its opening day, and I had a list of questions for Eli and Miriam about the medications he prescribed, and what other products I should stock.

Pulling out my ledger, I drew four columns. One for everyday goods, one for the soda fountain, the next for personal items, and the last for medications. "The pharmacy should be getting its State Board of Registration this week, and I'll need to place orders for the drugs. The front shelves are wiped clean and ready for personal and household goods, and the back laboratory is nearly ready for stock and compounding. I only need to sanitize the mixing area one more time to remove the dust particles. Tell me everything I'll need."

Miriam sipped her tea, considering his question. "How about we start with the retail area. If it turns out your license runs into a delay, at least you'll get people in the door and can sell merchandise."

"Good point, but I sure hope that doesn't happen. Those licensing exams were a bear." I began writing the list, thinking I'd start with personal items and later move on to household products and packaged food.

Eli said, "Don't forget, with all the families vacationing in this part, you'll need plenty of extra stock for things like cloth diapers, pins, and Vaseline for the inevitable diaper rash. If you run out, they'll drive south to Monticello instead. You want to keep them shopping up here."

Miriam jumped in. "And stock up on baby powder for the heat. People seem to like Mennen and Johnson &Johnson, although some of our parents are using that new Ammen's brand. My guess is the adults will need it for themselves and their older children as well.

They'd gotten the wheels in my head turning. I thought aloud, "Bugs will be a problem for those renting cabins without screens. I'll order netting for buggies and calamine lotion."

Over the next hour, I'd assembled three pages of supplies the average summer visitor would need. Although I could have continued another hour, I noticed Miriam's head had dropped onto Eli's shoulder, her eyes half closed, her lame leg propped on the coffee table. They'd had their fill for the day.

"One more question before I go upstairs for bed. Do you have a problem if I offer Ella some paid hours in the pharmacy to help me set up? I don't want to interfere with her obligation to you." I asked.

You'd think I clanged the dinner bell in their ears. Miriam shot upright, fully alert. Stunned at her oversized reaction, I scoffed, "You'd think I just announced incoming wounded! Is there a problem with Ella?"

Miriam was the first to react. "I know Ella, in strict terms, is not related, but be careful. There's still so much we don't know about her. I don't want to see either of you getting hurt."

"Hurt, how?" I asked.

She lightly cleared her throat. "Just take it slow. She's had a tough start in life, and I'd like to learn more about her past. I'm not quite sure what happened with her father. You know he's my older brother, but we were never very close. See what you can learn."

Eli smiled. "Darling, Albert's a big boy, and Ella is eighteen. I think we should stay out of things."

I nodded my head. They hadn't shared anything I hadn't already figured out. "I was also going to ask you if I could borrow the car on Saturday and snoop around Peterson's General Store in Monticello. They've been open a long time and probably have everything we'll need. I can make sure I haven't left anything important off my list. I figured Ella might like to keep me company. Do you need the car before noon?"

Chapter Six: Ella

Aunt Jenny's eyes narrowed as I gathered my purse and reminded Robbie about his Saturday morning chores. The Model T idled in front of the house, Albert waiting patiently behind the wheel. "Ella, I don't like this business of you riding around with Albert every day. You should be chaperoned. It's not right."

Exasperated, I sighed. "We're just going to Monticello; it's only a half-hour drive. It's for his drug store. Anyway, we'll be back by lunch." I dropped my shoulders. "It's only Cousin Albert."

Uncle Nate strode into the kitchen. "What's all the fuss in here?"

Robbie tattled, "Ella's going driving with Albert, and Aunt Jenny's mad at her."

Uncle Nate crossed his arms, surveying us both, first Aunt Jenny with her distrustful lips drawn in a piercing line and then me, my eyes pleading for him to give permission. Naturally, as the man of the house, Uncle Nate had the final word. In under a heartbeat, he resolved the matter. "Robbie, go with your sister. And Ella, I want you both back by noon. Our first boarders arrive tomorrow morning, and we need extra hands helping us set up this afternoon."

I knew better than to argue. My aunt and uncle had saved Robbie and me from a dreadful summer in the city. I now had a job and a family who genuinely cared about us. I knew it was best to comply and behave gracefully. In a show of gratitude for her peace-keeping efforts, I walked over to Aunt Jenny, bent down, and gave her a hug. She drew her arms around me, squeezing me so hard around my waist it took my breath away.

She then looked to the ceiling, seeking answers. "I just know boys, and they're not to be trusted when it comes to girls. Even my own boys thought about one thing only." She pulled my face towards hers and kissed each cheek. "You are too pretty for your own good, Ella Levine. Be careful."

"It's only Albert," I chided as Robbie, and I walked out the door.

She snorted, "He's still a boy!"

* * *

A half-hour later, we turned into Monticello, with its freshly asphalted streets. The air had warmed, and the smell of frying bacon and toast laced the air with a mouth-watering aroma. Compared to Liberty, with its bumpy gravel roads, the car moved with the grace of an ice skater. We glided into a parking space in front of Peterson's General Store. Its storefront glistened with freshly painted white clapboard and green trim. Even the floor of the front porch was painted green. An American flag, attached to the corner roof line, rippled in the light breeze as groups of older shoppers relaxed on wooden benches outside.

Although Peterson's was a General Store, not like the full-service pharmacy Albert had planned for the town of Liberty; it was a local landmark—a fully stocked mercantile store carrying practically every durable item a family needed. Best of all, it had a soda fountain. It was nearly impossible to avoid crossing paths with someone from town. Now, with Prohibition in full swing and the pubs closed, everyone met at the local soda fountain to socialize. I'd overheard in the city that the fountain was also a good place to buy illegal liquor and wondered if Peterson had a stock, too.

Robbie stood staring at the ice cream counter, his mouth wide as he walked in the door, his eyes assessing every inch of the soda fountain. Shelves holding coffee cups, cream-colored ceramic plates and bowls, as well as glassware in various shapes and sizes, waiting to be filled with ice cream sodas and soft drinks, lined the back wall. Beneath the shelves stood a waist-high counter holding a variety of syrups in glass containers, each topped with hand pumps plus rows of canisters. A small electric grill and two sinks were stationed along the back counter. On the opposite end, ice boxes storing milk, butter, and ice cream were built under the lower counter.

Every stool along the lengthy front counter, with its fifteen or more seats, was occupied. Half of them were filled with playful children twirling in circles on their round backless seats, sipping soda from tall glasses through straws, their ice cubes clinking. The other stools were filled with older men, their heads huddled together in conversation. In a deep hum, they pointed and discussed articles in the papers they'd spread out on the counter. All the while, they drank coffee and ate eggs with buttered rolls.

Robbie pulled on Albert's arm. "Are you building a fountain in your store, too?"

Albert laughed. "What's a pharmacy without a soda fountain? Of course, I am, and it should be ready by the Fourth of July when I open." He whispered in my ear, "Check out their menu."

A stool opened as we stepped toward the counter. I leaned down to Robbie's ear. "Hop up, and we'll get you a chocolate milk while Albert and I shop." I lowered my voice, "And don't tell anyone we're opening a store in Liberty. Got it?"

He nodded, pulling his thumb and forefinger across his smiling lips to seal them tightly. Oh, how he enjoyed being complicit in our caper. "Are you sure I can't get a soda?"

I shook my head. "No soda before lunch. Chocolate milk, like I said."

While I ordered for Robbie, Albert began walking the aisles, bending his body to study the lower shelves, displays, signs, and prices. Fully engrossed, he made quick notes on his pad with his pencil stub. He was so obvious. Some caper! I'd have to give him a lesson or two in sneaking around a store. My guess was he'd never done it before.

The soda jerk handed Robbie his chocolate milk and straw. "Here you go, son."

"Try not to get your drink all over your shirt, and no spinning. I'll be right back," I said, then froze in place, watching an older man wearing an apron approach Albert's side.

"What are you up to, young man?" the older man asked.

Albert answered, reaching out to shake the man's hand. "Nice to meet you. My name's Albert Kahn. I'm opening a pharmacy in Liberty next month. I'm just waiting for my license from the state so I can dispense medication. Thought I'd take a visit and introduce myself." Albert looked about the bustling store. "Looks like things are hopping down here."

The man hesitated momentarily, shook Albert's hand, then crossed his arms tightly against his chest. His right eyebrow lifted halfway to his hairline. His voice was loud and gruff. "Mahlon Peterson. I'm the owner. Didn't think we needed another store in these parts."

What was wrong with Albert? He was showing his cards so quickly; a foolish lamb heading to slaughter. From the corner of my eye, I noticed the older man sitting to my right twisting around to watch Albert and Mr. Peterson's exchange. I turned back to Robbie, pretending I didn't know Albert. I could hear Mr. Peterson speaking only an aisle away.

Albert switched the topic, seeking common ground. "I went to high school with your sons. How're they doing?"

Disarmed by Albert's familiarity, Mr. Peterson responded, "Local boy, eh? Nathan's fine. He moved to the city. Found life here in the country too dull. The others work for me. Timmy's still in school and works at a nearby farm this summer. None of them are here today."

Albert continued, "I grew up in the city til the war years. Then, I came here to help train the horses for France. Never went back. I love the country. I'm stocking medications for my aunt and uncle's patients." He stopped talking momentarily, then kept it up. "You know Dr. Drucker?"

I felt like screaming. Next, he'd be telling Peterson what he ate for breakfast. Couldn't Albert see that this Peterson character was just toying with him? Quit running your mouth!

Now recovered from Albert's personal questions, Mr. Peterson shot him a crooked smile. "Of course I do. But we use Doc Barker. He's been in these parts longer than any of us. My Pa opened the store years before your uncle came this way."

Albert said. "It seems silly to send folks all the way to Poughkeepsie for their medicines. It's much further than Liberty. And with the extra summer visitors, my bet is our two stores will barely keep up. We should support each other when we run low on supplies. Don't you think?"

Mr. Peterson coughed twice, not quite ready to draw a truce, ignoring Albert's remark. His tone hadn't warmed one bit. "I've been living well here, keeping food on the family table for the last twenty years after my pa passed. Don't go poaching my business. Ya hear me, son?" He drew out the word son, like he didn't mean it in a friendly way.

Albert's eyes darkened as he stared back at Mr. Peterson, straight in his eyes. I had to hand it to him. Albert kept his patience longer than I could have. His voice stayed even, but its neighborly tone had disappeared. "That was never my intention, sir. I'm sure there's plenty of business for both of us. As a matter of fact, I meant what I said about backing each other up this summer. Many city dwellers are relocating to the county to escape the summer heat. Things are changing up here, fast."

Mr. Peterson turned his back on Albert without having the good manners to say goodbye. He walked to the older men sitting near Robbie and me at the counter. Those men hadn't taken their eyes off Albert the whole time. Mumbling in a low voice, Peterson said to the huddle, every one of them sitting frozen as ice statues, "Boys, it looks like I've got myself a little competition from the Jews up in Liberty. There are too damn many of them coming this way for the summer. They don't believe in our Lord and don't talk our language."

Robbie opened his mouth to speak. I squeezed his wrist tightly, leaning toward him, whispering into his curious ear with the lightest touch of my voice. "Not a word...."

My skin crawled with anger. Our family was just as American as Peterson's. As a matter of fact, Aunt Jenny and Uncle Nate's son, Jake, died in France from the Spanish Flu, gasping his final breath in Eli's hospital. And Eli and Miriam were war heroes. Word of their bravery during the Great War and their care for wounded soldiers had, in just a few short years, turned them into local legends, both in the city and in Liberty. Eli, with his limb-saving surgeries, and Miriam, despite her polio brace, worked with her Uncle Ben at the American Hospital in Paris, with patients who had sustained facial injuries. They saved hundreds of American boys, if not thousands. How could that Peterson character not know? Didn't their time in France, Eli's lost eye, count for anything?

I could barely contain myself. Just as I was about to react, one of the old men pulled a large copper coin out of his pocket. I'd never seen anything like it. Indeed, it was too large to be currency. Out of the corner of my eye, I peered at the coin, reading its content, "One Country, One Flag, One Language" embossed around the edges. In the middle of the coin were imprints of a scroll, a crucifix, a Bible, an American flag, and the words "Constitution of the United States." The old man told his tight cluster, "It's time to call a meeting and see about this invasion."

* * *

An hour later, we were back at the farm, sharing news of our outing with Uncle Nate.

"God damn it, Albert! What were you thinking?" Uncle Nate shouted after he received the lowdown. "When will you learn to keep your words inside that noggin of yours?" His face was beet red. I knew he was ready to wring Albert's neck.

We gathered around the kitchen table. Aunt Jenny set a platter of chicken sandwiches before us. I was nervous, watching Uncle Nate explode. Had he simply held his temper with me for arriving at the farm unannounced, or was he more comfortable yelling at Albert because he was a boy and had lived for years in their home like a son? I couldn't take my eyes off them.

"I don't get it. I had my hat in my hands. What's their beef with us?" Albert implored, beads of sweat shining on his forehead. "Eli and Miriam deliver their babies, drive to their houses all hours of the night, and stitch their wounds, for God's sake." He wasn't about to stand down.

Uncle Nate took a calming breath. "Albert, not everyone uses your uncle for doctoring. They keep to themselves, like us. Young people don't understand how dangerous the world is. You think just because we sacrificed during the war, people will change overnight."

I blurted out. "Can someone tell me what you're talking about? What was that copper coin they slapped on the table? And what did he mean about a meeting?"

A dark silence fell upon the kitchen. Aunt Jenny rotated one of the ladder-back chairs, scraping it along the oak floor, and faced her husband. She lowered herself onto the rush seat. Reaching for Robbie's arm, she firmly pulled him onto her lap.

Robbie tried to pull away, but she held on. "Sit, Robbie, and listen to your great uncle. This is important for you to hear."

We turned our attention to Uncle Nate, who leaned back against the kitchen counter, crossing his arms at his chest, his face lowered. He lifted it and looked at Robbie and me. "Have you heard about the Ku Klux Klan? Some call them the KKK or Klan."

Robbie laughed, "I haven't. That's sure a funny name."

"Hush, Robbie. Listen and hold your tongue." Aunt Jenny scolded.

I shook my head, ignoring Robbie's remark, curious to hear Uncle Nate's explanation.

Uncle Nate sighed loudly, shaking his head in disgust. "It's a secret organization of evil men who think the country only belongs to them. It began after the American Civil War, when their slaves were freed. They did some very, very bad things down in the Southern states."

I gasped, realizing where this was heading. "You're telling us the Klan is up here, too?" Goose bumps broke out on my arms. My skin turned cold against my sweat.

Uncle Nate cleared his throat. "I'm afraid so. It seems a chapter started in Binghamton right after the men came home from the war in 1918, and they've been gaining steam ever since. Rabbi told me that there's a new group forming in Monticello."

I'd never heard anything so ridiculous and scary at the same time. "Why? There are hardly any Negroes around here."

Albert broke in. "They hate anyone who's not just like them, Christian and lily white. That includes Jews, Catholics, Italians, and anyone with a foreign accent. In other words, us!" He threw his cap across the room, yelling, "Uncle, if I had any clue whatsoever that Peterson was one of them, I'd never have gone there with Ella and Robbie. The whole thing makes me sick!"

I watched Albert and Uncle Nate closely as silent words pass between them. There was more to this problem than had been shared. "What else?" I asked. "What bad things have they done around here?"

At this point, Aunt Jenny could no longer restrain herself, blurting out, "They've started harassing us. In the South, they hung African men and women, and the law let them get away with it. They're monsters!" She shuddered. "They've gone after women and children. Burned houses and barns down."

Robbie's eyes opened wide with fear. I thought he'd cry. But instead, he turned to face her, placing his arms around her neck. "Don't worry, Aunt Jenny. I'll protect you."

Aunt Jenny sniffled. "Oh, my beautiful boy. *Ve* won't let any harm come to our family. It's not like where I came from, when *ve* couldn't fight back. This time, *ve* have guns, too. And we're not afraid to use them!" She latched eyes with Uncle Nate. "Tell them what happened last month."

An eerie silence settled in the room. Finally, Uncle Nate said, "Let's not scare the children, Jenny."

Aunt Jenny shook her head with vigor. "They may have grown up in the city, but they're lambs out here in the country. And right now, we're surrounded by wolves. They must know the truth and stay on guard."

Albert said, "She's right, Uncle."

Uncle Nate squirmed, still quiet.

I urged him on, my voice soft. "I want to know what happened. And I want to know what's up their sleeve. They said they were having a meeting."

"Alright, alright, already." Nate cursed under his breath. "The week before you showed up, they burned one of our Jewish neighbors' barns. It was nighttime. A milk cow was inside the barn. Burned alive!"

I gasped. "How do you know it was the Klan who did it?"

Albert answered, eyeing Nate with a determined expression. "They came on horseback, hooting and cursing, creating a big racket. When the owner looked out the window, he saw they were all wearing white capes with pointed hoods, holes for their eyes. They carried lit torches." By this point, his voice held a fury I'd never heard before. "It was them, alright."

Aunt Jenny caught a sob in her throat. "Why aren't you telling them the whole truth?" She shouted. "It was our boy, Martin's barn. Pure evil! They're criminals and must be stopped."

Uncle Nate tried to calm her, his voice lowered but strained. "Settle yourself, Jenny."

She rose from the chair. "I will not be settled. I will not lose another son! What if it had been their beautiful new house where our son and daughter-in-law live, and not the barn? Martin's expecting their first child this summer." Her voice had become shrill with anger; her face contorted and red. "I'm of a mind to burn their barns to a cinder and show them exactly how it feels! It's a damn pogrom. Just like we had in Belarus." Aunt Jenny stormed from the kitchen out the back door, the screen door slamming.

My jaw dropped with disbelief. An acrid sickness circled in my belly. Here, I'd thought it would be idyllic in the country—no scorching temperatures, no arguing, just nature and family love. But now, I couldn't deny this land was fraught with dangers of its own. First bootleggers, now the KKK. Stupid me. How could I have imagined that if I taught Robbie to swim, all would be fine?

* * *

The remainder of the weekend passed without incident. Robbie and I helped Aunt Jenny prepare for the boarders, making beds with her handmade quilts and colorful pillows, the likes of which I had never seen in the city. We placed fresh towels at the foot of each bed and stocked the kitchen pantry with more groceries than I'd ever seen in a home. Despite the excitement, I had little to say, but my head flooded with visions of this KKK, a vicious group I struggled to imagine. Hoods, torches? It was the stuff of nightmares.

By noon Sunday, the Farkas family arrived from Brooklyn. They were a group of five, including a nine-year-old girl, a boy Robbie's age, and a three-year-old girl. In their typical fashion, Aunt Jenny and Uncle Nate welcomed the family, waving towels in the air, as they drove up the driveway, Robbie and I following close behind. Road dust coated their black Model T, but the engine still hummed smoothly. The family poured out of the car seconds after Mr. Farkas pulled to a stop.

Aunt Jenny took the woman's hands in hers. "*Velcome* to our home in the country. You must be *Vilma*. How was your drive? I'll bet you're all hungry!"

Wilma stood quite still, taking in the scenery as the children scrambled onto the grass. Her face broke into a smile. "It was a long ride, but it's lovely to be here now. A slice of paradise."

Robbie edged his way to the boy and, without a pause, said, "I'm Robbie. What's your name? Wanna see the pond?"

The child smiled. "I'm Noah, and my sister is Adina."

Adina added, pinching her brother's arm. "Don't forget, Maya, our little sister. She's three, and I'm nine."

Noah pulled his arm away. "I'm glad there's a boy here. My sisters are driving me crazy." Noah drew finger circles around his ears.

I extended my hand to shake Wilma's. "I'm Ella, Robbie's older sister. Do the children swim?"

Adina called out, "Noah and I do, but Maya sinks. She doesn't know how at all."

I smiled, facing Mrs. Farkas. "I've been teaching Robbie, and if you'd like, I can work with your children so they're safe around the water."

The husband introduced himself to Uncle Nate as Sandor. "Sounds like a fine plan, but first we unpack and have lunch. Jenny's right. We're all hungry, and I must start back by midafternoon."

Wilma pinched her face in alarm. "But I thought you said you could stay the night."

Sandor threw his arm around Wilma's shoulder, pulling her close. "Don't fret. I'll be back Thursday evening, and we will have a nice long stretch together next Shabbat. By then, you'll be so familiar, you can show me all the sights."

I walked around to the back of the car with Uncle Nate. "We'll help carry your things upstairs to your rooms so you can settle in."

Tilting his head toward me, Uncle Nate whispered, "Thank you, Ella. Appreciate your help."

Aunt Jenny opened her arms, appearing relieved to get the process underway. "And I'll pull lunch together. *Ve'll* meet at the picnic table behind the house in half an hour." She fanned her hands in front of her face. "It's getting too hot to eat indoors."

Chapter Seven: Miriam

The following Monday evening, after a busy clinic and day with the children, I lay in bed listening to Eli's soft breathing. He was the only person I trusted with my secrets. It was clear to me that now, more than ever, I must know what was happening with Julian, but not by rattling Ella for more information. The circumstances around my brother had changed in magnitude since he and I struck a deal after the war.

Hearing that Julian expected the two children to share one bed was the last straw, but I still sensed Ella was holding back. There was more. And it was unfair to pressure her, taking the last shred of her innocence and dignity away. If I wanted to know the truth, I'd have to buck up and face my older brother head-on. The idea left my stomach sour. Our last exchange was unsettling, leaving us with only distrust.

Julian was seven years my senior. With little in common as children, and parents who raised us as different as night and day, outsiders could presume we were unrelated. We played separately, and as the years advanced, Mama and Papa had household help to care for me, never asking Julian to step in while they were out. In their later years, both Mama and Papa regretted not filling the void between us with more children, but by then, it was a moot point.

Unlike my busy social world full of girls my age, Julian had few, if any, friends. He'd return from school and hide out in his bedroom, reading or solving number puzzles. If I interrupted him, even with a soft knock on his door, he screamed for me to get lost. I knew Mama worried about his temper and isolation, but he was at the top of his grade. The teachers called him a genius with numbers. And so, Papa and Mama accepted our different natures with as much grace as they could muster, Papa often saying, "These two are the wonders God has given to us. He expects us to take their good parts along with their challenges." I always knew he meant Julian's challenges.

Mama worried about Julian constantly, hoping he'd straighten out in college, where there were other students equally intelligent who might outshine him. She hoped wrong. There were only three other young men beside Julian who excelled to his degree, all of whom graduated with the newfangled actuarial degree. They were extraordinarily gifted, but equally odd. When Julian graduated, there were no invitations to his classmates' graduation parties. After four years, he still had no friends. Our family celebrated alone.

Within a few weeks after college. Julian grabbed his first job offer and, by the end of the summer, had moved to Brooklyn. Every day, he walked to work from his one-bedroom apartment across the Williamsburg Bridge to the Jarmulowsky Bank, located in the thick of the Lower East Side. Julian always had a ready excuse when Mama peppered him with invitations for an after-work dinner.

That November, six months after graduation, he met and married Selma. She quickly moved into his apartment. He informed the entire family they had eloped. My parents were fit to be tied. They had done nothing to deserve his disregard for their feelings. To no one's surprise, Ella was born soon after.

Despite the doting love my parents had bestowed upon Julian, his simmering anger and rebelliousness, all that ran counter to our parents' values, grew over time. Julian had always loved playing cards and was passionate about the game of poker. I didn't know about his excessive gambling until he approached Papa for money two years after Ella was born. It was at that point my trust in Julian began to erode.

The shouting between Papa and Julian made the walls of our apartment vibrate. Once things escalated, Papa sent me to my room. Was he planning to strike Julian? Did he think I couldn't hear every word, every breath through the thin walls? Julian's angry voice grew more vicious by the minute. "You and Mama think you're better than us. Selma says you German Jews look down on her because she came from Belarus, has a thick accent, and wasn't born with your golden slippers. She's right, you know!"

I knew my Papa like the back of my hand, and his silence after that remark did not bode well for Julian. Papa had far more patience than Mama, but when his temper flared, it was formidable. Pushed too far, all hell could break loose. Finally, he spoke in a deep, strained voice. "How can you say such an ugly, hurtful thing? Is that how you ask for help? A grown man, a father with a good job at a bank?"

More silence ensued. I stood with my ear to the door, the seconds ticking like drumbeats in my head as I waited for Julian's rebuttal. His tone had cooled. "You know how expensive children are. Their medical bills, clothes, and food. It's never-ending."

Papa retorted, still holding onto his fury, "Son, you make a good living. Tell me the truth. What's the money for? What have you done?"

Julian waited a moment, then answered, "I only need a few hundred dollars."

"Only?" Papa's patience had thinned. "Only?" The volume of his voice grew. "That's a small fortune."

Julian spat out, "Otherwise, they'll shatter my knees." He paused. "Are you going to help me or not?"

Papa roared, "You're still gambling? Now, consorting with loan sharks? Outrageous!" As he stretched out the last word, I shrank to the floor like a puddle, splayed out on the bare wood, utterly flabbergasted. "What does your wife say?"

Julian scoffed with his typical imperious tone, "I don't need to explain myself to you, or her, for that matter. Besides, your money will eventually be mine in the end."

I was shocked to my core at the height of Julian's disrespect. Although my parents tolerated a considerable amount of back talk from Julian, I'd never heard anything so full of entitlement and disregard for their support and love for him.

Neither had Papa, now pushed over the top. His outrage was explosive, "How dare you! You come to me, acting like a prince, demanding your inheritance? You know damn well neither your Mama nor I was born with, what did you call it, golden slippers? But you were." He stopped for a moment, then added, "We worked ourselves half to death providing for you, giving you the education neither of us ever had. Now you speak to me this way? You're a disgrace!"

Julian's voice came through in a sneer, not registering a word Papa said, "So what's it going to be? Are you giving it to me now or after the worms eat out your eyes?"

"Ungrateful *mamzer*! Get out of my home and don't come back until you're ready to apologize and respect us for everything we've provided."

By this point, I had curled into a shaking ball, my head between my knees. Indeed, never a big fan of Julian, I still knew how much Mama and Papa loved him, never backing down to defend him in a pinch, even when they knew Julian was in the wrong. How had his gambling escalated to this point? He had pushed Papa past his brink.

I was thankful Mama was grocery shopping and wouldn't hear about the argument until Papa had a chance to cool off and work out a truce with Julian. I waited for close to an hour, embarrassed for my parents, while Julian stormed out, slamming the door slam behind him before I finally left my bedroom.

Papa didn't cool off one iota. Julian had broken the last pillar of Papa's trust, ending his lifelong devotion to his son. During the following days, I overheard Mama crying and arguing with Papa through our closed bedroom doors. My brother's problem had been kept tightly under wraps, brewing for years. This was the first time I understood the corrosiveness of his gambling habit. One they had unwittingly supported for years.

In those often-muffled conversations, I knew decisions about Julian and the future were at stake. My parents' angst had grown from a passing worry in high school to a full-blown distress that his gambling habit had become a lifelong problem. Beyond their broken hearts at the thought of estrangement, they worried about their substantial estate, particularly knowing Julian was sizing it up, waiting to take his share. At night, I struggled to find a comfortable position in bed, curling up with my pillow. I must try to stop dwelling on this crack in my family, or I'd be too tired for my nursing classes the next day.

Drifting, I recalled the arduous path leading my parents to their real estate fortune. Shortly before the turn of the century, Mama and Papa sold their garment businesses: Mama's dress kits and Papa's buttons. They invested the money in half a dozen apartment buildings, living off the rental income. On paper, at least, they had acquired a sizeable wealth despite continuing a frugal lifestyle.

For two more weeks, Papa and Mama debated until Papa finally put his foot down. "Tillie, it's time we face things head-on. He's a gambler. It's a habit he can't shake, and for years, we've been part of the problem. We will no longer feed the monster! I'm going to our attorney."

"But Abe," she drew a loud breath. "He's always been so good with numbers and cards. He can't help himself. We have so much. Why make such a big *tzimmis?*"

"You know what happens to gamblers?" he grumbled.

His question was met with silence.

"They borrow and take from anyone who will give money, even loan sharks! He'll ruin us if we allow him to drag us down. All our hard-earned money, everything we hoped to leave for our innocent little grandchildren will be squandered at gambling tables. You want that?"

Days later, one evening after returning home from my nursing classes at Beth Israel Hospital, they sat me down after dinner to share their final decision, one certain to destroy any future relationship I'd ever have with Julian.

Papa explained Julian's problem in excruciating detail as if they thought I'd been deaf to their arguing all these weeks. Out of respect, I remained silent, nodding my gloomy head as they described the years of Julian's lies and money disappearing from the house. I recalled the coins and dollar bills missing from my bureau. That must have been Julian's doing, too.

Finally, Papa said, "We've come to a painful decision. Your Mama and I agree it's our only choice if we want something left for our grandchildren."

I watched his face. Papa's eyes were hooded with disappointment, looking down at his hands as if he wished they held one last option. Finally, he lifted his eyes to mine. "We are giving you an important responsibility. It's either you or our attorneys. I trust your judgment and prefer to keep our family business under this roof."

I knit my brows, my hands grew clammy, bracing for what he was about to say.

Papa's eyes bore into mine. "Given the seriousness of Julian's gambling, we are placing our real estate holdings in a Trust under your name. You will be the sole trustee, with your Aunt Hannah serving as an emergency trustee in the event you are unable to fulfill your responsibilities. Julian will be forbidden from drawing any income or selling the real estate. Only you can."

I gasped. I knew nothing about real estate. "But Papa, all I've studied is nursing."

Mama reached for my hand. "We understand and have people at the bank and an attorney to help advise you. But for the most part, you don't have to do anything but deposit the rent checks in your bank account. We have a super in each building who can handle repairs and rent collection. And don't forget, they will be under Mr. Lieb, our attorney's watchful eye."

Papa continued, "Miriam, you're just as smart as your brother and far more sensible. Unless something unexpected happens and you're forced to sell the properties, the buildings generate a steady stream of rental income each month. Your mama and I live very comfortably on that income. We suspect you will, too."

So far, nothing he said concerned me greatly. But when he unraveled the next layer of his plan, I was aghast.

Papa hesitated. "It's your mother's and my wishes that Julian's half of the estate is left untouched until it's time for his children's education and their adulthood. Unless there is reasonable cause, such as illness, we will completely skip over Julian."

"But Papa!" How did he expect me to handle my brother with such devastating news once Papa and Mama were no longer there to back me up? Having witnessed the blistering arguments and name-calling between Papa and Julian, I knew it wouldn't take long for Julian's anger to redirect my way. "Isn't there some other way?"

"There are a million other ways, and when we're gone, you will face those options. But don't fool yourself, any of our wealth that goes into Julian's hands will run through his fingers like water. You must stand strong against him."

Mama dabbed her nose with her lace handkerchief, sighing a deep resignation. "Your father's right."

In the years following that discussion, I lost Mama to illness, and later Papa to apoplexy. Then the Great War overshadowed the country and our lives for two additional years. Both Julian and I were stationed in France, and I didn't have the time or stomach to deal with Papa's estate before departing. Instead, I left matters in the trusty hands of our attorney with Hannah's input if needed. But soon after returning from France, I received a cold, curt letter from Julian.

February 12, 1918

> *Dear Sister,*
> *Now that we've returned to the States unharmed, it is high time we meet with Papa's attorney to review the will. I would like to schedule this meeting in one week.*
> *Your Brother,*
> *Julian*

Unharmed? Perhaps he was unharmed, but with Eli's medical condition hanging in the balance, Julian's attitude left me irate. I took the letter to Hannah for her advice. She convinced me to get the meeting over with so I could move on. A week later Julian and I met in Papa's attorney's office.

For the first time in three years, Julian and I faced each other. Unlike so many emaciated veterans, his body had filled out, no longer the slender frame of an adolescent. His eyes were clear with purpose.

I shook his hand, still too annoyed with him for a hug. "You look well, Julian. Glad you sidestepped the shrapnel and Spanish Flu."

He answered in a flat tone. "They had me working on the supply chain. Didn't see much battle. For once, my clumsiness may have saved my life."

So that was it. Julian feigned being a klutz, allowing others to take horrible risks in the trenches on his behalf, yet still able to claim he served his country. In the meantime, Eli and I were deep in the action, serving in evacuation hospitals, facing the horror our boys encountered on the battlefield every minute of every day.

The grandfather clock ticked loudly. Although I was apprehensive, my annoyance and the year I spent in France had toughened me up. After a full year working in the war hospitals and then tending to Eli's devastating facial injury for the following six months, I knew I could take on my brother. It was a drop in the bucket compared to all I'd witnessed.

Hannah had updated me on his plight. Julian had lost his pre-war employment. News of the Jarmulowsky Bank's closure was no secret. Most of its depositors had been recent immigrants from the Lower East Side. When the Great War began, bank customers withdrew their deposits en masse to lend support to relatives in Europe. The shrinking bank's coffers forced the institution to relinquish its glory days and file for bankruptcy. I assumed Julian was unemployed.

"How's the job search going?" I asked, expecting a tirade of complaints.

Instead, he had uplifting news. "Good. I just accepted a position at Metropolitan Bank. Maybe I'll finally put my actuarial degree to use."

Was this the same man who'd stormed from the house years ago? Had he finally changed? I pressed, "How're Selma and the children?"

He snipped back, throwing me off balance. "The marriage is kaput. Selma caught me with another woman, and she finally has grounds for divorce. Better for both of us."

"Oh, Julian, I'm sorry." I knew adultery was the only way out of a marriage in New York, short of death. "Selma and the children must be devastated." I wondered if he bothered trying to fix things with Selma, recalling how heart-wrenching it was for Eli and me to find our way back to each other during our war separation.

Julian captured my eyes with a coldness that left a spray of goose bumps on my arms. "I couldn't care less. I'd wanted out of that marriage before I left for France. I shouldn't have given her a farewell *schtuppe*. Now I have one more kid to feed."

I was shocked at Julian's callousness. Those poor children. Then my blood boiled again as I realized he hadn't bothered to ask about Eli's condition.

A secretary poked her head around the door jamb. "Mr. Levine and Mrs. Drucker, Mr. Lieb is ready for you."

Chapter Eight: Albert

Tuesday evening, I sat with Wilma Farkas on Nate's front porch and picked her brain. I figured she'd be the right person to ask about household goods I should stock in the store for boarders. After all, she'd already spent a couple of weeks at the farm and seemed to have no trouble sharing her views on just about everything.

Wilma sat back, closed her eyes as she rocked on the porch, the chair's rhythmic creaking reminding me of the war tune "Over There." Once I got the tune in my head, it was near impossible to shake off.

Wilma began rattling off a list. "Rainy day toys, Lincoln Logs, and Tinkertoys. Perhaps marbles and jacks. When it rains, the children can't run about outdoors and swim. They get bored and wear on my nerves." An hour later, I had a full page of additional items to order.

I loved sitting on the front porch of the farm, my second home since my eighth year of school. Uncle Nate's and Aunt Jenny's house was as familiar to me as my folks' place in the city. My father, known to most as Dr. Kahn, was uniquely gifted. Not only was he a brilliant surgeon, but his ability to empathize with others, including my struggles, while he tended soldiers in France, set him apart from most fathers. From the time my natural mother was killed in a carriage accident, he understood the hole she'd left behind. Papa's time in the service picked at the same scab until I could no longer resist battling back at the world, at all the people who cared for me. Knowing I was healing on the farm, he did not object to leaving me with my aunt and uncle to finish out my childhood. Despite the distance, with a high-speed train from Poughkeepsie to New York City, we saw each other frequently.

And for Aunt Jenny, especially after losing Jake, having another young boy to care for was the salve she needed.

It was time for me to head back to Liberty. Ella walked me to the car. "I'm free on Saturday. I can bring Robbie along and help you stock shelves."

That girl never shied away from hard work. I'd hire Ella to handle the soda fountain and storefront in a heartbeat if Eli and Miriam allowed me to take her on. I knew I couldn't do the front and back of the pharmacy on my own, and she was damn smart, someone I could trust. Besides, my heart beat a few steps quicker when in her presence. Some days, I counted the minutes until I drove her home. But I couldn't read her; she remained a mystery to me. I had no clue if Ella was also churning warm feelings in that secretive heart of hers.

As two weeks rolled into three, we eagerly looked ahead to Friday's Fourth of July celebration. My state license had arrived days ago, and now I could legally dispense medications. I scrubbed every speck of dust from the store, leaving it pristine. The shelves were neatly stocked with everyday needs: cloth diapers, toys, bandages, laundry soap, and toothbrushes. The soda fountain stood ready for its first ice cream float. All the ingredients for breakfast, lunch, and the usual in-between meal treats of sodas, sandwiches, and ice cream floats were in the refrigerator and supply shelves. My brand new, top of the line Toastwich electric stove was a marvel. The confection display near the cash register held various candy bars and lollipops, while tobacco products were behind the register.

I covered the large picture windows facing Main Street with old newspapers. Ella had painted our announcements atop the newsprint. "Grand Opening, July 4th—Free Gifts for the Kiddies!" The town parade would be marching down Main Street on the Fourth. No one could miss us. Last weekend, Robbie and Ella filled fifty small bags containing Baby Ruth bars and peppermint sticks for the children. I had also purchased sparklers for those in the community, celebrating Independence Day in their lodging.

My favorite space in the pharmacy was the laboratory in the rear of the store, separated from the front merchandise and soda fountain by a locked door bearing a chest-high window. The lab was where I would make my mark, compounding much-needed medications for the sick, working in tandem with Eli's medical care. Eli and Miriam's experience during the war was a powerful magnetic force, pulling patients from all over the county to their practice in Liberty. But it was peacetime, and trauma was infrequent, so besides handling accidents on farms, they became a highly skilled pair at the day-to-day medical needs of delivering babies and making house calls. Both kept abreast of the new medicines like insulin, a long-awaited miracle treatment for diabetes management. It took less than two years for their clinic to become the top medical practice in the county.

* * *

After I returned from the farm, Eli and Miriam reviewed the list of medications and compounding ingredients I planned to order. Once we exhausted the list, I inched my way to the taboo topic. "Will you be prescribing whisky? I heard there're a few legal distributors like Buffalo Trace and Old Forester." I thought for a minute. "I can find out where Walgreens gets their supply."

Eli chuckled. "That's a loaded question if I ever heard one. Once we open that door, who knows what might happen."

Miriam tsked, "Honey, you recommend a shot of whiskey or schnapps for anxiety all the time. After four years of Prohibition, lots of your patients are running low or out of their personal supply. Where will they buy it? They'll have to go to Canada to smuggle in Seagrams."

"It's not so easy to get whiskey legally, even for pharmacists, and the Canadian border has gotten tighter in the past couple of years," Eli said.

The solution came to me in less than a second. "What about that Dutch guy? I'm sure he'd be happy to supply us. According to the State guidelines, I can keep a modest supply on deck in the back of the store."

Miriam bolted up from her chair, whispering loudly through her teeth as she looked to the stairs. "Are you crazy? He's a gangster!"

I wasn't sure what difference that made, but the last thing I wanted to do was wake the children with an argument. "Slow down, let me check around and see where they get whiskey in Poughkeepsie. I have a college friend up there who works at Borroum's Drug Store."

Eli was sitting deep in the pillows of the couch. He looked at both of us. "You're right. Some of my patients really benefit from a small amount. It settles their nerves, just like it did for the soldiers in the trenches. We will need to keep a stock on hand."

To me, they were making a lot out of nothing. The facts didn't add up. Both Robbie and Ella had spent a full day with Dutch, and he hadn't touched a hair on their heads. How bad could Dutch be? I also recalled Ella saying that Dutch gave Uncle Nate a bottle. Maybe I should have a swig and see if it's any good. If it tastes like some of the gut rot many of the bootleggers were distilling, then it would be a moot point.

I wanted to change the subject and prod Miriam to share more about Ella's family. No one was really talking about them anymore now that Robbie and Ella had been here a while. I knew there was a bigger tale behind their estrangement.

It was astonishing how easily Ella and Robbie had melded with the rest of us, always happy, always helpful. I picked up a children's book from the coffee table, spinning it in my hands, glancing up at Miriam. "I'm surprised neither of Ella's parents have shown up."

Miriam shot a glance at Eli. He lifted his brows, tilting his head toward his wife. "I'm afraid that's your department."

Miriam exhaled. "I spoke to Julian last week, and he's going to let them stay put for the summer."

I shrugged my shoulders. "That's it? Does Ella know you spoke to him?"

She snapped back, "No, she doesn't, and please don't tell her. There's far more to the story with that man than any of you know, and it's best the kids are kept out of it."

I screwed my face with disbelief. "Ella's not a child anymore. She's smart. She wants to go to college and is saving every nickel she earns this summer. Why is the man such a bastard to his children?"

Miriam shook her head in disgust, rose, and walked upstairs, leaving my words hanging in the air.

Finally, Eli looked me hard in the eyes, "I agree. There are far too many secrets in this family. But I promised Miriam I wouldn't discuss it. Let it sit until she's ready to share."

63

Chapter Nine: Miriam

I was ready to explode, leaving Eli and Albert behind in the parlor, storming up the stairs in my stocking feet brace and all, trying not to wake the children. That damn brother of mine hadn't stopped gambling for a minute. Mama and Papa had worked themselves to the bone, saving to ensure their family would never struggle, providing a good education, and a strong start to their adult lives. Instead, Julian drove them mad with his wretched habit until he was disinherited, convincing himself he could outsmart every other New York and Brooklyn gambler with his superior number skills. Julian dug in, just like the impostor he'd been during the war, deceiving his family and friends, leading them to believe he spent his time in France fighting, instead working far away from the battles and under the cover of the supply lines. I simply could not make sense of his warped mind.

I partially blamed it on my parents, stoking Julian's self-importance, telling him he was much brighter than his classmates throughout his childhood, as if being smart could offset his atrocious social skills. Julian was terrified to let others see his flaws. His undeserved conceit with numerical wizardry boomeranged back to destroy his life. With gambling odds constantly stacked against the player and Julian's inability to quit when he was ahead, he never beat the poker table for long.

Papa's warning rang in my ears. "Don't fool yourself. Any of our wealth that goes into Julian's hands will run through his fingers like water."

I opened the doors to the children's rooms, tiptoeing in and silently promising them a future protected from broken platitudes and untrustworthy parents, so they never felt compelled to run away. I bent down, kissing each of them on the cheek to calm myself before leaving their rooms to prepare for bed. A wave of guilt ran through me, knowing I should have provided equal financial support for Ella and Robbie all those lost years.

As I washed my face with the bar of Palmolive left swimming in a pool of water in its soap dish, my irritation resurfaced. When would my family stop wasting our luxuries? I switched my angry thoughts back to my visit to Mr. Lieb, Papa's attorney, a month after returning to New York after the war. Julian had lied through his teeth the entire time, bamboozling me.

Once Julian and I were summoned from the waiting room, we sat silently in Mr. Lieb's office, a formidable space filled with heavy wood furniture and cheerless, dark fabrics covering the chair cushions and windows. A pair of gold tassels encircled the heavy drapes, holding them open. The cords were hooked to the outer frames of the tall windows, allowing a block of afternoon light to pour through the soiled glass and illuminate the carpet with shattered rays, while particles of dust sparkled in the air.

Mr. Lieb, who had known Julian and me since childhood, had handled all of Mama and Papa's business affairs. His first assignment had been to advise Mama with her early Butterfield Pattern Company struggles during her years producing dress kits. After Papa and Mama sold their garment businesses, he handled their apartment building acquisitions and wills.

The door opened, and Mr. Lieb, now a bent older man, shuffled in. "Good morning. I'm relieved to see both of you well and in one piece after France."

We stood and shook hands. "And how are you feeling these days?" I asked.

His craggy face broke into a smile. "Always better, Miriam, once I see you. Next month, I retire. I'm handing the practice to my son, Samuel. He's excellent and will take over your parents' affairs after our meeting today." His face shifted between Julian's and mine as he adjusted the wire glasses on his aquiline nose, a nose skilled at sniffing out frauds. He asked me, "How are things going with that brave husband of yours?"

Julian interrupted, "Enough chit-chat. Get on with the matters at hand."

Rude, as expected. My anger boiled through my belly. Keep your control, Miriam. I reminded myself that it was simple; follow Papa's instructions.

Answering Mr. Lieb, I said, "Eli and I are getting through the end of his face surgeries. We're beginning to think about what we'll do next." I shot Julian an angry look. "We'll start the meeting when you're ready, Mr. Lieb."

After positioning his short, round body in the desk chair, he adjusted the old steel Bauhaus lamp with its curled arm to shine on the papers he'd extracted from the folder on his right. After turning a few pages, he said, "Oh, here we are. Let me read this portion aloud to you both."

I knew what the will contained. Mr. Lieb's words melted into a sonorous drone as I watched Julian's menacing face turn beet red, the blood vessels in his temples distend, pulsing with anger.

Julian glowered, "How dare he!" Then, he shot out of his chair, practically tipping it over, and paced the rear of the room, spinning in circles. "Papa had no right to do that. I'm his rightful heir. I'll contest!"

While Julian's outburst turned my stomach on end, Mr. Lieb's calm response astonished me. His face didn't move a muscle as he sat still, eyes glued to Julian, waiting for the tirade to cool. "Young man, not only is this document entirely legal, but your father struggled with your reckless gambling for years. It's all documented in the file; every dollar he spent to bail you out of your financial holes. Abe spent endless hours sitting in your exact chair, sorting out ways to handle you. The decision to remove you from his will was perhaps the most difficult of his life, and I'll have you know, well-documented with your sordid history. But rest assured, your children will be entitled to your half when they become of age."

Like a chameleon, Julian's temperament shifted from anger to calm, his face composed as he envisioned a path to the money. He walked to the edge of Mr. Lieb's desk, leaning into the man's face. "Didn't you know? I haven't gambled in years. If I haven't gambled, then how could this be true? That would make the document null and void."

Mr. Lieb's brows and chin dropped, and pity crossed his face. "Good luck with that, son. You'll spend what little money you might have, losing your case." He scrunched his brows, "And I must tell you with complete honesty, it's not worth the gamble."

At that, Julian stormed from the room.

Ten minutes later, I left after expressing my gratitude to Mr. Lieb for enduring Julian's tirade and arranging to direct all the apartment rental earnings to my bank account. When I stepped out of the building onto the sidewalk, Julian was still pacing, waiting for me.

He charged my way; his hands spread helplessly at his sides. "Miriam, you must believe me. I'm a changed man. No more gambling. I have too many responsibilities with the children..." He hesitated, grumbling, "and alimony."

It didn't add up, but I detested fighting, struggling to find a way through the impasse. "Why can't you make ends meet with your salary? Eli and I aren't going to spend any of the extra income. We plan to save it for the clinic we're building and our children's education."

But Julian didn't hear a word. He was just warming up. "My children are much older and have endless needs. Besides, I need to pay a lawyer for the divorce and rent a second apartment. My expenses are far greater than yours."

I stood still as a statue, repulsed by his pleading, atrocious behavior in Mr. Lieb's office, and inability to behave like a grown man. "Julian, as much as I'd like to help you, these were Papa's wishes, and I intend to respect them. Your children's portion will remain safe and sound in the Trust. In the meantime, let me know if they have special needs."

Like a sudden streak of lightning, he unleashed his fury, contorting his face into a sneer. "You conniving bitch! You plotted with Papa to do this all along, didn't you?"

I looked at him with pity, my shoulders dropping, remembering the intensity of his arguments with Papa, Mama's crying, and me cowering behind my bedroom door. Julian didn't have an inkling or care how much pain he'd inflicted on our family. "That's ridiculous." I turned away, walking to the bus stop at the corner. "Good day, Julian."

He called back to me in a singsong, menacing voice. He wasn't done with me. "I know your dirty little war secret, Sarah Rosen. That was the name you hid behind in France, you lying worm. I wonder what might happen to your flawless reputation if that got out."

My blood froze.

* * *

Eli's footsteps, padding up the stairs, pulled me back to the present. He was the only person I trusted with the truth about my parents' money and Julian's gambling. He entered the bedroom and wrapped his arms around me. "Are you alright, darling? Why did you tell Albert you'd spoken to Julian?"

I sighed, "I suppose I shouldn't have lied, but I wanted to end the discussion. I know I must face my brother again now that I know he's been gambling. I've no choice but to cut him off from the rent income I send monthly. It's obvious he's not spending it on the children. It's been five years, and the scoundrel has the two of them sharing a bed. It's absolutely appalling." I began to cry. "I'm a horrible, foolish person for keeping it up all these years. How could I have waited so long without checking in on them?"

Eli squeezed me tighter, caressing my back, comforting me. "If I were Ella, I'd run away too. But despite their deprivation, somehow, what's underneath their bedraggled coating is decent. They are strong children, and if anything, they prove that money alone doesn't make for good people." He rocked my body, pulling me into his safe cocoon. His familiar scent drew me in; not the scent of a man who worked in the fields with his hands, but the scent of a thinker and healer—antiseptics, soap, medicines. As tempted as I was to pull him in tighter, I tenderly moved back, at least for the moment.

My eyes pleaded for guidance. "Am I handling Julian the right way?"

He leaned his lips to my ear. "Hold off for now. Let the children recover this summer. Besides, Julian must know you're onto him. Let him stew in his own bilious soup."

Chapter Ten: Ella

It was the Monday evening before Albert's Drug Store Grand Opening. We had only three days left to prepare for the Fourth of July. I'd spent the early evening hours helping organize the pharmacy laboratory in the back of the store. Workmen were still banging nails into the walls, applying touch-up paint to the areas marred with black smudges and scratches.

Finally, Albert drove me back to the farm. Before I jumped from the car, he leaned his head to mine. "I need to tell you a secret, Ella."

The corners of my lips lifted, curious to hear what he would say.

His eyes held a flirtatious squint. "I could never have gotten this set-up done without you. I'm certain you came to Liberty for a bigger reason."

I shifted my head to the side to face him, smelling his minty breath from the candies we'd eaten on the drive home to the farm. "And, what's that?" I ribbed back.

Before I could react, Albert kissed me gently and pulled back ever so slightly. His lips, delicious pillows of softness and affection, drew me in for more. Just one more kiss, I thought, but Aunt Jenny's caution about boys stopped me.

He sensed my hesitation. "What's wrong? You must know I'm wild about you."

I shook my head. "I've never kissed a boy before. Well, except for Robbie, and that was always on the cheek."

Albert's sincere brown eyes searched mine. "How do you feel about me?"

I sighed deeply. "You are the best cousin in the world, and I like you very much. But aren't we first cousins? Is this permitted?"

Albert threw his head back and laughed. "If we were blood-related, it might not be okay, but we aren't. Anna and I are adopted. My parents are not tied to your bloodline."

I leaned toward his face, and Albert's next kiss lingered, sending tingling sensations from my lips to my toes. This time, I gasped. "Holy Smokes!"

Albert pulled back, his eyes twinkling with mischief. "Enough for now. Don't want your bodyguard, Aunt Jenny, getting riled up."

Slightly rattled by the sensation but thrilled by his affection, I said, "That was my very first, divine kiss." I struggled to find something to say that would put the brakes on. "You must know I have a lot to figure out, especially what's up with Robbie and me going home at the end of the summer. And I need a plan for college. My responsibilities should come first, right?"

Albert's smile hadn't left his face. "But did you like the kiss? How do you feel about me, aside from all those excuses?"

"I like you very much. Those were not excuses. We must take things slow, or you know it won't work."

He lifted my hand, kissing it in a demonstration of Victorian chivalry, ignoring the second half of my answer. "See you in the morning."

I walked into the house with a wide grin. After two weeks, worrying about everything under the sun, it was a joy to experience my first unforgettable kiss.

When I entered the steamy kitchen, Aunt Jenny was in a frenzy, perspiration coating her forehead as she filled platters of food, ferrying them out to the picnic table in the backyard. The fragrance of salted steamed vegetables and a savory meatloaf filled the air. Freshly baked rolls in a wicker basket on the counter were covered with a red checked napkin, keeping them warm. "My goodness, Ella. Why are you so late? I could have used your help the last hour."

I set my purse on the table and took the platter of meatloaf from her hands. "I was helping with last-minute preparations at the pharmacy. I'm so sorry."

The entire scene was unexpected. Guilt raced through me, leaving me with a sour stomach. Knowing Aunt Jenny for the last two weeks, she was a woman who kept her calm, thriving on chores and family energy. "Where's Wilma? Doesn't she usually help?"

"We'll discuss it after dinner." Aunt Jenny slipped back into her edgy silence.

Something had happened that day. I hoped for Aunt Jenny's sake it wasn't too bad. She'd come to enjoy Wilma and the children in just a week. "What else can I do to help?"

She pointed to the platters. "We need to get drinks and glasses out. The table's already set."

I scurried outside with the platters, rushing in and out of the house, retrieving the rest of the dinner, a pitcher each of lemonade and cold water. Then Aunt Jenny clanged the dinner bell. One by one, Wilma and her children rushed into the kitchen, stopping to wash their hands. Uncle Nate and Robbie followed close behind. I pulled Robbie aside before we reached the table. "After dinner, we need to talk."

He nodded; his eyes downcast, glued to the grass below.

I wanted to know what had happened after I left for Aunt Miriam's that morning. Robbie's guilty face told me he was complicit. I'd never forgive him if he spoiled the summer for both of us.

Dinner passed with an uncommon quiet. The only noise was the evening breeze blowing through the fluttering leaves above and the passing of platters, forks scraping plates, chewing. Wilma's younger children were the only voices indifferent to the silence.

I gathered the dinner plates and platters at the end of the meal. "I'll be right back with honey cake and cookies for dessert. Anyone care for tea?"

The heads shook. Robbie got up from his chair and lifted an empty platter. "I'll help."

We entered the kitchen, waiting for the screen door to shut. "What's going on, Robbie. What happened today?"

He began to cry. "I was supposed to look out for Noah, but I forgot."

"Just tell me."

Robbie wiped his nose on his undershirt sleeve. "We were exploring the farm, beyond the orchard, looking for ripe fruit. Then we saw two men coming our way. They looked familiar to me. At first, I thought they might be neighbors."

I bent down to his face, staring him straight in the eyes. "And?"

"They called out, "Hey, you two boys, come here." Noah ran their way, and I followed." He hiccupped a cry, then gasped for air, settling. "I knew one of them. He was one of the old men from Peterson's soda counter. You know, the ugly guy with that big copper coin."

My stomach tightened, never realizing the boys could get in trouble on Uncle Nate's land right before our eyes. "What happened next?"

Robbie's lips trembled. "They laughed and looked at each other as if they had a secret. Then they asked if we wanted to visit their farm with them, in their car."

"Oh no!" I whispered, alarm sending chills down my back.

"I knew right then they were bad people. Strangers. I grabbed Noah's hand, and we ran home as fast as we could. Now everyone's mad at me for taking Noah too far from the house."

I hugged Robbie hard, then handed the dessert plate to him. "No, you're not getting blamed. I'm sorry they scared you and everyone else. You did the right thing, grabbing Noah and running home. I'll talk to Uncle Nate. In the meantime, take the honey cake outside to the table and try not to spill it on the grass."

Oh my God, the Klan was casing out the farm, planning their next attack. Fear laced through my body, my stomach flipped over so quickly I barely had time to turn to the sink, throwing up every bite of dinner. I ran cold water across my face, wiping off the dampness with Aunt Jenny's red checkered dish towel.

Her voice came through the back door. "Ella, are you alright?"

I turned away from the sink. "Not really, what are we going to do? What if—"

Aunt Jenny set her hand on my back. "We'll talk later when the children are in bed. Right now, I'm worried we'll lose Wilma and the kids." She exhaled a deep sigh. "Just when we're all settling in. Let's try to stay calm. I have a mind to go after those evil men with Martin's old gun."

I nodded, while a bit amused by her feistiness. "I'll handle the clean-up. Better that you and Uncle Nate stay with her."

I was left alone for the next half hour, barely aware I was cleaning the kitchen, scraping leftovers into small containers for the icebox, washing and stacking dishes to dry on the drainboard.

All the while, my thoughts were immersed in this new threat, the Ku Klux Klan, a terror group I'd never heard of in New York City. I wasn't naïve; I knew the city was fraught with perils. People were mugged and hit by cars every day—dangers that could kill you in minutes. I knew to hold tightly to my pocketbook and not swing it around like a toy. From the time I was small, I heard the adults banter that Jews were scorned by the uptowners, even the wealthy German Jews. I understood most colleges didn't accept Jewish students, and I would go to City College if I went to college at all. For that matter, countless businesses wouldn't hire us either.

But this KKK disturbed me in a more penetrating, sinister way. Small mobs lurking around, torching barns, men disguised in pointed hoods. It was something out of a pulp magazine. How would we ever protect ourselves from such shadowy villains? Would the law help us, or might they be in on it, too?

* * *

Finally, all the children were settled down in bed, leaving Wilma, Uncle Nate, and Aunt Jenny settled in the parlor. I was in the kitchen preparing tea when Uncle Nate began. I listened intently.

His voice was gentle. "Wilma, I know this event today disturbed you. It unsettled us as well."

She began to weep. "Who are these terrible people? What do they want from us?"

Aunt Jenny interjected in a calm voice. "Mostly to scare us away. They started with their terror in the southern states after the Civil War, tormenting the freed slaves. Then found their way north to the country up here since the boys returned from the Great War."

Wilma crumpled her face in disbelief. "Terror? But why such behavior? That's not what America stands for."

Uncle Nate shook his head, exhaling a loud sigh. "They think because their people came to America first, they have some ungodly claim over the land. They don't like our languages or our religions and think by scaring us, they'll drive us out."

That was my Uncle Nate, telling the stark truth with no histrionics. I entered the parlor holding the tray, setting it gently on the coffee table. A waft of lemon and spices curled into the air. I poured and handed a cup to each adult. "Is it alright if I join you?"

Aunt Jenny motioned for me to sit, adding, "Of course, they want to scare us, but they are still dangerous. They burned Martin's barn and killed a milk cow."

Wilma gasped. "Where's the law?"

Uncle Nate drew a long sip from his cup. "They know about it, but don't have proof of who started the fire. Before we get them involved again, I think Eli and I should take a ride down to Peterson's and have a neighborly word with him."

I could picture Eli making his case. The man was a peacemaker and healer. During the war, he'd performed more surgeries than most doctors had in their careers. Would he have to pull his eye patch off to prove his sacrifice for America? How many of those hillbillies had even fought for this sacred country they held as if it were theirs only? Showing the hole in Eli's face would set them straight. Or was prodding at the men's cowardice a way to trigger them further?

I leaned forward toward my uncle. "Should I come along? I can vouch for Robbie. I saw the men at the soda counter, too."

My uncle's calm with Wilma was a thin façade. His anger cracked through, startling me with his fierce words. "Absolutely not! This is a conversation for grown men. Not for the ears of young ladies." He sat momentarily, breathing loudly through his nose, restoring his composure. "But you make a good point. I'll have Albert come with us. He was there with you at Peterson's."

Soon after our talk, Uncle Nate was on the phone to Eli and Albert, arranging a ride down to Monticello the next day.

In the meantime, Aunt Jenny sat beside Wilma, patting her hand, assuring her in their shared accent that this would end the torment. Aunt Jenny changed the subject to a discussion of the types of pies they would make the next day.

I wasn't convinced a conversation at Peterson's would do a damn thing. I'd seen the hateful looks on the faces in that store.

Chapter Eleven: Ella

The following day, Albert dropped me off at Miriam's before collecting the men for their ride to Monticello. Our morning drive from the farm was strained, fraught with unsaid words, so different from our typical rides. For the last week, we both burst with contagious chatter, a feeding frenzy of plans for special drug store events during the summer, everything from free balloons to contests with peppermint stick prizes. Albert believed that if he delivered a superior service to customers, he'd win them over for life. Now, with Peterson's hostility, he no longer cared about poaching customers in Monticello or pretending to be civil. The presence of the Klan on our farm in broad daylight was the last straw. Our men had a burning anger, ready to dust off old guns, bayonets, and defend their families and land with their lives. How dare the Klan approach our children?

"Albert, you must try to be peaceful. What they did at Martin's farm was…." I searched for the right words.

"An act of war. That's what it was!" Albert shouted into the wind that poured in through his open window, blowing his dark curls helter-skelter. "We'll answer with violence next time they try anything. Today is their final warning."

I thrust my head back against the seat. "Who do you think you are, Jesse James?" I shouted back, my exasperated voice filling the space between us. "None of you are sharpshooters. You'll get yourselves killed if you show up with rifles." I thought for a moment. "Are you inviting the sheriff to join you?"

He turned to me, spitting out his words. "No. These thugs showed up on our property unprovoked, without the law. We plan to do the same."

Were all three men equally stupid? Eli, with one eye, Uncle Nate, who hadn't shot a gun in who knew how long, and Albert. Gotta love the man, but he didn't have a mean bone in his body. They'd all likely get themselves killed in a scuffle. I tried to talk some hard sense into his head. "Whatever you do, don't go in that store with a weapon. If you have a gun and things heat up, they can always accuse you of taking the first shot. You'll end up in prison—the perfect solution to getting rid of us."

Albert didn't answer, but I could tell from his jumpiness he was thinking, eyes squarely on the road. All I got in return was a harumph.

I shouted at him. "Are you a damn fool? Did you hear what I said?"

The best I could get was a nod as he screeched to a stop beside the sidewalk before Miriam and Eli's place. Glaring at Albert as I opened my car door, I said, "There are better ways to handle goons." That's when it hit me. The solution we needed might be close by.

Closing the door with a bang, I entered the house. Baby Sarah was crying upstairs. Miriam called out, "Ella, is that you? Is something the matter?"

What was I thinking? I had no right taking my anger out on her little family. I answered in a loud whisper. "I'm so sorry. I was arguing with Albert. The men have lost their marbles!"

The cries from upstairs quieted. She waved me into the kitchen. "Come, talk to me. The twins are still sleeping. We have only moments before everyone is awake."

I followed her into the kitchen, not wanting to worry her, but needing reassurance. I dropped into a chair by the breakfast table. "What did Eli tell you about today? Do you think going to Monticello is a good idea?"

Miriam leaned against the counter. "Perhaps if the Klan knows we've seen some of their faces, they'll back off."

I figured I'd get right to the point. "Is Eli taking a gun?"

She snapped back. "Good God, Ella. Why would you think they'd bring weapons?"

"It's just…just that Albert was so angry. He was seeing red."

Miriam pulled a chair close to mine and sat. "There are no weapons. Trust me. That's the last thing anyone wants. Including those awful men."

"But look what happened to Martin's barn and his poor cow?" I implored. "These are terrible people."

Miriam reached out to touch my arm and calm my frayed nerves. "I'm sorry they told you about that."

A storm cloud of secrets enveloped me, surrounding my body like a scratchy wool blanket, leaving me restless and unsettled. I wondered how many more I'd discover this summer. Would they find out my secrets, too? The money I stole from Papa. Although, if truth be told, my misdeed was a drop in the bucket compared to what was going on around here.

It was a perfect time to change the subject. Albert told me Miriam spoke to Papa this past week, but Miriam never said a word. Full of gab every morning over breakfast, I thought it strange she hadn't mentioned anything. Especially since the first thing Papa would have told her was about the money I stole. "Albert told me you spoke to Papa. What did he say?"

Miriam dropped her head. "He told you that?"

"When did you speak to him? What did Papa have to say?" I repeated, no longer allowing her to stall.

She paused. "I wasn't truthful with Albert. I didn't speak to your father yet."

I shook my head. "Why did you say you had? I don't understand."

Her contemplative green eyes searched mine. "Your father and I have a complicated relationship. I will eventually need to clear the air with him, but this is not the right time. Not while you and Robbie are getting settled in." An infant's cry pierced the air. "I'm not even sure how much you know. Can we let things sit for now?"

Exasperated, I heard little feet descending the staircase. The house was awake.

I nodded, more confused than ever. My hunch was right. There was a secret around every corner.

Chapter Twelve: Albert

Uncle Nate, Eli, and I entered Peterson's General Store with a clear mission. This time, Peterson and his cronies would be put on official notice. It didn't take a genius to figure out these men were the ones who burned down Martin's barn. We would hold them personally accountable for any further injury or damage.

Mahlon Peterson was behind the soda counter when we entered. The bell over the door clanged as we walked in. Peterson was bent over the bar, deep in conversation with the same four cronies who sat at the counter last time I came. As if they were one colossal filthy insect, their eight eyes turned to us in unison, glaring straight at us. I had a bad feeling this conversation would not go well.

Uncle Nate stepped forward, extending his hand to Mr. Peterson. "Mornin', Mahlon. Any chance I can have a private moment?"

Mr. Peterson twisted his face away from the men toward the three of us, keeping both hands firmly on the counter. "Anything you need to say can be said right here."

I watched Uncle Nate, unintimidated, as he cracked a tiny smile. "Mahlon, I've known your Papa since I came up to these parts forty years ago. God rest his soul. Watched you grow up. Our families have been peaceful, living and farming together since before the new century. We've shopped in your store for decades, our kids schooled together, have never had any cause for dispute. What's all this ugly business, now?"

Mr. Peterson, a half head taller and ten years younger than my uncle, stood straight, gazing down at him. "No idea what you're talkin' about,

Nate."

Uncle Nate scoffed, anger lacing into his voice. "You've always been an honest man. No need to deny things." He turned to the huddle of tough older men. "My nephew saw two of you scouting my property, trespassing, only a few weeks after my son's barn burned to the ground. Did you know his milk cow was roasted alive? What kind of decent man on God's green earth tortures innocent animals?"

Peterson was ready for a fight, his legs planted far apart, sleeves pulled up his arms, without any provocation from us. What happened to the middle ground where sensible men found peace and resolution? I'd never seen this type of animosity in all my years growing up in the county. The Klan had brought with it a hateful tide of violence.

Eli stepped forward. "Look, fellas, there's no reason we can't get along. The county is big, and there is plenty of space for us all. Besides, your business is booming."

A burly man in his forties stood, eying Eli. His unshaven face barely concealed a deep scar across his chin. "Here's the problem. You Jews are crawling through the countryside like swarms of rats. It's making the land ungodly. Un-American."

I was stunned. His words curdled under my skin, arousing an unexpected anger I could barely restrain. Before thinking, speaking through clenched teeth, I'd dug my forefinger into his chest. "Un-American, you say? Do you know who you're talking to?" I drew a deep breath, my body burning, hands clenching. "Who among you served in the Great War?"

Quiet. Not one man stepped forward.

I pointed to Eli, my voice rising to a fevered pitch. "Dr. Drucker is a goddamn war hero. Lost half of his face for this country you think is yours alone." My voice rose to a scream. I leaned into his face, my nose filling with the stink of his unwashed body. "Can't get more American than that!"

Uncle Nate reached out and yanked my arm backward, drawing me away from the counter. "Calm down, Albert. Let's settle things like civilized men." Returning to Mr. Peterson, he said, "Look, Mahlon, we don't want trouble. Never have."

They locked eyes; the veneer of friendship had dissolved. Uncle Nate continued, "But it's wise for you to remember, we have a right to defend ourselves if provoked." He paused and turned his head, scanning the other men, speaking with a firmness I hadn't heard in a long time. "And we will. That's a promise." He took a long breath, eying each man. "You stay off our properties and away from our families."

The men stood, glaring, noses twitching, itching for a fight. Our warning only moved us closer to a conflict.

Leaving the store, I heard one man utter. "No way I'd have gone over there and fought to defend frogs. Besides, I've got German family who fought against us. Those Jews are a bunch of fools. Probably killed some of their own, fighting on the wrong side in that god-forbidden war."

Chapter Thirteen: Ella

The ear-splitting decibels of horns and drums in the marching band on Main Street rattled the front windows of the drug store. The Liberty Band led the Fourth of July parade played familiar war tunes *"It's a Long Way to Tipperary"* and *"Over There."* The melodies made my spirits rise. Singing along with the band, I realized I was singing alone. I turned to Albert. "What's the matter? It's your big day. You should be excited."

His face was grim. Albert had been brooding since his harsh encounter at Peterson's

General Store. "Those thugs don't give a damn the sheer number of immigrants who fought for America. Twenty percent of the U.S. Army were new Americans, and so many perished, like Jake."

I shrugged. "They probably don't care. They only have one thing on their minds, and that's to push us out of here."

Barely listening, he added, "Did you know that seven Jewish soldiers received Medals of Honor? Or that many soldiers weren't even citizens and couldn't speak English? We chose to defend a country that offered all Americans refuge from the torment in Europe. We made it safe for the Klan, too. How can they be so blind to their hypocrisy?"

I winced, trying to set the discussion on track and lift his spirits. Although I shared his sentiments about the Klan, France could have been another planet for all they cared. Like Robbie and me only weeks ago, these goons probably hadn't once ventured more than a few miles from home. How could they grasp the enormity of the Great War when I couldn't? "They're a bunch of ignorant cowards, hiding behind white hoods, trying to act tougher than they are. We can't let them dictate our lives or spoil the fun." I placed my hand on his sleeve. "This is your day. What you've worked so hard for."

He studied my face a few seconds, until his scowl melted off. Then, out of the blue, asked, "Can I kiss you again? That will distract me."

I stifled a laugh, not knowing if he was kidding or manipulating me. Were men truly that simple? Either fighting or loving? I leaned toward his face and gave his cheek a quick peck. "We're not going to start romancing in public. But Albert, it's your day. You worked hard for this moment. Think about how you graduated from pharmacy school and are now opening a drugstore." I took a deep breath, spun in a circle, stretching the skirt of my yellow checked gingham dress to the sides, and added, "You didn't even notice my new dress. Look at how cute it is, short with a low waist. Now I'm as fashionable as the city women. Aunt Miriam gave it to me. After the baby, she doesn't think she'll squeeze into it ever again."

Albert smiled broadly, throwing his arm around my shoulder, pulling me into a side-ways hug, tipping me off balance. "You are adorable. You must know I'm falling for you. Whether you like it or not."

Out of the corner of my eye, I spotted the marchers making their way up Main Street behind the band. I pointed them out. "Look, here come the veterans! And Eli and Miriam, dressed in their medical uniforms, are leading the parade with their kids."

As they passed the drug store, pushing Sarah's baby carriage and holding the twins' hands, Eli held up a sign in the shape of an arrow, pointing it at Albert's Store. It read, "Welcome, Liberty Drugs!"

That did it. Surprised and delighted, Albert snapped out of his temper, waving and jumping in triumph, his eyes misting with emotion. He pointed to the large banner in the store's front window, shouting back to the marchers, "Get your free Fourth of July treat!"

Men and women shouted back. "After the parade. Save something for us."

I tugged at the sleeve of Albert's new white pharmacy coat. "Take this off. Let's lock up and join them. No one will come into the store for at least another hour. And bring a stack of business cards. We'll hand them out."

Ten minutes later, a crowd of several hundred townspeople formed at the western end of Main Street. A temporary platform had been constructed over the last week, specifically for this day. An American flag, fluttering in the light breeze, hung from an oak tree's thick branch that extended behind the podium. Townspeople and farmers followed behind the marchers to this spot, spreading out among the vacant chairs, some unfolding family-sized blankets on the grass.

The County Commissioner, a portly middle-aged man with a bushy mustache sporting a pinstriped summer suit stepped up to the podium, waving his straw boater hat, welcoming the crowd. The Commissioner approached the microphone, tapping it for sound. The microphone emitted a loud screech, quieting the audience. Holding it farther from his mouth, he said, "Well, that got your attention. How about we start by standing? Men, remove your hats, and let's recite the Pledge of Allegiance. Please remain standing."

The crowd chanted in unison, "I pledge allegiance to the Flag of the United States of America, and to the Republic for which it stands, one Nation, indivisible, with liberty and justice for all."

Band members arranged their scores, then played "The Star-Spangled Banner." The conductor swung his baton with vigor, straining it upwards to the clouds when they reached, "The bombs bursting in air."

As I looked about, men and women were wiping their eyes. I wondered how many were still mourning family members they lost during the war. Finally, the band sat.

The Commissioner cleared his throat. "Welcome, citizens of and visitors to Liberty, New York. Today, we celebrate the birth of our country and the democracy we hold dear. Thank you, veterans, for your service, and a special heartfelt thank you to the families whose sons made the ultimate sacrifice defending our beloved country. Please honor them with a moment of silence."

The men held hats to their hearts with one hand and wrapped their wives in their other arm. Eli's eye patch was daily proof of our family's sacrifice in the Great War. But what about the men buried in France and Belgium, like Cousin Jake? Or the ones who returned so impaired that they still had trouble stringing sentences together or remembering their names? I couldn't fathom how difficult it was for families to have their children's graves thousands of miles away or to have them home, alive but lifeless. My heart ached as I scanned the crowd, finally understanding the gravity and cost of the war Papa always derided as the greatest folly of the century.

The Commissioner began his speech. "You can take your seats now. That is, if you can find one." He waited a moment for the crowd to settle. "Our country is entering a period of modern growth. Now, with cars and trucks transporting farm goods to local cities, our state is becoming more connected, and commerce is growing in our rural areas. Main Street, almost a decade past the Great Fire, is being rebuilt. As a matter of fact, where you now sit is the site of a future gasoline station and food market. But today, we are delighted to announce our first pharmacy, Liberty Drugs, has opened its doors."

From deep in the back of the crowd, a group of men heckled. "Go back to where you came from, Jews, I-talians, foreigners. You're not welcome here!"

The townspeople hushed, shocked at the foul-mouthed interruption, waiting for the Commissioner's reaction.

From the center of the stage, his eyes scanned the audience until they landed on a group of men patting each other on the back, praising one another for the disruption.

The irate Commissioner shouted into the crowd. "Show yourselves. Who made those disrespectful comments?" he yelled. "Behave like gentlemen or leave!"

While the gathering stirred, I scanned the crowd for the troublemakers. I slipped away from Albert, weaving through the congestion toward the back of the audience, edging closer to the disruptive men. Far more furious than afraid, I had a mission. I wanted to see their faces and uncover what they were hiding. As I drew closer, I spotted two men who had been in Peterson's General Store the previous week. They blended in with the others, many of whom wore overalls and straw hats. I turned my back on them and listened.

"Once we burn another barn, they'll get scared and leave. It will rattle um good," said one man.

"They'll be watching for us," said a second.

"Nah, they'll never figure it out with our hoods. They'll run for the hills like a bunch of scaredy cats," said the first.

"I don't know, Ralphie. Probably should wait a few weeks until they think the threat is gone," said the second.

I gasped, covering my mouth with my hand.

"I say, strike while the city folk are pouring in. Look around, we're getting outnumbered. We need to make our move now."

The first man added, with a sinister sneer, "Make 'em reverse direction and run back to where they came from. Burn 'em out like rats."

A new gravelly voice I hadn't heard before said, "How many of us do we have?"

I turned my body slightly toward the voice, peeking in their direction, my dread growing by the second. Damn, it was the same man with the copper coin! I had to find out his name. These people were monsters!

"Near fifty, I reckon," another man answered.

About twenty people deep in the crowd, I spotted Albert looking for me. I stopped eavesdropping. I didn't want to draw Albert closer to the Klan and spoil my ruse. Besides, some of them from Peterson's might recognize him. I backtracked in Albert's direction, guiding him to the front of the audience.

He stopped, tightening his stance, his hands open at his sides. "Where'd you go? Had me worried."

I searched his face. "I snuck over to spy on the men. Albert, I'm sure they don't remember me." I drew a deep breath, releasing it slowly. "There are fifty of them. They plan to burn another barn. But maybe not right away. They want to scare us off."

He glowered, eyes ablaze, teeth clenched. "I knew it."

* * *

We left the field and headed back up the street to the pharmacy. "Look, now we have real information. Before we do anything, we should meet with Eli and Uncle Nate. It may be time to call the police," I said.

Albert grunted.

I had no idea what that grunt meant. I wished Albert would speak English and stop acting like a child.

I thought about their fire threat. Although we were only a few weeks into summer, the temperature had turned warm and dry. Even the evenings gripped the day's heat like a mother bear guarding her cubs, reluctant to release them. The sparse grass in the open lots had browned. The town could go up in flames in minutes, and the new pharmacy along with it. I didn't recall one drop of rain since the ferry trip three full weeks ago. Was it only three weeks? I felt as if I'd lived here all my life.

I broke the quiet. "We should be getting a lot of people in the store soon. Didn't you say your mom and papa were driving out from the city and staying overnight? Can we hold off on a serious discussion until everyone leaves at the end of the weekend? I'm sure we'll come up with a solution."

Albert snorted with a loud "Humph. The only way to deal with the Klan is to turn it right back on them. They've made up their minds, and nothing short of violence will change a damn thing. We've got to snuff out the brush fire before they burn the whole place down."

He might be right, but ours was an army of three men against their fifty. And we didn't know their names or where they lived. If we were going to fight back, we needed to gather a heck of lot more information.

As we reached the final bend in the street, I turned my head from Albert to look at the pharmacy. A man stood hunched forward against the door, his black fedora tilted downward, shading his face from the afternoon sun. The sleeves of his white shirt were rolled up to his elbows, and a cigarette smoldered between his thumb and forefinger. I could smell the woodsy tobacco a half block away. He lifted his head, watching us as we approached.

His face broke into a smile as he recognized me. "Well, if it ain't my favorite girl, Ella Levine. How're tricks?"

Chapter Fourteen: Albert

As we approached my pharmacy, I noticed a shady figure leaning against the door dressed like a city gangster, fedora tipped forward, cigarette hanging from his lips, and an unclipped tie. A cold sweat swept over me. I instinctively grasped Ella's hand, preparing for the worst.

The signboard, freshly painted with the store's name, Liberty Pharmacy, glistened in the afternoon sun. Usually, this would have brought great joy. But today, it only added to my concern. The shimmering heat reflected off the sidewalk and tension in the air heightened as I watched a moment of recognition pass between Ella and the man.

"How can I help you?" I asked. "This is my pharmacy."

Ella interrupted in a voice edged with a healthy measure of annoyance, "What are you doing here, Dutch?"

Dutch drew his lips together, one side of his mouth curling up in a smirk. "Haven't changed a smidge. Feisty as ever." He continued to leer at Ella.

It hit me like a jackhammer. So, this was the infamous Dutch Schultz. I stood straighter, using my most commanding voice, tired of fending off bullies, refusing to sound intimidated. "I asked how I could help you. I'm about to open, and we have only a minute. Speak now if you have something to say."

Dutch turned to me; his eyebrows raised in appraisal. "It's a business visit. I have a proposition for you." His eyes drifted back to Ella and then returned to me. "Didn't expect to run into an old friend."

I snipped back. "Well, now is not a good time for a social visit or a business transaction. As you can see from the window, we're about to open, and the townsfolk…." I pointed down the street, "are coming to the store as we speak, to check out the pharmacy and for free gifts. Should be mobbed in here any minute." I wished I hadn't used the word, "mobbed."

Dutch shot out his hand, missing the pun. "The name's Dutch Schultz. I've found in my experience that there's always enough time for a business discussion. How about we go inside?"

Now, more annoyed than nervous, I exhaled, shook his hand quickly, and unlocked the door.

As we entered the pharmacy, Ella said in a tone laced with sarcasm, "I had a bad feeling we'd be seeing you again."

Dutch chuckled. "A gal smart as you is usually right."

The screen door slammed closed behind us. I turned to Ella, "Remind me to oil that hinge later. Or maybe we should attach a bell, anything but that irritating slam. I need to know if someone's in the store while I'm in the laboratory."

Dutch made himself right at home, browsing up and down the aisles, pulling items off the shelves to inspect, then setting them back down. In the meantime, I put on my white jacket and name tag. Finally, I walked over to him. "Tell me what this business is about."

Dutch sat on a stool at the soda fountain, facing the window, surveying the sidewalk. Reaching into his back trouser pocket, he pulled out a flask and unscrewed the top, handing it to me. "Taste this."

Ella challenged; her face pinched. "What's in it? How do we know it's safe to drink?"

There he went again with that annoying bark of his. "Har. Har. Cause half of New York City is drinking it. Safer than city tap water."

I took the flask from his hand and smelled. The scents of oak, spice, and alcohol reached my nose in seconds, not the harsh smell of moonshine. "You have a distillery?" I asked.

Dutch winked at me. "You bet. You got yourself a good nose."

I took a small sip and swirled it in my mouth, letting it sit on my tongue. The liquid was smooth and spicy. "Rye? From here or Canada?"

Dutch's eyebrows shot up. He pulled his head back in surprise. "Where'd you learn so much about whiskey?"

Ella stepped closer to me. Her eyes widened with surprise. "I want to know the answer to that, too."

I chuckled. "I may not have served overseas, but half my family did and came home thirsty for the stuff. I've had good teachers."

"Customers in the know are my best. Do you have a supplier yet?" Dutch asked.

About to take another sip, I saw a group of townspeople walking by the front picture window, heading to the door. I handed the flask back to Dutch. "We need to do this another time."

He pushed my hand back. "Keep it. I'll be back this way next week with your supply. We'll talk more then." Dutch stood as he watched a family enter the store. He took a paper napkin from the counter, scribbled his phone number with Ella's pen, then handed the napkin to me. "Time to head out. Good luck today."

I could feel my resolve slipping as he ambled out of the store. If I had a mind to throw him out at first, it had softened. The man was more confident than anyone I'd ever met. And with a swagger to boot. With whiskey as fine as he was selling, I wanted to know more. Once outside, Dutch reached into his pocket, drew out a cigarette, and bent forward to light it. Then he vanished.

With barely any time to consider the strange visit with Dutch, my pharmacy filled with customers—some looking for free gifts, but most browsing, ordering a soda or ice cream from the counter. Standing outdoors on a hot day had left everyone parched. Ella stationed herself behind the soda fountain, filling orders for ice cream and soda with ice cubes and a straw, her arms moving at lightning speed, making change faster than anyone I'd ever seen. She had already lined the counter with water-filled Dixie cups that customers could take for free. When I asked why, she told me she could fill ice cream and soda orders for the paying customers faster if she wasn't bogged down getting everyone free water. The gal had natural business smarts.

In the meantime, Robbie appeared with Aunt Jenny, helping distribute gifts. Robbie handed bags to the children as they left the store and showed others where to find the pantry supplies. That left plenty of time for me to speak with the adults about their medication needs.

By dinnertime, the store emptied. My chest filled with pride. I had joined the world of adults, with a full-fledged business and license to dispense drugs. If I was very lucky, perhaps a sassy young girl at my side. Not bad, not bad.

Moments later, the screen door slammed again as my parents entered. I cringed. Ella washed the last of the glassware, carefully turning each glass upside down to dry on a towel before replacing it on the shelves. I looked up from my broom and waste pan. Greasing that door was my top priority for Saturday morning; otherwise, the slamming would surely drive me crazy.

My family entered with a commotion of their own. They had made it, after all. "Hello, son. Congratulations on the pharmacy." Pop said with a full smile. He pulled Mama and my sister, Gilda, close to his side. "I got tied up with hospital matters and couldn't leave the city until after lunch. But we're staying the weekend and got here on time to celebrate with you at the farm." His eyes drifted to Ella, still standing behind the counter.

But before he could say a word, Mama strode over to her. "Goodness, you must be Ella, Julian's daughter. I'm your Aunt Hannah, Uncle Nate's younger sister." Then she placed her arm around Gilda and said, "And this is Gilda, Albert's little sister.

Gilda's shoulders dropped; her face pinched. "I'm not little. I just turned nine."

Ella hugged them both. "Have we ever met? I can't believe how much family I have." She cocked her head at Gilda. "I hope you're planning to spend time at the farm. My younger brother, your cousin Robbie, is there and will love meeting you."

Pop said, "That's where we'll be staying. Can I interrupt for a moment? I have something to show you, Albert. We'll be right back."

"Of course," I said, following him out the door. Mama and Ella were deep in their own conversation.

The outdoor air held the cumulative warmth of a hot summer day, bottled up by the hour, only to release itself like a hot furnace into the evening. I said, "It would have been nice to have a breeze to blow the heat away."

Pop and I walked a half block to his car. "It's worse in the city, and the hospital corridors reek. Maybe we'll get lucky, and a wind will pick up." He pointed. "Check out the new car."

I was surprised at what I saw. "That red Model T looks spanking new. Did you sell your old one?"

Pop laughed and gave me a pat, handing the car keys to me. "It's yours, Albert. Our gift from your mother and me. We're both deeply proud of you."

My mouth slackened. Pop had, without fault, been a generous father, respecting and supporting every important decision I'd made, beginning with my request to finish upper school in Liberty after the war. But this? A car was so extravagant. I said, "It's too much."

Pop chuckled, "It hasn't hurt that I've had quite a run in the stock market lately. I decided to pull money out and replace my car." He pointed down the street at a gleaming black Model T. "And while I was at it, I decided it was the perfect time for you to own your first car."

My head spun. "I had been talking with Ella about delivering medicines to customers in a year or so. I can start now." I hugged my father, thinking about Ella's reminder of how lucky I was. "You are the best father a son could ever hope for."

Pop cocked his head. "So, tell me more about this Ella. Are you serious about her?"

Chapter Fifteen: Miriam

Aunt Jenny outdid herself this evening. She was a terrific cook and always prepared sumptuous dinners, but tonight was something special. Since the war years, the Fourth of July had always held special meaning for Nate and her, having lost their younger son, Jake, to the Spanish Flu while he was serving overseas in France. Unlike the somberness of Memorial Day, they viewed the Fourth of July as a happy event, not so much about the future he sacrificed, but about the wonderful memories he left with them. This year, she was feeding a bigger crowd than usual and wanted to impress her guests.

Uncle Nate had filled the fire pit that afternoon with seasoned wood from last winter's stack. He burned the logs until they shrunk down to a bed of scalding red coals, then placed a grill over the top and set the chicken to slow cook. The secret ingredient was Aunt Jenny's special tangy molasses, pepper, and peach sauce, the peach preserves from Jenny's canning last harvest. Uncle Nate spread the sauce over the skin as he continually turned the chicken, never taking his eye off the food until the skin was perfectly brown and crisp and the meat beneath was melt-in-the-mouth tender.

While Uncle Nate tended the chicken, Jenny steamed the remainder of her early peas and green beans in the kitchen, finishing them with slabs of butter, salt, and pepper. She served the meal with two braided challahs she'd baked.

Earlier that morning, the older children had scrambled down the hill to Aunt Jenny's berry patch, carrying two tin pails each, with instructions to fill the pails to the brim with the ripest blueberries and raspberries they could find. While the children were picking, she and Wilma sprinkled flour on the kitchen table and rolled out Jenny's pie crusts, baking three berry pies before leaving for the parade. I got off easy with the simple task of bringing fresh vanilla ice cream from Albert's pharmacy.

I watched Hannah and Ben melt into the backyard crowd, welcoming Wilma, Sandor, and their three children. It was a marvel, though not surprising, to see how fast Hannah won over Wilma's heart. My aunt had a magical touch with women. As an obstetrician, she knew women inside and out. Her welcoming smile and soft manner put thousands of her patients at ease during her years of practice. It was never long before Hannah was sidetracked away from the main conversations, gently pummeled with medical questions and personal concerns.

The boys scattered about the yard, engaged in running games, a constant blur of motion. There was no such thing as walking games for them. My younger cousin, Gilda, made friends with Adina, Wilma's eldest, both disappearing with tin pails back to the berry patch. Hannah called out, "Don't go farther than the patch. I want to be able to see you. Pick the ripe berries before the birds get to them, and we can bring some back to the city."

The Fourth of July events were the perfect remedy to lift our spirits. After a week of worry about the Klan, the holiday united the community, reminding us of our mutual support during the war years, the sacrifices made, and our love of America. With Albert's pharmacy and more businesses scheduled to open along Main Street, Liberty was growing into a full-fledged year-round community.

Albert's grand opening, Sandor's return to the farm, and the feast Jenny had prepared were the perfect ingredients Wilma needed to erase the worried frown off her face. Hopefully, it was enough joy to convince her to remain all summer. I knew Aunt Jenny would be devastated if she left.

Sandor lifted little Maya onto his shoulders. "Oy, the traffic was terrible. Remind me never to drive from the city on a holiday weekend." He had changed from his dark suit into linen slacks and a white collared shirt with two buttons open at the top, his carpet of curly black chest hair peeking out. His sleeves were rolled up to his elbows, revealing pasty white arms.

Wilma sidled up to him, pulling at her open collar to allow more air into her blouse. "It's only the beginning of July and already quite warm."

"Nothing compared to the city," Sandor said, turning his head to Wilma. "That reminds me, I brought two fans with me. I must have grabbed the last ones from the hardware store. They're still in the car. I thought you could put one in the kitchen when you girls cook and one for our bedroom." He shifted his eyes to Aunt Jenny. "After you're done in the kitchen for the night, feel free to bring the second to your bedroom."

Robbie and Noah had been kicking a ball that rolled into the adults' seating area. Overhearing the conversation, Robbie perked up, his eyes wide. "What's that about a fan? Do we get one, too?"

Uncle Nate said, "Many thanks, Sandor." Turning to Robbie, he continued with a smirk. "Only the adults get fans. You kids get a cool swim in the pond before you turn in."

Albert, who had been sitting at the picnic table, muttered to himself, "Fans, hadn't thought of that. I'll place an order tomorrow for the store."

We finally squeezed in around the table. The men reached into a box in the middle of the picnic table to grab a circular black yarmulke from a stack, placing it on the crowns of their heads. A short Shabbos prayer preceded the meal. In our family, traditions were skewed to our needs and beliefs, which were far more liberal than those of many other Jewish groups in the city. The only night we prayed before a meal was on Friday, the Sabbath. Fortunately, the Farkas were like-minded and did not object to our peculiar selection of observances.

Dinner was relaxed, extending well into the evening. Midway through, the Rabbi appeared, filling his plate with chicken after reciting a prayer before eating. Later, when the dessert plates were cleared and dishes replaced in the cupboard, the children separated off. Running, always running, collecting fireflies and placing them in Aunt Jenny's old Mason jars, attaching wax paper lids with rubber bands. Holes were punched through the paper to let fresh air inside. Before bed, they would release the fireflies back into the air. I sighed, grateful that the young ones were experiencing a childhood of innocence. Every year, the war slipped further into the past, becoming a distant memory for the older children who could still recall the nightmare of adult separation.

Once the children headed down the hill to play, Nate brought an old bottle of schnapps he'd stored in the root cellar to the picnic table. Eli strode from the house with two handfuls of small glasses.

Wilma remarked, "Isn't that illegal?"

Eli chuckled, "Not if it was bought before Volstead. We stocked up our supply, hoping to have enough to last until the Feds regain their senses. You watch. It won't be long until alcohol is legal again."

Sandor took a glass, holding it out to Eli, "Well then, I wouldn't mind if you pour a bit of that. It's been a while. Could use some after that endless drive." He raised his glass, took a long draw, smacking his lips. "Excellent. Haven't had anything quite that tasty in a long time." He set his glass down. "Now that it's only adults here, I want to know what's going on with this Klan Wilma called me about. I'm not liking the sound of it."

The Rabbi was the first to speak. "Of course. The appearance of the Ku Klux Klan is very disturbing, but I had a long talk with the sheriff and am confident he has matters under control."

Albert interrupted, "No disrespect, Rabbi, but were you at the parade earlier today? Did you hear those men in the back? I didn't get the sense they were anywhere near under control."

"How does the sheriff plan to keep them away from us?" Uncle Nate asked as Aunt Jenny cast an angry eye at Uncle Nate.

I knew she did not want to scare the Farkas family away.

Rabbi shushed the men. "He has a good idea who they are and is planning to make a visit. Let's leave things in his hands for now."

Listening to the men grumble about how little they trusted the sheriff to do anything of substance, I thought about what I knew about the Klan, surprised they'd drifted this far north. The atrocities they committed in the deep south made my hair stand on end. The hangings, castrations, and fires were shocking. So many fires. But the new immigrants, all of us, were tough people, not anything like the newly freed slaves who never forgot the shackles they'd worn. We weren't afraid to fight back. Thousands of Jews and Italians served in the Great War and were intimately familiar with the guns and bayonets they used in the trenches. If the sheriff had any brains at all, he would find a way to call off the Klan before our boys got to them, or he'd be facing brutality more vicious than anything they could dream up behind those white hoods.

Albert knew enough about the horrors Eli and I faced in the army hospitals and had little patience with the Rabbi's words. He was no longer listening to the Rabbi and was undeterred by Jenny's angry stares, her fierce expressions commanding us to shut up. "I've seen these men and know first-hand they're up to no good. As far as I'm concerned, the sheriff has little time on my clock to straighten the Klan out. If he's not successful, they'll be facing professional fighters who won't cower to their cartoon clothing and fire spears."

The Rabbi studied Albert's face. "You shouldn't go riling everyone up. Give the sheriff a chance."

By that point, Hannah motioned for me to follow her inside. I gathered she wanted to hear more about Julian, Ella, and Robbie. Once through the kitchen door, I followed her through the house to the front door, exiting onto the porch. We sat on the oak bench Nate built for Jenny's front garden. The light was fading as we gazed at the hilly landscape, the children in the berry patch, and the pond sitting in the distance like a painting.

I guessed right. She was determined to know more about Ella's past.

Hannah's brows were drawn together. "What's going on with Julian's family? You'd think the war would have straightened him out."

I sighed. "Well, it didn't. His neglect of the children is inexcusable. Wants to put them to work hauling ice, has them sleeping in the same bed, and doesn't bother to come home at night. That's why Ella took Robbie and ran away. I'm just thankful they came here."

Hannah studied my eyes, nodding her head, in the know. "He's probably still gambling. It certainly sounds like it to me. Have you cut him off yet?"

A wave of shame flowed through me. "I'm not sure how much Ella knows about Julian's gambling problem. I know when I do cut him off, he's sure to complain to anyone who'll listen. And I don't want to spoil the children's summer. They're both happy here."

Hannah asked, "What have they been up to since they arrived? I hope they haven't been a burden for Jenny and Nate. Those two are getting on in their years. Both are over sixty."

I laughed, leaning back on the bench. "If anything, Jenny has a renewed energy. She's wild about Robbie. The poor kid is starved for attention, and he follows Nate around like a pup, helping him with small jobs all day long. He loves feeding the chickens. With Martin married and in his own home, they've been lonely for youthful energy."

"What about Ella? She's very pretty and at an age where she can get herself into a lot of trouble. What's she like?"

I thought about Ella and her unique blend of city smarts and innocence, completely opposite to how either Hannah or I was raised. Tillie watched over both of us like a hawk. "Ella's single-minded and smart as a tack, saving every nickel she earns for college. She does a lovely job watching the children and helps Albert in the pharmacy. She has no idea I have her tuition all tucked away."

Hannah's face pinched with confusion. "She doesn't know about her grandparents' trust? Why?"

I exhaled heavily, knowing my time was running out. "It's such a can of worms. Once I tell her, and I know I'll have to…." My shoulders drooped. "I'll have to share everything about her father. Honestly, I'm not ready for that conversation."

Hannah nodded, understanding the dilemma. "She and Albert seem close. Anything going on with them that Ben and I should know about? Is she suitable for him?"

I smiled. "As I said, she's single-minded about college. Ella was at the top of her grade, despite her crazy parents. Both children have turned out well."

Hannah raised her eyebrows. "You're not answering my question."

"There's not much I can say from her end. Ella appears to like Albert, but I don't think she has serious romantic interests. She's quite different from the boy-crazy girls we used to know." I paused a moment. "But he's mad about her. He doesn't let her out of his sight for long and hangs on her every word. He's the one you should be watching."

Chapter Sixteen: Ella

In under a month, this ever-growing family of mine had wormed its way into my heart. Bit by bit, I learned more about my roots. Unlike the fairytale versions I was hearing from my Sullivan County family, Papa's edition was only shared to make some sort of cautionary point, never with love. I knew Papa was bitter, but the way he spoke of his parents, sister, and other relatives made one think they were atrocious people. In his version, he was always the victim, the one family member singled out and misunderstood. If it hadn't been for my memory of Uncle Nate years ago at Bubbe Tillie's home and his generous invitation to visit Aunt Jenny and him at the farm, I would have been afraid to venture with Robbie all the way from Brooklyn to Sullivan County.

I couldn't understand why Papa would choose to distance himself from a warm and protective family. I'd had an inkling for years that something bad had happened before I was born, but it was a dark secret, never shared. If I peppered Papa with questions, he'd scold me, so I stopped asking. Now, if I was patient, I'd get the truth from Aunt Miriam. As his younger sister, she must have witnessed some of the events. And knowing Papa the way I did, I was sure it involved money. Because that's all he cared about.

Learning about Bubbe Tillie's garment business made me proud of her grit, pushing against the men of her time who were determined to see her fail. And Hannah's endless bravery after she was framed and incarcerated in Blackwell's prison gave me a new respect for all she endured to improve medical care for women. I would have treasured more moments with them.

I'd missed out on a lifetime of memories. So many birthdays and holidays had slipped by Robbie and me. Our lives would have been richer with their love. For us, birthday and holiday celebrations were austere. No special meals or gifts. Worst of all, no words of endearment.

Mama never seemed to have money for fine cuts of meat nor gifts, insisting Papa wasn't giving her enough allowance for new shoes, clothing, and food on his pay days. Gifts were a luxury we could never imagine. Although presents and birthday cake would have been lovely, what we had really missed all those years was the warmth and supportive spirit surrounding us now on the farm.

Mama badgered Papa nonstop. The friction between them made my skin crawl with dread. "You get paid a good wage, Julian. Where's it all going?" Papa would storm out of the house without answering. When he did give her cash, I'd spy her slipping a few dollars into the bottom of her rag bag, somewhere he would never look. Hiding money from each other was something they both did even after the divorce.

That Sunday evening, we sat around the fire pit roasting marshmallows on sticks, watching the sun set in the western sky. The delectable smell of charred sugar made my mouth water. I asked Uncle Nate to tell me more about his parents and their farm before it moved from Harlem to the country in New York State.

He drew a deep breath. "My parents, your great grandparents, Sarah and Sam, were immigrants from Germany. Conditions in the old country had become terrible for the Jews, and the two of them married illegally. You see, the Germans only allowed the oldest son to marry, and Sam was the third son in his family of eight. After your grandmother, Tillie, was born, he and Sarah decided it was no longer safe to stay in Germany. They packed up a wagon, made their way to Hamburg, and boarded a ship to New York. It was a time when many German Jews came to America."

That's the first time I've heard that story. Do you know what year it was?" I asked.

Uncle Nate smiled. I could see he enjoyed retelling the memory. "I sure do. It was 1866, a year after the War Between the States ended, decades before our Lady Liberty stood in the harbor or the Immigration Center at

Ellis Island was built. They came through the first official intake center, Castle Garden."

I'd never heard of Castle Garden. "Was that near Ellis Island?"

Uncle Nate nodded his head. "Not too far away. It's impossible to imagine my folks crossed the sea close to sixty years ago. At that time, the northern half of Manhattan was mostly farmland with a few scattered houses. Central Park was partially built, and there were no cars yet. Imagine…." He waved his hand at the horizon. "The buildings stood only five to seven stories high because there were no elevators or electricity. Harlem was still rocky country land, mostly used for livestock farming. Loose farm animals roamed the dirt streets."

Albert cut in with a quick laugh, pantomiming a cow strutting down the avenue. "Can you imagine a cow gracing its way down Fifth Avenue in front of the construction of the Vanderbilt mansion. That must have been a sight."

Visualizing a rural Manhattan stretched my imagination. Now a modern city, so much had happened in a single generation. In school, we learned that after the Great War ended, there was a competition to build the tallest building in the city, surpassing the sixty-stories-high Woolworth building. Bank and insurance buildings were rising on Wall Street in a race to claim that bragging right. City roads were paved, and cars hummed through the avenues, replacing horse-drawn carriages and wagons. New York had become a whole new world since the time Tillie arrived.

Uncle Nate continued reminiscing. "The Harlem farm was far smaller than this one. Moving was the smartest thing we ever did. It gave us a chance to expand and specialize. Once a Kosher butcher set up a business here in the county, we didn't need to leave the area for butchering."

"Did Bubbe Tillie leave the city with you?" I asked.

He paused, "Your grandmother, Tillie, had no interest in leaving New York City. She wanted to finish school and imagined a future far more exciting than life on a farm. So, at sixteen, she married your grandfather, Abe, and moved downtown to the Lower East Side, near where your father, Julian, now works."

"Is that where Papa and baby Sarah were born? In the tenements?" I asked.

Aunt Hannah, touched by the magic of recollection, added, "I lived in Tillie's tenement apartment after the twins came. I was almost five, about to start school. My best friend lived across the hall. What a time that was. Once little Sarah passed, the more delicate of the twins, Tillie was determined to rent a decent apartment with indoor plumbing, electricity, and an elevator. We moved in the summer, before school started, and lived in the next apartment until Tillie and Abe both died. That big sister of mine was one determined gal."

"Did Bubbe get to finish high school?" I asked, wondering if her dreams were fulfilled after she married Abraham. Would my dream of college come true for me?

Hannah said, "No, she didn't. She learned quickly how fast life passes and the many challenges crossing your path, derailing your dreams and good planning. But Tillie and her best friend, Sadie, invented a dress kit for women to sew at home. For women who couldn't afford to order through dressmakers or stores. They bought them up as fast as Bit-O-Honey bars. Sears and Roebuck sold the kits nationally. The packet contained every part needed for a finished dress and apron: cloth, thread, needles, and a pattern. It was an extraordinary idea and very successful. The kits sold all over the country for many years. It was especially popular in the prairies, where each element could take forever to receive by mail. This kit had it all."

I wondered how she and Sadie came up with that idea.

"Tillie was a woman with tremendous vision. Abe kept selling his buttons, and together, they made quite a good living," Hannah said.

Miriam interrupted, sending Hannah a warning look, her face tense. "Enough stories for now. You are making me miss Mama and Papa."

In an instant, I sensed Miriam put the brakes on the conversation to avoid spilling another family secret. I was beginning to learn their silent language, the starts and stops that signaled the conversation was heading too far into treacherous water. Although I wanted to know more, I could be patient. Miriam couldn't keep secrets from me forever. It served no purpose to force her tonight.

While the others broke into smaller conversations, I moved closer to

Albert, leaning into his ear. "Want some help in the pharmacy tomorrow? I'm free all day."

His eyes sparkled with delight. "You bet. I love having you there with me." Albert winked, making me blush a deep red. Then he glanced at his mother, who was watching our interaction, quickly turning back to me. "Besides, you've been such a big help, especially with the soda fountain. It gives me more time to fill customers' medications in the laboratory. Pick you up at eight?"

* * *

The following morning was another scorcher. Part of me wanted to stay back on the farm, staying cool in the pond, teaching the children their swim strokes. But I'd offered to help Albert and always kept my word. Besides, he let me sample the ice cream and sorbet flavors, treats I rarely had in the city.

Settled in Albert's car with the top down and windows open, the gravel below creating a steady bounce, I said, "It'll be a smooth ride once these roads are all properly paved. They won't be so bumpy." I grabbed my straw hat before it flew off my head. "This is quite a swanky car your Papa bought for you." I felt a pang of jealousy. It would be a cold day in hell before my father ever spent that kind of money on his children.

When we pulled up to the store twenty minutes later, it was already 85 degrees inside. "Albert, still thinking about buying fans? I think we'll need them in the store, too." I pointed to the thermometer mounted on the outer wall.

A small cluster of customers stood on the porch, waiting for us to open, the women fanning their faces with their straw hats. Greeting us warmly, they said, "Saw your displays yesterday. This store will be a lifesaver this summer, especially the ice cream."

Albert smiled broadly. "That's the idea. We needed a pharmacy in town." He turned to prop the door open, leading them inside, trading conversation about new products and shelf items customers could buy. He said to the crowd, "Let me know if I'm missing anything or if you need a special order.

I'm always happy to help."

As I wrapped the apron strings around my waist, the screen door slammed, causing Albert to jump and face the door. "That gets fixed this week." His last word hung in his mouth as he faced Dutch Schultz. "Good morning. I didn't expect you back so soon. What do you need?"

Dutch scanned the entire store with his hawkish eyes, not missing a particle of dust, avoiding eye contact with the customers. "Thought it was a good day for a drive and an ice-cold drink from my favorite girl, Ella."

I side-eyed Dutch from the counter, then turned to face him. "Oh, please! I'm putting up some lemonade. Just about ready." And then, "How about you cool off and get on your way? You must have better things to do than have a cold drink in Liberty, New York."

One by one, customers slipped out the door, possibly realizing who Dutch was. I considered encouraging them to return. Better yet, if I could get Dutch to leave for good, the problem would be solved.

Dutch snickered, "You do have a mouth on you, Ella. If you're not careful, I might think you don't like me too much," he said, drawing his drink through a paper straw.

I rolled my eyes back. "What's there to like? Besides, you're scaring our customers away. Want to run the store into the ground? Right after we opened the doors."

Albert stiffened, staring at Dutch. I was sure he was worried Dutch wouldn't react well to my wise mouth.

Dutch guffawed, "You'll like me in good time." He ran his eyes down my body. "Besides, I can't resist a sparky young broad. Now, how about that lemonade?" He reached into his jacket pocket and fished out a flask, pouring amber liquid into a glass. He turned to Albert and winked. "Add that lemonade right on top of my medicine."

I sighed, shaking my head. "You're going to get us into a heap of trouble if you're not careful around here. I don't want to be accused of aiding and abetting in a crime." I watched Albert handle the remaining curious customers and send them on their way.

Seconds after the last one left, the screen door slammed again. I looked away from Dutch, who was sitting on a stool by the counter toward the front door. My eyes darted to Albert's. He saw him, too. It was Mahlon Peterson. What in God's name was he doing here?

Albert strolled over, extending his hand. "Welcome. What brings you up in this direction?"

Mr. Peterson ignored Albert's outstretched hand. "Same reason you came my way. Getting information about the competition." Mr. Peterson took out his notepad.

Albert laughed, overlooking the handshake slight. "My goodness, Mr. Peterson. We only opened yesterday. We can't possibly be competition for anyone."

Dutch leaned over the counter, signaling for my ear. "Who's he?"

I shook my head. "Oh, nobody. Just a storeowner in Monticello."

Dutch squinted. "When a man refuses a handshake, it means trouble. Don't a smart city girl like you know that? Now, what's the story?"

Was there no pulling the wool over Dutch's eyes? He continued to peer at me, waiting for me to spill. I asked Dutch, "What do you know about the KKK in these parts?"

For the first time, he drew back, revealing a crack in his otherwise calm demeanor. "Him? No foolin."

I nodded. "Do you know anything about him?"

"I've heard of his store. They sell local crap bootleg gin. But I didn't know he was in the Klan." He tilted his head. "Have they bothered you?"

I was torn about sharing anything, but a fury was growing inside me, fast enough to outpace my good judgment. "No... well sort of. We're pretty sure they burned down my cousin's barn before Robbie and I arrived, and a milk cow inside was killed." I knew I shouldn't tell Dutch about this, but my anger continued to escalate. How could I stand on the sidelines and do nothing? It was eating me alive. And, just a few days ago, I considered asking for his advice. I knew a man like him wouldn't shy away from a fight. I said firmly, "They don't know who they're dealing with. My uncles fought in the war. They used machine guns and bayonets. They're not afraid to fight back."

Dutch bit down at the end of his straw, turning halfway around on his stool, watching Mr. Peterson and Albert. "You don't say."

Mr. Peterson picked up right where he left off. "Sonny, you're competition to me. And that's not going to go well for you or your people. Why don't you consider taking your store somewhere else?"

Albert stepped forward, practically rubbing noses with Peterson. "I've tried to be friendly, but you don't want any part of it. And there is no way in hell I'm moving anywhere. So why don't you turn around and crawl back under the rock you came from? This is a family store, just like yours. No place for threats or violence."

Mr. Peterson smirked. "This ain't the end of it. You Jews are going to get run out of here whether you like it or not."

At this point, Dutch spun around in his chair, took three full strides directly into the middle of the two men and faced Peterson. "Did I hear you right?" He pulled open the side of his jacket, revealing a sidearm. "Exactly, who are you thinking of running out of town?"

The blood drained from Mr. Peterson's face as he recognized Dutch, perhaps from the newspapers he sold in the Monticello store. His eyes bulged open. "Mr. Schultz, good to see you. I was just leaving."

Dutch gave his back a firm push, and Peterson stumbled out the door. "Get outta here, and don't come back, or you'll answer to me."

For a moment, I felt giddy, imagining what it would be like to have my face, like Dutch's, trigger so much fear. But on the other hand, Peterson and his gang had now officially become our enemies. We needed a plan to protect ourselves.

Dutch was quick to serve up his solution. "You can't be putting up with that shit. If they smell weakness, they'll burn this place to the ground. You know, I—"

Albert cut him off mid-sentence. "Dutch, I think I know where you're going with this, but it's our problem to solve, not yours. Thanks for your help today, but I'm not looking to start a full-out, bloody war."

Dutch, wearing a half-smile, crossed his arms on his chest and leaned back against the counter. "Albert, that right?"

Albert nodded.

"You got a lot to learn about mean people. You're softer than you think."

Albert protested, "I'm not soft."

"Hum." Dutch shook his head from side to side. "What would you do if I gave you a punch in your choppers right now?"

Albert began rolling up his sleeves. "Give you one back twice as hard."

Dutch laughed. "You say they killed your cousin's cow and burned down a barn? That's a hell of a lot of property damage." He watched my face, waiting for me to see his point. Then he switched back to Albert. "Why didn't you swing back, then?"

I interrupted, "No one saw their faces. We weren't positive at the time it was them."

Dutch pinched his lips, rocking his head back and forth. "Now he comes into your business, doesn't shake your hand like a gentleman, tells you to pick up and leave." Again, he waited. "What are you going to do now? Give him free samples?"

The screen door slammed. Uncle Ben and Aunt Hannah walked in with Miriam's twins and Gilda in tow. My stomach pooled with acid. The town of Liberty was closing in on me by the minute. Aunt Hannah said, "Good morning, kids. We're here to lend a hand."

Could their timing be any worse? Albert walked over to the door, hugged Aunt Hannah, and then shook Uncle Ben's hand. I gave them a warm wave. Dutch sat back at the counter, his back to them.

Uncle Ben peered at the back of Dutch's head, "Did we interrupt something? Who's your guest?"

Dutch spun his stool around, facing my uncle. Albert had already told me how brilliant his Pop was. Uncle Ben was the one person on earth who read a daily paper cover to cover every single day. It took him a half-second to recognize our guest, Dutch Schultz, the infamous bootlegger.

Uncle Ben's lips formed a perfect 'O.' "Well, this is a surprise. My name is Dr. Ben Kahn, Albert's father." He extended his arm to Dutch, and they shook. Uncle Ben turned back to Aunt Hannah. "Why don't you head back to Miriam's and take the children with you?"

Aunt Hannah turned to me. "Ella, you come along, too."

Dutch laughed. "Ella and I are good friends. Aren't we, sweetheart? She stays." The firmness of his reply left a quiet in the air. Hannah met Ben's eyes, and he dropped his chin.

Albert swallowed hard, his hands flailing at his sides. "You can't make this kind of stuff up. My first day of business—a Klansman, a bootlegger, and my parents, no less. Who the hell will be next, the President?"

It was the perfect response to release the tension in the air. Dutch laughed loudly in that God-awful cackle. Uncle Ben raised his heavy gray brows at Albert, both smiling. I was in a daze, never before privy to so much drama and comedy mixed into one morning.

Uncle Ben said, "Albert, I think it's time for you to fill in the blanks. I can see quite clearly you have not told me everything these last months."

He then turned to Dutch and me. "I'd like Ella to head up to Miriam's, too. And, Mr. Schultz, although it's been a pleasure, right now I need time alone with my son. Perhaps you can move along, too."

Boy, did that man have confidence in the face of a gangster like Dutch. Was it from serving as a doctor in the Great War?

Dutch pinched his face, and for a moment, I wasn't sure what he'd do. But a second later, he put the fedora back on his head, tipping it to the three of us. "I'll be back tomorrow, Albert. To talk business." He ambled to the door, then spun back to shake Uncle Ben's hand again. "And it was a pleasure to meet you, doc."

I cringed at his insincerity. Did that creep ever stop with the saccharine? Tomorrow was Sunday, and I would have to come back, too. I couldn't leave Albert here alone when Dutch returned. I had an instinct that I understood the likes of Dutch better than Albert ever could, even in a lifetime.

* * *

Dutch walked up the sidewalk, waiting for me. I couldn't imagine what Uncle Ben thought was going on. Dutch had just told Uncle Ben I was his friend—a gangster, no less. "Oh no! What do you want now? To completely

109

ruin my life?"

Dutch sidled up to me, keeping my pace. "Of course not. I've been here to help you from the very start. Remember how you and the kid got here in the first place?"

I stopped in my tracks, looking straight into his eyes. "What exactly do you want? Just tell me."

He nodded his head. "Okay, doll. I want the liquor business for the drug store."

My gut told me he was hiding something, just like Papa did when I asked why there wasn't money for food. "And?"

"And nothing." His voice sounded sincere, but his eyes hinted there was more.

"You're lying. What else?" I insisted.

Dutch cleared his throat. "A location for whiskey storage. Not too far from here. Can't keep it all at the distillery. Your family has a mighty big farm nearby."

I knew there was more, but I had no clue how much storage he was talking about or what kind of trouble our family could get into if we were caught. "Just for the record, tell me what's in it for us?"

Dutch smiled. "Doll, it's clear what you need. Do I need to spell it out for you?"

I glared at him.

"Protection from those bullies out there, the Klan. They're coming for you."

Chapter Seventeen: Miriam

Hannah stormed into the parlor as I nursed Sarah. The twins were setting up a game of checkers on the carpet. Hannah fidgeted, waiting for their quick game to end, and then crouched beside them. "Children, could you take that upstairs and play in your rooms for a little while? I need to speak to your mother, you know, grown-up talk." As they clomped up the stairs, she turned to me in an exasperated whisper, "What in tarnation is going on around here?"

I stared at Hannah, my mouth agape. "Why are you back so soon? Something happen?"

Hannah dropped into the chair opposite me, leaning in so the children upstairs could not hear. "There's a dangerous bootlegger at the pharmacy. Ben threw us all out!" She drew a deep, shaky breath. "Dutch Schultz. He's been in all the papers—a gangster. And he seems well acquainted with Ella."

I fell back against the sofa, throwing a diaper over my shoulder, placing Sarah upright for burping. "I guess he's back."

Hannah's eyes opened wide, her questions spewing. "You guess! He's been here before? Why haven't you told me? Albert's now consorting with felons?" She didn't wait for me to reply. "There's more to Ella's background than you've shared. This Schultz character appears to know her quite well." She huffed, waiting for my answer.

I stayed calm, for the first time feeling protective of my niece. Having Julian as a father already gave her plenty to handle. Her childhood was no picnic. In fact, it was hardly a childhood at all. From what I could tell so far, she was a surprisingly pleasant and honest young girl, a blend of innocence and street smarts. "I know plenty. She's been here with me for the past few weeks, helping with the children. On the way up from the ferry, Robbie went gaga over Schultz's fancy car, and he gave them a ride to the farm. She knew they shouldn't take the ride, but he convinced her Liberty was on the way to his turkey farm. The kids had no idea who he was."

Hannah huffed. "That didn't show good judgment."

I continued, ignoring Hannah's barb. "I suppose he wants to supply medicinal alcohol for the pharmacy. Albert talked to us a little the other night about where he'd get his whiskey for prescriptions." I paused. "This familiarity with Ella is all part of his rough guy *shtick*."

Hannah drew a sharp breath. "And you didn't think you should tell us Albert is considering a gangster supplier?"

My doting aunt was beginning to get under my skin. How dare she treat us like disobedient children! I felt my milk let down in my other breast, leaking onto my blouse. I glanced at the circular stain. "Now, see what you've done? Making me hot and bothered." I quickly set Sarah to work, emptying my full breast. "Everything is under control. You don't need to be told every little thing, Hannah. We are adults."

Hannah crossed her arms, giving me a quiet space to settle Sarah. She whispered, "We need to discuss this. Albert's our son, and if he's breaking the law, I want to know about it."

The front screen door slammed shut as Ella walked in. She was breathless and angry. Hannah glared at the poor girl.

Before Hannah could start in, I said, "Ella, would you fetch me a glass of water and come sit? We're concerned about that Schultz character and why he was at the drug store." I adjusted the pillow under Sarah, so she wasn't pulling so hard on my breast.

Moments later, the three of us sat, Ella filling Hannah in on her relationship with Dutch Schultz from the moment they met, reminding us that Schultz found the pharmacy on his own, not through his earlier contact at the ferry. Hannah listened politely. Knowing she could be a tigress about Albert, I was grateful she gave Ella time to finish her sentences.

Ella retold the morning's events. "Dutch wants to supply the pharmacy with whiskey, but today, after he met that awful Peterson character from Monticello, he told me he wants more. The Klan's a problem for him, too. He's sure they make their own gin and compete with his whiskey." She sighed. "So now, Dutch wants to send an army of goons to protect us – for a price."

I interrupted, turning to Hannah. "This wasn't the Klan's first threat. They burned down Martin's barn in June. At the time, we weren't certain who started the fire. Now we're sure it was them."

Hannah was reeling. "Good Lord, when did it get so dangerous up here? And how on earth could an eighteen-year-old girl know so much?"

Exasperated, I exhaled loudly. "The Klan came after the war. We're only learning about it now." Turning back to Ella, I said, "What do you mean for a price? What price?"

Ella rolled her eyes. "He was waiting for me when Uncle Ben shooed me out of the store. I made him tell me. He didn't at first, but I knew he wanted something more than to sell Albert a few bottles of whiskey." She sighed. "He wants a place to store his goods, probably at the farm. Somewhere the Feds wouldn't think of looking."

Hannah jumped up from her chair. "My God! The Feds? Just when we thought we were safe again, the world's turned on its side." She glared at Ella. "And you didn't answer my question. When did you get so comfortable chatting with gangsters?"

Ella narrowed her eyes, avoiding Hannah's question. "At least we know what he wants. That gives us time to figure out how to handle him." She released her breath slowly. "Aunt Hannah, aside from Papa, he's the first crook I've ever met."

I said, "Sit down, Hannah. You know Ella's got more street smarts than we had at her age. She was raised in the city with that father of hers." I waited a moment. "Think about it. Compared to a few years ago in France, this seems like child's play. The Volstead Act is ridiculous, to say the least."

Hannah stared back at me.

I continued, "Honestly, do you truly believe a bunch of Puritan laws could stop Americans from drinking? Why couldn't the government give us all a break, especially after the sacrifices we made for the country? My God, they issued booze to the soldiers to keep them warm and calm in the trenches. Now it's illegal?"

Ella nodded her head. "Besides, Albert hasn't made any decisions yet. He may be a little naïve with Dutch Schultz, but I think he's much more worried about our safety with the Klan, especially after the incident with the boys last week."

Hannah's eyes met mine in lightning speed. "Incident with the boys? It seems you left something else out. How many more nuggets of information are still tucked into your sweet head?"

I sighed and shared last week's scare with Hannah. "Now you're fully informed. Happy, now? What concerns me most is this Klan. They are driven by an irrational hatred towards us and reject any reason."

Ella's voice was even. "I think we ought to consider Dutch a wildcard weapon. It might be worth his price."

Both Hannah and I turned her way and stared, speechless. Who was this girl?

* * *

Moments later, Ben walked into the house, head down, seemingly lost in thought. He faced us. "It seems you're already huddling about Dutch and God knows what else."

Hannah asked, "What did Albert have to say? Why hadn't he told us about any of this?"

Ben dropped into a chair as I closed my blouse and burped Sarah again. I said, "Ella, would you mind holding onto the baby, and I'll get some cool drinks for everyone. Maybe that will lead to cool heads."

"I fail to see any humor in this." Hannah snapped, her annoyance trailing after me like a long tail into the kitchen.

The parlor was quiet. I could hear the twins playing upstairs. At best, we had time for a quick discussion before they asked for a snack.

I brought a tray into the parlor. Ella had put Sarah down for a morning nap and cleared the children's books off the coffee table to make room for the drinks.

Ella remained standing. "I'll head to the store and give Albert a hand while you talk. I promised I'd help him out at the soda counter today." She edged to the door. "See you later."

Now it was the three of us facing each other with a new world of problems.

Hannah repeated, "What did Albert have to say?"

Ben answered evenly. "His big worry, of course, is this Klan and their likelihood of harming the family and community. His lesser issue is Schultz, although he said the rye from his distillery is exceptionally good."

I tried to suppress my smile, knowing how opposed Uncle Ben was to Prohibition. For that matter, most New Yorkers viewed the dry movement and law as a direct affront to all immigrants, particularly the German and Irish. The Act had curtailed their long-standing social gatherings at now-closed pubs throughout the city. Little by little, local soda fountains, with their under-the-counter liquor, had begun to substitute. Not to mention the speakeasies that were scattered north to south all through Manhattan.

But Hannah didn't find his words amusing. "He's a gangster, Ben. Gangsters surround themselves with other lawless people, all carrying guns, killing people on the streets. I don't want us to have survived the war only to get killed here at home."

Ben sighed. "There's a greater chance of getting killed by the KKK than someone who shows his face in daylight on the street."

I added for Ben's benefit, "It seems Schultz talked to Ella after she left the pharmacy. He offered protection from the Klan in exchange for storing his whiskey. Did Albert know about that?"

"No, but I figured it would amount to something along those lines. That's a topic to discuss with Nate and Jenny. They're the only ones with enough land to speak of."

Hannah stood. "Am I hearing you right? You think we should get in bed with this criminal?"

I cringed, hating to hear them argue. The two of them could be pigheaded when angry, digging in for a long time. "How about we table this until we can include Nate and Jenny. We need to hear their thoughts."

Hannah and Ben quieted, but their anger remained palpable.

Chapter Eighteen: Albert

Moments after Papa left, Ella returned through the pharmacy's screen door, closing it gently. We'd only been open a short while, and my nerves were already shot.

Ella asked, "How did it go with your father? Is he very upset? Your mother sure was. I think she hates me."

I released a deep sigh. "My mother can get emotional like a mother bear. But Pop is the most level-headed of all of us. He gave me a great idea."

Ella's mouth turned up to a half-smile, her eyes amused. "Let me get this right. Father. Levelheaded. In my world, those two words are never used in the same sentence." She laughed, eager to hear more. "What's his idea?"

I shook my head. "I really should have thought of it on my own. It's so obvious. He said I need to stop in and visit Doc Barker, introduce myself, and see what he'd like me to stock in the laboratory. Maybe he can be the voice of reason with Peterson. He's been around since the Lenape tribe was making pottery in this valley. They may just listen to him."

Ella chuckled. "Does Uncle Nate know him well? Perhaps he should go with you?"

"Absolutely. They grew up in the county together when Uncle Nate first came as a kid with our great-grandfather, Sam. Doc Barker delivered Jake and Martin and was the only doctor in this part of the county until Eli arrived after the war."

Ella crossed her arms on her chest, looking pleased. "Your father is one sharp man. When are you going to see Doc Barker?"

"First thing Monday morning. It would take a huge weight off if we could put this Klan nonsense to bed."

She nodded. "You're right. They're a vicious mob. If they're not stopped, we're going to see a tidal wave rather than a ripple."

Just as I was about to ask Ella if Dutch said anything else to her, more customers arrived. The young couple, wheeling a baby carriage, pushed it to the soda counter and sat. They were both well-dressed, the man in a light blue summer suit and straw boater, the wife in a white short-sleeved Swiss dot dress with a sash at the waist, outfitted for a pleasant walk around town, even if it was only our humble hamlet of Liberty. The young man flipped off his boater, fanning his face, and looked at Ella. "What are you serving for breakfast. Heard you had fresh eggs, straight off a local farm."

Chapter Nineteen: Albert

Uncle Nate and I passed Peterson's General Store as we pulled into a parking spot further down the street, in front of Doctor Barker's medical office.

"Do you think it's ok to show up without an appointment?" I asked.

Uncle Nate laughed, "You know, Albert, for most of the years Doc Barker's been here, no one had a telephone. People just arrived at his door with no warning. He won't blink."

I'd never considered how far back their history went. I imagined Doc Barker being pulled out of his office hours to tend a birth or care for a sick, home-bound family member. The telephone changed the way we lived day to day and communicated with our doctors. It was a brilliant invention.

The two of us entered a large front room the doctor used as a family waiting area. A small elderly woman wearing wire spectacles sat behind a desk. Behind her was the door leading to the examination rooms. Uncle Nate strolled up to the woman. "Good morning, Gladys. Don't you look like the picture of good health?" He twisted to me. "Gladys is Doc's wife. She holds the office together."

She raised her eyes above her metal bifocals, taking him in thoroughly before smiling, "Nate Levine, as I live and breathe. How's the family?"

Nate's face lit up into a smile. "We are all well. Just stopped by to introduce my nephew, Albert Kahn to Doc. He opened a pharmacy in Liberty. Just got his state license."

"That's lovely. What a great help, having medicine without driving all the way to Poughkeepsie. That's been quite a hike all these years." Gladys said.

I added, "And I make home deliveries too."

Just then, the door behind Gladys opened. Doc Barker peeked through the crack. "Gladys, have my first patients arrived?"

She answered. "Nate Levine and his nephew are here to see you. Do you have a few minutes to meet?"

Doc Barker opened the door fully, extending his hand for a hearty shake. "My God, Nate, it's been years. How are you?" He looked from Uncle Nate to me. "And this must be Albert? My, you've grown into a man." Turning to his exam rooms, he said, "Come on back to my office."

Seated in his small office, I surveyed the chaos. There was no way I could function in such a cluttered space. Journals and books were stacked in precarious towers on his credenza, desk, and floor. Sunlight reflected off the dust particles, as they sparkled in the air. There must have been six empty coffee mugs on his desk, all with varying shades of brown coffee sediment ringing their interiors.

Doc saw the curious expression on my face. "Don't fret, Albert. This room is my cave, reserved for my best thinking. Gladys is forbidden to clean in here. The other rooms in my clinic sparkle with daily applications of Clorox."

I was never particularly good at disguising my emotions. "I apologize. I was just surprised."

Uncle Nate drove right to the point. "Doc, I wanted to introduce you to Albert personally. Just this week, he opened his pharmacy up in Liberty on Main Street. Albert completed his Pharmacy degree in Albany this past spring."

I interjected. "Are there medications you'd like me to stock or compound for your patients? I'm happy to do whatever you need to support your practice. I'm even planning to make home deliveries."

Doc sat back in his chair. "You don't say, a local drug store. Now that's progress."

Uncle Nate smiled. "We've come a long way since our fathers started out here."

Doc said, "Speaking of new practices, how's Dr. Drucker doing? I met him a while back. Took quite a trauma to his face."

Uncle Nate nodded. "He was shot on Armistice Day. Imagine getting through all those battles, and then a demented German shooter finds his way into an American operating room near the Front. Besides shooting Eli, the German soldier killed two nurses."

Doc shook his head, his eyes downcast. "Such a senseless shame."

I redirected Uncle Nate's answer. "His practice is going well, especially with all the summer renters. But he misses the operating room."

Doc cocked his head to the side. "How so?"

I said, "He'd become one of the best surgeons near the trenches because of his limb repairs. Saved many arms and legs that would have been amputated by most surgeons."

Doc's eyebrows lifted with interest. "I didn't know that. What a sad state, all those boys without their limbs." He dropped back in his chair, turning to Uncle Nate. "I was so sorry to learn about Jake. I'll never forget the day I helped him into the world. Quite a big baby if I remember right. Just awful to have his life cut short."

Nate nodded, looking at his lap. Then, as if on cue, he lifted his head and locked eyes with Doc. "There's something else I want to discuss with you while we have a serious moment. Are you aware a branch of the Klan has formed up our way?"

Doc froze, gazing out the window. "Yes, I am."

I added. "They burned down Martin's barn and yesterday threatened our children. They congregate at Peterson's, and he's in on it."

Doc Barker stared back at our faces, alternating between Uncle Nate and me. He didn't utter a word.

"Any way you can talk some sense into them? Not sure they'll listen to the sheriff. They think they're above the law." Nate paused, staring Doc in the eyes. "We've been living peacefully together for decades. Now, since the end of the war, these rabble rousers come into town and have stirred things up, destroying property, killing animals, scaring folks."

Doc pushed his glasses up his nose, rubbing his chin. "Very disappointing to witness such unneeded violence. And I don't enjoy the thought of patching up people after fights. Not at my age."

"So, you'll try to talk sense to them?" Nate asked.

Doc rose from his chair to shake our hands. "I will try. But no promises. It's like they caught a fever and refuse to shake it off." He chuckled lightly. "Most of them were not exactly at the head of their class, if you know what I mean."

I didn't want to end our meeting on a sour note. So, I reminded Doc, "If you give Gladys a list of your medications, I'll make sure I'm stocked. Please tell Mrs. Barker I'll follow up tomorrow with a call."

Moments later, we were out of town, heading back to Liberty. I asked Nate, "You think he has any influence on those goons?"

"Don't think he's involved, but I also don't think he's going to change anyone's mind," Nate answered.

I glanced in the rearview mirror. There were two old, rusty Model Ts spewing exhaust from of the back of their cars, driving mighty close to us. Their engines could be heard a quarter mile away. "Looks like we might have trouble following close behind."

Uncle Nate's voice was tight. "Step on it, Albert."

My new car, straight off the assembly line, could accelerate up to forty-five miles per hour. In minutes, we left them in the dust. I was never so thankful for my generous Papa.

Chapter Twenty: Ella

The following day, after a massive breakfast of challah French toast and berries at Aunt Jenny's, Albert dropped me off at Miriam's. The house was uncommonly quiet. I figured Miriam was upstairs nursing the baby.

The gentle morning sun filtered through the curtains, casting a warm glow on the now-familiar surroundings. Back in Brooklyn, I 'd never noticed the serenity of sleep or the stillness of the morning air. The noise of city traffic persisted deep into the night, with horns honking every few minutes, delivery trucks barreling down the avenue, followed by the clamor of people awakening.

From downstairs, I could almost feel the children stirring in their beds, their last moments of sleep slipping away. I hurried to the kitchen, eager to have their breakfast ready when they came downstairs. I'd brought a container of the ripest purple blueberries I'd ever tasted from Aunt Jenny's patch, planning to bake a dozen muffins from a recipe she'd scribbled down that morning for me. In a separate bag, I had a set of finger paints from the pharmacy to try outside with the twins. Finger paints were the new rage this summer, a much messier form of painting for children and some adults. I thought they were a fad, with not much of a future.

Albert filled me in on his visit to Doc Barker on the ride up. The more I thought about the Klan, the more convinced I was that building a bridge between Eli and Doc was a smart move since Doc knew everyone, having met the townsfolk one by one in good and bad times.

Albert said, "The man is older than the hills. He's got to be retiring soon.

Not sure he can change anything."

"It's worth a try. Besides, he needs to know Eli better. Neither of them ever has a night off. Some days Eli is so tired, he walks around like a mummy. They should be helping each other. I'll suggest to Miriam that they invite him to dinner," I said.

But I was taken aback when Eli mentioned that Dutch had not returned the next day as he'd indicated. Had something happened? The unexpected news left me with a sense of unease.

Two hours later, Miriam was in the clinic, working with Eli, the baby upstairs, fast asleep. The twins and I were assembling their favorite jigsaw puzzle, Jig-a-Jig. The phone rang, startling all of us. I jumped to answer it before the next ring woke the baby.

"Hello, Drucker residence," I said, out of breath, expecting the caller to have confused the clinic number with their home.

There was no confusion after hearing Papa's whiny voice. "Is this Ella? Well, aren't you fancy! We need to talk."

Although I'd been dreading a conversation with Papa, that thought paled in comparison with his complete lack of concern for Robbie and my well-being. But there was no changing this man. "What is it, Papa? I'm watching Miriam's children and don't have much time." I paused, "Why didn't you tell me I have so many cousins?"

Papa kept his voice even at first, then the anger poured out. "Who the hell cares? I want my money back. How dare you steal from me!"

I exhaled slowly, taking care to control the conversation. "Don't worry, I just moved it to a bank here, didn't steal it. We haven't spent a penny."

He spat, "I have a mind to teach you a lesson, you ungrateful child."

"I plan to return it at summer's end when we get home. Robbie is having a great time on the farm, and so am I."

He grew more irritated. "End of the summer? That won't do at all. I need it now."

"Why, did you lose your job?" I asked with a growing concern.

"No, I did not. The why is none of your business." Papa yelled. "I'm coming to get it."

Just then, I heard a cry from upstairs. "If you do, you won't get a red penny, and all your family will see for themselves the kind of father you are. Besides, I can't talk now. I'm watching the children, and the baby just woke up, crying. You'll have to wait a few weeks for the money. It's all here. Bye, Papa." I set the receiver in the cradle, heading to the stairs to change Sarah. Would Papa heed my warning and stay home? Perhaps it was time to discuss the honest situation with Miriam. After all, she knew Papa best. She was his younger sister.

Midmorning, I made blueberry muffins with the children. The mouthwatering aroma filled the kitchen. Everyone took their chairs and ate, licking their fingers as a finale. Tamara begged, "Oh, Ella, could we make more tomorrow morning?"

"Of course," I answered. "How about you and Jake head back upstairs, get dressed, and make your beds while I talk to your mother?"

Jake's eyes lit up. "What about?"

Miriam looked at me curiously while she burped the baby.

"Boring grownup stuff, like parents talk about," I answered, rolling my eyes to the ceiling. "Then we can play a game while the baby naps again." The children scampered up the stairs.

"What's this all about?" asked Miriam

"Ugh, Papa called this morning. He's furious with me."

Miriam's eyebrows shot up. "Why is he mad? He's known you both were here for a few weeks now."

I hesitated, ashamed to admit my wretched behavior. Finally, I took the plunge. What was the worst that could happen? "Before I left Brooklyn with Robbie, I found his hidey hole and borrowed his cash." I quickly added, "But I haven't spent a penny. It was just in case we needed to pay train fare to get here. I figured I could return it at the end of the summer, and he might not even know it was gone. He gets a paycheck every two weeks." I exhaled, figuring I might as well spill the rest. "He threatened to come up and take his money back."

Miriam laughed in a knowing, deep, evil tone I'd never heard come from her mouth. "You really have no idea about your father, do you?"

I shook my head, surprised she hadn't scolded me, waiting for her to unveil another secret. "What do you mean?"

She placed Sarah on her other breast. The baby, entirely indifferent to the conversation, went to work sucking and gulping in her infant glory. "Your father has a serious problem. One that began before he left for college and has only grown worse over time."

I lifted my brows, tilting my head to the side, silently nudging her.

"Oh, Ella, he's a gambler and cannot stop himself. He'll win for a stretch, but then goes on a losing streak, gambling away everything but you children." She stopped, studying me carefully. "Haven't you noticed that he's strange with money?"

How could I not notice? I was always preoccupied with my mother's nonstop concern about paying for the rent, food, and clothing. Deep down, I feared he was living a double life, the kind with a second family, one he loved.

Miriam continued, speaking carefully as if applying a coffee filter to the story, holding back the gritty parts. "Before your grandparents passed, your Grandpa Abe put his sizable inheritance in a Trust to keep it from your father. Up until that time, and now for that matter, Julian couldn't stop gambling and was always asking our father for more money." She sighed. "Your grandpa put me in charge. That's why your Papa stays clear of me. He doesn't want me to know anything he's up to."

Like the Jig-a-Jig puzzle, the pieces were dropping out of the box of secrets and snapping together. The source of our fractured family was starting to make sense. A twist of sadness tightened my chest, realizing I'd always seen money as a solution, not a source of problems. "Can't he control himself?" I stammered, struggling to grasp the extent of Papa's years of this vile habit.

"Apparently not. Nothing devastating enough has happened to stop him. Your grandpa and grandma were at their wits' end. Even during the war, he got involved in gambling, setting up fights with dogs and roosters. His reputation was well known in France."

By this point, Sarah had finished nursing and was sitting happily on Miriam's lap while her Mama patted her back. A loud burp practically knocked her backwards. We both smiled.

She had a complete disregard for table manners or family troubles.

Miriam wiped the milky drool off Sarah's face and kissed her rosy cheek. "Yes, sweetheart, we all agree. Your Uncle Julian's got himself in another pickle." She turned to me. "I'll call him tomorrow and warn him to leave you alone. Do you mind if I put the money in the bank for safekeeping? Knowing Julian, that won't appease him, but it is the right thing to do."

* * *

At noon that morning, I walked down Main to the pharmacy. Baby Sarah was sleeping in her carriage after her midday feeding. The twins shot directly to the soda counter, climbed up on the stools, and twirled in circles. I jumped behind the counter to help Albert with the lunch customers, frying hamburgers on the electric griddle along with melted cheese sandwiches for Tamara and Jake. Within his first week of business, Albert's pharmacy and fountain had become a regular stop for locals, always hopping with activity.

"What a relief you've come," said Albert as he removed his cooking apron. He'd been working at the grill and was finishing. "Do you think you can help me out for an hour while I fill prescriptions? I'm getting behind, and some customers are returning after lunch to pick up their medicines."

I leaned to his ear, whispering, "Maybe it's time you hired someone in the morning to get you through the breakfast and lunch shifts. It's an awful lot to do by yourself. Aunt Jenny or Miriam may know someone looking for work."

Albert cast his pleading doe eyes at me. "But I was hoping you could help."

I laughed, "No way with three children to watch at the same time. Consider this a helpful visit." I looked about. "You're lucky the baby's sleeping. Once she's up, I need to leave."

Albert said, "You're right. On another note, Dutch stopped by earlier. I plan on using his whiskey for the prescriptions. Nothing more."

"What happened with using the legal suppliers?"

Albert shook his head with a mischievous grin. "Turns out the legal supplier in Albany is getting his best whiskey from Dutch and labeling the bottles with his pharmacy's name. If I did that too, I stay legal while getting Dutch's good stuff. These bootleggers think of everything."

"Well, isn't that something?" I said, "Your father's right. The law is ridiculous. All it did was start a huge black market." I needed to find out more. "Did he ask you about storing the stuff in exchange for protection?"

Albert squinted his eyes. "No, he didn't mention it. Did he say something to you?"

That damn Dutch, trying to suck Albert into his scheme little by little. He was far more savvy than the rest of us. "Be careful, Albert. We didn't get a chance to talk the other day. Dutch wants to get Uncle Nate to store his goods somewhere safe."

Albert huffed, "I'll be damned. What a sneak. Never said a word about that."

"Why would he? Just be careful what you agree to. Right now, Dutch has you nibbling at the bait," I said.

Albert buttoned his clean white lab coat. "Maybe it's not such a bad thing. Let's see if the Klan decides to take another run at us. I'd love to see their expressions when Dutch's men retaliate. The Klan will be out of their league, gone from here in no time." With those words, he disappeared into the laboratory to fill orders, leaving me to tend a rush of new hungry customers.

Chapter Twenty-One: Miriam

With Hannah and Ben back in the city, and the house mostly to ourselves, I had time to mull over the rapid changes in Eli and my lives. The addition of baby Sarah in the spring and Albert as a semi-permanent guest made the house tight. We barely had any time alone to talk.

In the six years since the Great War, a conflict that shaped our medical practice and our move to the country, the clinic had experienced explosive growth. This growth was due in part to the number of city dwellers moving north out of the congestion in Lower New York, and to Doc Barker's younger patients drifting away from his practice, seeking a more youthful, modern physician.

All this led to a discussion after we put the children to bed. Eli and I sat in the parlor sipping tea. "Albert suggested we invite Doc Barker and his wife, Gladys, here for dinner. He thinks Doc is getting close to retiring. If that's the case, we may need to bring on another doctor," I said.

Eli set his head back on the couch, closing his good eye.

"Are you falling asleep? Right in the middle of our first conversation in months?"

Eli chuckled. "No, I'm thinking about your question. Remember that young couple who came in this morning. The one from Monticello?"

I thought back to the appointments earlier that day. "The tall couple, pretty wife with the big blue eyes? If I recall, they were newly married."

"That was them. I was sworn to secrecy. The gal is pregnant and plans to use us for her delivery in five months. Their parents are from these parts and don't want to be seen as abandoning the ship," he said. "There's a lot of loyalty to Doc Barker.

I nodded, thinking aloud, "Albert's right. A dinner is a good idea. If Doc agrees to another physician, he can help us recruit a new doctor into the fold, and we can keep two offices, one in Monticello and one here. That will help cover the geography, all the calls at night, and during the weekends. While we're at it, should we bring on a nurse-midwife?" My mind had begun racing with ideas. "Have you heard about the nurse-midwifery program in the city? The profession's come a long way. We can always try to pull from there."

Eli nodded. "Good thought. I haven't been this dog tired since the war. It's time for another doctor, and yes, a midwife, too. Births are way up since we got back in 1918. I was thinking we should add a non-Jew. Set an example for the townsfolk, and it will be easy to cover all the holidays. Times are changing, and we need to build trust in the community. Show them we can all live and work together." He paused, "After all, their men trusted each other with their lives in France, no matter their religion or skin color."

He'd set my thoughts in motion. I knew we couldn't chase the Klan out overnight, and Eli's plan might be optimistic, but it was a good start. I'd call Gladys Barker the next morning and set up dinner. "Best we lead the charge."

Our lessons in building talent were hard-earned. We had nearly two years of combat experience in France, working with medical staff from every religious and ethnic background on the globe. If we hadn't a good eye for talent before entering the war, we sure learned how to judge skills and character in lightning speed, working with extraordinary levels of trauma. A solid nurse and doctor's hallmarks were strong intellect, steady hands, and the ability to focus on the patients' needs. A good practitioner was judgment-free and came in every possible size and color. Yes, this was an excellent way to lead by example.

* * *

To my delight, when Eli mentioned his plan to Nate, he and Jenny insisted they host. In Jenny's typical efficiency, Doc Barker and Gladys joined us at the farm that Saturday evening for one of Nate's sumptuous outdoor meals.

It was a perfect summer evening. The intense heat had lifted from the air, leaving behind a dry, balmy temperature. I finally had a chance to wear the new sleeveless drop waist dress I had bought in Poughkeepsie a month ago. Still too bare for the clinic, it was a comfortable frock for a summer evening. And the loose body made it perfect for my postpartum figure.

A soft breeze blew east, diverting the distasteful odor of the chickens below into the valley far from the eating area high on the hill. Aunt Jenny had a jar of citronella oil for everyone to smear on, warding off the bothersome evening mosquitoes.

As always, Jenny's dinners tasted the best when grilled outdoors by Nate with her secret sauce. She had a full pot of steamed fresh green beans and a platter of early tomatoes. Jenny drizzled French dressing over the tomatoes, a brand-new salad dressing made by the Heinz Company. It was all the rage, smooth, with a touch of pepper to liven it up. She claimed, "This bottle of dressing is better than any I've ever made."

After dinner, Ella rounded up the children, and she and Albert led them down the hill to the pond for a swim, cooling everyone down before bed. Doc, Gladys, Eli, Nate, Jenny, and I were left to discuss business. We settled into Nate's Adirondack chairs arranged around the fire pit. Doc screwed his face. "These are comfortable enough once I settle in, but how in tarnation am I supposed to climb out with such a deep seat?"

I laughed as I handed everyone a glass of iced tea. "Don't worry, we'll haul you out of there when you're ready.

Eli placed his hands on his knees. "Doc, you and Nate have lived here a long time, seen many changes. Have you thought about what the county will be like ten years from now?"

Doc cocked his head to the side, contemplating my question. "Funny you asked. I thought you might want to discuss the future when you invited us for this lovely dinner." He cleared his throat. "I'll be turning seventy this year and am not the young buck I used to be. But my nose still works."

Eli laughed, "What does that mean?"

Doc smiled back, "I can smell what's going on. I know some of my young patients have been driving up to Liberty to see you. Can't really blame them. Every year, it gets harder to keep up."

Eli's voice was soft. "My hunch is the population is going to keep growing. With better roads and faster cars, people will move out of Poughkeepsie and live west of the city. The whole country is going through the same thing, spreading out and filling up with people."

Gladys rocked her head. "It's the times we're living in. The stock market is booming, and people can afford more land. They want to get out of the city and spread their wings. I've been reading the papers. It's all over the country, even the West."

Eli nodded at Gladys then switched back to Doc, watching him with care. "My best guess is, at this rate, we'll need one more doctor and a midwife between you and me. Have you given the future any thought?"

Doc observed Eli for a moment. His simple words surprised me. He was not as gullible as I had imagined. "You could have grabbed it all for yourself. Anyway, that's what the Klan would've accused you of doing. But you had the decency to come to me, asking to build a plan together." He paused a moment, cocking his head to the side. "I like you. You're a respectable young man."

Eli shot his hand to Doc, shaking it slowly. "You have my deepest respect. You've been taking care of folks out here for decades. I don't know how you ever managed it alone. How about we figure out the future, so everyone wins in the end?"

I couldn't have felt prouder of my husband. It was impossible to believe only a few years ago, in France, he had wandered so far off course that I almost left him and our marriage. Since those dark days, he has proven, time and time again, I'd made the right decision.

Chapter Twenty-Two: Albert

It was the second week of July. Despite the thick summer heat, and after only two weeks of business, my pharmacy was thriving. Between the locals who'd patiently waited for the store's opening and word of mouth, we had a constant stream of customers at the soda counter and ordering prescriptions. Both Doc Barker and Eli were keeping me busy in the laboratory, compounding medicines. As usual, Ella's advice to hire a worker for the counter was spot on. Miriam helped us find a reliable high school girl who was fast, accurate with the register, a good cleaner, and needed a summer job. But it wasn't the same as when Ella worked in the store with me. It was only then my heart soared.

The quick trips back and forth to the farm in the morning and night were frustrating. I needed to find another way to spend time with Ella. An idea came to me Friday evening when I was driving her home from Miriam's. As I pulled into the farm, I turned to her. "What do you think about doing something fun on Saturday afternoon or Sunday? All we do is work."

Her eyes sparkled with curiosity. "What did you have in mind?"

I shrugged. "Have you been to Poughkeepsie?"

She shook her head.

"You've refused to take money for your help at the soda counter, and I thought we could shop for you. My way of thanking you for your help. Maybe I can take you to a nice clothing store, and you can select a couple of outfits."

She stared back at me. At first, I thought she might be angry, that my suggestion was too personal, suggesting that her clothing wasn't acceptable, then I saw tears fill her eyes.

"Ella, I didn't mean to upset you. I saw you admiring Miriam's new dress and just thought…."

She interrupted, "No one's ever taken me shopping for new clothes. That's the most extraordinary, generous idea." Ella leaned over and kissed my cheek. "You do like me, don't you?"

My eyes widened in surprise. "You've got to be kidding. Can't you tell I'm crazy about you?"

"But aren't we first cousins? Is it okay for us to…?"

"I told you the first day that we're not blood related and it's not against the law."

She pursed her lips in a tight line. "Doesn't it still matter, you know, in principle?"

I sighed. "Only if you're looking for an excuse not to be with me." I was getting frustrated, my heart falling. "Why don't you talk it over with Miriam. She's always given me good advice. And if you don't want me to bother you, just say so, and I'll respect your wishes."

Ella shook her head. "You're getting me all wrong. I'm so happy when we're together. I just don't want to make mistakes I'll regret. Especially when everyone has been so good to me." She paused a moment. "Also, I think your mother feels I'm too rough around the edges for you."

The girl never ceased to amaze me. It was as if she dropped out of the sky from another planet. Beautiful, wily as an alley cat, but afraid of trusting kindness, as if it were so fragile to the touch it could shatter into a million pieces. "Don't worry so much, Ella. You're the best surprise this family's had in a long time. My mother will come around."

* * *

I closed the pharmacy after the lunch crowd left and headed to the farm on Saturday, the next day. Ella had said "yes," and Aunt Jenny agreed to an afternoon of shopping and dinner only if we brought Robbie along. I had a vague feeling we would wind up watching Robbie more than enjoying each other. As soon as I pulled up in front of the house, my suspicion was confirmed. Before I opened the car door, Robbie was calling out, begging us to bring Noah, too. "I promise we'll listen, oh please."

Finally, I sent Noah inside to ask his parents, knowing my great plan was crumbling to bits.

Moments later, Wilma followed Noah and Robbie to the driveway. "Noah said you invited him to go with you?"

I laughed. "Sort of, if their arm-twisting counts as an invitation. It was Robbie's idea, but Noah's welcome to come, if they promise to behave."

Wilma sighed. "Honestly, I'd enjoy a rest from their antics this afternoon while the little one naps. Would it be too much trouble to stop at House of Cards on Main Street while you're in town? I can use some more stationery." She opened her purse and removed two dollars, handing them to Ella. "Nothing too fancy, maybe just a few sprigs of flowers on the paper. The change should cover Noah's supper. Please, no *trafe*."

The price for a date with Ella was getting steeper and more crowded by the minute. Now we needed to find something for Noah's dinner that wouldn't set Wilma's quasi-Kosher diet on its side. I figured anything that wasn't pork would suffice.

Ella stifled a laugh as we got into the car. "Looks like grilled cheese sandwiches for dinner. I was kind of hoping for a hot dog." She sat silently for a moment. "I can't get used to all the food rules."

"What do you mean, food rules?" I asked.

She chuckled, "It's easier to be Jewish with no rules, like my family. We eat anything we can get our hands on. Up here, some people won't get in a car on Shabbos, eat pork, or wear a bathing suit, but there's no guessing where one person's rules start and another one's end. Everyone picks and chooses. It's far easier, having no rules. I say if you're hungry, eat. Or hot enough, put on a swimsuit and jump in the pond. Here, I've no clue what a person might eat or do."

She saw hints of humor in everything. That is, if you count cynicism as humor. Despite her keen observations, Ella enjoyed people. She might tease a bit, but she was always generous with her compliments.

Despite her deprived childhood, there was no judgment beneath her lighthearted observations. I wondered how I would have fared with her rough upbringing. Where did her huge heart come from? From everything I'd heard, it couldn't have come from her father.

A world filled with adversity, like Ella's, left her skilled at smelling danger, tenacious as a badger when it came to facing down tough guys like Dutch, and quick to find solutions when a decision was needed. I could use a dose of that.

My youth wasn't a picnic for me, either. The two years Papa was away in Paris almost crushed me. I'd no patience to wait out his absence amid the endless fear I harbored for his safety. If it weren't for Mama and Uncle Nate, I would have become a street urchin, looking for a fight in every alley.

The two-hour ride to Poughkeepsie sped by with Robbie and Noah reciting and repeating ridiculous jokes, and me holding Ella's hand in the front seat. Once in town, I decided we'd stop at Luckey-Platt's first. They'd just opened their new store on Main, and I wanted Ella to find something special.

Lucky for us, I found a parking spot near the department store. Once inside, we located the women's department upstairs. In seconds, a sharply dressed saleswoman wearing a yellow summer suit and sporting a bob style haircut approached. "How can I help you this afternoon? My name is Helen."

Ella and the boys gawked. Compared to their mothers at home in housedresses and aprons, this woman could have walked straight off the cover of a fashion magazine.

I stepped in, extending my hand in Ella's direction. "We're here to find this lovely young woman, Ella, a summer outfit or two. Can I leave her in your hands?"

Helen looked at me and then the two boys, who had dropped to the floor, wrestling, already making a ruckus. She said, "Perhaps you can walk about the store or explore the town for an hour while Ella and I find something suitable. How does that sound?"

"It sounds great. Just give us a moment." I led Ella to a display, reaching over to a dress, flipping over the price tag. Then, pulling out my wallet, I handed her several bills. "This should cover a couple of dresses and a new pair of shoes."

"Oh no, Albert. It's way too much." Her eyes opened wide at the bills in her hand. "Are you toying with me?" She snorted. "It's not a nice joke."

Without thinking twice, I pulled her into my arms. "No, I'm dead serious. You've been such a help in the pharmacy, and I want you to have pretty things. Now take it, and we'll meet at the stationery store down the street when you're done. I'm getting the boys out of here before we get thrown out."

With the instincts of a fox and the determination to make a good sale, Helen linked her arm through Ella's. "Come with me, dear. I have some beautiful new outfits that just arrived. They'll look stunning on your slender figure."

An hour later, Ella floated into the stationery store wearing a linen canary yellow drop waist dress with two-tone T-strap shoes and a smile bright enough to light up Broadway.

"You're as beautiful as a movie star!" I laughed, watching her spin in circles before us. "How about next time we come here, we go see that new Buster Keaton movie about Sherlock Holmes? You can wear that pretty dress." I reached into my trouser pocket and pulled out a box. "By the way, I picked up a watch for you. I thought it might come in handy."

Ella's eyes sparkled with delight. "My first watch. Thank you so much."

I was having one of the best days of my life. It was the first time I had money of my own to share with a girl, bubbling with happiness to treat Ella, who returned appreciation and joy for new things in the most heartfelt fashion.

After a quick purchase for Wilma at the stationery store, we passed the barber shop with its red and white barber pole and arrived at Borroum's Drug Store, perfect for a quick bite at their counter. The boys' nonstop antics were wearing on me. I'd save the nice dinner out with Ella for another trip.

Opening the door, I spotted four open seats at a long soda fountain across the store. His counter, at least twice the length of mine, required two young men to keep pace with the customers, one at the grill and the other clearing plates and taking orders on his small pad. I wondered how long it would take for my counter to become that busy?

I placed my hand on Robbie's shoulder, pointing ahead. "Boys, go get those four seats." As they scampered over to the stools, I said to Ella, "Can you place an order for everyone? I'll have a hamburger and Coke. I want to say hi to Mr. Borroum in the back. I've known him for years. I'll be out in a minute."

Leaving my hungry group settled at the soda fountain, I walked to the door to the pharmacy. As I was about to knock, my closed fist hanging in the air, I heard men arguing. I opened the door, only to come eye to eye with Dutch and a darkly dressed goon holding Mr. Borroum by the shirt.

In a flash, Dutch spun toward me, reaching into his jacket, pulling out a pistol.

"What the hell is going on?" I yelled, acting on sheer impulse. "You planning on shooting me, Dutch? Ella and Robbie are having lunch at the counter. What do you plan on telling them after you're done?"

He screamed back at me. "What the hell are you doing here? Aren't you wandering a little far from the homestead?"

I didn't like Dutch's tone and his implication that I should somehow be chained to a tree in Liberty like a dog. I lowered my voice. "Why are you shaking down my friend?" I was certain Dutch had no idea we pharmacists were few and far between in the northern counties. We all knew each other and stuck together.

Dutch slid his gun back into his vest holster and laughed that insipid, grating bark of his. "Just an accounting misunderstanding. Right, Borroum? We'll get this straightened out next week."

Mr. Borroum's face was chalky white. I thought he'd pass out right on the floor.

As Dutch approached the back exit, I called out to him. "Dutch, we need to talk."

All he said was, "Next week." And then he and his sidekick were gone.

I turned my attention back to Mr. Borroum. "Are you alright? Did he hurt you?"

He brushed off his white coat. "Prohibition smoked out all the bullies looking for a quick buck. First the gin moonshiners, and now this creep."

"What do you mean? Why was Schultz here?" I asked.

"He found out I was splitting my liquor order between two suppliers, trying to keep everyone happy. But they're all crooks and no one's satisfied unless they have it all."

Borroum got me thinking about what Dutch told Ella about liquor storage. I was sure that would be our next hurdle as he forced pharmacists to buy from him. "Who are the gin moonshiners?"

He tsked. "A sleezy group of hillbillies south of Monticello."

I knew exactly who he was talking about. They were supplying Peterson's, too. The Klan. "I think I know who they are. Did you have any idea they're part of the Ku Klux Klan?"

"The who?" Mr. Borroum's face squeezed into a knot. "Never heard of them."

Didn't the man read a newspaper? He sold them in his store. I began to explain the Klan and what they were out to do. By the time I was done, Mr. Borroum was sitting at his lab table holding his head in his hands. "My grandpappy must be rolling in his grave. Not in a million years could we have imagined a bunch of thugs would be running our town."

Chapter Twenty-Three: Miriam

Another scorcher, and only seven-thirty in the morning. Now in the depth of July, it was all we could do to keep the children cool during the day. With baby Sarah still on a tight feeding schedule, I couldn't let Ella take the three children to the farm. Sarah hated a bottle. They'd have to wait for the weekend to swim in the pond. Instead, every morning we lugged pots of cold water into the backyard with some toys, and the twins ran about in the shade splashing each other. Meanwhile, Ella watched them from nearby, drinking iced tea or lemonade, and I scooted back and forth from the clinic to nurse the baby. I would fix a pitcher of tea the day before, and we drank it the following day with sugar and ice chips. Last night, after the heat lifted, I made hard-boiled eggs and a roast chicken, now cold in the icebox. That would get us through lunch and dinner.

The front door opened as I tiptoed down the stairs. Waving to Ella, I whispered, "Good morning. Right on time. How was your trip to Poughkeepsie this weekend?" I immediately took in her blue dress. "My, you look very pretty. Something new?"

She stood at the bottom of the stairs, waiting for me to come down. As I caught her eyes, I sensed a new emotion. "Did everything go well?"

She launched right in. "Albert gave me money to shop for clothes as a thank you for helping him set up the store. No one's ever given me money for new clothing before. I found two dresses that should keep me cool. What do you think?"

I cocked my head to the side, my lips pursed. She was both strong and vulnerable, like so many of the nurses I'd encountered in the war years. Life had already toughened those who served, enlisting for service with a hide of steel and something to prove. But their hearts were fragile from life's punishments. "Honey, you deserve special things. You are a remarkable young woman."

She drew a deep breath. "I have something a little odd to ask you. Please tell me the truth. It's important."

I hunched my shoulders, waiting for the shoe to drop. "Sure, what is it?"

She wrung her hands. "Albert would like to step out together. I'm not sure it's proper. You know, being first cousins. He says it's alright since we're not related."

How could I not realize this was coming? From the second they met, Albert couldn't take his eyes off her. I'd never seen him out of bed so early every day with a smile on his face. I wondered when their romance began heating up. "There's really no danger in the two of you being together, you know, down the road regarding healthy children. So it shouldn't be an obstacle. But the bigger question is if you're ready to court Albert. What are your feelings toward him?" I asked.

Her eyes held an uncertainty I hadn't witnessed on her face before. "He's wonderful, but I've never had a boyfriend. He was my first kiss." She drew a sharp breath. "Was it okay I told you that?"

I smiled, remembering my first kiss and how that relationship did not work out so well. "Of course. But it's not all about kissing a man and settling down. Or letting a man pick you. You're such a smart girl. Have you thought about college? What are your dreams?"

"Dreams? Or what's truly ahead? Girls like me don't get many options." Ella said with a sigh.

I placed my arm around Ella's shoulder and led her to the kitchen. "Let's talk while we get the children's breakfast ready." I pointed to the wall peg holding my aprons. "Be sure to wear an apron to protect the front of that pretty dress. Don't want to soil it. You're going to need to wear that outfit a few times this week with the heat."

I hadn't spoken to Julian yet, and until I did, wouldn't tell Ella about the Trust. Besides, she was a motivated saver, and as the conversation unfolded, it became clear she'd already had an idea for her future. Ella had decided to apply to nursing school.

While scrambling eggs for the twins, Ella shared her research. "I thought there was a school in Poughkeepsie, but the hospital there is mostly for people with mental problems. The big nursing school in Albany is three years long, and close to five hundred dollars a year, over half is room and board. It'll take a lifetime for me to save that much." She sighed, "If I go back home, Mama's going to want me to work and help pay her bills. That will be the end of any dreams for me."

My head was filling with other options. There were plenty of nursing schools in New York City: Bellevue, Mount Sinai, and Beth Israel, where I trained. Although most had housing, I could also speak to Hannah and see how she felt about a boarder if Ella went to school uptown at Mount Sinai.

I heard Sarah's morning hunger squeal. "Looks like we have a lot to think about. But before I get Sarah, a word of advice. If you want to go to Nursing School, and I think you should, you two must be careful in the lovey-dovey department. You know what I mean?"

She smirked, nodding.

I said, "Or else you'll be taking care of little ones and can kiss nursing school goodbye." I headed for the stairs and squinted back at Ella. "It would be a damn shame for the nursing profession to lose someone as talented as you."

Our words left me deep in thought for days. Before the week was out, I would call both Julian and Hannah to discuss Ella's future. With school over, Albert panting about her, and an uncertain future back in Brooklyn, it was high time to help my niece. In only three weeks, she had proven herself multiple times over to be an extraordinary young woman with unshakable values.

Chapter Twenty-Four: Ella

With the adults next door at the clinic, baby Sarah down for her morning nap, and the twins playing tag with pails of water in the backyard, I finally had a moment to think about Miriam's words.

Was it possible to turn my nursing school dream into reality? I knew I was taking the right steps, working every day for Miriam and saving every penny, but college had always felt an arm's length away, just out of reach. Was I ready for a serious relationship with Albert? Did I know for sure he'd be the right person with whom to share my life?

These questions left my head spinning. I had always looked at life in the short-term, convincing myself to stay the course, avoid making mistakes, and trust in myself. Miriam had jolted me out of my bubble, forcing me to see a larger picture. The one advantage I had was time. I'd just turned eighteen in the spring, offering room to maneuver. Most girls I knew married in their early twenties, which would give me plenty of time to earn a nursing degree first. In my case, the insurmountable issue was how to pay for it.

Just as I was brewing on the dilemma, Jake approached me in a fit of giggles, holding a cup of water he'd scooped out of his pail, his sister at his heels. "Come on, Ella. Play with us! Or we'll splash you." On days like this, I wished Robbie were here with me. But from Aunt Jenny's reports, he was having the time of his life with Noah at the farm.

I jumped out of my chair and roared, "I'm the summertime monster. You'll be hanging from the clothesline when I catch you. Better run fast!" We ran around the backyard until I was flushed, drenched in my own perspiration.

I could not take another step.

The children dissolved into laughter, ready to hang me on the line to dry out.

I raised my hands, "Time for the monster to take a rest and drink some cold water. If you're good, we'll go for ice cream floats later at Albert's."

Cheers ensued. Ice cream was always the perfect antidote for the heat.

* * *

Two hours later, after lunch, the baby cooing in the carriage, the twins and I sat at Albert's soda fountain counter in front of the fan. The children were concentrating on their ice cream bowls, Tamara stirring her chocolate ice cream into soup. I sipped my strawberry float, relishing the cool relief traveling from my mouth to my chest as the fizzy mixture slid down my insides. Baby Sarah sat propped up on my lap, held securely in my arms, watching me closely. I asked Albert's new staff how she liked working behind the counter.

Her smile gave me the answer I needed. "It's the perfect summer job. I ring up the purchases, serve the orders, get tips at the counter, and a paycheck—all in a half day."

Not a bad job for a sixteen-year-old. "What do you do in the afternoon?"

Without batting an eye, she said, "Swim, try to stay cool with friends. Then I help my mother fix dinner and clean up."

The baby began fussing. I knew she wasn't hungry. It was probably the heat.

I held a spoon to her mouth. "Would you like a teeny taste?"

Unaccustomed to a spoon, her tiny pink tongue jutted out of her mouth to taste the speck I left on her lips. A moment later, her eyes widened, and she began stretching, making guttural begging sounds. I gave her a little more, and a smile crossed her face. I wondered if Miriam would be bothered that I fed Sarah ice cream. The outside temperature had climbed into the nineties, and she was miserable, too. This morning, before we left, I changed Sarah's wet diaper and found a sizzling heat rash on her bottom. A cool mouth was just the distraction to keep her happy.

Albert wandered out of his laboratory into the store. "Hot enough for you? We've been serving ice cream floats since ten this morning. I'm going to have more supplies delivered. At this rate, we'll run through two weekly ice cream deliveries in half the time."

He lowered himself onto a stool and searched my face. "Did you check in with Miriam, about, you know…the cousin thing?"

The corners of my mouth turned up. "I did. And we're good. But there is one thing."

He knit his brows, eager to hear the catch. "What's that?"

I sighed. "I really want to go to nursing school before we fall into anything serious. I'm not ready for more commitment right now." There it was out on the table.

He sat watching me. "And?"

"And I understand you're a few years older than me and may be looking for a partner, a wife. It's not right for me to hold you back." Had I spoiled everything? Would he stop wanting to be my boyfriend?

Albert reached for my hand, still sticky from the spoon. "I'm not going to lose you unless you no longer want me. I've told you before, I'm crazy about you. You'll go to nursing school, and if you need my help, I'll be there for you."

Where did these generous people come from? I left the dark shadow of my Brooklyn family less than a month ago and entered an entirely different world, one with abundant light, people concerned about others, about me. My eyes filled.

Albert reached for my arm, squeezing it. "Did I say something wrong?"

Tamara looked up from her bowl. "Are you alright, Auntie Ella? Did your teeth freeze?"

I smiled at her. "No, they're happy tears."

The phone in the laboratory rang. Albert jumped up to answer it. "Be right back. Hold that thought."

I heard his yell clear to the counter. "I'll gather extra supplies and be right there."

A wave of goosebumps spread across my arms. I gently placed Sarah back in her carriage and hurried into the back laboratory. "Who was that? What happened?"

Albert was pulling bandages, tape, and drugs off the shelves, placing them in a cardboard box. He half-turned to look at me, his eyes wide with horror. "Something horrible has happened to Peterson's son, Timmy. He caught his arm in a thresher. Can see clear to the bone. Doc is driving him up now. He wants Eli to save his arm."

My chest deflated. "That's crazy! Why isn't he taking him to Poughkeepsie? That's the closest hospital. Eli will need more backup." My thoughts caught up to the moment. "And he has no depth perception. How can he operate?"

Albert didn't pause, filling the box. "Not enough time. Besides, he has Miriam to help, and they'll just amputate in Poughkeepsie."

As Albert looked around for any missing supplies, he fully turned to face me. "Stay here for another hour, then close the place for the day."

With those words, he tore out the door, running down Main Street to the clinic with the box of supplies in his hands, his white pharmacy coat flapping behind him, leaving the rest of us speechless.

I took a deep breath, needing a moment to think. Nothing about this sounded right. Peterson's son? My God! What would happen if Eli couldn't save the arm, or if the boy died? I couldn't imagine how Doc Barker convinced Peterson to bring the boy to Eli. Peterson hated us.

Forget sitting around the pharmacy. Looking about, there were only four customers left at the counter. They were practically finished eating. I said, "I'm so sorry. The counter is now closed."

The customers eyed me, eyebrows raised. One man asked, "What happened?"

"There's been a serious accident nearby. All hands are needed at the clinic. We'll reopen tomorrow. I apologize, but you must leave now. The ice cream is on the house."

I called Uncle Nate from the phone in the pharmacy. Deep down, I knew that no matter how things turned out—good, bad, or the worst—everything would be better if Uncle Nate was here with us. Together, he and Doc Barker could prevent things from spiraling out of control.

Uncle Nate didn't wait for me to finish explaining. "Jenny and I are on our way. Sit tight. We'll leave Robbie with Wilma."

A half hour later, the children and I were back at the house on Main Street. I settled the twins in the parlor, reading their books. Aunt Jenny, who arrived minutes after me, took Sarah upstairs to bathe and powder her bottom before placing her in the crib for an afternoon nap. Uncle Nate settled on the couch, cracking open the Sullivan Times. Looking up from the paper, he said, "Check things out and let me know how I can help. I'll be right here if you need me."

"Ok, I'll be right back. Just want to see what's going on." I opened the connecting door to the clinic and stepped through.

The clinic was a whole different world from the cozy house on the other side of the door. Antiseptic smells, partitioned rooms, and the high degree of order were not present in the main house filled with young children. I wondered how Miriam managed the back and forth over the course of a day. With Sarah's feeding schedule, Miriam alternated the high-pressure world of a doctor's office with the deep relaxation of an infant feeding every three hours. My head would swirl off my shoulders.

The pull into the medical suite overpowered me as I entered the rear hallway. The door to the large procedure room was closed. I heard noises, but they weren't coming from Timmy. I figured Miriam and Eli had started anesthesia. Blood splatters covered the walls and floor of the hallway, emitting a metallic smell that nearly knocked me over. I heard a man down the hall in the waiting room, crying. Was it Mr. Peterson? Creeping in that direction, I saw Doc Barker beside him, holding his hand, and on his other side, a woman. Was she Timmy's mother?

Mr. Peterson chanted between his chocking sobs, repeating the same words, "I knew it was a mistake to come here. If Drucker kills him, he'll have hell to pay."

Doc gently reassured him, "Eli Drucker is your best bet. No one within a hundred miles of here can do the kind of surgery he does. Do you have any idea how many limbs he spared during the war?"

Mr. Peterson sniffed, "That was when he had two eyes, Doc. He's not the same man he was then."

Doc persisted, "He's your son's best bet, and I know in Poughkeepsie they'd just take the arm. They don't have anyone there with his surgical experience. At least here, Timmy has a chance. After all, he is a righty."

The woman lamented, "He can't lose his right arm. He's a boy. I'll mark him for life." She sobbed, "My boy."

I stood in the hallway, watching the men, frozen and unsure what I should do. Having never been in a situation this dire, I began with something I knew well, cleaning. Walking into the second, unoccupied exam room, I filled a small pail with soapy water and a sponge. Moments later, I was washing down the soiled walls and floor.

Doc called out to me. "Young lady, who are you?"

I set the wash pail on the floor and sat in a chair beside them. "I'm Ella Levine, a niece from Brooklyn. I watch the children and help Albert at the pharmacy. I was there when the call came in and thought I'd find a way to help. How long have you been sitting here?"

Mr. Peterson stared at me; his eyes were on fire. "I know you. You've been in my store."

I nodded. "I called my Uncle Nate to come and help with the children so I can be an extra set of hands."

Mr. Peterson barked, "You're just a kid. What do you know about attaching arms?"

Years of experience dealing with my father's biting anger gave me the confidence to simply ignore his harsh words. I understood he was overwhelmed with fear and looking for a place to set it. "I'm going to be a nurse and will do whatever Uncle Eli or Doc Barker needs to help your son. Can I start by bringing you some coffee or lemonade while you wait? You must be terribly parched."

Doc Barker's face relaxed. "You're a natural, Ella. Yes, please bring some drinks. It's going to be a very long afternoon." He then patted Mahlon's shoulder and gave the woman's hand a reassuring squeeze. "Maisy, I'll poke my head into the room in a little while and see how Timmy's doing."

I drifted back into the house. Happy to be back in the kitchen, the first thing I did was check on the children, Uncle Nate, and Aunt Jenny. The heat had exhausted everyone, and I found the twins fast asleep on the parlor couches. Not a peep came from the baby upstairs. Aunt Jenny was sprawled out in a chair, her legs stretched apart, apron dipping down between her legs, hands folded across her round lap. Uncle Nate was snoring up a storm, the newspaper spread flat across his chest. How I wished I could join them. But I knew next door was teetering on the edge of disaster, and my gut told me to stay on the other side of the connecting door.

I set up a tray with a pitcher of lemonade, iced tea, and some glasses and brought them to Doc and the Petersons. "I'll be back in a few minutes with something to eat in case you get hungry."

Doc gave me a careful smile, and Mr. Peterson bent forward, eyes on his clenched hands, knuckles white with fear. I wondered if he was praying.

Just as I popped back into the kitchen, Albert ran in from the clinic procedure room. "I need to get Mr. Borroum, you know, the pharmacist in Poughkeepsie, to meet me halfway with intravenous fluids from the hospital. Eli's amazing. There's no doctor's office in the world giving fluids in this way. He's practicing battlefield medicine in Liberty, New York!" He dialed the phone to get Mr. Borroum on the line. While he waited for the other line to pick up, he continued talking. "The kid's lost a lot of blood. He's severely dehydrated."

The last thing I heard Albert say was, "See if you can get blood from the hospital. We need type O." Then he was out the door, practically tripping over Uncle Nate's outstretched legs.

Uncle Nate shook the sleep from his head. "What can I do? Is Doc here?"

I pointed to the children, still conked out on the couch, placed my index finger on my lips, and pulled Uncle Nate into the kitchen. "Doc is in the waiting area with Mr. Peterson and his wife. He's angry his son was brought to Eli. I just got some drinks and am going to make sandwiches for them. It would be helpful if you can keep them company while the twins are asleep."

Uncle Nate walked through the doorway into the clinic and headed to the waiting area. In the meantime, I pulled out cold chicken and bread from the icebox and prepared sandwiches, cutting them in half and stacking them on a large plate with pickles and sliced tomatoes. I set the tray with napkins and leftover cookies Miriam had in her jar and headed back to the waiting area. The men were deep in conversation, Uncle Nate listening carefully to Mr. Peterson's recounting of the accident.

"Timmy's been working for this family since he began high school. There's nothing he don't know about handling a thresher, but something must have caught in the motor, and when Timmy reached in to free the jam, his arm got caught." Mr. Peterson explained, appearing less agitated.

Talking to Uncle Nate and Doc about the accident helped calm him. But Maisy Peterson, Timmy's mother, was falling apart. She sat weeping, stopping every few moments to pray, chanting, "Please God, help my little boy, my little boy." I had never seen anything quite like it. But I noticed one peculiar thing. The more Mr. Peterson helped comfort his wife, the steadier he grew. Her desperation gave him the courage he needed. Was this normal behavior? Do nurses see this every day?

I caught Doc's attention. "Do you want me to poke my head in? Albert left a little while ago to get supplies in Poughkeepsie."

He took one last bite of the sandwich and rose from his chair, checking his watch. "Thanks for the refreshments, Ella. It's been over an hour. I'll stick my head in."

I glanced at the wall clock. It was already four in the afternoon. "Doc, would you see if they need any help from me?"

Doc stopped at the lavatory and washed his hands before lightly knocking on the procedure door. He didn't wait for an answer, opening the door, saying, "How's the boy doing? Albert's on the road." I stood behind Doc as he spoke. I had an open view of the room.

Eli locked eyes with Doc. "The kid's lost too much blood. We don't have time to wait for Albert."

Timmy's body lay flat on the table, his injured arm extended out to the side, resting on an instrument table, blood and ooze dripping from his wound into Miriam's roasting pan on the floor. My stomach curled in knots. Were they going to use that same pan for cooking after this?

Eli's voice was urgent, "I don't want to lose this kid, Doc. We can't wait for Albert to get back with blood. I have a transfusion kit in the cabinet. I needed Type O an hour ago. Timmy's close to death."

Miriam rose from her chair on the other side of Timmy and grabbed the kit, which included droppers and tubes, handing it to Doc. "Test the parents first, then Nate and Jenny." While Doc took the kit to the front room, I followed Miriam to the second exam room where she set up the transfusion equipment, including a long, sharp needle, thick tubing, and a canister. She added several drops of a chemical to the canister.

Forgetting I hadn't been invited into the room, I asked, "What are you putting in the jar?"

Miriam startled, looked up at me. "I didn't know you were standing there. Are you alright watching this?"

I was transfixed. "Oh yes, it's fascinating. I'm going to be a nurse."

Miriam glanced between the kit and the waiting room, tapping the toe of her shoe. "The chemical keeps the incoming blood from clotting, so we deliver unclotted blood into Timmy's body. Check Doc and see if he's ready. We have no time to spare."

I was out the door before she finished asking. Doc was nodding his head. "Excellent, Type O, a match." He looked into Peterson's eyes. "Come with me. You're going to share some of that liquid life with your son."

But Peterson sat, glued to the couch, his voice breathy. "What do you mean? You already stuck me. Isn't that enough? I hate needles."

Doc reached out his hand to pull Peterson up. "Mahlon, I know this is the worst day of your life, but you really don't have a choice. Your son is on the edge of death. He's lost way too much blood. This has become a far bigger issue than saving his arm."

Maisy gasped. "Mahlon, shake it off. Doc, test me."

Peterson's face was pasty white. "I think I'm going to pass out."

Doc squeezed his shoulder. "That's ok, we're going to have you lie down anyway. You can sleep through the whole thing if you want."

I cleared my throat. "Test me, Doc. Maybe I'm an O. I don't mind giving Timmy my blood."

Peterson straightened up so fast I thought a bolt of lightning had struck his body, his face filling with red-hot anger. "I'm doing it. He's not taking Jew blood."

His wife cracked a smile through her tears, shaking her head. "Good God, Mahlon. Now go! He needs you, now."

I didn't know what to think. The man was bursting with so much fear and hate I thought he'd explode. But I let his words slide off, reminding myself that if Albert didn't get back in time, I could let Miriam know I was willing.

Doc led Peterson into the second patient room. "Ella, help him lie down and roll up his sleeve. Get him comfortable. It's going to take a little while."

Mr. Peterson was shaking as I tried to settle him down, fixing a pillow under his head.

"Eli and Miriam performed this surgery more times than you can count when they were overseas." I looked down into his eyes. "I'm sure it must feel strange and frightening having Timmy a few feet away, but you're the hero of the day. Your blood is going to save his life."

Mr. Peterson watched me closely. "Why are you being nice to me? I've been a total brute to you – no gentleman."

"It's like Doc said, 'Today is the worst day of your life.' Why would I want to be mean to you on such a bad day?" I smiled, my eyes sparkling with a hint of mischief, "Even if you deserve it."

Doc and Miriam entered our room and had the intravenous blood line working in seconds. My God, they were fast. As Miriam checked to see how quickly the small jar was filling with Peterson's blood, she pointed to a level near the top of the jar and said to Doc, "Get me when the blood level reaches here. Should only take a few minutes. I'll bring a second container, and we'll fill another."

Peterson drew a pained breath. "You didn't say two. Agh!"

I rubbed his free arm gently. "Mr. Peterson, you can do this. Let's talk about other things. None of us wants to see your Timmy die."

He sniffled, grabbed my hand, and squeezed. "Stay with me. I don't want to be alone. And I don't want Maisy to see me as a coward."

So, I stayed. I sat for over an hour holding his hand, talking about everything from the history of his life to his customers' favorite products. He shared with me how surprised and joyful he was with Timmy's birth, years after they thought their family was complete. As a small child, they could already see that Timmy was a gentle and studious child, an opposite personality from his rambunctious older siblings.

After Miriam came for her second small jar of blood, I helped Mr. Peterson to a chair, brought a second chair into the room for Mrs. Peterson, then fetched water and a sandwich.

"Mrs. Peterson, let me know when he finishes the water, and I will get another. Miriam wants you both to sit a while until Mr. Peterson can stand without feeling dizzy. There's no hurry at all."

I left and poked my head into the procedure room. Timmy's condition seemed to have changed dramatically for the better after receiving his father's blood. But there was no time to spare. Eli and Miriam jumped back into the repair as Timmy's color pinked up.

"Can I watch a while? He looks much better. Timmy's skin color almost looks normal." I said, my voice hushed.

Miriam was bent over the wound, stitching tissue together with tiny knots at Eli's instruction. She answered me without looking up. "Yes, but check on the children in a little while. It's awfully quiet over there."

Eli was administering the anesthesia, lightly adding chloroform to keep Timmy immobile and asleep. They worked seamlessly, without speaking, with Eli occasionally pointing at a stretch of tissue and whispering, "Avoid this, it's the radial nerve, looks intact. Keep it up, Miriam, you would have been an excellent surgeon."

Doc peeked his head through the doorway. "Are things promising?"

Eli looked up and said, "Yes, indeed. Good chance we'll save the arm so long as no infection sets in. He does need more fluids. Still dry. If Albert is lucky enough to get more from Poughkeepsie, it will help."

Doc answered, "Anything more I can do?"

Miriam said, "Make sure Mahlon's feeling ok. He needs to rest for now. Don't need two patients." She glanced at Doc. "And tell them things are looking up, but it will be a while till we're out of the woods. I probably have a couple more hours sewing him up. Right, Eli?"

"Tell them three or four hours more," answered Eli.

Doc stood beside me, placing his hand on my shoulder, "This niece of yours is really something. Has us all fed and the place clean as a whistle. Even managed to tame that rascal, Peterson."

Miriam nodded, both eyes focused on her delicate work, "Ella, it's time to fix a bottle for the baby. I have breast milk in the icebox. I'm going to miss at least one more feeding." She took her free arm and squeezed it across her chest. The leaked milk had penetrated her apron, leaving saucer sized circles of dampness.

"I'll get the bottle ready now," I knew her breasts were filling with milk, becoming painfully engorged. All that baby did every waking hour was nurse, coo, and then back to sleep before she started another round. In my eyes, Miriam was the definition of grit.

"Do not overheat the milk, and afterwards, give her a hearty burp." Miriam paused, continuing her instruction in her all-business manner. "Get the children dinner, too. There's lots of food in the icebox. And thank you, Ella."

Just as I walked back into the house, I heard the children's voices. The twins were outside, playing a game with Uncle Nate, and Sarah was wailing after her nap, an empty belly ready for milk. I opened the back door, calling out, "I'm back, everyone. Would you like some lemonade and a cookie?" I set up two places in the kitchen, took out the milk from the icebox, and scooted upstairs to help Aunt Jenny with Sarah.

Sarah was kicking off her wet diaper, screaming at full throttle. That wet diaper must be scorching her tender skin.

"She's an angry little girl," Aunt Jenny said.

"How about I take care of changing and washing her? I took milk out for her next bottle. Could you warm it for her? Miriam told me to use a saucepan, but not to let it boil."

"Of course." Aunt Jenny turned to head down the steps, waddling, stepping carefully, holding the banister.

I turned to the baby. "Oh, Sarah, I know this nasty diaper must be burning you up." I undressed her, propping her over my shoulder while I ran the upstairs sink, splashing cool water over her irritated skin. She calmed down immediately. I sat her in the sink, soaking her bottom for a couple of minutes, and then lifted her out, patting her dry against my chest as I headed back to the nursery. Miriam had a jar of Vaseline next to the changing table, and I spread some on her rash. That seemed to help. Now it was time for her bottle.

I brought Sarah down to Aunt Jenny, settling her in strong arms. The bottle was perfect, warm but not hot. While baby Sarah sucked at the nipple, I poked my head in the refrigerator, thinking about dinner. I could barely wrap my head around food again. The day had been exhausting, and I was drained. How did Miriam and Eli keep the pace? They were like machines.

Walking into the parlor, I said, "Aunt Jenny, any chance we could switch places? My feet are killing me, and I don't know what to do about dinner. You're so good at that."

In a flash, she said, "I was hoping you'd ask. I'd also like to take a good look at what Miriam has in the ice box. I have a feeling she will need a few extra things. I can bring more food from the farm tomorrow. Wilma called. She's itching to hear how things are going and wants to help, too. Maybe I'll get her to fix a couple of pies this evening to bring back tomorrow."

I smiled. There was no end to their goodwill. "By the way, did Albert come back?"

"I sent him back to the pharmacy after he returned. Told him you had the blood," said Aunt Jenny, pointing to the corner of the room. "He left the other provisions in that box over there. He should take care of his customers."

"That's great," I said. "I'll bring the box over to the clinic now, then feed Sarah."

The hours crawled by. It was seven in the evening when Eli and Miriam finished working on Timmy. During that long stretch of time, numerous Peterson family members filed into the waiting area, supporting their kin, their arms full of platters of food. As their number grew, they overflowed into the backyard and parlor of the house. I was on my feet constantly caring for the three children, leaving the drinks and food for the crowd to

Aunt Jenny, who was always one step ahead of their needs.

As I watched the faces come and go, it struck me how much everyone wanted to help, offering to bring fresh food the next day, checking on the Petersons' house, sitting with Mrs. Peterson. The strong bond of community far outweighed our ridiculous grievances. While I assisted in the kitchen, Mrs. Peterson's sister held Sarah, cooing and keeping the baby content.

After closing the pharmacy for the night, Albert joined us back at the house with a canister of vanilla ice cream and cones, preparing one for each child in the backyard. The twins and other children who had arrived with their parents ran around the backyard, licking drippy ice cream cones and later catching lightning bugs. Someone brought a pail of water outside from the kitchen and cleaned the children off.

In the meantime, at six-thirty, I crept back to the clinic. Eli and Miriam were tying the last stitch, attaching two rubber tubes to the surgical site, holding them in place with gauze and tape. Miriam explained, "These are Penrose drains. They help reduce swelling and prevent infection, accelerating the healing process. But they also introduce risk. We must watch them carefully, looking for any extra redness since the tubes can sometimes introduce infection. Today, we are willing to take that chance. Timmy's young and strong, and we'll watch him very closely."

I returned to the clinic again an hour later. The door to the procedure room was open. Mr. and Mrs. Peterson stood at Timmy's left side, holding his uninjured hand. Eli, Miriam, and Doc were carefully explaining the extent of his injury, the steps Eli and Miriam had taken during the lengthy surgery, and the long road to recovery.

Mr. Peterson, exhaustion written all over his body, bent over, stroking Timmy's forehead. "We must take him home to rest. He can't stay here."

Miriam answered in an even voice, "I understand how frightening this has been, but he cannot be moved for at least a week, and that's if everything goes according to plan."

Eli added, "Once he's stable and beginning to mend, I'd like to transfer him to a hospital bed in Poughkeepsie for a few more weeks, like we did overseas after limb repairs. His injury was remarkably like what we saw during the war. Healing takes many weeks. We must all be patient."

Mr. Peterson's body slumped further. "Will he be able to use his arm? His hand?"

Doc Barker wrapped his arm around Mr. Peterson's shoulder. "Mahlon, the body heals according to its own clock. Timmy is out of the deep woods but has a way to go to reach the clearing. I think it's best that you kiss him good night, take Maisy home, and both of you get some rest now that you know he made it through this terrible day. Come back first thing tomorrow, and you can sit with him then."

"In a little while," said Mahlon. His eyes were puffy and red. His body sagged with exhaustion. He was not going anywhere too fast.

Chapter Twenty-Five: Albert

My shirt was drenched in sweat. From the moment Miriam called me at the pharmacy, I'd been running flat out, with no time to think. The trip to Poughkeepsie took longer than expected. By the time I returned to the clinic, Timmy had been transfused, so I returned to the pharmacy. People were milling about the sidewalk, hoping I'd reopen the store. After all, I had a business to run.

I returned to the house hours later, after Timmy's arm was repaired and we were on the other side of the chaos. I took two glasses of lemonade from the kitchen and walked out to the backyard to sit with Eli. Miriam remained indoors, nursing the baby while monitoring Timmy in the clinic. Maisy kept her company while Mr. Peterson drifted back to the waiting area.

I plopped next to Eli on a picnic bench, handing him a glass. "This is what you were doing day and night in France?"

Eli nodded. "But trust me, it was much easier with two healthy eyes." He sighed, "I could never have handled Timmy without Miriam. With her brain and steady hands, following every one of my directions, she could have been…" He paused, "Should have been a surgeon. She has a natural gift."

I patted Eli's shoulder. "You are both incredible. The town is lucky to have you."

"We'll see how Peterson feels about it when he sees just how slow the recovery is. Timmy almost lost his lower arm, and the radial nerve was mashed in places. I'm not sure how much use he'll have. If the nerve doesn't regenerate, his arm may be lame, more decoration than anything else," Eli said.

"How long before you know?" I asked.

"Months, probably more time than Peterson has patience for. I can't imagine how anything less than perfect won't circle back at us."

The back screen door slammed. I twisted around to see Doc Barker ambling out. "Mind if I join you two?"

"Take my seat." I said, "I'll get you a drink."

"Have anything stronger than lemonade?" said Doc.

Eli chuckled, "Do we dare get Peterson out here for a nip? It's been a hell of a day."

Doc did an about-face, talking back to us over his shoulder. "You bet he can use one. I'll get him."

While Doc went back inside to get Peterson, I walked into the clinic to see how Miriam and Maisy were holding up. When I got to the procedure room, Timmy was beginning to wake up, struggling to free his arm from the splint.

Miriam cooed in a soft, reassuring voice, handing the baby to Maisy. "Timmy, you're fine. Try to lie still, and I'll give you something for the pain."

Mrs. Peterson chewed her lower lip, repeating, "Thank God you're alive."

Panic laced through Timmy's eyes as they darted about the room, taking it all in. "They dared me to unclog the thresher! They called me a coward." He gasped, crying. "My God, it hurts so much."

Miriam ignored everyone but Timmy, administering a shot of morphine. "This will help settle you. We can talk about the accident later when we have a better grip on the pain. You're a very brave soldier, young man."

Timmy's eyes dropped half closed, his breath shifting to even intervals. Miriam turned to us. "Morphine is a wonder drug. There's no way we would have gotten through the war years without it. The pain from an accident like this is indescribable."

I had nearly emptied my pharmacy's stock of the drug. Tomorrow, first thing, I'd call my pharmaceutical supplier and ask for a rush delivery. It would take some time before this boy was out of the woods. "Will you need more fluids? I'm going to place an order in the morning and restock. Let me know everything you'll want when we get up tomorrow," I said.

Just then, Doc entered the room, having retrieved Mr. Peterson from the chair in the waiting room. I followed behind as Doc led us to the backyard bench where the men sat, filling their cups with shots of Dutch's whiskey.

"That hits the spot," said Doc, admiring the content. "Color is fine, and it tastes like a good Canadian whiskey."

Eli turned to Peterson. "How are you holding up, good man. Not sure who that was harder for, Timmy, or you and Maisy."

Peterson's voice hitched. "One hell of a day. The worst in my life. Thought I'd lose my kid." He took a swig, slowly raising his eyes to Eli's. "I owe you thanks. I mean it."

I directed my words to Eli. "Miriam just gave Timmy a shot of morphine. He was coming to. In a lot of pain." I sat. "Seems to have settled him back down. That stuff is a wonder drug. She said you used a lot of it in France."

Eli snorted, "That's an understatement. If soldiers had any idea of the pain from injuries, they'd never be willing to fight in wars."

Peterson looked back at Eli. "What do you think, Doc? What's ahead for my son?"

Eli took a moment, watching his hands, and then looked into Peterson's bloodshot eyes. "It will be a long road, months, before we know how much function will return. The bones were practically intact, and blood flow was adequate, but the nerves and muscles took a real beating."

Peterson said, "Won't it mend?"

Eli continued; his voice controlled. "Miriam has the steadiest hands I've ever seen, and she stitches better than most surgeons I've worked with, but the body is God's creation, and we will not know his future until the healing begins. Right now, Timmy needs to get past the day's trauma. No movement, lots of fluids, and pain medicine. In a couple of days, once the risk of infection has subsided, we'll know more."

Doc said, "Like I said, Mahlon, he would have lost the arm if we took him to Poughkeepsie. Now, he stands a good chance of keeping it."

"Can we stay with him?" asked Peterson. "Please?"

Doc answered, "Best you take Maisy on home. If you get worried, someone will be awake in the clinic with him through the night. Just call. Remember, you need to stay rested, too."

Eli placed his palms on his knees, raising himself to stand. "I'm going to check on the boy and see what Miriam has to say." He turned to face us. "If he's stable, we'll work out a rotation so, like Doc said, one of us is attending him around the clock."

I couldn't put my finger on it, but Peterson's demeanor had shifted for the better. No longer belligerent, picking a fight, he'd become quiet and compliant. Was it the force of our cohesive team saving his boy, the camaraderie of throwing down whiskey together after the ordeal, or sheer relief? But Peterson appeared to be a changed man. Had he begun to trust us?

When Eli returned to the backyard ten minutes later, Peterson was already three sheets to the wind, barely holding himself upright. He chuckled, "I'll get one of Maisy's relatives to take us home and leave the car here for the night." With those words, he half-stumbled into the house.

Eli took one look at Mr. Peterson and called out, "Good plan. We'll see you in the morning." Then he turned to Doc. "I'll take tonight, then Miriam, Eli, Albert, and Ella after we've prepared her. Doc, maybe you can encourage the Petersons to sit with him during the day and leave the nights to us. That way, Miriam and I can run the clinic, and Albert can keep the pharmacy open."

Doc drew his brows. "Put me in the rotation, too. Do you think we can move him to the hospital in a week? I know his parents will want that."

Eli cocked his head, lips drawn tightly, "Let's get him out of the woods first. If there's no infection and he can handle a little jostling, we'll move him. But I'd rather talk about it once I feel more confident."

* * *

By the grace of God, the first five days passed without fever or complications. Timmy was one tough lad, determined to do everything he could to power through the early days of healing, insisting on sitting up, drinking broth, and using a bedpan independently. That kid knew how to follow directions.

By the end of the first week, he was standing with his arm in a protective splint and walking around the clinic.

Every day, platters of food were delivered from the Peterson's extended family to Miriam and Eli's home, feeding the eight to ten visitors who arrived daily from all over the state, as well as those of us involved in Timmy's care. Baked hams, breads, biscuits, creamed chipped beef, and noodle casseroles piled up on the kitchen table as Miriam's icebox continued to run out of space. On the counter was a bakery's worth of cakes and cookies. Always a full coffee pot on the stovetop. At the end of each day, Ella packed a carload of food for Maisy to take back to her home for overnight guests.

By the sixth day, Miriam confronted Eli and Doc, dragging them to the picnic table in the backyard, the only available seats in sight. "This is getting to be too much. We need to move Timmy to a hospital. We're not equipped to run a hotel. The twins don't know their right from left with all the strangers in the house. Frankly, neither do I."

Eli nodded. "I'm thankful he's healing well." He lowered his voice and began speaking directly to Doc. "Timmy's in a bigger hurry than his father to mend, and I don't want him hurting himself. If Peterson agrees, I'll request an inpatient bed at Vassar Brothers Hospital in Poughkeepsie for three more weeks. That will give him a month of recovery under physician and nurse supervision."

Doc chimed in. "Maisy's exhausted with worry and all the visitors at their home has worn her to a thread, too. I say we try to get him to the hospital before she falls apart. I'll talk to Mahlon now. We can make the transfer once they have an open bed for him." He rose from the bench and headed back to the clinic.

I watched Doc as he walked into the building, moving slowly then stopped, looking noticeably tired. "The old guy needs a good break, or he'll be your next patient," I said to Eli. "You two joining forces is a smart move. And I hope it fixes our problem with the white hoods."

Eli sighed loudly. "That would certainly be one good thing to come out of all this. But I can't tell how much use of his arm Timmy will get back now that the risk of infection is lessening. He still can't bend his fingers."

Since Timmy's accident, Ella and I had learned volumes about medicine from Eli and Miriam, I thought my head would burst. Daily, we participated in Timmy's care, taking his blood pressure, heart rate, temperature, and measuring fluids in and out. The indicators of health seemed endless. Staying overnight with him and following the hourly measures of his vitals kept us attuned to the life-and-death nature of healing and its byproducts, pain and fever, not to mention the precarious pace of healing during the initial hours and days. "Does he have any sensation at all?" I asked.

Eli nodded. "He can feel a pin prick in his wrist and palm. Those are good signs. I hope together, working with Miriam, we were able to pull that radial nerve together. That would be a triumph."

"When will you be able to tell more?" Doc asked.

"Once we remove his splint, we'll check for wrist control. But that won't be for a few more weeks. Until then, we need to ensure he's monitored and doesn't injure himself trying to do too much. You know how reckless young men can be. Always determined to beat the train to the station."

Chapter Twenty-Six: Ella

After the past week, working in our Liberty make-shift hospital, I was more determined than ever to attend nursing school. I sent away for applications from Albany Hospital, Mount Sinai, Beth Israel, and Bellevue, hoping I'd figure out how to cover my tuition. With all the chaos going on around Timmy, I knew Miriam hadn't time to make calls. I figured if I had admission letters in hand in a month or so, her conversation with Aunt Hannah about Mount Sinai would have more impact. By living with Albert's parents in Manhattan, I could save money on housing and meals if I went to nursing school uptown. In the meantime, I did everything possible to help care for Timmy and the children so Eli and Miriam could see their regular appointments in the clinic.

On the days I returned to the farm in the evening, I slipped into my bathing suit and swam with Robbie in the pond, splashing each other, washing away the haunting memory of Timmy's relentless pain. One evening, Robbie put on his clumsy goggles and dove to the bottom, exploring. Up he swam, breaking through to the surface, holding a penny in his hand. "Look what I found. The light was reflecting off the coin."

I laughed, enjoying his delight.

In my early fantasies of Uncle Nate's chicken farm, everything was idyllic, safe, and peaceful. In just a few weeks, my senses had sharpened. Just like the city, the country had its dangers: machines, bootleggers, and vengeful people. The biggest difference, was here, at the farm, my family was kind to Robbie and me. And Albert, my first kiss, the first man to give me money for new clothes, had me thinking about my future.

Robbie dove under the water and grabbed my legs out from under me. Down I went, hair and all. "You little stinker! When did you become a fish?"

He laughed, gulping mouthfuls of water and spitting them out at me. "I'm not a fish, I'm an explorer, looking for lost treasures."

I dunked his head under the water for a second before he could swim away. I could play this game too. Childhood—I was determined to have my last taste of it here, even if I was already eighteen.

* * *

When I woke the next morning, I felt like a new person, fully rested and ready to face the day. It was Monday morning. There was nothing like a good night's sleep and one of Aunt Jenny's pancake breakfasts to set me right. Smelling the butter sizzling in the cast-iron pan on the stove had my mouth watering before I lifted my head from the pillow.

According to Miriam, Timmy would be taken by ambulance to Vassar Brothers Hospital in Poughkeepsie later in the day. Eli wasn't taking any chances with Timmy's arm and wanted Mr. Peterson and Timmy to know he meant business. I heard Eli tell Mr. Peterson yesterday when he protested the cost, "I'm telling you, Mahlon, we will not get a second chance to repair his right arm. Under no circumstances do I want any additional jostling. We've only come a short way on the healing journey. You and Timmy may think he's better because the food is making him stronger, and he's getting his spark back. But don't be fooled, the arm and hand tissues have their own healing clock. Believe me when I tell you, it's much slower than you think."

When Albert arrived at the farm to pick me up, he insisted on first finishing off the leftover breakfast. He sat with Aunt Jenny and Wilma, sharing the upcoming specials at the store. Finally, I hopped into his car, eager to hear the update from the past evening. "Is everything on schedule for Timmy's transfer?"

Albert laughed. "After this past week, the Petersons have a new appreciation for what goes on behind the closed doors of clinics and hospitals. When the word of how we saved Peterson's kid gets out to his cronies, we

165

won't be hearing a squeak from them in the future."

I sighed, "Peace comes at a terrible cost. That boy almost lost his right arm. He's still having a lot of pain. He has a way to go."

"But at least he'll be at the hospital for the rest of it. Everyone needs a break, including the Petersons. I heard poor Maisy telling her husband that if their family visitors didn't leave soon, she was going to lose her mind. All they did was eat and ask her for every small item under the sun, more pillows, towels, and toothpaste. It never ended. Some didn't even wash their dirty plates, just left them on the counter for her to clean. She told Mr. Peterson, "What do they think, I'm running a hotel?"

I sat back in his car, enjoying the ride into town. "You know, after last week with Timothy, I'm determined more than ever to study nursing. Miriam knows so much medicine. I want to be just like her."

Albert turned his head to meet my gaze. "You never cease to amaze me. Sometimes, I think I know you so well, but then, I realize I've just scraped the surface." He took a deep breath. "You must know I've fallen head over heels in love with you."

I reached for his hand, squeezing it gently, encouraging him, but not quite ready to say those words. I needed more time, knowing he was impatient to hear the same feelings from me.

We pulled up in front of the pharmacy. Eli said, "Stay here, I'll be back in a minute. My list is inside. I'm going to take a ride to Poughkeepsie to properly thank Mr. Borroum. I'll drop you off at Miriam's on my way."

"That's alright. I'll walk. After that huge breakfast, I could use a stretch." I leaned over and kissed him on the cheek. "I'll see you later. Drive carefully."

* * *

It was only seven-thirty in the morning, and the early heat was already seeping into the air. My mind filled with plans for the day as I walked to Miriam's house. Knowing it would be another scorcher, I'd set up water games in the backyard for the twins. Hopefully, with Timmy's transfer to Poughkeepsie later today, I wouldn't be needed much at the clinic. With all the attention on the Petersons and their constant flow of well-wishers, the twins had become ornery, missing their dose of daily attention. A full day of fun, cool activities would do them a world of good. Albert had received a case of squirt guns last week, and I grabbed two a day earlier before they sold out, hiding them in the kitchen.

Scattered gravel lay on the sidewalk along Main Street. I kicked a few pieces as I walked. Today would also be a great day to teach the kids hopscotch. It was one of my favorite outdoor games in Brooklyn, where sidewalks surrounded us, and stones were plentiful. Back in those days, we'd pinch chalk from the classroom. I had asked Albert to order some and had a full supply on hand.

I'd come to care for Timmy, for the first time appreciating how familiar nurses and doctors became with their patients. All those hours together led to a friendship beyond Timmy's medical needs. He shared stories about high school and farming friends. To his father's dismay, Timmy wasn't an outdoorsy kind of boy. Instead, as an avid reader, he had his head in a book during his spare time, a regular at the library. Peterson wanted to see him work in the family store, but Timmy had a far grander idea—the study of law.

At one point later in the week, once we'd established a friendship, I asked him if he knew anything about the Klan and why they hated Jews and other immigrants. His answer surprised me.

Timmy laid his head back. "They're a crazy group and think you have some kind of mystical dark powers. They even think you have a stub tail and tiny horns hidden under your hair."

I took his left hand and placed it on my head. "Do you feel any horns? Good God, where do they get this stuff from?"

Timmy laughed; the first joyful sound to come out of his mouth all week. "Can I check for a tail now?"

I spanked his good hand and said, "You just try it, big shot, and Albert will be kicking you out of here on your own tail."

But as much as I enjoyed the medical lessons and the excitement of the week, returning to babysitting, filling out nursing school applications, and assisting Albert in the pharmacy suited me just fine. The overnight shifts were wearing everyone out, the tension growing, and petty arguments flared at the slightest provocation. Two days earlier, after Albert had spent the night caring for Timmy, Miriam practically took his head off. He couldn't wait to recount the story to me.

Miriam had picked up Timmy's medical chart, now pages long, assembled in reverse chronological order on a clipboard by Timmy's bedside, and began reviewing the entries from the night. She snapped, "Albert, how many times do I need to remind you to put the vitals in the correct columns? You have his blood pressure in the heart rate column and over here, the respirations where his pulse should be. Don't you know by now they're entirely different things?"

He rubbed his eyes, "Sorry, I'm so tired, I'm seeing double. Can I head up to bed for a few hours?"

Her voice rose, "Did you hear me? Accurate charting is fundamental to good patient care. Mistakes lead to more mistakes, and guess who bears the brunt of your errors? Not you, the poor patient."

"I heard you. Can you hand my head back so I can place it on a pillow? I only have a few hours to sleep before I open the pharmacy." A day later, Albert's pride was still singed from her tongue lashing.

Yes, it would be good to have Timmy tucked away in a hospital bed and restore our normal lives. I knew once he was bedded in at Poughkeepsie, we would return to our amiable selves and get on with the summer.

As I approached Miriam's house, I heard gravel crackle on the street. A car pulled up beside me. The engine sputtered and whined as if it were breaking down. I stopped, turned to look at the car, and offered my help.

A man's voice shouted out the window. "Any chance you're Ella Levine?"

I approached the driver's window to peer inside, curious how they knew my name. "Who are you? Do you need help? Your car sounds like it."

Just then, the back door of the car opened, and a tall, burly man twice my size with a grey and white scraggly beard stepped out. I recognized him. The man with the Klan coin at Peterson's! Before I had a chance to run, he grabbed me, shoving me into the back seat beside a stumpy, mean-looking man. I screamed for help. "Shut up, Jew bitch," he said.

I was on fire, burning with fear and anger. I thrashed my arms, tried to claw his eyes, but he pressed me back against the seat. I couldn't move. "What the hell is your problem?" I screamed.

"Tell her, Gus," shouted the driver.

Gus sneered from the front seat, "You kidnapped the Petersons. It's time for payback."

I struggled to explain, but he gagged me, yanking a burlap hood over my head.

I sat in the backseat of the car, tied, muzzled, angrier than a badger. What did they think a skinny girl like me was going to do? What did they expect from me? Cry? Beg? They wanted to put the devil's scare into me. After all, Timmy told me they thought of Jews as devils. I sniffled. Slightly at first, then louder, finally giving it all the force I could. Then the tears turned real as my body reacted to the loss of control. Would they hurt me? Oh God, please set me free.

Gus mumbled, "Oh, here we go. She's hit her breaking point."

The stumpy man said, "Let me take off her muzzle. There's no one out here on these country roads. Don't want her to suffocate."

He removed the hood and gag, giving me a good chance to check out the men. I recognized the two in the front seat from Peterson's and the Fourth of July event. I sniffled. "Please untie my hands so I can wipe my nose."

All three men exchanged glances as if they were thinking with one brain. Gus, the coin man, said, "Go ahead. She'll kill herself if she tries to jump out of the car."

I wiped my eyes and nose, as if I'd been crying buckets. I asked in a meek voice, "Why did you take me?"

The stumpy man answered. "We already said. Your family's holding the Petersons."

I argued, "No, they're not. Who started that rumor?"

The driver, a tall farmer wearing a straw hat partially hiding a scar that ran from his right eyebrow up to his hairline, shouted back. "Peterson and his family have gone missing. They're not answering the phone, and the store's been closed all week. We heard they're being held up in Liberty by the Jews."

I scoffed, "Yeah, because Timmy almost lost his arm in a thresher. Doc Barker brought him up to Dr. Drucker." I gave my words a moment to settle in. "You know he was the best at repairing arms and legs in the war. He saved the kid's life! Timmy's getting transferred later today to a hospital in Poughkeepsie."

The man with the coin sneered. "Likely story. You're not going anywhere till they release the kid and his family."

I said, "Check it out. Timmy is waiting at the clinic for an ambulance to Vassar Brothers Hospital. They're all going there this afternoon. Call Doc Barker or the clinic and hear it for yourself." What a bunch of rot. Only hillbilly idiots could have drawn such a dimwitted conclusion.

The men were quiet, then the driver said, "No phones where we're goin."

That shut me up. I wondered if they'd heard a word I said. For them, kidnapping was easier than learning the truth.

I insisted, "Didn't anyone tell you about Timmy's accident? He was with other people working in the field. He was bleeding to death. They took him to Doc Barker's first."

Again, the man with the coin answered. "Nope. And while we're at it, shut your pie hole or else I'll muzzle you again like a wild dog."

We drove for an hour or so into a part of the county I'd never seen before. Finally, we veered off the main road and headed further west on dirt roads. Where on earth were they going? The road dust billowed in the air, making me cough. We rattled down the narrow dirt road to a dilapidated farm. Would anyone find me here? They could bury me alive, and no one would hear my screams. I looked about, wondering if I could outrun these geezers. But we were miles from Liberty, tucked into KKK territory, and I'd probably die of thirst in the horrendous heat. Besides, I wouldn't be able to trust a soul. I covered my face as my eyes filled again.

The car slowed by the farm, pulling to a stop in front of a barn and silo. The stumpy man beside me retied my hands while the driver got out and pulled open the barn door. The man's hands were the size of a giant's, thick and scarred. He yanked me from the car.

I cried out, struggling to pull from his grip, "Please, no. For the love of God, don't put me in there! It's hot enough to kill me."

My words hit deaf ears. Without a pause, the tall man dragged me inside the barn and tossed me onto the hay floor as if I were weightless. He then slammed the door shut, locking me in with the clang of a metal latch.

Shaking with fear, I drew my knees to my chest, wrapping my bound hands around my knees like an infant. These men were off their rockers. What was their plan? Would they hurt me or demand ransom? My imagination went wild, wondering how long I could survive without food or water. I prayed they'd find a phone and check out my story, learning I was telling the truth. Or would they choose to believe their own lies? After all, they'd burned Martin's barn and cow. Did they see me as a human or a rat, like they'd called us at the parade?

"Let me out. We didn't take anyone!" I shouted through the locked door. No answer.

I trembled as the tears dropped. Through my blurry eyes, I checked the new watch Albert bought for me. It reminded me of my new family. People who loved me. It was going on ten. In the next couple of hours, Albert would be returning from his trip to Poughkeepsie, opening the pharmacy. It wouldn't take long for Miriam to realize I was missing. Thank God Timmy wasn't getting moved until later in the day. They still had Peterson under their thumb at the clinic. I had to believe they could get the truth out of him and learn where I'd been taken.

I stretched out on the hay; my tied hands set on my belly. Thinking about Albert and Miriam helped give me a new dose of courage. Studying the upper barn windows, I saw the sun in the eastern sky, casting heavy rays of light through the small windows onto the opposite side of the barn. I settled in, knowing it might be hours before anyone came, thankful I had a very full belly from Aunt Jenny's hotcakes. I sure hoped those thugs would bring water and let me use their outhouse.

Chapter Twenty-Seven: Miriam

I checked my Elgin wristwatch, the very same watch I'd worn in France during the war. Elgin was as reliable as the sunrise. Eight-thirty. Where was Ella? She had never been late before. I called the farm, and Aunt Jenny said she had left with Albert more than an hour ago. Then I called the pharmacy, knowing Albert was planning to make an early trip to Poughkeepsie to restock supplies. There was no answer there either. Ella must have gone with him. But it wasn't like her to leave without telling me she'd be late.

The girl had been a tremendous help all week. Smart as a whip, Ella was also compassionate, a salve with the Petersons and Timmy, continually moving back and forth from the clinic to the house. Once again, I was thankful we had constructed the connecting door in the renovation. Although she supervised the children most of the day, Ella made frequent stops to check on the Peterson parents, carrying drinks, sandwiches, and cookies over from the house for them and their supporters. It didn't make sense for her to act irresponsibly now.

Ella knew we needed to prepare Timmy for a hospital transport, which meant reviewing his chart for the umpteenth time and discussing the details with Maisy and Mahlon so they wouldn't panic over every decision along the way. Most people in these parts still viewed the hospital as the last stop before the grave. They had no idea of the wonders that had begun occurring inside those walls, especially since the war. In fact, over the last three years, Eli delivered numerous lectures to the doctors and nurses, sharing those advances, elevating their procedures. We'd learned volumes about infection, anesthesia, and healing while serving overseas, and now the hospital had modernized with those new methods. Timmy would do well under their care.

The morning dragged by. Eli was on his own at the clinic without my help while I watched the three children. And I couldn't ask Maisy to do more than bounce the baby. I needed Ella's set of hands. By our lunch break, I asked Eli to run down to the pharmacy and meet them.

Chapter Twenty-Eight: Albert

Eli was standing on the sidewalk in front of the pharmacy, shifting from one foot to the other, when I pulled up at 11:30. I called out, "What are you doing here? Run out of something?"

Eli ran to the car window, scanning the car. Then he explained in a panicked voice, "Ella never made it to our house this morning. We were hoping she was with you."

My body turned cold. "What do you mean? She didn't come with me. She was on her way to your house, walking in your direction when I left. Said she needed a stretch after Aunt Jenny's hotcakes."

Eli's forehead creased with concern, blurting out, "My God, where could she be? Do you think she's with that Schultz character? How do we find him?"

Dutch always made his visits to the pharmacy on his own time. So often in fact, that I couldn't think of one reason why I'd need his phone number. "I shook my head. Do you really think he could have taken her? Ella knew she had to be at your house."

"Who else could it be?" Eli lifted his open hands to his sides. "We've got Timmy all fixed up. The Klan shouldn't be bothering us now."

It didn't make sense. Dutch loved flirting with Ella. And only a week ago, in Poughkeepsie at the pharmacy, he told the goon to put his gun away the moment he heard she and Robbie were at the soda counter. I thought hard into my hazy memory talking to him weeks ago at the soda counter, Dutch leaving his flask, handing me a paper with his phone number. Yes, I might have stashed it somewhere in the laboratory. I jumped from the car, pulling the key from my wallet. "Eli, I need your help. I think I might have his phone number somewhere in the back."

Immediately, I racked my brain. What did I do with the paper? I was always organized in the laboratory. The place sparkled. What in God's name did I do with it? It was so busy that day we opened. "Eli, check the counters and drawers in the main room. I'll search the laboratory."

Five minutes later, Eli walked into my laboratory. "I didn't see it."

I'd come up empty, too. I searched my mind for the day Dutch gave me his phone number and if it had been before or after my last trip to the dump. I might still have the trash bags in the shed. "Sorry about this, but we must sift through the garbage. I hope it isn't too rancid."

A half hour later, four full cans of garbage were emptied, their contents strewn about the backyard dirt, stinking to the heavens from all the soda fountain trash roasting for days inside the hot shed. It was pure misery holding our breath while sifting through the mess. We found nothing.

Walking back inside the store to wash our hands, I said, "I'll rake up the garbage later once we figure something out. I wonder if he left a number with Nate. I know he tried to sell liquor to him in June." We dried our hands. I grabbed my white coat. A paper crinkled. I slid my hands into the pockets and quickly pulled the paper out. A surge of relief ran through me. I ran to the phone on the counter, dialing Dutch's number as fast as I could.

A gruff voice answered on the fourth ring. "Harvest Homestead Farm. We aim to serve your needs."

"It's Albert Kahn at Liberty Pharmacy. I need Dutch. It's urgent."

"Hang on."

Minutes passed. I heard men's voices mumbling in the background. Finally, Dutch got on. "What's up?"

Frantic, I yelled into the phone. "Do you have Ella with you? She's missing."

"Why the hell would I have her?" He paused, "Missing? You say Ella's missing? Anyone else?"

"No." I knew in my gut he'd never hurt her, but it didn't add up. "We just fixed up Peterson's son. You know, the guy from the store in Monticello.

The Klan shouldn't have a reason to bother us."

"Why not? They're the Klan. Crazy sons of bitches." The phone was silent for seconds.

I shouted back into the phone. "Dutch, are you there?"

"Just thinking."

"Can you come to the clinic on Main. We still have Peterson there with the kid."

"What? Why are they there?"

"His kid mangled his arm, and Eli fixed it. They've been here for days."

He barked back, "I'll be there in no time. Don't let Peterson leave. I'm getting my Ella back."

I winced. My Ella? Who does he think he is?

* * *

Knowing we had a full half hour to wait for Dutch, Eli picked through the shelves, filling a box with new supplies to carry up the street to the clinic. Moments later, we arrived with boxes of replacement supplies—sutures, gauze, surgical tape, and the like.

Miriam pulled us into the kitchen. "Where in the world have you been? Where's Ella, and why didn't she think to tell me she wasn't coming this morning? It's been a madhouse!"

Eli stood, still as a deer. "We're trying to figure out what happened. She's gone."

Miriam raised her hand to her lips. "Ella's gone? Where would she go?" She turned to me. "Weren't you two together this morning?"

I shook my head. "She was walking from the pharmacy, on her way here when I left. She wanted to walk off breakfast."

In an instant, Miriam's eyes shifted from blazing hot mad to brows drawn in concern. "It must have been that gangster."

Eli kept his voice low. "We think she was kidnapped. But not by Dutch Schulz. We think it was the Klan."

"How can that be? We've been helping one of their men's family members."

Miriam shook her head in disbelief.

I interjected, "I know it doesn't add up, but it's not Dutch."

Miriam cringed, "Have you called the police? Why would the Klan bother us now? We've saved one of theirs. It must be that Schultz character." She emphasized, her nostrils flaring. "How do we find him?"

Eli said, "We already did. He's on his way here to help. Let's keep the police out of it for now."

Her eyes shifted to the waiting room where the Petersons sat, enjoying their sandwiches and lemonade. They had allowed Ella to wait on them hand and foot this whole week. "Those double-crossers."

Eli walked to the waiting room and returned a moment later with Mr. Peterson. It took no time at all to explain the situation. Peterson's face went white. "That mobster is coming here, to your clinic? I don't know anything about a kidnapping. We were wondering where Ella was this morning. She's a sweet kid. Always here to help us."

Eli barked, "When's the last time you heard from your men?"

Just then, we all looked out the window. A honking car was tearing up Main Street.

I ran to open the door. Dutch's Austin sped into town, spraying gravel and dust everywhere. I waited for him to reach a stop. Dutch sprang from his car, leaving three men sporting black fedoras behind, sitting in his car, guns pointed out the windows.

I stepped in front of Dutch. "Tell them to put their guns away. Someone's going to get hurt."

Dutch barked, "That's the idea, genius."

As much as I knew Dutch could never hurt Ella, his disrespect toward me burned. We entered the clinic, and I said, "Eli's been talking to Peterson. Let's see what he found out before pouncing."

Dutch sneered back. "What kind of weakling are you? Pouncing, as you call it, gets me to the answer fast. No one wastes my time."

"I'm not fooling, Dutch. I don't want Ella hurt in a crossfire."

But Dutch didn't listen to a word. Within seconds of walking in the door, he had twisted Peterson's shirt into a tight ball around his fist, pinning the terrified man to the wall. As Dutch held his other fist back, ready for a punch, he shouted into Peterson's face. "Tell me where Ella is, or you'll have a nose even your mother wouldn't love."

Eli stepped in, grabbing Dutch's arm, yanking the balled fist downward. "Mr. Schultz, show some restraint. Mr. Peterson has been trying to reach his friends, but they don't all have telephones, and those who do aren't home."

Dutch pulled his arm free from Eli's grip, holding Peterson up higher. "Take us to them, you scum. You know where they'd hide her."

Peterson stammered, "But we're waiting for the ambulance to take Timmy to the hospital."

"To hell with that. The wife goes with the kid. You're coming with us!"

Chapter Twenty-Nine: Ella

My watch read 11:30. The sun was inching overhead, driving the heat in the barn up to a suffocating temperature. I banged on the door, begging for water and a trip to the outhouse. Finally, I heard footsteps. "I'm coming. I'm coming. Don't get your knickers in a twist."

The stumpy man opened the barn door. A blinding light hit my face, forcing me backward. He grabbed my upper arm, leading me to the outhouse on the edge of the pasture. As he untied my hands, he said, "You got two minutes. Then you're going back."

After taking care of my business, wiping myself with gross newspaper crawling with ants, I exited, pleading, "Please don't tie my hands again. There's no way I can hurt any of you."

He ignored my request. "We're not taking any chances."

There was no point in arguing. All I really cared about at that moment was water. I croaked, "My mouth is so dry. Can I have a drink?"

He pulled me across the yard, close to the well. With one hand, he slung a pail over the arm beneath the faucet and began cranking the pump. When the water rushed out, he tipped the pail to my face, splashing me, cold water sliding down the front of my blouse. I didn't care. The cool water, restoring my parched throat was divine.

I took a few long draws, for the first time in my life, appreciating the purity and relief of water. "Can I bring the pail with me? It's steaming hot in the barn."

He grunted, removing the pail from the arm of the faucet, carrying it while dragging me back to the barn.

My eyes took in the scenery, realizing the two of us were alone. "Where'd the other men go?"

He sneered back, shoving me inside the barn. "Stop asking questions." Then he slammed the door closed. The metal bar slid into the latch with a loud scrape.

My head cleared from the fresh water. I wondered how long it would take to be found. I laid back on the hay. Somewhere in my exhaustion, I drifted off to sleep, but not for terribly long. Loud, deep voices of men arguing woke me.

A man yelled, "I'm tellin' you; no one kidnapped the Petersons. The girl was sayin' the truth."

"Says who?" Stumpy man barked back.

Another voice said back, "We went to the farm where Timmy works. Last week, their thresher practically took his arm off. They wrapped his arm tight and took the kid to Doc Barker, who drove Timmy to the Jew doctor. The one who sewed on arms and legs in the war. He's been up there since, with Mahlon and Maisy. Lots of family, too."

Stumpy man yelled, "Holy shit. Mahlon's going to bust a gasket. What are we supposed to do now? It don't seem right to hurt her."

At those words, I began banging on the door. "Let me out. I promise I won't tell anyone. Just let me go home."

Just then, I heard cars pulling in fast on the dirt road, horns blaring.

"Let her out," shouted one of the men. "Untie her hands. Don't want it to seem like we've done harm to her."

The door opened, and the man wearing the straw hat untied me.

As I stepped into the light, I saw Mr. Peterson, Eli, Albert, and Dutch jump out of their cars. Dutch's three men poured out behind him, brandishing rifles.

Peterson shouted to the men. "What the hell is going on?"

Gus yelled to Peterson, "Mahlon, we didn't know. The store was locked, no one at home. 'Thought those Jews kidnapped you."

Albert ran to me, sweeping me up in his arms. "My God, you gave me the scare of a lifetime. Are you alright?" He led me away from the barn toward his car.

Dutch bent to light a cigarette, took a long drag, and smirked. "Christ, this is the kind of mush ya get in movie houses." He walked past us directly to Gus. "Were you the knucklehead who decided to pull this innocent girl off the street?"

Gus, a full head taller than Dutch, sneered, "You Jews are wrecking the place. Putting stink on everything you touch with your black magic. This here used to be God's country."

Dutch began laughing, leaning his head back, guffawing at the top of his lungs. "Black magic, you say? You, the genius who burned our barn and milk cow, too?"

Our cow? That man was galling. He didn't even know about it until I told him.

Gus grunted. "Didn't know a cow was in the barn."

What a dope. He walked right into Dutch's trap, admitting to the fire.

Dutch opened the door to the barn. "Sure, you did. It was nighttime. Couldn't you hear the innocent creature braying, begging for mercy?" He pointed to the inside of the barn. "Any animals in here now?"

Peterson jumped in. "Can we take a moment and cool off? Ella's safe. No harm done. Let's get back to Liberty and leave things be."

Dutch sneered at Peterson. "You say no harm done. Your goons kidnap a young girl off the street, and that's not harm? Especially since she was on her way to help your precious little boy. And you cost me a day of work and have the gall to say, no harm done?" He laughed again, its sinister edge echoing; its ominous pitch caused everyone to freeze in place. "You say this was God's country. Any chance you've read the Bible?" The men were all quiet. "Anyone?"

The Klansmen nodded, looking at the ground, realizing Dutch was no ordinary man. He was not the least bit scared of them.

"Ever hear of an eye for an eye?" Dutch flicked his cigarette into the barn. "Whoops, better stand back."

Within seconds, the dry hay in the hot barn ignited, spreading the fire, engulfing the floor of the barn as embers shot through the torrid air. The Klansmen ran to the well for water. Dutch raised his gun to the air and shot. Everyone froze.

Dutch commanded, "You goons stand right where you are and watch until the barn burns to the ground. If any of you decide to pull another stunt with any of us, it won't be just your barn that burns. Get it?"

They stood, meek as sheep, watching the fire lick its flames around the structure.

Dutch shouted, "You're dealing with me and my men now! And don't forget it."

Chapter Thirty: Albert

Eli, Ella, and I stood in a tight knot away from the barn, shielding each other from the inferno. The torched barn added even more heat to the already suffocating day. Ella turned to me, "Can we go home? I've had enough of this place."

I held her close to my chest. "Yes, of course. You had me scared there for a minute." Ella reached up, kissing me on the cheek.

She broke away and walked over to Dutch. "Thank you."

His angry face broke into a smile. "For you, doll, anything. I told ya you'd need protection."

Ella's eyes were dead serious. "I haven't forgotten." Then she turned back to me and said, "Let's go home."

Peterson's face, a now deflated balloon, faced us. "I'll get a ride back with the boys. We need to have a little talk."

* * *

I sat in the back seat with Ella while Eli drove us back to Liberty. Eli twisted his head, glancing at her. "You sure you're not harmed?"

Ella shook her head. "I'm not hurt. But I'll admit, I got scared when I told them the truth about the Petersons, and they wouldn't believe me. I guess they decided to find out for themselves while they had me locked in there. Two of the men left and returned to the barn right before you arrived."

Eli said, "I can't believe this Schultz character helped out of the kindness in his heart. And frankly, Ella, he's a crook, so I don't think he's seriously smitten."

"Not sure he'd care about her age, but Dutch is going to want something for today. Men like him always do, and I don't think it's Ella," I said.

Ella drew her lips together tightly. "I agree. He told me on the Fourth of July, we were going to need protection."

"He was right," Eli said. "But for what price?"

Ella's eyes went from mine to Eli's. "He needs a place to store his whiskey."

Chapter Thirty-One: Miriam

Uncle Nate dropped Aunt Jenny off at the house within an hour of my call for help with the kids. But I still felt like an octopus, running the clinic myself, answering phones, checking vitals, and keeping an eye on Maisy and Timmy. I couldn't take my mind off Ella. Why would the Klan take her, and what would that insipid gangster do when he faced the men? I couldn't shake the sinking feeling that the day was heading from bad to worse like an out-of-control train.

Maisy, also distressed over Ella's disappearance and her neighbors' possible involvement, sniffled in her chair, dabbing her eyes.

I approached her, furious that she could hate us privately but take over our lives with her family's needs when a crisis hit. Despite my anger, I extended my hand. "Why don't you wait with Timmy in the back? We'll have patients coming in any moment, and you can use a little privacy."

She sniffled, "I feel horrible. I only thought they were playing harmless pranks, not up to serious mischief."

My brows scrunched, "I would hardly call kidnapping Ella mischief. She's only eighteen and did nothing to deserve such horrid treatment. The poor girl must have been scared out of her wits. I have a mind to report this to the police."

"Oh, please don't. Let us set things right. Your family has been so kind to Timmy and me," she said, sweeping her arm outward. "To all of us, our big family. I'm ashamed that such a terrible thing was done to that poor girl. She's been an angel."

I softened a smidge. The poor woman truly had no idea just how ugly things had become with the Klan. "I don't get it. Why are your men so despicable to the Jewish farmers? We've done nothing to harm you."

Maisy said, "Some folks get so set in their ways they just can't change. For a long time, this part of the state was wide open, with a few scattered farms like Nate's poultry farm, and everyone had plenty of space for themselves and each other. No one bothered anyone. Now, it's filling up with people who don't speak English and have strange customs. It's natural to feel discomfort."

I shook my head slowly, studying her eyes. "I disagree. It's natural to be curious and helpful. Isn't it the Christian way, to welcome strangers? To treat them as one of your own? It's the Jewish way. It's in the Book of Leviticus."

Maisy squirmed uncomfortably. I could see their discrimination had been encouraged and accepted as a norm in this backwater country. She simply hadn't questioned their vicious words. Maisy looked down; her face drawn with regret. "We've strayed far from the Bible. I can see now. I should have questioned Mahlon."

Timmy shouted through the door. "Ma, I want to know what happened. Is Ella alright?"

I opened the door to his room. Timmy's books and personal items had been packed away. It looked very different from days earlier that week when the walls were covered with Get Well cards. Magazines and books had been spread across every surface.

"I want to know what's going on. What did those creeps do now?" he asked.

As Maisy shared the morning's drama, his eyes grew wide, filling with angry tears. "If they touched a hair on her head, I'll kill them myself."

I knew the conflict wasn't over. I didn't trust any of them. Even if Mahlon, Maisy, and Timmy were convinced of the absurdity of grabbing Ella, they couldn't stop this powerful wave of hatred. And Lord knows how far Dutch Schultz, with his trigger-happy finger, would go and at what cost to us. Although we would involve the police, I didn't trust they'd do anything. I knew that I must alert the highest authorities. But where to start – the

County Commissioner, the Governor? I'd talk it over with Nate and Eli once Ella was back home, safe, and settled in.

* * *

It was one in the afternoon when Eli, Albert, and Ella arrived back in Liberty. Ella collapsed into my arms. "I'm so thankful to be home." Then she rushed to Aunt Jenny, who tucked her into her ample bosom.

Aunt Jenny spoke in Ella's ear. "This is reminding me of those terrible years in Belarus. You are a strong girl, Ella, a fighter, like I once was. *Ve* understand each other."

I stared at the two of them, realizing both were different kinds of women from the rest of the family, never blessed with the protection we took for granted. I could read between the lines; they were bonded by the hardships and risks they endured to move forward and survive.

I said to Eli. "Is someone going to tell me what happened?" I grunted, thinking of the clinic next door and how backed up it was becoming. "Maisy is sitting with Timmy, still waiting for the ambulance, and you have a full waiting room of patients. I did what I could to hold them off. You should probably go over there now and let Albert fill me in."

Aunt Jenny stayed with the children inside the house while the rest of us settled into the backyard chairs. Albert started. "You can see that Ella's fine. The Klan goons snatched her because they thought we kidnapped the Petersons. They locked her in a barn about an hour southwest of here. By the time we got there, they'd realized their mistake and were letting her out. Dutch muscled his way in, scared the crap out of them, then burned down the barn."

Preposterous. That's what it was. We had to distance ourselves from characters like these, or we would never see the end of it. "What now?"

Albert continued, "We left Mahlon to deal with his people, and he'll find a way back here for his car. In the meantime, we know Dutch wants a secret place to hide his booze. And that means the farm."

Aunt Jenny's ears perked. "Who does that crazy *mamzer* think he is?"

187

I shouted, "Are you crazy? There's no way Nate and Jenny will become accomplices to a crime like that." I crossed my arms. "Absolutely not!" In the meantime, I was counting the minutes until I could talk privately with Eli that evening and come up with a different plan. "How about we all get back to work. The day is more than half over."

Ella stood there, tears streaming down her face. "Don't worry, Miriam. I'll come up with something. I'm so sorry for this mess."

Albert took Ella in his arms. "It's not your fault. You didn't invite the Klan or Dutch."

I thought about the Petersons inside the clinic. "Ella, why don't you look in on Maisy and Timmy and let them know you're safe? They were both worried sick about you."

Chapter Thirty-Two: Ella

That evening, after Timmy was on his way to Poughkeepsie and business hours at the pharmacy were over, Albert and I drove to our cousin Martin's farmhouse to discuss the situation. He lived close by his father's farm and was the one who'd lost the most because of the Klan's misdeeds. Although they'd given me the fright of my life, I knew I'd manage to get over it. But Dutch was a problem that wasn't going away. Albert and I figured we'd take a shot at solving it on our own without dragging everyone into the process. After all, I was the exact person who led Dutch to Nate's farm.

The biggest issue with Dutch was he took matters into his own hands when no one was asking for his help. Albert just wanted to make sure Dutch's impulsiveness didn't cause more damage than good, as his first reaction was to rush over to the clinic, scare the dickens out of Peterson, and then burn down a barn. Then he wanted more in return as a type of compensation. The only way to handle him was to even the score and tell him to get lost.

After clearing and burying the debris from the barn fire in May, Martin had begun rebuilding. He hadn't anticipated the high cost of lumber and labor, and was spending more money than expected, about to draw a bank loan to finish the job. He seemed to have the most to gain from a financial arrangement with Dutch. And both Albert and I knew he was strongly opposed to the Volstead Act. In fact, Martin already had quite a stock of his own liquor in the house cellar. But that was no guarantee he'd want to get dragged into business with a big city criminal.

When we pulled up, Martin and his wife, Fanny, were just finishing dinner outside. Fanny's belly was tremendous. She must be a few weeks from delivering their first child. I began having second thoughts. Didn't they already have enough on their plates? I leaned over to Albert, "Maybe we should reconsider getting Martin involved. They have their hands full, and we shouldn't bring danger around a new infant."

Albert said, "Let's not ask for anything, just pick their brains and see what they have to say. If they're not interested, they may know someone else who is."

"True." Somehow, I knew I'd feel a lot better if Dutch stayed clear away from my family. All he brought was trouble.

We sat at the picnic table with Martin and Fanny, sharing what had happened over the past day. Fanny kept interrupting to ask, "Ella, are you sure you're okay? They didn't touch you, you know, spoil you, did they?"

I shook my head. "Only scared me half to death, roasting me in that awful barn. They roughed me up a little, but that was all."

When we finally finished our story, and Fanny was convinced my maidenhood was intact, Albert searched Martin's face, "What do you think?"

Martin leaned back and laughed. "Good God, it's nice to see those white hooders have finally met their match, another bloodthirsty fool. And this time he's Jewish like us."

"Even though Albert and Eli didn't ask Dutch for help, he's going to want something in return. He's been telling us all along that we need protection from the Klan," I said.

Martin sat quietly, his face shifting in thought. Finally, he said, "You can simply refuse him and see what happens."

Albert scoffed, "You have not met this guy. He travels with a carload of gangsters, all wearing sidearms. The biggest difference between the Klan and him is he doesn't hide behind a hood."

Fanny gasped, placing her hand on her protruding belly. She then lifted it and reached outward. "Here we are in this beautiful country, trees and sky all around us, and it's infested with bullies and tyrants."

Martin stood up. "Fanny, can you handle the cleanup if I clear? I want to head over to the farm with these two and discuss some ideas with my folks."

We grabbed the platters and dishes, carrying them into the house. I sidled up to Albert. "But I thought we were going to keep Uncle Nate and Aunt Jenny out of this? Miriam is not going to be happy."

* * *

An hour later, we were seated at Uncle Nate's backyard table. It seemed comical to me, a city girl, conducting the most serious business at hand at a wooden picnic table full of splinters, originally designed for eating. Aunt Jenny approached Uncle Nate, Martin, Albert, and me with a full tray of lemonade and sugar cookies. I jumped up to take the pitcher from her hands.

"Thank you dahlink," she said.

Uncle Nate and Aunt Jenny, already involved with Dutch and the Klan, were familiar with the basic facts. Nate's curious eyes studied Albert's. "So, what do you think this character wants in return for his unsolicited help? That is, if you can call burning someone's barn down to the ground, help."

I poured the lemonade, giving Aunt Jenny a chance to get off her feet. She sat, hands clenched, listening intently.

"He has chutzpah." She spat out in anger. "And Martin, with your new baby coming, I don't want to see any more funny stuff from these *mamzers* with hoods."

Martin interjected. "Look, everyone. The guy commands a team of mobsters. If we get in with him, there's no telling where things might end. He's like a renegade unit in the army. We know he needs a place to hide his booze, so it's not all at his distillery. But what's it going to be next? And at what cost?"

Albert flicked his hand. "I don't think he's going to lose a wink of sleep if we all end up behind bars on his behalf."

I gazed at the stunning scenery—the well-kept chicken pens and barns, the orchards, and the immense pond. My eyes froze at the pond, my head forming a solution. The pond! My lips curled up. "What if there's a way to help Dutch hide his whiskey without any of you knowing where it is? Somewhere the Feds would never think to look."

Uncle Nate raised a bushy brow. "Ella, what are you driving at?"

Martin added, "The Feds have gone so far as pulling out walls and flooring to search for hidden booze. They'd have no qualms about digging up the yard or chicken coops."

My smile grew.

Albert elbowed me in my side. "Tell us. Ella."

"I can't tell you. If I did, then you'd know where it was. Do you think you can leave it to me? Trust me?"

The men all eyed me with skepticism. But Aunt Jenny didn't doubt me in the least. She followed my eyes to the pond. "I trust you. You're a clever young lady. Could have used you back in Belarus when the Cossacks were chasing us." Turning to the men, she said. "I trust this girl to protect us. Let Ella do her magic and the rest of us stay in the dark."

Chapter Thirty-Three: Miriam

The silence after the Petersons departed for Poughkeepsie left me euphoric. I could finally focus on the children singing outside and baby Sarah's cooing. The sounds of my family tucked in their home brought great comfort, restoring and centering me. I knew I had to deal with several nagging issues in my path, but for the moment, coming up for air was my top priority. I forced myself to bring order back into our house, straightening the pantry shelves, cleaning out the refrigerator, and entertaining the children, while Eli finished with his patients. Then we'd formulate a plan.

Eli and Martin weren't the only ones left rattled and scarred by the war years. Having left months after the conflict, nursing Eli's facial injury in Paris, then England, and finally New York City, I could not distance myself from the torturous memories of the wounded. Even now, years later, I would examine Eli's scars while he slept. I studied his face to ensure the skin grafts were not pulling at the neighboring skin, wondering if one more surgery might help smooth out his cheek. Somehow, while in his slumber, Eli sensed my wakeful presence and would mutter, "No more Miriam. I'm done. It's time to live."

It wasn't his appearance that troubled me, because my love for Eli was near spiritual. I worried about further injury and distortion to his face. And perhaps, I was still shaking off my own shell shock from the war. No one who hadn't personally witnessed war could imagine the insanity and horror of the battlefield. And the hospitals were only marginally more controlled than the trenches. It was inhuman. Impossible to leave the frightening memories behind like shedding a snakeskin. I knew we'd all carry the memories with us until the day we died.

But today, we had double trouble. Neither issue was something we could have anticipated. If we could force the Klan to go away, perhaps that would also put the brakes on that Schultz gangster. I planned to submit a formal petition to the Commissioner and Governor, appealing to their pledge for democracy and freedom for all.

But home was not without its challenges. The practice was growing quickly, and we were poised to plan for future community needs. Talks with Doc Barker needed to move along in time to secure a new doctor for next summer. It took at least twelve months to recruit a new physician. And I couldn't delay a heart-to-heart with my brother, Julian, a day longer.

On her own, Ella had sent her nursing school applications to programs in the city and Albany. Every school admitted her for the fall term. It was time to make decisions, and that meant a serious discussion with her father. The more I pondered the matter, the more convinced I was that this should be handled through our new attorney, Mr. Lieb's son, Samuel. That way, I would keep my distance and ensure the hostile emotions were kept in check.

Over the course of the day, the house descended into the sweet silence of midafternoon napping, the steady breathing of my three beautiful children resting in their beds, rebuilding their energy for the home stretch of the day. Eli was still catching up with patients next door in the clinic. It was high time to start writing my letters.

August 4, 1924

Dear Mr. Lieb,

I hope you are enjoying the summer season despite the heat and have purchased a fan for your office. Even up in Liberty, NY, where the mountain breezes are steady, the heat has climbed into the 90s on many days.

I'm writing to update you on family news and seek your assistance with a decision I made. As you may know, Ella Levine and her younger brother, Robbie, have been staying with the family on the farm this summer. Ella recently graduated from high school at the top of her class and has applied to nursing programs in the area, and in New York City. With her standing, she's been accepted everywhere. It's time to tell her about her father's gambling. Presently, she has no idea.

Julian has not reached out to the children all summer to check on them. He shows no interest in his parental obligations. Although we do hear from their mother, Selma, it is typically in the context of Julian's failure to pay alimony and child support. It comes as no surprise that she scrapes by.

Since the war, in exchange for Julian's promise of responsible fiscal management, I have continued to send him half of the rental income from Mama and Papa's apartments. However, he has disregarded those critical commitments and left his entire household in a state of dire need.

I have come to the decision to redirect half of his portion of the rental money to their mother, Selma Levine, for her ongoing care of Robbie, and use the balance to pay for Ella's nursing school. It seems to be the correct course of action and in line with my parents' wishes.

Please inform Julian of my decision. Effective September 1, 1924, he will no longer receive any income from the estate.

Thank you for your ongoing support as I navigate these unpleasant circumstances.

And send my warmest wishes to your father.

Yours truly,

Miriam Drucker

Satisfied with my decision, I poured a cold glass of lemonade and sat back on the sofa in the parlor to relax. The baby's feeding needs had soared to new heights, and I was drinking water and juice like a madwoman in the desert to keep up. But before I could finish my glass, I fell asleep, slipping into a familiar dream so vivid, I thought it was real....

I woke to the sound of ambulances racing to a screeching stop in front of the canvas-draped hospital. Oh, how I wanted to keep sleeping. The constant demand caring for new patients in an Evacuation Hospital left me in such deep fatigue from the moment my eyes opened until I set my head on a pillow late at night. I'd all but forgotten what a refreshing night's sleep felt like.

The armistice was signed, and the fighting was supposed to be over. But the fact was, artillery smoke continued to rise from the trenches. Soldiers were not sated. How could they want more? Were their bodies so stoked with fear and hate they couldn't trust the end?

We had sent truckloads of staff, beds, and provisions back to Paris on yesterday's train, leaving us with the minimum. I rose from my cot to see the extent of injuries, silently calculating the supplies and staff we had left, preparing to assign them to cover the carnage.

Shaking off the fatigue, I walked through the front flap of the hospital and faced the driver. "How many do you have?"

"Too many." He pointed to the four ambulances behind him. Two head injuries in each. "A rogue German shooter got into the operating room and unloaded a magazine's worth of ammunition. I'm not sure how many are still alive."

My stomach sank. This was never supposed to happen. The war was over. Hospitals were safe havens, not battlefields. I walked around the back of the ambulance as he opened the door. He gently edged the stretcher out. I saw the remains of a face. My belly turned as a sickening faintness overtook me. "Oh no! It's Eli!" My hand caught the edge of the door. "Get him onto a table right away!"

In a panic, I ran into the hospital and pulled every doctor and nurse I could find to receive Eli. "It's my husband. My husband. You must save him."

The medics were carrying Eli in as I shot back out the door to see who else needed care. There was one body left in Eli's ambulance, lying next to the indentation in the blanket where Eli had lain. The patient was dead. That pretty nurse. The same one I saw him with in Paris. He'd lied!

"Miriam, darling, wake up. You're having a bad dream." Eli tenderly stroked my shoulder.

I opened my eyes, still entrenched in the nightmare. "You lied to me. You didn't end things with her." I cried.

"Of course I did. You're having that dream again. Shhh, you'll wake the children."

Chapter Thirty-Four: Ella

The kidnapping had left me shaken. Although I put on a brave face, it was the first time my personal safety had been violated, leaving me reeling inside. Once I hit the hay Friday night, I fell into such a deep slumber Aunt Jenny became worried I was ill. Saturday morning, around ten, she roused me from my sleep. Still deep in my dream, I thought I was in that nasty barn. I woke panting, unfocused, unable to let go of the horror. She held me in her arms and rocked me as the reality of the morning came into focus.

"Such an ordeal for a young woman. But, Ella, you are a very strong girl. You will shake this off in no time. I see how you take charge. Just like I did in Belarus. You are a leader." She pulled me to her chest with a passion she'd never shown me before. "I know your childhood was lacking, but trust me, it was a picnic compared to the pogroms. We constantly worried for our lives."

I pulled back. "Will you tell me about those times?"

Aunt Jenny groaned, "It was so long ago, dahlink. I don't like to dredge up all the bad memories. *Ve* lost so many people dear to us. By the time I was your age, I was on a boat to America. It was my good fortune to meet your Uncle Nate a few years later. I used a matchmaker in the Lower East Side who remembered your grandmother, Tillie, and reached out to Nate to see if he was married."

As she stroked my back, Aunt Jenny continued, "Nate gave me a life I could never have imagined in Belarus. If it hadn't been for Jake dying of that horrid Spanish Flu in France, everything would have been perfect. And now, what more could I ask for with Martin and Fanny's new baby coming any day, and you and Robbie? With life's hardships come unexpected gifts."

I leaned up to kiss Aunt Jenny on her soft cheek. I loved this woman.

She glanced at my eyes; her lips bent up in a small smile. "I've learned to live with the tragedies, then keep my eyes on the gifts. Life is much happier that way."

I tried to absorb her words, knowing what she said was true. The discovery of my extended family this past summer was nothing short of a miracle. And who guaranteed miracles came without hitches and challenges of their own. Yesterday was horrible, but I came out of it unscathed because I have family who love me. And even Dutch, in his maniacal way, was trying to express concern for my safety.

Aunt Jenny straightened my shoulders, turning me toward her. "You go ahead and use the pond for his hiding spot. It's a brilliant idea, and the two of us will keep it our secret. You're right, the fewer who know, the better, my little warrior."

Nodding back, I planned to reach out to Dutch on Monday, unless he found me first. The only condition in our arrangement, one he couldn't mess with, was keeping the location of his whiskey an airtight secret from my family. My carelessness had pulled Dutch into our lives from the beginning. Handling him was my burden. I didn't want these well-meaning people dragged in. And what they didn't know shouldn't hurt them.

* * *

Monday came all too fast. I climbed into Albert's car after breakfast. He whisked me off to Miriam's, staring hard at me before he depressed the accelerator. "I don't understand why you're so mysterious about the liquor."

"I've told you already!" If he didn't stop pestering me, I'd stop getting rides from him in the morning. I knew the secrecy was eating at him, but I wasn't going to change my mind. Some things in life we take to the grave. As my mother, with her old country superstitions, would say, pew, pew, no kinehora. "Quit asking. I brought Dutch into our lives, and I will handle this."

"Yeah, but…."

I cut him off. "But nothing. If you don't stop, we're over, Albert. I'm that serious. There's no future without trust."

He sighed loudly, shrinking behind the wheel. "Alright already, but you better not scare me again. I'd die if something bad happened to you." We drove in silence for a few moments. Then he asked, "Why didn't you come up to the drug store on Saturday? Don't you like spending time with me anymore?"

The man had no idea how whiplashed I'd been from the kidnapping. What did he think? That after being manhandled, I could brush myself off with no time to recover. I might be a city kid, but I wasn't that tough. "Oh, Albert, I needed some rest before another crazy week started. Besides, I saw you yesterday. Wasn't that nice?"

He nodded slowly, "I suppose I'm just feeling like I can't protect you. And isn't that partly my job as a man? To keep you safe?"

I laughed, "You're my boyfriend, not my bodyguard."

Albert pulled the car to the side of the road, idling the engine. "I fail to see anything funny about this. You're my girl, not Dutch's. He seems to have gotten it in his head that he's got some claim on you."

My laughter bumped up a notch. "For goodness sakes, that's ridiculous. Do you think so little of me? Why would I ever allow a creep like Dutch to claim me, as you call it?"

"It's not funny, Ella. He's a very dangerous person."

"That's right. With a bizarre set of morals. But he'll go away soon. I have it all figured out. You just need to leave it to me." I kissed him on the cheek. "I promise."

Albert tsked, "I'll try." He pulled up to Miriam's house, leaning over to kiss me on my lips. "You sure are a different sort a girl. One of a kind."

I shouted through the open window as he pulled away. "See you at the fountain after lunch for ice cream." I scanned the area. "Looks like it's going to be another scorcher." Then I chuckled, attempting to lighten the mood. "Don't see any kidnappers today! Coast is clear."

He scowled back at me.

* * *

The familiar cooking smells of breakfast wafted into the parlor. Despite just finishing breakfast at Aunt Jenny's, the smell of toast made my mouth water.

"Good morning, Miriam. You have no idea how great it feels to have a normal day. Let's hope the whole week stays that way," I said.

But I knew it wouldn't. Tying up business with Dutch was at the top of my list. There would be no real peace until I had that ugly task behind me. But first, I'd have to get his phone number from Albert or wait however long for Dutch to appear on the scene again. I had a strong feeling that making the first move might serve to my advantage, a tactic taken straight out of Dutch's own book.

I spent the next hour going through the motions of my job as a nanny, feeding the twins, changing and dressing baby Sarah, showering her face with kisses, and then handing her off to Miriam for her second morning feeding. All the while, I wondered where Albert might have put Dutch's phone number. It was probably in the pharmacy, most likely in the back. I'd wait until later to search when the children and I were at the store for ice cream.

In the meantime, I sat with Miriam while she nursed.

She asked, "Tell me the truth, Ella. Are you alright after Friday? That was a true initiation under fire."

I sighed. "Everyone keeps asking me the same thing. I was exhausted and slept most of the weekend. But I feel fine today. All back to normal."

Miriam scoffed, "I'm beginning to wonder what normal means these days. Everything is changing around us. It was calm as a windless pool of water a few years ago. Now, with Prohibition and the Klan, things have gotten stirred up."

I looked down at my hands, clasped on my lap. "I was hoping it wasn't me who stirred things up."

She snorted with a tight-lipped smile. "It was simply unfortunate timing on your end. You and Robbie had nothing to do with it…." Miriam cleared her throat. "By the way, with the twins playing upstairs, it may be a good time to have that talk about your father. I didn't forget. And, as I understand, you're hearing great news from nursing schools."

I sat forward in my chair. "First, let me get you something to drink. I have a feeling this won't be a short story."

After bringing Miriam a cold glass of water, I sat ready to listen, hoping her explanation would make sense out of the strange world of my childhood.

Miriam started slowly, choosing her words carefully. I knew she was selecting what to share, trying to present Papa in the best light possible, leaving out important details. I decided to listen patiently, then I'd ask her to fill in the gaps.

She inhaled through her nose and started. "Your father was always a brilliant, yet awkward child. He had few friends and amazed everyone with his advanced math skills. Mama and Papa were proud but also worried how he'd fit in as an adult. Secretly, in high school and college, your Papa began gambling, counting cards, and beating his classmates at poker and other card games, although he sometimes lost big. That's when he'd ask for more money."

"From your parents?"

"Yes, and later, after graduation, loan sharks. Do you know what they are?"

I nodded. I had heard rumors about the tough men on the streets who'd lend money to unsuspecting individuals at exorbitant interest rates and then beat them up if they didn't pay on time. No wonder Papa limped around so often, covered in black and blue marks.

"The problem was, he could never resist the urge to return to the gambling tables and try to recover his losses. He was so confident in his game skills that he believed his bad luck was just an anomaly. Between fixed games, the size of his bets, and bad timing, he was pulled deeper into debt. Finally, Papa cut him off—not only from occasional financial help but also from his inheritance." She wrung her hands. "And the hardest part, at least for me, was that they put me alone, in charge of their estate. Of course, that ruined your father and my relationship.

My eyes opened wide as I took in the news. I had no idea this was the reason our family had become a lonely island in Brooklyn, inhabited by two children, a distraught mother, and a hateful father. "He really couldn't stop? Gambling was worth losing everyone who ever loved him?"

Miriam shook her head sadly, her misty eyes brimming with memories. "It was heartbreaking to watch. You have no idea how hard your grandparents tried to push him to change his ways. Finally, after the war, when it was just the two of us left. He swore to keep his promise to Papa. Julian claimed he'd quit gambling during his service in France." Miriam swallowed hard and reached for her water glass, gulping down half. "I knew he couldn't, but I had done something wrong during the war, too. Somehow, he discovered I had a secret and was using it against me. He bribed me to give him the rent income in exchange for concealing my secret."

I was filled with curiosity. "I want to know your secret."

Miriam scoffed. "I was a foolish girl at the time and entered the war illegally. The Red Cross and Medical Corps had refused to accept me because of my leg brace from polio. Eli and I had just gotten married, and I couldn't bring myself to stay behind in New York. Somehow, your Papa discovered what I'd done and threatened to share the information with the Medical Corps, ruin my reputation, and jeopardize my nursing license. Today, seven years later, I no longer care. Just let him try."

From my position, Papa's story was nothing near as exciting as Miriam's. Many unfortunate families in Brooklyn were headed by one parent. Between death and abandonment, there were numerous single parent households who didn't have time or money to indulge their children. But I'd never heard a tale quite like Miriam's. "Promise you'll tell me more this summer?"

"I promise." She adjusted baby Sarah onto her other breast. "When you and Robbie arrived here last month, I realized your father must be gambling again. You both looked half-starved, wearing rags. I was absolutely outraged and ashamed of myself that I hadn't kept tabs on you. Your grandparents worked themselves to the bone so their family would never go hungry. I knew it was time to stop funding his gambling habit. Besides, I needed to give you and Robbie the support you deserved, the support your father promised to give you. He never kept his word. Honestly, I don't think he was capable."

I'd never thought Papa had lost control of himself. He always came across as in command with his bellowing voice and threats to us. But now I realized it was a cover for his own inadequacies. He'd perfected his own style of lying and covering up his thievery.

Miriam stroked Sarah's head, gently twisting her short curls into ringlets. "He's gotten his last check. As of September first, he's cut off. That will give your mother enough to properly care for Robbie, and I'll take care of your nursing school."

My mouth dropped open. Just like that, my nursing school was paid for. "Why are you telling me now?"

Miriam had no time to answer me. The twins came galloping downstairs, eager to engage in activities, and it was time for the baby's morning nap. Miriam went upstairs to put her to bed and then scurried to the clinic to help Eli with office hours. I spent the rest of the morning in a daze, digesting this new information. I'd been taking my nursing school dream one step at a time, hoping by the end of the summer I'd come up with loans or some other way to pay the tuition. Now, my future was secure and Robbie's, too. I knew Mama wouldn't waste a penny on anything frivolous. Robbie would have the childhood he deserved.

By 10:00 am, the twins were deep into playing cops and robbers with their water guns in the backyard, and I seemed to be the desired target for their misfirings. Dripping from head to toe, I walked into the kitchen to grab a towel, only to discover Dutch standing at the interior doorway.

Shocked, I whispered, "What in God's name are you doing here? Who invited you into the house? Don't you have any manners at all?"

"Heh, heh," he barked out in his gruff laugh, ignoring everything I'd just said. "Thought it was a good time for you and me to square things up."

"Keep your voice down. There's a baby sleeping, and I don't want anyone to see you here."

"Big words for the little lamb trapped in the barn." He sneered, a menacing grin forming on his face.

I looked hard at him. "I have a plan. But before I tell you, you must swear it's take everything or leave it." I enunciated each word slowly. "And I mean everything."

My bravado only seemed to add to his pleasure. "Swear, like a pinky promise?" he began laughing at his joke. "I like negotiating with you. How'd you get so brassy?"

I sat, thinking about the volumes I'd learned from evil people in only a few weeks. It was nearly the end of July, and I'd just about had it with all of them, the Klan, Dutch, and now my crazy father.

I squinted at him, filled with disgust as he stalled. "I'm dead serious, and I don't hear you agreeing to my single term."

He threw back his head, spreading his arms out like an eagle about to pick off his prey. "Oh yeah, your way or the highway. Ok, babe. Let's hear it."

I motioned for him to sit in the chair, turning my head to the window to check the twins were still engaged in their game. Little did they know, while they were having fun playing cops and robbers, two bad guys were sitting only feet apart inside the house. And one of them was me. "I have a place to hide your product. But my family can't know. No one. Ever. Period."

He cocked his head to the side. "Interesting. And where might that be?"

I had his interest. Spreading out his whiskey was his top priority. As far as I knew, most of it was stored on his turkey farm. "At the bottom of Nate's pond, beside the apple orchard. You can drive to it from behind the pond without coming anywhere near the house. Deliver the bottles late at night while everyone is asleep and be out of there before dawn. Only you, your men, and I will know where it's hidden. It's over twenty feet deep."

His mouth broke into a smirk. "Why don't you want your family to know? I would have paid you for storage."

Always looking for the angle. The man didn't have a pure thought in his head. "I want them unaware in case something goes south. They're not interested in doing business with you or any other bootlegger. But I know you won't go away without getting something back from us. Will you?" I continued to stare into his light brown eyes. Soft eyes that would otherwise look innocent, but I knew better.

"You are a wily cat. And you're right about getting something back."

"The last part is you disappear. Between you and the Klan, my family's been a wreck all summer. Afraid their boarders will leave and never come back. They need peace, especially the older ones."

"Free storage, you say?" He wasn't listening to a thing I said. It was crystal clear Dutch had no interest in peace or my family. All he cared about was his cargo and money.

I nodded, imagining him out of our lives. "Agree? Total secrecy? Disappear?"

Dutch stood, then extended his hand. "Sure, sweetheart. You got it." I couldn't read his calculating eyes. But I knew he wasn't done. I dreaded hearing his next words. What if he didn't agree? "You sure you don't want to come work for me? I could use a smart dame like you."

I shook his hand, relieved his words had not been romantic. "Not a chance in hell."

Chapter Thirty-Five: Albert

After lunch, Ella entered the pharmacy with a bounce to her step. The twins were excited to have their ice cream treat, jumping up on the stools, hooting with delight. And after all the vanilla ice cream we'd been slipping to baby Sarah over the last few hot weeks, I expected her first word would be "ice cream." Although her portion was barely enough to coat the tip of a spoon, Sarah, at four months, knew the ice cream was coming once they walked through the banging screen door, her arms flapping with excitement once inside.

I strode to Ella, placing my arm around her shoulder, pulling her into my chest. "You look happy today. Anything new?

Her face beamed with excitement. "Let's get the kids settled, and I'll tell you all about it. Bottom line, I'm going to nursing school."

Moments later, Ella shared the secret about Julian and the family Trust. Money I never knew existed. But it made sense since my mother had told me Tillie and Abe invested in real estate after they sold off their garment businesses.

"It seems Papa has been gambling away Mama's child support for years. He has a very serious gambling problem on top of being wickedly mean," Ella said.

"Amazing. I had no idea!" I thought back to those years after the war and how quickly Eli and Miriam pulled the clinic together and fixed up their house. Miriam must have had money piling up while she was in France. "What I don't get is why she didn't cut off her brother years ago. It would have helped your mother take care of you and Robbie. And she could have set some aside for your education."

Ella raised an eyebrow, smirking. "That's where the story gets interesting. Apparently, my Papa knew a secret about Miriam. He threatened to reveal it if she didn't continue paying."

That Miriam was a shrewd woman. I always sensed there was more to the story. "Well, spill," I said.

Ella raised her shoulders, her lips drawn in a thin line. "Miriam's secrets are for Miriam to share."

My God, that girl could be frustrating, leading me down a dead-end path like that. "Did she tell you her big secret?"

"No, I don't know any details. But I sure would like to find out more. She promised to tell me before the end of the summer. After all this time, and meeting Robbie and me, Miriam decided not to give Papa any more money or power over her."

As delighted as I felt for Ella's success funding nursing school, her deal with Dutch continued to niggle at me. I wondered if she would keep her plan a lifelong secret or, after a few years, when all was a distant memory, share it with me. For now, I knew better than to pester her. Instead, I'd focus on enjoying the last few licks of summer together, the little that remained.

"I have an idea," I said.

Ella spooned a speck of ice cream between Sarah's cupid lips. "What's that?"

"How about I take you to see the Albany nursing school next weekend and then we can go the following weekend to the city, and you can see Mount Sinai, Beth Israel and Bellevue?" I watched her face light up. "It may help you make the right choice for yourself."

Before I knew it, Ella had thrown her arms around me. "You are the best, Albert. Now that I know I can start in September, I was beginning to worry about where I should attend. All the schools will want a commitment soon."

"Then we'll work it out, and I'll close the pharmacy on Saturday. All we'll need is permission from Aunt Jenny and Miriam."

I preferred Ella stay with my parents and attend school at Mount Sinai. Her secret pact with Dutch weighed heavily on my mind, and my family offered her an additional layer of protection. It would take a very reckless man to tangle with my Pop.

Later that evening, after dropping Ella back at the farm and the children were tucked in for the night, I settled into the parlor with Miriam and Eli for a cup of tea.

Miriam eyed me with curiosity, "What did she tell you?"

I took a sip of the tea, inhaling the smooth aroma of honey from the farm. "Let's see. Julian was a gambler, you're cutting him off, there's money for nursing school, and you have a dirty little secret you haven't shared." I smiled broadly. "That's about it. Time to spill, Miriam."

She dropped back against the couch, exhaling deeply. "I really don't want to keep discussing it. I'll tell you both when the three of us are together."

"Who else knows?" I asked.

Eli waved my words away. "You heard her. Topic is closed for the evening."

Accepting momentary defeat, I pushed forward with a more pressing concern. "What do you think about her nursing school choice? Where do you think she should go?"

"Honestly, I haven't given it a lot of thought yet. What does she have to say?" Miriam answered.

The baby's cry pierced the air. "Hold that thought." Miriam rose from the couch. "Sarah will get her final big feeding for the night. The last few days, she's begun sleeping ten-hour stretches. Keep your fingers crossed."

Moments later, with baby Sarah sucking loudly, we resumed our discussion.

I put my own thoughts on the table. "I was hoping Ella would go to Sinai's nursing school. That way, she has some insulation from Dutch and his goons. If she's living in a city dorm, there's no one to keep an eye out for her."

Eli nodded. "I share your concern, Albert, but what about Albany? That may be far enough away from his stomping ground, and she could get a fuller experience living in a dormitory."

Miriam turned to Albert. "Have you spoken to your parents? Do you know how they'd feel about making such a long commitment?"

I shook my head. "I wanted to pick your brain first."

"Eli and I know lots of people at Beth Israel and can make sure Ella has some immediate contacts who'll look out for her. They have a very safe dormitory, and your parents are right uptown. I think Hannah still spends a great deal of time downtown at the Jewish Maternity Hospital." Miriam said. "She can check in with Ella."

Thinking about having Ella away for long periods made my heart drop. Would she meet someone new? Or decide Liberty was only a small backwater town lacking the excitement and culture of New York City?

Chapter Thirty-Six: Miriam

I should have been celebrating Sarah's milestone, sleeping through the night for a ten-hour stretch. Instead, I woke after four hours, filled with apprehension.

Today, I promised myself I'd call Mr. Lieb, our family's attorney to follow up on my request for an official letter to Julian. If I had any remaining mental energy, I'd also draft a letter to the Commissioner of Sullivan County and the New York Governor about the Ku Klux Klan and their misdeeds. I'd send the same letter to both men and give them time to commiserate. In that letter, I'd ask for an in-person appointment to hear their recommendations.

By mid-morning, there was a lull in the clinic. Ella had the children busy in the house, and Sarah was still napping. I used the quiet moment to call Mr. Lieb. I kept his phone number in my clinic contact book. MU (rray Hill) 3 – 4895. I dialed the rotary phone. His secretary picked up on the third ring. "Law practice of Samuel Lieb. How can I help you?"

My memory snapped into place. The senior Mr. Lieb had mentioned his retirement. He told both Julian and me that his son would be taking over the practice. I only hoped his son had been debriefed on Julian's sad circumstances. "Hello, this is Miriam Drucker. Mr. Lieb senior has been our family lawyer for many years. Is he still there?"

"Oh no, I'm sorry to say he passed away two years ago. His son, Samuel, has taken over the practice. Perhaps he can assist you?"

Seconds later, I was on the phone with Mr. Lieb's son, a young attorney with a confident and clear, youthful voice. "I am terribly sorry to hear about your father. He was a trusted part of our lives. You may know, your father handled the Levine family's business and estate for many years. It was arranged through my parents and your father."

"Of course, I am familiar. I was planning to call you. I assume you've heard about Julian's predicament."

My heart stopped. Just hearing Julian's name gave me a sour taste in my mouth; it was always some disaster. What did he do now? "No, I haven't. Tell me."

I heard a deep sigh through the receiver. "Julian was arrested yesterday morning as he entered his workplace, Metropolitan Bank, on charges of embezzlement."

I dropped into the closest chair, a wave of despair shooting through me. How could I possibly be surprised? I should have anticipated Julian's problem would keep getting worse. "Dear God," was all I could say.

"He then called my office, asking me to represent him in these charges. But you see, I don't handle criminal law, so I referred him to a friend of mine who's quite good in that area."

"Where is he now? Does he have money to pay an attorney or bail?" I asked, an annoyed edge encasing my words, ready to attack my vile brother. Why did I care if he had the money or not? My words were bitter. "I gather the crime was committed to support his gambling habit."

The other end was silent. "He's in the Tombs downtown. He hasn't permitted me to share anything quite yet, so I have client attorney confidentiality issues to consider, but I can say, you're barking up the right tree."

"Would you advise me about next steps? You see, I was all set to discontinue his support as I indicated in my letter. That's why I was calling." I twisted the phone cord around my finger. "His children ran away to the family farm in Upstate New York in June, hungry and dressed in tatters. He hasn't kept true to his parental duties in any sense of the word. It's disgraceful. Things must change."

"I'm very sorry to hear that. He seems to be sinking to another depth. Perhaps you should see him and decide for yourself. The Tombs are located at 125 White Street. He's unable to make bail, and I don't think they'll move him to Blackwell's for some time. Maybe you could talk sense into him."

Visit him in prison? He brought all his misfortune on himself! Why should I subject myself to such a filthy place? I remembered Papa's words, "We can no longer feed the monster!"

Instead, I said, "For years, the family's been trying to help him reform. Nothing will work except the harshest response, cutting him off from money." I drew a slow breath, calming myself. "I will not see him. You can tell him that. And there will be no more money. Julian can send a letter to me if he has something to say."

"I see. I will pass along the message." Mr. Lieb said in a soft tone as if he understood the gravity of our family pain was not short-lived, but a decades-long struggle.

"I mean it, no more money. No matter what he threatens. He's made this bed for himself. Now he can sleep in it." I hung up the phone, wondering how long it would be before Ella found out and if she would agree with my decision.

* * *

Later that night, I sat at my writing table and penned a letter to the Governor and Commissioner. I hoped I'd receive a quicker response if they both knew I sent the same letter to each.

Dear Governor Alfred E. Smith,

I am writing with growing concern that our peaceful rural county of Sullivan has fallen into the hands of thugs. Specifically, I refer to the quaisi-secret organization known as the Ku Klux Klan, an evil group who has taken it upon themselves to define a "true America." Their idea of a true American excludes the recent European immigrant groups as well as the Africans. I'm certain you don't need to be reminded, this diverse population from all over Europe comprised twenty percent of our armed forces during the Great War, fighting and dying in France in the name of American freedom. Having been in France myself, serving as a nurse, the soldiers were equally brave and, unlike the KKK, believed in America's principles, rejoicing in our country's welcoming arms to others.

Over the last couple of years, the KKK membership has grown in Sullivan County, with a hub forming in Monticello. Not only have they disrupted social gatherings (County Commissioner's speech was rudely interrupted by their chanting earlier this summer on July 4th), but recently, they admitted to burning the barn of a Jewish family. The family's innocent milk cow, still inside, perished in the blaze. Only last week, they kidnapped a young Jewish woman in an act of ill-conceived retribution for a non-existent crime. Fortunately, we were able to retrieve the victim before she was harmed. But these acts are intolerable and wholly un-American. Without appropriate action by the government and law, they will continue to grow and flourish.

We all know the heartache and havoc they reeked in the deep south with hangings of innocent freed slaves, and our community is determined they will not repeat that behavior here in our county. But, if the officials in our great state choose to turn a blind eye, citizens of this beautiful county will act on our own. This is not a county of cowards. Practically every family has a member who either perished in France or returned scarred from the war. None of us are intimidated by men hiding behind infantile hoods. Our men are the very same ones who fought eye to eye with an enemy brandishing bayonets and guns in hand-to-hand combat.

Please respond post haste so this conflict does not spiral out of control. A copy of this letter has also been sent to our Commissioner.

With due respect,

Miriam Drucker, RN

Chapter Thirty-Seven: Ella

A week passed without calamity. Aunt Jenny had returned to entertaining Wilma's family. Once again, laughter filled the air in our backyard during dinner. Wilma's husband, Sandor, reported he was making a killing in the stock market, so their family would return the following summer. I wondered if Wilma would be bored without the drama of Dutch, Timmy Peterson, and the KKK. Even though she worried every time one or another crisis bubbled up to the surface, she had a three-ring circus to hold her interest. And her berry pies had become the talk of Monticello, with Maisy asking her for a dozen every week to sell in the Peterson's store.

Miriam's household had also settled back into a calm daily routine. With baby Sarah sleeping through the night, the dark circles under Miriam's eyes faded away. Without those exhausted shadows, her lovely face glowed.

The best part for me was that Dutch and his goons had disappeared into thin air. I could only hope he'd dumped his whiskey into the pond while we were in the thick of slumber. But now, thanks to his and the Klan's absence, we had a perimeter of peace surrounding our world in Liberty.

I was thrilled, having received acceptances to every nursing school where I applied. My immediate decision was to select one. As I became more analytical about the choices, I realized moving north to Albany was too far away. I wanted to be closer to Albert, Robbie, and my new family. I was torn between Bellevue, Mount Sinai, and Beth Israel. Even without visiting the hospitals, I was pulled to Beth Israel, following in Miriam and Eli's footsteps. Both were so knowledgeable. I knew part of their expertise was in part due to serving in the war, but I also believed their hospital training at Beth Israel gave them an excellent foundation. Now that I could afford lodging, I would live in a dormitory with other students, making friends with my classmates, having a full experience. That left me with Bellevue, Beth Israel, and Mount Sinai. That is, if I didn't live with Aunt Hannah.

When I opened the door, Miriam was waiting with an envelope in her hand, a frown on her face. "Good morning. This came for you yesterday. It was in our box at the post office. I wanted you to see it right away. I think it's from your father."

The envelope was filthy, scuffed with dirt on both sides. The handwriting was unmistakably Papa's. "What do you think he wants?" I asked Miriam.

She shrugged her shoulders. "Why don't you read it first, and then I'll fill you in on what he didn't share."

I took the letter to the table in the backyard and stood, my shaky hands tearing it open, dreading its contents.

Dear Ella,

The time has come to ask for the money you took from the apartment. I find myself in an unfair predicament. Last week, I was arrested and thrown into the Tombs. Trust me, I am entirely innocent of the charges, but I will need my money to hire a lawyer to resolve this situation.

It seems your Aunt Miriam cut me off from the family Trust, and your Mama hasn't a penny to spare. So that leaves you.

Please help me. The men in this prison are atrocious, the very scum of society. I won't last long.

Your Papa

I sat numbly, digesting this terrible news. Just by looking at Miriam's face when she handed the letter to me, I knew she already knew, hiding the truth from me. But why? I wondered how long she would have kept it up if he hadn't sent a letter. I'll bet my Mama knew, too.

I sighed and walked back inside, letting the screen door slam behind me, once again feeling shut out. Miriam was waiting, sitting at the kitchen table, sipping her morning coffee. The toaster was browning bread, filling the kitchen with the aroma of breakfast. She looked up at me. "I've been hemming and hawing about telling you about your father. I found out last week when I called our family attorney to send him a letter about cutting him off."

I handed the letter to her. "Read this!"

Miriam read, sighing, shaking her head. "He's a sick man, Ella. I think he's probably guilty. Is this the same money you asked me to hold?"

I plopped into a seat. "Yes, I feel like a thief, too."

She mused, "I wonder why he hadn't told me about the money. Did something else happen I don't know about?"

I nodded. "He called here a few weeks ago, and I told him I'd give it all back as long as he let us stay." My eyes filled. "I'm not a nice person, Miriam. I stole, too."

She pulled me into an embrace. "Honey, you were just trying to survive. People will do things out of desperation when they're in a life corner."

I sat for a moment, then wiped my face with the sleeve of my blouse. "You have every penny of his that I took. I've kept my earnings from this summer separate to use for nursing school. I always planned to give his money back at the end of the summer. I just didn't want Robbie and me hauling ice."

Miriam's eyes welled with tears; her lips set in a soft line. "This is my fault. I never should have let things get so far out of hand. Giving him money all these years emboldened him. If I had cut him off sooner, as your Grandpa advised before he passed, he might have turned things around. I'm so sorry."

"I should give his money back. And I want to see him."

Miriam gasped. "The Tombs are no place for a young woman and certainly no place for cash. It stays in the bank, and I'll disperse it to pay bail and his attorney."

"I must face him. I'm going." I repeated. So much for visiting nursing schools with Albert.

* * *

"How in God's name did I let you talk me into this!" Miriam whispered in my ear as we climbed out of the taxi at the City Prison. The train ride from Monticello went smoothly, but we had to wait for the ferry in Weehawken for an interminable amount of time, all the while with baby Sarah fussing. Then, of course, a long taxi ride across town to the Tombs.

"You didn't have to come. Albert offered to take me." I reminded her. But Miriam insisted on going, not trusting Papa for a second, convinced he would manipulate me with guilt and persuade me to hand over a lot more than the money I took from his home library.

"I'm the only one who has witnessed his sneaky behavior with my parents' money. And he's very skilled at manipulating people," she huffed. "You might have dealt with your father's temper, but his gambling was his best-kept secret. And of course, he's going to deny stealing from the bank."

My eyes scanned the sidewalk. Discarded cups, chewing gum wrappers, and newspapers were strewn about. City people could really be pigs. There was a heap of garbage on the grass. Were those feet sticking out from under a stack of open newspapers and rags? Ugh. I already missed my life in Liberty.

"You're right about that. I can't believe I didn't see it all along. He was always secretive about money. None of us knew anything about our grandparents' wealth," I said.

We stood together, staring at the old prison. Shaped like an Egyptian tomb with a partial flat top, it stood adjacent to a larger building encompassing a full block shaped like a pyramid. There was a walkway high above the street connecting the court building to the prison, called the Bridge of Sighs, like in Venice, Italy.

The wind blew our way, engulfing us in the smell of rotting sewage mixed with garbage. "This place is disgusting." I covered my nose with one arm, jostling the bag of food I'd brought for Papa with the other.

"The entire prison was built on a polluted pond, first drained, but never fully dried out. So the structure sinks inches every year." Miriam covered Sarah's face with a blanket. "I fear what it's going to smell like inside."

"It's a bad idea to take Sarah in there." I pointed to a coffee shop down the block. "Why don't you wait with the baby, and I'll be back as soon as I can. Visiting hours start in ten minutes, and I already have permission to see him."

"You're right, and she's going to need a feeding soon." Baby Sarah had awakened, squirming in the carriage. "But I hate to send you in there alone. You must promise me you'll be extremely careful."

I smiled, despite the horrid setting. "I'm a grown woman and far sturdier than you might think. Besides, I would never bring the baby inside that infested building. I'd die first." I glanced down at Sarah, already fussing, writhing her body in anger, hungry for her meal. "I'll tell you everything when I come out. Besides, all Sarah does is sleep and eat, sleep and eat. There's nowhere inside you could possibly feed or change her."

Miriam was already surveying the block for a women's store. "You're right. I think I'll take her into a dressing room and then meet you over at the coffee shop. Remember, be careful."

Determined, I turned on my heels and headed towards the entrance. I drew a deep breath, summoning my courage. The front door was older than the hills, heavy, splintering, and half-peeled of paint. I was hit by the smell first, an amplified version of the stink outside. Before I knew it, stomach acid filled my mouth. I breathed in through my mouth and pulled a handkerchief from my purse, covering both my nose and mouth.

It was hard to imagine such a medieval building plopped in the middle of bustling New York City. The air was cold and damp, completely cut off from the warm weather outside. Goose bumps ran down my arms as I approached a guard for directions. Weathered and stern, he pointed to a corridor. "Visiting is that way. Mind your purse."

Covering my nose, I forged forward, entering a nightmare of the worst kind. Steps into the hallway, I heard screams and swearing echoing off the stone walls. How long could Papa survive in these horrid chambers without losing his mind?

Another guard at the end of the hall released a bar lock, pulled a metal door open, and led me into a large room with rows of tables and chairs for visitors. Most were empty and remained that way. No one was coming to see family. Could I blame them?

Papa entered the room through a rear door. Spotting me, he turned to the guard behind him and pointed my way. He was hardly recognizable. In only two months, he was noticeably older and more emaciated than I'd ever seen him. He bent forward, shuffling his feet in my direction.

Papa was a man who always took pride in his appearance, a real dandy, as Mama used to say. Now, dressed like a bum, his hands were bruised, caked with dirt. I'd never seen his fingernails so broken and jagged. The guard pushed him into a chair opposite me.

Attempting to ignore his appearance and unwashed smell, I handed him a chicken sandwich. He gobbled it so fast, I gave him another. Papa's eyes filled with tears. Finally, he spoke. "They starve us so we're too weak to revolt. They treat animals better than humans." Tears filled his eyes.

Having never seen him cry, I bit back my own tears, my courage dwindling. "We're going to get you out of here. You must stay strong."

His crusted eyes met mine. "Did you bring my money? Let me have it."

In a flash, I knew he was up to his old games. "I never knew you had a gambling problem. That's why we grew up poor, wasn't it?"

Papa's face darkened, red as a beet. "It's none of your damn business what I do with my money. Now give it over."

"I don't have it. Miriam opened a bank account with your money so we could post bail and pay the attorney."

His eyes bulged wide, temper exploding. Papa slammed his palms on the table. The guard's eyes shifted to us. "I knew that bitch would take it!"

I tried to reason with him. "Papa, keep your voice down. I thought you wanted to get out of here. Who hands over that much cash in a prison? You know it would be nuts." I said, realizing at that instant that his temper no longer scared me. He was reduced to a pitiful man.

Papa's anger deflated. Dropping his head onto the table, he began sobbing. "I just want to die."

I'd seen plenty of his temper, but never anything quite like this. Papa was losing his mind. "I know you like to control your money, but the bank account is for your own good. You need to get out of this hellhole before you do die."

He lifted his head, wiped his nose with his sleeve, and nodded. Then, rising from the chair, he signaled the guard to take him back to his cell.

I handed the bag of sandwiches and fruit to him. "Take this with you. I pulled it together this morning, so you'd have something to sustain you."

Chapter Thirty-Eight: Miriam

An hour and a half later, with the new straw hat I had bought at the clothing store after nursing the baby, I was settled at the diner, eating a slice of fresh peach pie and sipping coffee, flipping through a copy of the Tribune while the baby slept. As if Ella sensed I was counting the seconds for her to return from that disgusting prison, a little bell on the doorknob tinkled, and Ella walked in, out of breath. A deep frown was etched into her youthful face. My heart dropped. That girl was carrying the weight of the world.

I waved her over to the table. "Come, sit. What can I get for you? Rough time in there?"

She flipped her hand in the air. "No food. Still feeling queasy from the smell. I'll never erase this terrible day from my memory." She stood, gazing down at the sleeping baby. "I've got to go to the lavatory and wash before I touch a thing."

Minutes passed before she returned, my impatience to hear more about her visit growing as I waited. Something could have happened to her in that awful place. Finally she reappeared, her eyes ringed in red. "Tell me what happened. How did your visit go?" I asked.

She continued to rant about the smell. "There are no words for how it reeked. A mix of the worst human odors. I thought I'd vomit. Why can't they clean the place better? There's really no excuse to treat prisoners so poorly."

"How did things go with your father?" I asked, attempting to steer her back on track.

Ella's breath was steady. "He looked terrible, dirty, and afraid. Crying and angry. Finally, he calmed and accepted our plan to use the money for bail. Can you believe he thought I'd bring that much cash into a prison? I'm not an idiot." She shook her head. "I think he's confused. This has thrown him completely off his game."

I patted her hand. "Oh, honey. His problems run deep. They may never get resolved. The only way to handle your father is by forcing him to start over. Only he can decide to reform, stop gambling, and earn his money legally."

"How can you be so sure he can't change?" Ella asked, her face creased with pain.

"No one loved him more than your grandparents. He was bleeding them dry before they finally said, 'no more.' They struggled with him for many years." It took little to remember those painful years and the arguments filling our home instead of laughter. "I know this sounds cruel, but I think the only reason he came to Mama's shiva was to see if she left him anything. Then, of course, I loosened the rope after the war and gave him his share of the rent so he wouldn't blackmail me. Biggest mistake of my life."

"Why?"

"Because he still gambled away every penny and allowed you and Robbie, his own flesh and blood, to live in poverty. There was always ample money to take very good care of both of you. It's my fault, my vanity, my fear, that allowed this to happen."

Ella studied me. "Why, what was the horrible forbidden secret he was holding over you?"

I glanced at Sarah, curled on her side, in a sweet slumber. Why? Why did life have so much cruelty, so much disease? I shifted my eyes from the baby to Ella. "I stole the identity of a dead nurse who was heading for France and went by her name during the war. At the time, I was desperate to help in the hospitals and be by Eli's side. We had just gotten married but with the leg brace, no one would accept me into the Medical Corps. Julian somehow found out and threatened to report me if I didn't give him a monthly allowance from the Trust. My nursing license would have been revoked."

Ella gently shook her head. "You are a firebrand. I always admired your courage and your nursing skills, but never knew you were that plucky."

Plucky? Perhaps single-minded, but except for that transgression, I'd always adhered to the rules. "For me, those were desperate times. I never imagined I'd be so lonely after Papa passed, and it had been months since I'd seen Eli." I'd no clue I'd be greeted with a picture of deep betrayal in Paris. Oh, how I wished I could erase those memories from my dreams. That secret would go to my grave. Eli had enough challenges adapting to his facial wounds. He'd earned redemption many times over.

Ella crossed her arms. "That weasel, he would have destroyed you over gambling money?"

"Your father can't stop himself."

"What do I do now?" she asked.

I thought carefully. "For the moment, you've done everything possible. You showed him heartfelt concern that he doesn't truly deserve. And you've returned his money in a responsible way, so it will be used to take care of his immediate fees. You may have saved his life, just helping him get out of that cesspool. It's his chance to start over." I paused, knowing there was no secret medicine to cure his ills. "Now it's time to step back and let him do the hard work, even if it means he has to serve a sentence."

Ella nodded, taking in every word. "Miriam, please don't punish yourself for handing over the Trust income. I probably would have made the same decision. As far as I'm concerned, it all led me to my incredible family."

Chapter Thirty-Nine: Ella

A couple of hours later, as the sun settled into the western sky over Central Park and the heat drained from the air, we sat in Hannah and Ben's apartment on the Upper East Side sipping a cold drink. There were fans in every room, inviting the cool air through the windows as the outside temperature gradually dropped.

Hannah had hired a nanny years ago, before the war, when she was pregnant with Gilda. And the nanny stayed all these years, becoming an extension of the family. Although Gilda was now nine years old and had outgrown the supervision she needed as a small child, their loyal nanny had melded into the family fabric, evolving in her duties to match the family's changing needs. Never having children of her own, she was delighted to help with baby Sarah.

"Aunt Hannah, it's so nice of you to invite us to stay here tonight," I said. "You have a beautiful apartment, and the sun setting over the Park is almost as enchanting as the farm." Nothing as pitiful as my poor Mama's view of the alley beside her Brooklyn apartment and the rats darting about the garbage cans, creating a racket every night. City life could be desperate for those with little money. But there was no doubt, both Uncle Ben and Aunt Hannah had worked hard for many years to live in their comfort and splendor. Neither one was handed any shortcuts.

"Please, it's time to call me Hannah, especially since in a few years, we'll be coworkers. And Miriam has been singing your praises since that boy's arm repair. Says you're a natural talent," said Hannah.

She smiled warmly for the first time. Was it our future working together, or that she was relieved I wouldn't be sweeping her son off to the altar any time soon? "So, tell me, will you see both Mount Sinai and Beth Israel nursing programs tomorrow before heading back to the farm?"

I had taken Mount Sinai off the list, but Hannah's warmth made me reconsider. Perhaps she and Uncle Ben would offer a haven. Besides, between them, they had an encyclopedic knowledge of the medical field.

Miriam leaned forward, interjecting, "I was hoping we could go to Mount Sinai in the morning and leave the baby here during her nap. It will be much faster, and I'd like to look around too."

Hannah smiled, "That shouldn't be a problem."

"Afterwards, we'll gather Sarah and head downtown to Beth Israel around lunchtime. Then we'll take the ferry back across the Hudson and a train back to Monticello. A long day to consider a big decision," Miriam added. "Ella has decided to take Bellevue off the list."

Hannah twisted back to me. "Miriam tells me you graduated at the top of your high school class. Have you given any thought to college and medical school?"

Was this a compliment or a challenge? I'd never thought about becoming a doctor. Turning to Miriam, I asked, "Have you ever had those regrets?"

Miriam eyed Hannah, laughing. "Don't mind Hannah. She did the same thing to me at the end of high school. Even though the two professions at their best meld together seamlessly, they are each quite different."

I cocked my head, spreading my hands in question. "How so?"

"Doctors generally make the final diagnoses, operate, set bones, and handle procedures. Nurses do pretty much everything else: safeguard the patient during illness and after surgery, keep a close eye on any physical changes, administer medications, change bandages, and so forth." Miriam gave me a moment to digest the information. "I have always wanted to have a fuller, longer relationship with the patient, guiding each through the healing journey."

I thought about how deeply her convictions were tested during the war. "Did you feel differently in France?"

"Interesting question. I not only felt more committed to my role as the nurse, but I also saw where the grey area was between professions."

Hannah interrupted. "For example? What grey area?"

Miriam turned to the window with a faraway look in her eyes. "When Eli sat with our cousin Jake as he lay dying from the Spanish Flu, he transitioned into a more traditional nursing role. Keeping Jake as comfortable as possible as he died, helping him breathe."

Hannah said, "But he was family."

"I know." Miriam answered, "But it is a beautiful example. One I will always treasure. As for the nurse crossing into the physician duties, we frequently helped debride wounds in the operating room, tie stitches when the second physicians were scarce, and so forth. Anything we were asked to do, or sometimes not directly asked to do, we did. We were working tightly as a team to save lives under an unthinkable torrent of injury and time pressure."

I thought back to Timmy Peterson. "Like Timmy. You and Eli worked as one."

She nodded. "That's when I knew you had that ability to see the whole picture, capturing all the needs—the family, the patient, the supplies, nutrition. When I saw you holding that despicable Klanner, Mahlon's hand, while he panicked over the blood transfusion, I knew you'd crossed into that very special place only great nurses inhabit. You extended comfort to a man in need, a man who was a threat to our family. It was similar from time to time when we cared for enemy soldiers."

I smiled. "I'll bet you wanted to show those German soldiers how much better the Allied nursing care was."

The corners of Miriam's mouth curled. "Yes, sometimes. Remember, I still speak a fair amount of German, so I could communicate with those men. It kept the prisoner-patients calm. They never gave me a moment of backtalk or concern."

Hannah sighed. "Ella, if you ever change your mind, I will be here to help you along. Mount Sinai is accepting more women into the medical school every year."

* * *

The next morning, I woke early, barely rested after a night of tossing and turning. Thoughts of Papa in the horrid prison haunted my dreams. The Tombs were so opposite to Hannah's home uptown. Had I helped enough, setting up a bank account? Was there sufficient money in his account to pay for his release? Although nursing school occupied hours of my thoughts during the summer, it paled in comparison to my family slipping deeper into a dangerous crevice. A crevice that would leave us without a shred of goodness to remember about our father.

On the way to the bathroom, Miriam approached me in her robe. Always astute to my moods, she asked, "I know you are worried about your father and want to help more, but trust me, he's the one who must act. There is nothing more you can do. Even your wise grandparents, the ones who loved him most deeply, realized the only way for your Papa to turn things around was to cut him off and make him face himself in the mirror. The strength to change must come from within him, not from you."

Although I knew she was right, having spent at least two decades watching the slow erosion of her childhood family and with it, her parents' heartbreak, the pain I felt was just as real. "I'm sad for him. I wish I could do more."

Miriam pulled me into a hug. "You will in time, but you'll need to be patient to see if he's fallen low enough to face his problem. In the meantime, you are going to get educated, your mother will have plenty of money to take care of Robbie, and you'll be close to Brooklyn so you can visit during school breaks."

Miriam was right. Everything necessary for the future was tucked into place. Now, I must let go of the image of Papa's filthy, crying face and move forward with my hard-earned plan.

Within the hour, we were touring the Mount Sinai complex with a guide from the nursing school. Both Miriam and I were impressed. Construction surrounded us. New buildings and renovated wards for different diseases replaced most of the old units.

Miriam was a reservoir of questions. "Is there lecture time, an anatomy lab for nurses, classes in medications and physiology?"

The tour guide could barely keep up with Miriam. Finally, she answered, "It's not medical school. Our student nurses spend most of their hours on the wards, learning by shadowing experienced nurses and eventually doing the work independently."

Miriam screwed her face. "I suppose my most foundational question is, do they understand why they're performing tasks a certain way, or why a certain medication is used to treat a disease?"

The guide turned her baffled face back to Miriam. "Certainly, they are encouraged to follow the physicians' chart orders, and as I say, they are welcome to ask."

Before long, we left the hospital to pick up the baby and our satchels. On the walk back to Hannah's, Miriam was quiet.

"What is it? What did you think?" I asked.

She walked on for a while. I repeated my question.

Miriam huffed. "I find it irritating when nurses are trained to be mindless servants to the physicians. Just follow the doctor's orders and don't formally learn the medicine. I can't tell you how many times I witnessed situations where the quick thinking of a nurse helped steer an exhausted or distracted doctor back onto the right path. If the basic elements of medicine are not taught in a systematic manner to new nurses, their education is left full of holes, like Swiss cheese. We lose our checks and balances. Besides, doctors always want to work with the most educated and competent nurses. It helps make their job so much easier, and the patients do the very best."

Two hours later, with Sarah and our satchels, we stood in front of Beth Israel Hospital, far more weatherworn from the outside.

Miriam drew a deep breath. "My head is overflowing with memories. This is where I learned what nursing was all about, from both sides of the drape."

"What do you mean, both sides of the drape?"

"Not only did I attend nursing school here, but I also worked in different roles in the hospital until I went overseas. That was the professional side of the drape." Her shoulders dropped. "But when I caught polio and became terribly ill…" she paused. "Well, that's when I understood the patient side of the drape."

"I keep forgetting you had polio. I'm so accustomed to seeing you in your brace that I don't notice anymore. It's barely slowed you down."

Miriam chuckled. "If I'm not careful, it slows me down with ulcers and pain. But that wasn't my point. What I'm trying to say is that aside from the important, but faceless, numerical measures of care such as mortality and infection rates, the only true way to gain insight into the patient experience is to become one. Then you get a very accurate view of what it's like to be sick and vulnerable. Pay careful attention to your patients. You'll learn the most from them. Talk to them, as you did with Timmy. You must always remember that."

I absorbed her words. There were volumes of knowledge to learn. Hours and days with Timmy and his parents had given me a small taste of the patients' experience, complete with all the emotions around trauma: fear, pain, and prayer for every slight improvement. Along with the compassion Miriam and Eli extended to Timmy, they still managed to run their busy clinic and household. I would try to never forget her words.

* * *

That afternoon, we nestled onto the upholstered train bench, stained from many coffee spills. After leaving Mount Sinai uptown and the possibility of living with Hannah and Ben, I thought my mind was made up. Left dazzled by the new buildings, sparkling wards, the nurses in their starched outfits, I was convinced I'd attend nursing school there.

Now I wavered. The intelligent and comfortable dialogue between the staff: doctors, nurses, and aides at Beth Israel was a sight to behold. Sure, they weren't dripping in the Mount Sinai money, with new wards and buildings, but they fostered a hospital environment I could see myself a part of, a world that made places of healing, like the Liberty clinic, a possibility.

Certainly, the corridor walls could use a fresh coat of paint, and some of the flooring was chipped, but the patient wards and rooms sparkled, not a dust bunny to be found. The privacy drapes were freshly washed, and the commodes and bed pans glistened. That diligence was the layer of care that counted most, as it prevented the spread of infection. Even a novice like me knew that fact.

But the best part was watching the staff make rounds, the physician taking the lead, turning right and left to the nurse on duty and the medical staff in turn, for an updated report, their clinical impressions, and finally sitting next to each patient to ask direct questions to them as well, sending a powerful message of their importance, the team's concern and cohesiveness.

Despite Mount Sinai's investments, I did not sense that level of warmth and unity. It appeared as if the staff worked in corn silos, with the medical students furiously taking notes, the nurse recording orders while the attending pontificated. No one spent much time looking at the patient or sitting beside him. The staff's attention was directed upward, impressing the attending, who seemed quite full of himself already. I hadn't noticed such things until I had the Beth Israel tour as a comparison.

Miriam left me with my thoughts for a few hours while she tended the baby. Sarah woke with a furious hunger, and we had to find a private place to feed her, causing us to almost miss the ferry. We were the last passengers to make it on board, and then onto the train, practically missing both. By the time we found seats for the final leg to Monticello, Miriam appeared exhausted, about to conk out herself.

"How's the leg holding up?" I glanced at the baby, content, sleeping in her carriage.

Miriam lifted her leg, setting it on the empty seat in front of us. "Would you mind taking off my shoe so the conductor doesn't get his knickers in a twist with a dirty pump on the couch?"

I gently removed the shoe. "Would it feel better if I massaged your leg?"

She chuckled. "Yes, but not here. They'll take it all wrong. My foot, yes. So sorry if it smells from the day."

I'd never given the smell a second thought, ready to work on her leg, too. "Of course, I will owe you a relaxing leg massage when we get home, for all you did yesterday and today. It meant so much to me—all of it. Especially helping me deal with my father," I said.

I removed her sock and cradled her foot with both hands, gently massaging her sole.

She began moaning in a low, throaty voice. "Oh, that's simply delicious. Please don't stop. But, Ella, you haven't shared your thoughts with me about the two nursing schools. I'd love to hear what you are thinking while I relax."

For the next hour, I spoke nonstop about the details of each tour, beginning with my first impressions of the buildings, wards, and equipment. Then I transitioned to the environmental factors, such as the presence of patients' body odors, routine cleanings, and overall sanitation to mitigate infection and disease spread. I spoke about the people, the roles of physicians and nurses, their scope of practice, eye contact with each other and the patients, and the ease of interacting. Finally, most importantly, I watched the patients. Were they calm? Did they appear fearful or comforted? Was there good eye contact between the physicians and the patients? I put myself in the role of a family member. How would I feel about the care if the patient was a loved one? Was there evidence of a strong trust?

I watched Miriam's expression throughout. She was awake, relishing her foot rub and listening to every word.

She took a deep breath. "It's no surprise your thoughts are so well organized. You hit all the right spots, including on my feet." We both laughed.

I slid her sock and shoe on. We were about halfway to Monticello. Hopefully, either Albert or Eli would be there to pick us up for the final half-hour ride to Liberty. For the next couple of weeks, I'd be here with my extended family, then off to school.

My voice cut through the soft chugging of the train. "Beth Israel is my choice. I'll send my paperwork in and call tomorrow to let them know I decided."

Miriam squeezed her hands together. "I'm delighted for you, darling. You will be a standout and in no time rise in the ranks as an example to all new nurses. I couldn't be prouder."

I felt satisfied with myself, and thankful Robbie would be returning to a home stocked with food, well-fitted clothing, and a far calmer mother. But as far as Papa, I remained worried that if he didn't get himself out of jail, he'd die. I decided to give things a week and then find out more.

Chapter Forty: Albert

I waited a full hour for the train to pull into the Monticello station. Already past our dinner, I imagined Miriam and Ella were hungry. I stood on the platform waving my hands when I finally saw the train pull into the station. As the train screeched to a halt, I ran to the exit doors to lift off the baby carriage, then extended my hand to Miriam and Ella.

"Aunt Jenny's been keeping dinner hot for you. Let's stop by the farm first. Everyone's there and biting at the bit to hear how things went." I watched Ella's face, hoping for a clue, but the best I could get was a cagey look. I'd have to speak to her alone to get the full story about her father.

Within the hour, we sat around the picnic table, discussing the nursing schools and Ella's decision to attend Beth Israel. Her face was lit up with excitement. Although I feared I may lose her to the thrill of New York and a city hospital, I was happy she was achieving her dream. It brought back memories of pharmacy school and the volumes of material I learned. The stimulation of other eager students and planning the pharmacy in Liberty filled my daily thoughts for months. I'd never want to deprive her of that experience. But still, I worried about losing her. And she hadn't mentioned her visit to the prison.

Just as we'd cleared the last plate, Eli pulled out two letters from his trouser pocket that had come in the mail. "Miriam, these are for you. Looks like one is from the Governor."

Miriam swiped it out of Eli's hand. "Let me take a look at that." She slid her finger under the envelope tab and removed the letter.

"Read it aloud to all of us." Uncle Nate said.

Miriam took a deep breath through her nose and exhaled, positioning it to read. "Alright, it's not too long."

Dear Nurse Drucker,

Before I respond to the issue at hand, I want to thank you for your service. Having had family who served in the military in France, I know the trials our soldiers and medical workers faced. My deepest appreciation goes to you for all the men you ministered to who healed and those you helped pass to a peaceful end. There are simply no words to fully express my deep gratitude.

With respect to the appearance of the Ku Klux Klan, we have been alerted to their growing activity in our state and it will not be tolerated. Not only are we compiling a list of their gatherings, but we plan to attend those meetings with armed police and run them out. I pray there is no need for our veterans to face another conflict on their home ground, as we are fully committed to preventing the destruction of our great state.

We are aware that there are several Klan events in the works before the last days of summer. Please give us an opportunity to make our stance clear and run them out before taking any action of your own. We share your concern along with our utmost commitment to make our beautiful state all it was meant to be—a home to those who bring their best talents to our shores and build a brighter future, through their deep love of America.

Respectfully yours,

Alfred E. Smith, New York State Governor

I pointed to the other letter. "Who's that from?"

Miriam turned the post over. Seems to be from the County Commissioner in Monticello. She opened the letter and read through it silently.

"Anything else?" I asked.

Her lips curled upward. "It's mostly a repeat of what the Governor said. But he added information about the Klan's next several rallies. That's odd.

Apparently, they have two coming up later this month. One in Binghamton and the other in Monticello. This Sunday, as a matter of fact."

I crowed, "Well, what do you know. Maybe it's his way of calling out reinforcements."

Eli snapped. "Don't even think about it, Albert. You'll find yourself arrested and Liberty will be without a pharmacy."

* * *

I stewed all evening in bed, brewing over a way to get even with the Klan. How could anyone expect me to shake off the fear I had when Ella was kidnapped? Burning the barn evened the score for Martin's barn, but kidnapping a young, innocent girl was an entirely other matter. Her beautiful face, dirty from the barn with broken stems of straw poking out of her hair, eyes red-rimmed from crying, was a sight I'd never erase from my memory.

By morning, I had made my decision. I'd make an anonymous call to Harvest Homestead Farm, Dutch's establishment, and let them take it from there. No arm-twisting, just an innocent communication. Knowing Dutch as I did, I imagined he'd jump at the chance to fire off another warning.

I pulled up to Uncle Nate's farm about fifteen minutes early. Wilma had announced the evening before that she was making blueberry muffins, and I didn't want to miss out. She made them with buttermilk, and they were delectable.

"Wilma, I've been dreaming about your blueberry muffins all night."

Robbie shouted out with a loud laugh. "You are very bad Albert, dreaming about Wilma's muffins!"

I jumped from the chair and chased him out of the kitchen. Turning to Wilma, "I hope you know what I meant. Robbie's starting to get to that age."

Ella walked into the room, her arms overflowing with pamphlets and papers. "I think I have everything I need today. I'm calling Beth Israel and accepting my spot."

I gave her my best smile. "I am so proud of you." Turning back to Wilma,

I added, "Any chance I can take a few of these delicacies back to Liberty for an afternoon treat? You know, your delicious muffins."

"Of course, dahlink. Take as many muffins as you like." She giggled like a schoolgirl.

And with that, we were on our way to Liberty and Miriam's house.

Chapter Forty-One: Ella

I closed the car door behind me, relishing the familiarity of Albert's car, his showered, sandalwood scent intermingling with the outdoor fragrance of crisp late summer grasses drying into straw. All in all, I was content. Life would never be perfect, but so many of my dreams were coming true. "This has been the best summer of my life. So many wonderful things have happened," I said to Albert.

He started the car and turned to me. "Like us? What do you think? Will we stay together through your time in nursing school?"

He'd wasted no time asking the most important question on his mind, and yet, I didn't have an answer for him. The entire summer was an exotic pudding of so many sweet and savory flavors: the love of new family, overcoming dangers I never could have predicted, my first kiss, and the deep friendship I forged with Albert as we tiptoed into a romance. I turned the question back to him. "What do you think will happen? Can you wait? Are you patient enough to give me time to fulfill my dream?"

He turned the car off the brown grass onto the gravel driveway, heading away from the farm in the direction of the main road. "I wish I knew what comes next." He exhaled loudly, "You know how mad I am about you. I don't want to lose you, Ella."

I reached for his hand. "I feel the same way. I wish we'd met in the future, when my school was behind me. So many things can happen between now and then, and I don't want to hold you back." I was surprised at the growing pain in my heart as I spoke. I did love this man. I didn't want to give him up. But I wasn't ready to commit my entire life to him. It was too soon. I still needed room to grow and explore without the responsibility of a husband and children. It was enough for me to keep a lookout on Robbie and my parents. Who could know what would happen over the next year? "Let's try to write every week and see each other every month. But I don't want to hold you back. I know you are ready for so much more."

Another deep sigh. "Darling, people wait for each other for many reasons. Think about a few years back during wartime. People waited with enormous fear. We're only talking about nursing school. Pfft. That's nothing. We'll keep in close touch, and I'll try to get into the city every month to see you. I'll take you out for a nice dinner. I say we give it a real chance."

I knew Albert was a special man. He was right, and there was no reason to add unnecessary drama to the occasion. He had a mother who was a doctor and knew the commitment women made with their careers. He'd never take something that important away from me. I tamped down my concern and switched the topic. "I saw my father at the Tombs. It was horrid. No place for a human being. Not only do I fear for his life, but his shame is a heavy load to carry." My eyes watered. "I've never felt so embarrassed for my family. I wish I never came from him."

Albert sat silently as we pulled onto the shoulder and entered the paved highway. "I'm so sorry, Ella. I can't imagine how terrible that visit was for you. He's really let you down."

I wiped my eyes with my cuff. "That's putting it mildly."

Albert's words were measured. "My Pop's always been the rock of our family. Even during the war, doctors and nurses looked to him as a steady hand. In the operating room, but also when strategic decisions needed to be made. I'd like to give you that, be your rock and unburden you of your responsibility, like my Pop has given me."

The pull of Albert's protection was powerful. Laced with comfort and safety, it was a soft down comforter to make my nights restorative rather than broken by nightmarish images and the horrid bodily smells of the Tombs—my days joyous, shared with a best friend who could be both my love and counsel. A world enveloped in his loving embrace. But not yet. If everything went according to plan, it could happen in a few years, and I 'd return to Liberty, marry Albert, and join Eli and Miriam's medical practice.

* * *

An hour later, I was elbow deep in meal preparation, stirring the Quaker oats in a small saucepan for the twins' breakfast and chatting with Miriam as she nursed Sarah. "I can't thank you enough for taking me into the city, being there for me at the Tombs, and helping me sort through the nursing school decision. You're incredible. I hope you slept soundly, too."

"Like a drunken sailor. But I'll admit, with this damn leg of mine, I don't have quite the stamina I once had." Sarah had unlatched from Miriam's breast and was ready for a burp. "Can you hold her for a moment? My leg has pins and needles. Let me walk it off."

I put Sarah over my shoulder as I served the twins their oatmeal and fresh strawberries. Miriam returned to her seat just as the baby let out a loud, juicy burp, sending a stream of breast milk down the back of my shirt. The twins pointed and howled with laughter. Miriam and I shook our heads. "Timing is everything," Miriam said, reaching out her arms for the baby.

I handed Sarah back to Miriam for the second half of her milky breakfast. "Want me to check your leg for any skin breakdown?"

"That's probably a good idea. It happens at the slightest provocation. Always best to catch it early."

Just then, an idea occurred to me. "What do you think about swapping jobs today? I'll help Eli with the things you've taught me, such as turning over rooms, taking vitals, etc., and you take it easy, stay off your feet for a day. I can take the twins to the pharmacy for lunch, and you can sit while rechecking the patients' charts from the morning."

Miriam shook her head, her immediate reaction to stand her ground, then abruptly stopped, her eyebrows shooting up. "Ella, that's brilliant. If you need me to administer medication or shots, I'll be right here and can come over. It's not an altogether bad idea to get off my feet today and give this damn leg a rest."

* * *

The children, delighted to have lunch at the soda fountain, ordered grilled cheese sandwiches, pickles, and chocolate milk. I asked the short-order cook, "Any chance you have more of those Saratoga Chips? They're delicious!"

She rummaged under the counter and pulled out a large wax bag filled with potato chips, placing a small handful on each of the twins' plates. "Everyone's asking for them. I'll see if Albert will add chips to our standard order."

I reached into the bag and put a handful on a plate for myself, chomping at them slowly, enjoying the salty crispness while thinking about that morning, assisting Eli. I couldn't feel more certain about my choice to become a nurse. Thinking back, I marveled at how every encounter I had with the office patients was a new step in expanding my knowledge.

Earlier, around ten that morning, Mr. and Mrs. Korn arrived for a last-minute appointment. I settled them in an exam room. Mr. Korn was a large man, his face beet red, his breathing labored.

"Tell me how we can help you today."

Mr. Korn turned to his wife. "You tell her. It's too much for me."

As soon as Mrs. Korn began reciting his list of symptoms, headaches, dizziness, chest pain, I knew I was in over my head, worried he was having a heart attack. "Please wait a moment. I'd like to bring the nurse in to check you."

I ran through the connecting door into the house. Miriam was stretched out on the sofa. "I need you. We may have a seriously ill patient across the hall. I'm thinking it's his heart, and Eli's tied up. His name is Mr. Korn."

Miriam sprang from the couch. She strapped on her brace while hopping toward the clinic door, turning back to say, "Stay with the children."

I pulled out the checkerboard, running an hour-long marathon while my own heart thrummed, waiting impatiently for Miriam's verdict. Finally, she returned, just in time for Sarah's feeding. "You have excellent instincts. He was in heart failure. I used Eli's brand-new blood pressure instrument. It's got a crazy name, sphygmomanometer." She added, "I think that blood pressure tool is going to help us understand the heart.

"Is there a medicine to treat his condition?"

Miriam shrugged. "The more we learn about the heart, the more we realize how little we know. But if his wife can get him to lose fifty pounds, the high blood pressure may improve. His poor body is working so hard, trying to push blood through the heart. He'll be on bed rest, aspirin, and a salt-restricted diet for weeks, if not months. Hopefully, if he's not in and out of the kitchen snacking, he'll shave off some weight."

It amazed me how much disease could be avoided if we took good care of ourselves all along. Fifty pounds of weight was a lot to gain and probably harder to lose. But after years of hunger, when many elders came to America, a little belly was seen as a sign of success. Even Papa used to pat his stomach after a meal and say, "I'm eating like a king. It cost me a fortune." Little did they know moderation was what they should be aiming for. I made a silent wish that Mr. Korn and his wife would be compliant, and he'd improve.

My thoughts shifted back to the soda fountain and the potato chip I was eating. "You're a hypocrite," I silently scolded myself. The snack was salty and full of oil. Delicious, yes, but because they were so hard to resist, companies were making a fortune off our lack of willpower. I took the remaining chips and dropped them in the garbage, taking a long pull of soda pop, wondering with each gulp what evils lurked in my drink. Was any food safe?

Sarah slept soundly in the carriage. Wheeling her close to the Laboratory door, I entered the back room to check in with Albert. "How'd your morning go?"

He swung his body toward me, drawing me into an embrace. "Well, aren't you a sight for sore eyes. I've been compounding medications all morning and am beginning to see double."

"Miriam and I swapped places today so she could rest her leg, but a patient came in with heart failure. It was awful but exciting at the same time."

"Nurse Ella, reporting for duty." He squeezed me tighter. "You will be a very fine nurse." He leaned down to kiss me.

Those soft, delightful lips. His kisses set me on fire, that is, until the twins began to call, "Ella, where are you? What are you doing?" waking Sarah. In seconds, the serenity had vanished, and my role as caregiver was once again in full swing. Nope, I was years away from motherhood. Albert had better stop kissing me like that, or I may not make it.

* * *

A short time later, I was back at the house with the children. Miriam had her leg elevated, and I headed into the clinic to help Eli.

Miriam called to me. "Check over the rooms and make sure they've been turned over properly with a good cleaning. Eli doesn't always do a thorough job."

I smiled inwardly. She and Eli were like conjoined twins, glued at the hip, but each with entirely different skills. Could Albert and I form that sort of partnership in life? Perhaps, with an example like Miriam and Eli staring us in the face, we had a chance.

As I walked into the clinic, Eli called out to me. "I ran out to pick up the mail at the post office during lunch, and something came for you. No return address."

"Thanks." I took the envelope, turned it over, and instantly recognized the handwriting. "It's from my father. I'll read it later. Right now, there is much to do to get ready for the afternoon patients."

The letter burned in my apron pocket all afternoon, calling to me. But the clinic was busy. It was a full schedule: regular adult diabetes check-ins, and children with rashes and fevers—plus a gash requiring sutures. Ever since Miriam's bout with polio, fevers had taken on a heightened importance, especially in children. Although 1916, the year of the first epidemic, had dwarfed the volume of cases every year since, we all remained vigilant. Unlike many diseases, polio appeared in the summer and, without a vaccine or cure, had remained a horrible fear for parents, doctors, and nurses. Eli routinely asked parents to either call or return with their children so he could rule out polio early or take quick action.

Later, back at the farm, I was determined to read Papa's note in privacy.

Eli, Miriam, and Albert were the only people who knew he was in prison, and I wanted to digest Papa's news before fielding the onslaught of family reactions. The entitlement to everyone's personal story was the singular aspect of my large family I didn't enjoy. The seclusion I'd grown accustomed to, living with a small family, all preoccupied with their own concerns, had afforded me an enormous amount of privacy. Perhaps too much.

After helping Aunt Jenny clean up dinner, I walked to the apple orchard and found a grassy spot to sit. The late August evening air was cool, sending hints of autumn, a reminder summer was near its end. Many of the stories Miriam shared over those unhurried summer dinners included the apples from this very orchard. She fondly recalled the Rosh Hashanah dinners here at the farm with my Great Grandfather Sam and Rebecca, her stepmother, when they were still alive. Her stories rang with deep sentiment. These were the very trees that nourished my family over the harsh years and brought sweetness to the Jewish holidays.

Now I gazed upward and could see the small green apples in their final growth spurt, full ripeness only weeks away. Would the new season and Jewish New Year bring blessings for all of us? I hoped so.

The letter was one and a half pages, longer than I'd expected from Papa.

Dear Daughter,

Thanks to you, I am out of that dreadful prison. Although I'm still angry at you for stealing my money, it may have been a blessing of sorts that I had hidden funds. It was enough to make bail. I am now staying on a friend's couch in the Lower East Side, where my life began. There is a certain irony, my being back where I was born. If only I could begin again, turn back time, and make decisions that would have steered my life in a better direction.

You see, the last few weeks have been the first time in many years I haven't sat at a card table or bet on horses. At first, the need was clawing at me, but something changed in the last week. I've felt a calm growing, an ability to see something was missing from my life before. Then, all I cared about was money and gambling. The compulsion and vicious cycle led me to make reckless decisions, costing me everything important: my marriage, job, relationship to my family, but most important: my children's love and trust.

I wiped my cheeks with the heel of my hand. Could it be true? Was it possible after so many years for him to see the light? I read on.

Right now, my plan is to remain here in the Lower East Side until the trial. I'm working odd, local cash jobs, putting money for the lawyer's fee into the same account Miriam opened. He thinks he might be able to get me off on a technicality, but down deep, I'm not counting on it. There is justice in serving a sentence for all the harm I've done. I'm prepared to take my punishment, and it's only right that I stop gambling away Mama and Papa's Trust income.

I did not share my address because I need to stay secure in my small bubble of repentance. When the time comes, you will know how things turn out.

In the meanwhile, please consider extending a little forgiveness to your damaged father. I'm terribly sorry I could not have been a better Papa for you. With God's help, maybe I'll get a second chance. I only wish there was a way to apologize to my devoted Mama and Papa for all the heartache I put them through.

Your Papa

I lay back on the grass and gazed at the darkening sky. A sense of peace traveled through me, easing the tension in my muscles in a manner I hadn't felt all summer. I prayed Papa could remain steadfast and Robbie would have everything he needed for a bright future. I hoped imprisonment wasn't in his cards.

I was the lucky child. Now emancipated, I could head off to nursing school and build a life for myself. Determined to use the next few years wisely, I brushed myself off and walked back to the house, glancing at the pond on my way. There was no visible change in the water level. It made me wonder how many crates of whiskey Dutch had dropped into its depths. Or did he find a different place to hide his liquor?

Chapter Forty-Two: Miriam

I could scarcely believe Ella had only one full week until the end of her summer. Next week, Albert agreed he'd would take Robbie home to his mother and help Ella settle into the nursing school dormitory at Beth Israel.

When I spoke to Selma last week to inform her of the new arrangement for support money, she could not stop thanking me. Each "tank you, dahlink," triggered another rush of guilt, knowing I'd kept her trapped in poverty for the last seven years, handing the money to Julian each month, sending it down the irretrievable gambler's drain, not a penny to help her feed and clothe the children.

I must stop berating myself. But deep in my conscience, I struggled with guilt. How could I have ever allowed Julian's blackmail to go on for so long? What would my Papa have thought of me?

No matter what I thought now, I had been forced to face the truth back in June when Ella and Robbie appeared at Uncle Nate's, dirty, emaciated, and in outgrown clothing. Certainly, it was a disgrace on Julian's part, but I, too, should have known. Now a mother of three, I knew full well the importance of taking proper care of children. My only solace was that Ella had grown to be an exceptional young woman, and Robbie was a fun-loving young boy who didn't seem any worse for the wear. Perhaps Selma's love for them had the power to keep her children on the straight and narrow. In the future, I'd see that Robbie was invited back every summer to pick up where he'd left off. And if Selma chose to come with him, I'd make those arrangements, too.

Eight o'clock on the dot, Ella swept through the front door. I was in the kitchen setting the table for breakfast. "My last week! Where'd the summer go?"

"Good morning. It is hard to believe. The weeks have flown by." She met my eyes. "There're a couple of things I wanted to ask you before the children are up. Eli mentioned you received a letter from your father. May I dare ask if everything's ok?"

Ella cast a crooked smile my way. "I'm not altogether sure, but he's out of prison, staying on a friend's couch on the Lower East Side, claims he no longer gambles, and wishes he could redo his life. He said that the little he makes goes into the bank for his attorney. He didn't say much else besides being remorseful."

I wondered if Julian had finally reached his bottom, as Papa once referred to. The lowest a man could go before forced to face his demons. "I'm sure he'll keep you informed. Sounds like he wants to work on his relationship with you."

"That's what I figure," she said, placing a bag of food on the counter. "I brought challah with me. How about French Toast and scrambled eggs? We haven't had that in a while."

"Perfect." I tipped my eyes to the ceiling, hearing the faint sound of Sarah, rousing from her sleep. "It's about to get busy. But the second thing, I was hoping I could take you back to Poughkeepsie for school shopping this Saturday. Would you like that?"

Ella's smile lit the room. "Are you kidding? I'd love it. I've never been back-to-school shopping before!"

My belly twisted. I must get used to this feeling and stop with the guilt. But Ella was eighteen and had never gotten new clothing for the school year. I would simply try my hardest to make up for lost time with these children. I hoped with effort, it would eventually feel right in my heart.

Chapter Forty-Three: Albert

I zipped up to the front of Miriam and Eli's house at the end of the day, idling in my car. Within seconds, Ella appeared, waving to me from the front door. My heart began thumping. It always did when I saw her after a long day. How I loved that woman. "Countdown week!" I called out.

Ella climbed into the car beside me, gently shutting the door. "I can't tell you how excited I am to start school. Only four more days of work." She took a deep breath, her eyes sparkling with excitement. "And guess what else? Miriam is taking me back-to-school shopping!"

Her joy filled me. Ella's joy was my joy. Her demons were my demons. We would share the ups and downs of two years of nursing school, and before we knew it, could plan a future without obstacles. "Guess who's the chauffeur? Eli gets to watch the children, and I'm driving you around town." I glowed.

"Eli's watching all three? That'll be a hoot. But knowing Miriam, she'll have it organized down to the last lollipop." She laughed, then switched to a thoughtful expression. "Speaking of lollipops, I was thinking yesterday, about how much food we eat that's really bad for our bodies."

I cringed. "Is this Nurse Ella talking now?"

"I guess. Last week, when we had the patient with high blood pressure, I came to the soda fountain and started eating Saratoga chips. Do you have any idea how bad they are for you?" She paused, but I knew she had more to say. "They're full of salt and fat. And the soda is practically all sugar. The food manufacturers have us thinking they're the next best thing for our meals. Now lollipops? The kids won't have any teeth left by the time they're adults."

I considered the merits of her words. The chips were selling like crazy. I made more money from chips and soda than I did from many of the medications. "What do you suggest I do? People may stop coming in if their favorite snack foods are gone. Next thing you know, we'll be told that smoking is bad, too." My words made me cringe, knowing how much income I made from tobacco.

"I'm not sure there's anything we can do right now. People will eat what they want. They don't connect their behavior with disease and would rather face the consequences later," she said.

I changed the subject, tired of discussing a problem with no clear solution. "I was thinking of taking a ride to Monticello on Sunday and seeing what the Klan is up to. Want to come?"

Ella knit her brows. "Do you think my kidnappers will be there? I'm not so sure I ever want to see them again."

"Maybe. I can't promise they won't be, but you may not recognize them wearing their ridiculous costumes. The Commissioner is on the program, and I want to hear what he's planning to say. When he wrote back to Miriam, he told her they're putting the kibosh on this nonsense. Don't you want to see if the government is good for their word?" With Ella's hesitancy, the last thing I wanted to tell her was that I had tipped off Dutch.

"How did you know about Sunday?" Ella asked.

I tilted my head toward her. "It was in the Commissioner's letter. I'm not sure Miriam read that part aloud, but she showed it to me later. Eli and I have been talking about going. I thought you might want to come along, too. You know, close the door on those villains."

"Let me think about it."

Chapter Forty-Four: Ella

Saturday was a glorious day for shopping. The temperature had dropped to a comfortable level, and the skies were clear. The shorter days foretold the annual anticipation of a new school year.

While Albert ran errands in Poughkeepsie, Miriam and I covered every square inch of Luckey-Platt's. Her first order of business was proper winter outerwear. "Ella, your grandmother, Tillie, always believed in spending money on a good coat. She'd say, "A warm, well-made coat will last for years. And God help us if your father and I left the house without a proper hat, boots, and gloves."

We selected a brown and gold tweed coat fabric. Miriam said it matched my hazel eyes. The winter wear was so heavy that we asked the store to hold the items while we continued shopping. By midday, I couldn't believe the amount of clothing Miriam had purchased for me: three dresses, two wool skirts, and five shirtwaist blouses—three white and two pastels. Then she directed me to the escalator, leading me to the second floor to buy a new set of foundations, hosiery, and sleepwear. In a million years, I could never show these treasures to my mother. She would buckle under the weight of guilt, knowing she couldn't afford to send me off to school with such lovely new things, or pay for nursing school. I'd tell her I'd bought it with my saved summer earnings, adding to the heap of fresh lies.

After a hurried lunch with Albert, Miriam took me for a haircut at a bonified beauty salon on Main Street, just like in the magazine pictures. There were four workstations lined up in front of mirrors, all busy as a beehive. The room pulsed with the sound of women's chatter and scissors clipping. It was the first time in my life a professional hair stylist washed and cut my hair. In the past, Mama or one of her friends would line up all the girls in her apartment kitchen for an annual trim. The woman used blunt scissors to cut off a few inches from the bottom. Most of us had wavy hair, disguising the poor-quality cuts.

This time, I asked the beautician to cut my auburn hair to my shoulders so it would be easy to pin back in nursing school, but not too long to wear loose. Miriam and I agreed the popular bob I was eyeing in the magazines was impractical for nurses. "Loose hair is a germ spreader, falling onto the patients and whatnot," said Miriam.

Afterwards, I couldn't take my eyes off my reflection in the mirror. My waves hung evenly around my face, and I'd never seen my hair shine so. "Oh, Miriam. Thank you so much. My hair looks beautiful."

"Honey, you are beautiful and deserve every good thing that comes your way."

* * *

Later that day, after dropping Miriam off at her home, Albert drove me to the farm. We passed stripped brown corn stalks in the fields. The first signs of autumn surrounded us. Summer, a less intense season in the country than the city, was brief before the cold weather rolled in. I hoped there would be a few ripe apples to take home to Mama.

From out of nowhere, tears sprang from my eyes. I reached for Albert's hand. "This was the best summer of my life. I can't believe we'll be leaving for New York in only two days."

He pulled the car to the side of the road and left it idling while he hugged me. "When I set eyes on you for the first time, I knew. I know it sounds corny, but for me, it was love at first sight. My feelings for you have only grown stronger since that moment. Every day, all summer long, through everything we've gone through together. I can't tell you how much you mean to me."

I looked into his brown eyes, full of intensity. "I love you too. It's going to be so hard not seeing you every day." I finally said, although the words felt dry in my mouth, hard to get out.

Albert turned to the wheel, wiping his eyes with the back of his hand. "How about I pick you up tomorrow around noon. We'll hit the rally in Monticello and be back by midafternoon so we can enjoy a last dinner and get the car packed for Monday."

A shot of fear ran through me. "I'm not so sure I want to go to the rally. I hate the Klan and don't want them wreaking my last memories of the farm."

Albert held my hand. "But the Commissioner is going to be speaking first, sending a message to them about tolerance. Don't you want to see the Klan cower under the hand of the law? Maybe they'll be the ones who go back to where they came from."

"I do." I gathered my thoughts. Albert was probably right. "I guess we can stop by for a few minutes, but I don't want Robbie to come. I want him safe at the farm."

I breathed deeply, hoping I'd made the right decision to join Albert and Eli at the Monticello rally. I had no trust in the Commissioner's opening remarks after the way the Klan behaved at the Fourth of July celebration. I could only hope that by saving Tommy's arm, Mahlon Peterson might have the influence to bring an end to the torment of the county's new immigrants.

Chapter Forty-Five: Ella

As we turned onto Broadway, the main road leading into Monticello, Eli said, "I think the rally is on Cold Spring Road off to the left. Let's check it out."

Twisting my watch around my wrist, I asked, "Can we park somewhere near the back of the lot. You know, in case we want to leave early? That way, our car won't be hemmed in."

"Of course. Just give me the signal, and we're out of here," Albert said.

I released a breath I hadn't realized was trapped in my lungs all morning. In my heart, I believed I needed to witness the event, but I didn't know how much more of the Klan I could bear. A quick way out of the rally was my insurance.

The dusty dirt clearing for cars was a distance from the stage. I studied the level field, the gathering of standing spectators settling down. The program was about to begin. Albert and I inched into the crowd, close enough to hear, but far enough from the stage to leave if I chose. Horn-shaped amplifiers tied to posts boosted the sound through the air, reaching listeners far off in the field, while the speaker stood on the platform before a large circular microphone.

First up was the Commissioner, delivering the opening Pledge of Allegiance, a somber reminder to those who made the ultimate sacrifice during the Great War. Then, like his Fourth of July speech, he spoke about growth in the county and an opportunity for all to prosper. Finally, he addressed the issue at hand: the balance between free speech and loyalty to the U.S. Constitution, particularly the part about all men being created equal.

"Let Sullivan County always be an example for the rest of the great state of New York, and others in this county, for not only its tolerance of newcomers to America, but our open arms to growing commerce together and enriching our spirits with the cultural assets all of us bring."

There was some clapping amidst low booing from the crowd. The Commissioner continued to say, "And last, let me make this last point crystal clear." He paused, reengaging everyone's attention. "It is with the authority of the Governor of our great state of New York that we will have no tolerance for illegal behavior. Intimidation, mischief, and other wrongdoings will be handled by the arm of the law. With that, I wish you all a good day."

Albert squeezed my hand. "Well, he's made the State's official position clear."

"But what about all that booing. I don't think the naysayers give a hoot."

Just then, about thirty members of the Klan, wearing their full regalia, marched single file onto the stage. One tall man stood in the center before the crowd and held the microphone stand. He stood there a moment while we absorbed the power of their menacing presence.

Eli shook his head. "I agree with Ella. They're just warming up."

A voice from the audience yelled out, "Show your faces. Who are you hiding from?"

Suddenly, a Klansman on the side of the stage drew a pistol from his white robe. The crack of the gun rang through the speaker system, across the entire field. Screaming emerged from the audience. "A man's been shot!" The crowd, turning in our direction, began stampeding away from the stage. A herd of buffalo.

I grabbed Eli's arm. "We must help that man. Come with me."

Together, the three of us ran to the side of the crowd, finding narrow escape alleys as the spectators tore in our direction. We pushed forward, through the smell of their sweat, their fear. A few yards from the stage, a man lay bleeding on the ground. It was Peterson. "My God, they shot Mahlon Peterson, one of their own. Why?" Eli shouted.

Eli and I bent over his body, searching for the bullet hole. Mahlon recognized us immediately. "You've come to save me. Bless you." He gasped for air. "My God, this hurts."

Eli was ripping away Mahlon's shirt. "I found it. Lower right quadrant. Missed the heart and lung."

I placed my face close to Mahlon's. "You'll make it, Mr. Peterson. The goon had a bad aim. We're taking you to the clinic."

Then Eli twisted back to Albert, "I'll get pressure on the wound. Grab some strong men to help us carry him to the car."

Albert pulled four men from the group who had stuck around, craning their necks with curiosity. They gently lifted Mahlon off the ground, making their way down the field to Albert's car.

Meanwhile, I searched the disappearing crowd and saw Dutch. How the hell did he know about this? He was surrounded by his own goons. They pulled out their rifles while Dutch shouted to the Klan, all still spread out on the stage. "Ya want to see a little target practice? You're cowards, hiding in children's costumes. You get out of this county! And while you're running, how about you leave the country, too?"

On command, his men aimed their guns and shot. The coppery smell of gunpowder filled the air as we picked up our pace, carrying Peterson toward the car. This was war, the endless, deafening ammunition pouring forth into the air. I didn't look back. At that moment, I didn't care how many Klansmen Dutch's men killed. I was only thankful most of the townspeople between Dutch's hail of bullets and the stage had cleared out.

I climbed into the back seat with Mahlon, sitting on his bleeding body. I hoped my full body weight was enough to stop the hemorrhaging.

Mahlon moaned, "The pain, the pain. Can't stand it."

I smirked and looked him in the eyes. "Just be glad I don't have a pointy Devil's tail like Timmy thought. It would be sticking smack into the wound."

His face relaxed a moment. An amused sniff.

"Oh, was that a little smile I saw? Well, we're taking you to the right place. Eli and Miriam are the closest to a combat doctor and nurse you'll find up here. We'll get you something for the pain as soon as we can."

I glanced up at Eli. "How far are we?"

"Ten minutes tops," He answered. "How's our patient doing?"

Mahlon moaned. "Still on this side of the grass."

I looked at Mahlon. "Why'd that man shoot you?"

"After the barn, when I quit the Klan…" he stopped for a breath, "they called me a turncoat. I shouldn't have gone to the rally, but I was furious with them. They had you Jews all wrong."

I cringed at the pejorative use of the word, doubting years of hate could vanish overnight, but it was a start.

"Albert, did you see Dutch and his men shoot them down?" I asked.

Mahlon gasped, "The gangster?"

Albert answered, "Yup, he hates the Klan. Dutch was probably pissed they didn't leave after his last warning with the barn."

We pulled up to the clinic. Eli's brakes screeched while he lay on his horn. The honk, so penetrating, drew the family into the yard. Albert yelled, "Gunshot wound. Get the kids inside."

Eli pulled me off Mahlon. Blood squirted. Eli took one look at the entry wound, placed his hand atop the bleeding, and rolled the body to its side. There was no exit wound. "Bloody bullet's still inside. Let's carry him in. Then we'll get him under. Gotta get the damn bullet out."

Between Miriam, Eli, Albert, and me, we were able to carry Mahlon inside to the same table Timmy had lain on only weeks before.

I turned to Mahlon, "I checked after Timmy was here, and my blood type is O, like yours, a match. Is it okay with you if we use it? I promise you won't grow a tail."

Mahlon nodded and squeezed my hand. "You are a cheeky thing. You bet it's okay."

Eli said, "Miriam, give him a shot of morphine while we prepare the anesthesia. Albert, I'll need you to stay with the children while Miriam gets blood from Ella. Once she's got her sea legs, she'll take over at the house, and you can run down and get more supplies. Don't forget to call Maisy."

While Miriam administered the morphine and Eli applied a pressure dressing, we all washed up carefully. Miriam pulled a box off the shelf. "Surgeons now wear sterile gloves as standard practice in the operating rooms to reduce patient infections. I ordered a box. Let's all put them on."

Eli said, "It's about time."

By this point, Mahlon was ready. Calm from the morphine, reciting a few prayers, he turned to Eli. "It was because of all of you that I became a better man. You saved my son, and he'll be home from the hospital soon. Please, I want to live and see him, again."

My eyes teared. "You will. Hold onto that beautiful thought, and we'll talk after you wake up."

* * *

Three hours later, the bullet was out, and Mahlon's wound was stitched and bandaged. Eli and Miriam were able to transfuse two units of my blood to Mahlon, and I was ordered to rest for the remainder of the day. Maisy had gotten a ride to the clinic from her older son. They both sat by Mahlon's side as he woke. We stepped out of the room to give them privacy. Ten minutes later, as Mahlon drifted back into his medicated sleep, we led the Petersons to the waiting room and sat.

Maisy dabbed her tears. "Just as we're getting ready to bring Timmy home, this happens. I told Mahlon not to go to that horrible rally."

I took her hand. "There were plenty of people there who wanted the Klan gone. He was not the only one. And let's thank God the shooter had a bad aim."

Eli piped in. "That's right. Mahlon should be fine in a couple of months. The bullet is out and missed his major organs. His pelvic bone stopped the trajectory. We removed the bullet, and now his bone needs to heal." He handed the bullet to Maisy's son. "You may want to keep this for him. A reminder of how deadly hate can be."

Maisy nodded. "Amen to that."

Eli continued, "He'll need hospital rest for a few weeks. Maybe we can ask the head nurse at Poughkeepsie to bed him with Timmy while he's still there. I'd like to move Mahlon tomorrow, as long as he remains stable. The hospital is a much better environment for recovery. They have staffing around the clock."

I smiled. "And ice cream when you're up for it."

***

Albert took my hand and led me to the backyard. We sat under the branches of the trees in the Adirondack chairs and soaked in the soft breeze. "How are you holding up? Need another day before leaving for New York?" He hesitated. "I really owe you an apology. I never would have expected such an outright disregard for the law, especially in front of the Commissioner. It was a disgrace."

Mahlon's son walked out the kitchen door and stood over us, extending his hand. "I can't thank you enough for saving my father. If you hadn't been there..." he hiccupped a weak sob, then inhaled, collecting himself. "Well, to put it bluntly, you folks saved my brother and now our Pop. There are really no words, other than you can trust, so long as the Petersons are around, that we'll always watch your back."

Albert nodded his thanks, and we both shook his hand. Then Albert asked, "Any idea what happened after we left?"

Mahlon's son set his hands on his hips. "I heard from one of my pals who was there that the police must have anticipated a riot because they had prisoner buses hidden about a half mile away. As soon as the first gun went off, they raced to the scene, piling in Schultz's gang and the Klansmen who'd stuck around."

I laughed, "I hope they were smart enough to put them in separate wagons."

Mahlon's son chuckled. "I hope so, too. But they got Dutch. All of them are to go to the city for arraignment and trial—that was the Governor's orders."

Albert asked the tough question. "Injuries, deaths?"

Mahlon's son shook his head. "I didn't hear a final count. We'll have to wait for the paper, but over twenty men lay on the ground. I don't imagine the Klan will stick around too much longer. They're not welcome in these parts."

His eyes drilled into ours. "I can't imagine how destroyed my mom and the family would be if you hadn't saved Pop. You two must be the bravest people I've ever met, running into danger to help him." And with those words, he turned and walked back inside the clinic, shaking his head in disbelief.

Albert and I stared at each other for the longest time. I finally said, "We make a perfect team. Take me to the city tomorrow so I can get back here soon. I want to start living our future without wasting a day." I said those precious words again. The same words I'd been holding inside, but this time they came out of me like a sweet melody. "I love you, Albert."

Albert pulled me up to standing and kissed me deeply. I felt myself melt into him, so ready for more, but knew it must wait. "I will love you till the very end. You are my other half."

"And you are mine," I said.

Epilogue

1969, forty-five years later – the site of Nate's chicken farm

op was resting in his cottage bedroom, speaking to Mom in his trademark stage whisper. The wall vibrated with his words. "I will not have Sharon seeing that *nebbish* back home. He has loser written all over his face. Maybe she'll meet a nice Jewish kid while we're here at Grossbergers Resort. When did she go from being a tomboy to a tall, blond stunner—in heat, no less?"

"Oh, Robbie. You worry too much about her. Sharon's a great kid," Mom answered.

Ugh. I hated when he pigeonholed me like that. Sure, all little kids are cute and fun, but I wasn't little anymore. He couldn't accept me as a young adult. As a matter of fact, it only made him more controlling. So once again, Pop insisted the family spend the entire month of July in the country, our annual pilgrimage to our family's once upon a time chicken farm in Sullivan County.

Despite my annoyance with Pop, I'll admit that Grossbergers, the new owners, was an exciting break from the summer heat back home. The resort had an Olympic-sized pool, tennis, endless contests, shuffleboard courts, and meals. Oh, those meals that kept on coming.

This year, leaving my new boyfriend, Erik, behind was a real bummer. I barely had enough coins to feed the payphone for a few precious minutes, speaking to him one time a week. Each time, his deep voice made my toes curl.

I shouted into the air, knowing I'd be heard. "We're going exploring. I'll take Leo with me."

"Wear your watch. Be back by 11:30 to clean up for lunch," called Mom.

It seemed like all we did was shout and eat in my family. Someday, when I get married, I'll make everyone take a moment to find each other, rather than yelling through the rooms. No wonder there weren't any secrets.

Leo, my eleven-year-old brother, was bursting with energy, eager to play outside, jumping at the chance to explore. We headed out the screen door, letting it slam behind us. I chuckled, "I'll bet Pop will have someone here within the hour to oil that door. The banging will drive him crazy."

Leo skipped ahead. "Where are we going?"

I pointed at the distant trees down the massive hill on the front side of the property. "You know that our Great-Uncle Nate had his chicken farm right here. They picked apples in the orchard and swam in a nearby pond. I've always wanted to check it out. It should be at the bottom of the hill somewhere."

"What did they grow?" Leo asked.

I spread my arms, rotating my body to absorb the warm morning sun. "Chickens, silly. You know that."

Leo screwed his face, puzzled.

I pointed back at the enormous hotel. "They probably had a small vegetable garden for the family somewhere near the house, but the whole place was once a Kosher chicken farm. Most of the farms around here raised livestock. He originally had the farm in Harlem, New York. Can you imagine?"

"A farm in Harlem?" Leo raised his brows. "That's hard to imagine."

"But after Great-Uncle Nate died and the depression years hit, the family sold off the chickens, and the Grossbergers bought the land for a song. By then, the house was falling apart, and everything was overgrown. But the Grossberger family had the right idea. They built a hotel and cottages and brought the place back to life. Once World War Two was over and people returned to work, the hotel was always full. And, according to a family legend, there's a secret mystery about the farm."

Leo's eyes popped wide. "What kind of secret?"

"Pop said his big sister, our Aunt Ella, knew a bootlegger the first summer they came here in 1924. The gangster was searching for a place to hide his whiskey. Rumor has it Aunt Ella might have had a hand in it." I turned to face Leo. "Can you believe Aunt Ella knew a criminal? I wished she had lived long enough for us to know her."

"That's scary." He paused, sorting out the family tree in his head. "The same Aunt Ella who was married to Uncle Albert?"

"Yeah, she may have helped the gangster find a place to hide his whisky. You know whiskey and beer were illegal back then during Prohibition."

"Beer? Pop loves his Pabst." Leo chuckled. "And Canadian Whiskey."

We trudged down the remaining hill to the large cluster of low trees on the southern edge of the property. The entire area had been abandoned for decades while the Grossbergers built and expanded the hotel complex at the top. The resort could host over one thousand guests at any time.

Looking about, I noticed prickly bushes and poison ivy growing willy-nilly. "Watch where you step, or you'll catch poison ivy, and then you'll be scratching all week."

Passing a few half-dead apple trees in the old orchard, I realized there wasn't much to see. Skimpy branches held small apple nibs, coming to life amid the tree's limbs, but the apples wouldn't be ready to pick for at least another month or more. "Let's turn around and see if we can find the old pond where they swam. Pop told me they were allowed to swim at night before bed when the weather was hot. It must be nearby, especially if there were underground springs feeding the trees."

"That would be so much fun to swim at night," echoed Leo.

I laughed. "They swam instead of taking showers. A great way to cool down before bed."

We trudged through the undergrowth, our eyes searching for the three slick leaves signaling poison ivy. I took Leo's hand as we exited the apple grove and headed further downhill.

"Why would the pond dry up?" Leo asked.

I sighed, saddened a land's history could be erased in only four decades. "I'm not an expert, but my best guess is they needed a large well, maybe more than one, on the top of the hill where they built the hotel and cottages. That may have drained some of the same spring water that flowed underground, feeding the pond and orchard here, at the bottom of the hill. But that's only a guess." I led Jake to the lowest point, a flat few acres covered with prickly shrubs.

"Where do you think the pond was?" he asked.

"Not positive, but we may be standing on it." The area dipped and was soggy, covered with low-growing wild raspberry bushes and other vegetation. We walked deeper into the wet soil, pushing the scrub to the side with our bare hands, my shorts beginning to look like a pincushion of brambles and burrs. Just then, my feet sank to my ankles in mud. I heard a crunching sound under my left foot. A shard of glass poked through the back of the rubber sole of my sandal, just missing my skin. I jumped away. "Don't move. There's broken glass everywhere."

Brown liquid pooled upward into the grass, seeping between the toes of my flip-flops. The smell was strong and familiar, just like Pop's Canadian Club whiskey. "Well, I'll be a monkey's uncle."

I grabbed a loose stick lying on the weeds and dug, right where my foot had sunken. About four inches down, I felt something hard push against the twig. I picked around with my bare hands until I could feel the outline of a bottle. Once I reached the neck, I pulled it out. A sucking sound startled us as the bottle popped out of the mud. In my hand, I held a brown sealed bottle with a shredded label still stuck to the glass. I couldn't make out the words; the many years the label was hidden beneath the ground had all but dissolved the ink.

"Look at this, Leo. It's the real thing, bootlegger booze!"

He stared at the bottle in disbelief.

"We discovered the hidden treasure. They hid the whiskey in the pond." I whispered. I grabbed Leo's hand. "Race you back! I can't wait to tell Mom and Pop."

A Note from the Author

The art of historical fiction requires a seamless blend of fact and fiction to accurately transport the reader into the story's time and place. To accomplish that feat, I took the liberty to bend a fact here and there while remaining true to the historical period. For example, the burning of Martin's barn, threats to Rob, and the kidnapping of Ella were envisioned to illustrate the random acts of hatred expressed toward the Jewish community. Although there were KKK rallies in Mayhem in the Mountain, this one was fiction, along with Dutch Schultz's involvement. However, there is historical evidence that the Ku Klux Klan was driven out of New York by the politicians and leaders of the state.

History never ceases to amaze me. One significant event could change the trajectory of time. Throughout crafting this novel, I wondered if the Borscht Belt would have seen its heyday if the Klan or Prohibition had endured. But aside from the financial ruin of many farmers during the Great Depression, the emergence of the grand hotels of the Catskills and their enduring mark on the minority cultures of the post-WWII era had an unforgettable impact on the region's history. One to be celebrated with an open heart.

The brief bibliography below provides additional information about the history of this time period.

- *But He was Good to his Mother*, Robert Rockaway
- *Kill the Dutchman*, Paul Sann
- *Tough Jews*, Rich Cohen
- *The Forgotten Kapital: The Ku Klux Klan in Binghamton, New York 1923-1928*, Jay Rubin
- *Prohibition in the United States*, Hourly History

- *Rum Across the Border, The Prohibition Era in Northern New York*, Allan S. Everest
- *Dress Codes, How Laws of Fashion Made History*, Richard Thompson Ford
- *Victorian and Edwardian Fashion, A Photographic Survey*, Alison Gernsheim
- *Our Crowd*, Stephen Birmingham
- *Bellevue, Three Centuries of Medicine and Mayhem at America's Most Storied Hospital*, David M. Oshinsky
- *Polio, An American Story*, David M. Oshinsky
- *The Gospel of Germs, Men, Women, and the Microbe in American Life*, Nancy Tomes
- *The Women's Suffrage Movement*, Sally Roesch Wagner

About the Author

"I run like the wind to stay ahead of my disease—living, family, writing—my refuge."

A cancer diagnosis unveiling a genetic defect, together with a lifelong fascination with the history of medicine, propelled Jane Rubin to put pen to paper. In 2009, then a healthcare executive, Jane poured her energy into raising research dollars for ovarian cancer, the Ovarian Cancer Research Alliance (OCRA), while learning more about her familial roots. Her research led her to Mathilda (Tillie), her great-grandmother, who arrived in New York City in 1866 as a baby, at sixteen, married a man twelve years her senior, and later died of "a woman's disease." Then, the trail ran cold. With limited facts, she was determined to give Tillie an exciting fictional life of her own. Jane was left imagining Tillie's life, her fight with terminal disease, and the circumstances surrounding her death.

Her research on the history of New York City, its ultra-conservative reproductive laws, and the state of medicine during that era has culminated in a suspenseful, best-selling, award-winning three-book historical series. Her engaging characters confront the shifting role of midwives, the dangers of pregnancy, the infamous Blackwell's Workhouse, and the perilous road to financial success. *In the Hands of Women*, 5/23 (Level Best Books) and its prequel, *Threadbare*, 5/24 (Level Best Books), have been enjoyed by fans of historical fiction. *Over There*, the third in the trilogy (6/25 Level Best Books), transports members of the Isaacson family into the heart of France in World War 1, challenging the family values they dearly cherish. *Over There* was shortlisted by the Historical Novel Society for the 2024 First Chapters Competition and is a Finalist for the 2025 Hemingway Awards for 20th-century wartime fiction.

Jane's other publications include an essay memoir, *Almost a Princess, My Life as a Two-Time Cancer Survivor* (2009 Next Generation—Finalist), and multiple magazine articles. She writes a monthly blog, Musings, reflecting on her post-healthcare career experiences and writing journey.

Ms. Rubin graduated from the University of Michigan (BS, MS) and Washington University (MBA). She retired from a 30-year healthcare executive career to write full-time. She lives in Northern New Jersey with her husband, David, an attorney. Together, they have five adult children and seven grandchildren.

Also by Jane Loeb Rubin

Over There (2025 Level Best Books)

Threadbare (2024 Level Best Books)

In the Hands of Women (2023 Level Best Books)

Almost a Princess, My Life as a Two-Time Cancer Survivor (2010 IUniverse)

www.ingramcontent.com/pod-product-compliance
Lightning Source LLC
Chambersburg PA
CBHW051142130726
47988CB00005B/1948